MANHUNT

James Barrington is a trained military pilot who has worked in covert operations and espionage. He now lives in Andorra and this is his sixth novel. His previous novels, *Overkill*, *Pandemic*, *Foxbat*, *Timebomb* and *Payback*, also feature Paul Richter.

JAMES
BARRINGTON

MANHUNT

PAN BOOKS

First published 2011 by Pan Books
an imprint of Pan Macmillan, a division of Macmillan Publishers Limited
Pan Macmillan, 20 New Wharf Road, London N1 9RR
Basingstoke and Oxford
Associated companies throughout the world
www.panmacmillan.com

ISBN 978-0-330-46270-9

1 3 5 7 9 8 6 4 2

A CIP catalogue record for this book is available from
the British Library.

Typeset by CPI Typesetting
Printed in the UK by CPI Mackays, Chatham ME5 8TD

Visit **www.panmacmillan.com** to read more about all our books
and to buy them. You will also find features, author interviews and
news of any author events, and you can sign up for e-newsletters
so that you're always first to hear about our new releases.

To Sally – for always and everything

Acknowledgements

As always, my friend and agent Luigi Bonomi has given me his unflinching support, guidance and encouragement in this and other literary adventures. He's the man who really calls the shots. At Macmillan, I'm delighted to be working with Jeremy Trevathan and Catherine Richards – an impressive and organized team – and my grateful thanks are also due to Peter Lavery for his meticulous editorial eye.

James Barrington
Principality of Andorra, 2011

Author's Note

To readers who've been following the various exploits of 'Paul Richter', a brief word of explanation is needed. *Manhunt* is chronologically the first volume of this series, despite its publication date, and introduces a number of characters who reappear later in the series.

Prologue

The KGB came to the village of Skel'ki, on the southern shore of the Kakhovskoye Vdkhr, as they had always done, in the hours before dawn.

The bitter easterly wind had picked up snow in its passage over Kazakhstan, and the officer in charge – a young captain – had ordered the snow chains to be fitted before the cars had covered even half the distance from the KGB headquarters in Vasil'yevka. In the village, the wind moaned and howled around that cluster of buildings, leaving deep drifts in the lee of anything that provided a shelter. The few cars and lorries in the settlement had been turned into anonymous white lumps, and the two slow-moving black saloons left clear tracks in the snow as they crunched and rattled over the poor road surfaces.

The small grey concrete apartment building stood on the western edge of the village, where the farmland intruded into the built-up area. Identification of the building was easy – the informer had described it very accurately – and the KGB cars circled it once before they parked, one vehicle at the front and one at the rear entrance. The drivers stayed in the cars to keep the engines running and the heaters on, and also to stop anyone trying to

1

leave the building. Although the absence of any lights suggested that it was an unlikely eventuality.

Within the USSR, it was said that the KGB always operated in groups of at least three. The logic behind this assumption was that, if faced with any temptation, one man alone might succumb to it, two men together might conspire to do so, but the third would always inform. Whatever the truth, the group that had arrived to arrest Pavel Ostapenko comprised six burly KGB men.

They climbed the stairs to the third floor, then headed softly along the passageway until they reached the second door on the left. There, the captain paused and took out his automatic pistol. He carefully moved back the slide, chambering a round, before he gestured to his men to prepare. One of them hefted a sledgehammer, while the other four pulled metre-long clubs from inside their overcoats.

The officer held up his left hand, three fingers extended, and silently mouthed a countdown. When his last finger vanished into his fist, he nodded, and the man with the sledgehammer swung it at the door lock. With a splintering of wood, the lock gave way. As the implement was withdrawn, another KGB man lashed out with his foot and the door swung violently inwards. One and half seconds later, all six were inside the tiny flat.

Pavel Ostapenko sat up in bed with a start, as the door splintered, and stretched out his hand towards the light switch, though he needn't have bothered. The bedroom light came on instantly and, before Ostapenko could react further, one of the KGB men had reached the bed and jabbed him viciously in the solar plexus with one end of his club.

As Ostapenko tumbled, gasping and helpless, to the floor, his wife began to scream. The captain slapped her hard across the face, breaking a tooth and starting a nose bleed. She struggled to her feet, holding a hand over her face, and staggered towards her daughter's bed in the corner of the room. The eight-year-old girl watched in silent horror, eyes wide and mouth open, at this invasion of her parental home, then she clung to her mother with an unnatural strength born of sheer terror.

Two of the KGB men dragged Pavel Ostapenko to his feet and pinned him against the bedroom wall, while another systematically beat him about the chest and abdomen with his fists. Marisa and her daughter watched, helpless, as his thin body quivered under the savage blows.

Finally, at a sharp command from the captain, the two men holding Ostapenko bent him forward, lowering his head so that yet another could take a swing at it with his club. The weapon descended, but, at the last moment, Ostapenko moved his head slightly, and the club cracked his collarbone instead of meeting the back of his skull. Ostapenko screamed shrilly, and the two released him, letting him collapse on the floor.

The captain strode across the tiny room to where Ostapenko now lay, kicked him hard in the lower back, and then in the stomach – blows which seemed to have little effect on the prostrate Ukrainian – and then he turned away.

'Who are you?' Marisa Ostapenka stammered, the words slurring from smashed and broken lips.

'Captain Yevgeni Zharkov, KGB,' the officer snapped

in response. 'And this man' – he gestured contemptuously behind him – 'is under arrest for anti-Soviet activities.'

'What . . . ? What has he done?'

'He was overheard criticizing the Party's ten-year plan, and also the performance of the manager of the Mikhaylovka Collective Farm.'

Marisa Ostapenka shook her head. 'He didn't . . .' she began. And then she stopped, appalled at what she'd just said.

The captain eyed her steadily, the beginnings of a smile playing around his thin lips. 'You are not suggesting, comrade, that we are wrong, I hope?'

'No, no,' she cried, desperately shaking her head, but she already knew it was too late.

'Pick him up,' the officer ordered, and the semiconscious Ostapenko was again shoved up against the wall. They kicked his legs apart and took a firm grip on him. 'We'll ask the man himself.'

Taking a club from one of his men, the captain rammed the end of it under Ostapenko's chin, forcing his head back. 'A question for you, Ukrainian,' he snarled. 'You do not even have to speak, just give a nod if what I say is true.' Zharkov withdrew the club and stood back. 'Are you,' he began softly, 'guilty in any way of anti-Soviet activities?'

Before Ostapenko could answer, even if capable of doing so, the officer thrust the club up, in a vicious underarm arc, into the Ukrainian's groin. Ostapenko's eyes and mouth opened wide with the severity of the blow and, despite the straining grip of the two KGB men, his body doubled up in agony.

'There,' the officer said, offering a bleak smile to the woman and child. 'We asked him the question, and he admitted to his crime. That was a nod, wasn't it?' he asked.

The KGB men were all smiling broadly, knowing how to play the Georgian captain's little games. 'I'm not sure that was a nod, Comrade Captain,' one of them said. 'I sort of think he shook his head.'

'Oh, really?' the officer replied. 'Then perhaps we'd better ask him again.'

'No, no, please . . . please don't.' Marisa fell to her knees in front of the KGB officer, her daughter dropping by her side. 'Yes, he nodded. We all saw it.'

The captain bent down towards her. This business was becoming more amusing with every minute that passed. 'You're probably right,' he said gently, 'but I think we'd better ask again, just to make certain.'

He stood up, gestured to his men, and then again swung the club. As before, Ostapenko doubled over, and then fell unconscious to the floor. His pyjama bottoms were stained crimson with the blood pouring from his ruptured scrotum, and the bedroom wall he had been held against was now stained and splattered with gore.

'Now, that was definitely a nod.'

Marisa Ostapenka had retreated sobbing to a corner of the room and was crouching on the floor, with her eyes tightly shut. The captain stared at her with disappointment: it didn't look as if there was much further entertainment to be found in this apartment tonight.

He turned back to his men. 'Right,' he said, 'get him into the car. You'd better wrap him in something warm – it's snowing outside and we wouldn't want him catching cold, would we?' His men chuckled dutifully. 'It's bad enough that we had to restrain him so forcefully, for resisting arrest,' he added. As two of the KGB men dragged the unconscious Ostapenko towards the door, the captain called after them. 'And make sure he doesn't bleed all over the seats.'

In fact, Ostapenko wouldn't bleed for much longer, because he was already in the process of dying and would be dead long before the KGB cars got back to Vasil'yevka. The savage kicks delivered by the captain to his back and stomach had ruptured the man's liver and right kidney, causing massive internal bleeding. The combination of shock, pain and cold would do the rest.

At the door, the officer turned and looked back into the bedroom. The young girl, he noticed, had not made a sound since they had burst into the apartment, but had watched everything, with wide blue eyes. She remained kneeling beside her mother, her arms around the older woman, but her eyes were locked on his.

After a moment, the captain dropped his gaze, unable to face her any longer, then shrugged his shoulders and followed his men out of the door.

The officer was a Georgian, who had only been stationed in the Ukraine for a few months. He had never bothered getting to know anything about the local inhabitants, regarding them almost as a conquered people, subjects to be monitored and kept in order by the KGB, who were Russia's 'sword and shield'. He knew he would be moving on within a couple of years, his future postings taking him ever closer to Moscow, and that was all he really cared about.

MANHUNT

He didn't know that the Ukrainians can bear grudges, sometimes lasting for generations, and nor would he have cared even if he did. Marisa Ostapenka was pure-bred Ukrainian, as was her daughter, and, as they tried to rebuild the ruins of their lives in the months and years which followed that dreadful night, they would be driven by a single, unspoken purpose . . .

Russians may have long memories, but the memories of Ukrainians are longer still.

Chapter One

'Look,' Paul Richter said, exasperation showing in his voice, 'I don't even know why I'm here.'

'Yes, you do,' Baldwin replied. 'You're here because you need a job.'

Gerald Baldwin was tall and spare, with a hooked nose and deep-set eyes, and he looked like a senior naval officer in mufti. Despite this, he was actually a colonel in a tank regiment, and Richter still didn't really know why he was sitting in front of him.

In the afternoon sunshine, the room was oppressively hot, for all the windows were tightly closed. Baldwin didn't seem to notice but, if you've spent most of your working life jammed into a tiny unventilated armoured steel box that you share with two or three other men and a twelve-cylinder internal combustion engine, the discomfort of a warm day in London is going to be barely noticeable.

'Not a particularly impressive record, Mr Richter,' Baldwin remarked, glancing down at the file lying open on the desk in front of him. 'Just over twenty years in the Navy, and you leave as only a middle-seniority lieutenant commander. An early promotion to lieutenant, but after that the drive seemed to go, and you didn't even

8

make it to two and a half until your fourth selection board.'

'I had some personality clashes,' Richter said.

Baldwin favoured him with a brief smile. 'The word used here in your file,' he said, 'is insubordination.'

Richter shrugged. 'It doesn't matter much what you call it,' he said. 'I was working for an illiterate idiot. I knew it and everyone else knew it. What I shouldn't have done was call him an illiterate idiot to his face.'

'No,' Baldwin agreed, 'and especially not in the middle of the Yeovilton Wardroom bar on a Friday lunchtime, with half the senior officers from Flag Officer Naval Aviation standing there watching.'

'That shouldn't be on file,' Richter said.

'It isn't,' Baldwin replied, another smile slowly forming, 'but word gets around.'

'So,' Richter said, 'good timing was never one of my virtues.'

Baldwin went back to the file. 'Seems you've got no real qualifications,' he observed.

'Are you trying to cheer me up, or what? Most of the skills anyone learns in the services are completely useless on the outside.'

'Not necessarily,' Baldwin said. 'You still have some abilities that could be in demand.'

'Like what?' Richter asked.

Baldwin shook his head. 'I'll come to that later, if I may.'

'I'd rather you came to it now.' Richter was looking at his watch. 'It's nearly three o'clock, and I was hoping to get back home tonight.'

'Ah, yes. You live in Cornwall, don't you?'

As Baldwin had already signed the chitty for his rail fare from Falmouth, Richter assumed that this was a rhetorical question and ignored it.

A colleague had once, rather unfairly, described Richter's cottage on the east side of the Lizard peninsula as 'a shithouse with an adjoining ruin'. It was better than that, of course, but not by much. Richter had bought it when it looked as if he would be spending about every third tour of duty at the Air Station at Culdrose, just a ten-minute drive away. After he had exchanged contracts, the Royal Navy had, probably deliberately, then posted him only to the Air Stations at Portland and Yeovilton, or to carrier-based squadrons and staff jobs in the London area.

Baldwin continued turning over the pages of the file, perusing them in a somewhat disapproving fashion. Finally he closed it, tapped the cover in a fatherly manner, and looked over at the stocky and slightly untidy man sitting in a chair on the other side of his desk.

Richter was one of those people who could look scruffy, even in a morning suit. His fair hair had obviously been combed at some point that day, but still looked badly cut and untidy. His suit was clean, but needed pressing, and his shoes definitely lacked the mirror-like polish that a batman laboured to achieve every morning on Baldwin's footwear.

But the most arresting thing about Richter, Baldwin realized, was his presence. He didn't seem to blink quite as often as he should, and his blue-green eyes held the gaze of anyone he was looking at perhaps a shade too intently. He seemed to exude an air of stillness and tension that was almost menacing, and the colonel could see why he had sometimes not meshed well with his superiors in the Navy.

'You've had no success yet with finding a job outside?' Baldwin asked.

Richter shook his head. He had almost lost count of the applications he had sent out, and all of them – apart from eliciting three cautious interviews with insurance companies looking for an employee who could legitimately put the rank 'Commander' on his business cards – had been firmly rejected. It had been a very frustrating three months, and Richter didn't like being reminded of this.

'If I'd found myself a job outside,' he replied, starting to get irritated, 'I wouldn't be sitting here now in this greenhouse, listening to you pontificating.'

Baldwin gave him an unfriendly stare. 'Careful, Mr Richter,' he said, tapping the file again. 'Insubordination is no more welcome outside the services than within them.'

'Neither is procrastination. If you've got a job for me, why don't you just tell me about it so I can either take it or leave it, and then get the hell out of here?'

Baldwin eyed him for some moments further, then opened the file again. He leaned across the desk to take a pencil from a small grey plastic tray, minutely inspected the point – presumably to ensure that it had been correctly sharpened, in the proper military fashion – and then wrote a short note on the minute sheet inside the file. Like most Old Admiralty Building staff, he regarded the introduction of the fountain pen as dangerously reactionary, and much preferred pencils.

'One of your other reporting officers commented

11

that you lacked patience and didn't suffer fools gladly, Mr Richter. I hope your present attitude is not an indication of the way you might conduct yourself if we did offer you employment.'

'That rather depends,' Richter said, 'on the fools I would be working for.'

Baldwin looked up sharply. 'I'm not sure I like the tone of that remark,' he said. 'Are you trying to suggest that I'm a fool?'

'I don't know,' Richter replied evenly. 'I don't know you well enough yet.'

Baldwin stared at Richter for a few moments, then made another note on the minute sheet, and underlined it twice. Richter was beginning to feel like a schoolboy in front of the headmaster.

Unfortunately, the only halfway interesting offer of possible employment Richter had received, since departing from the service of the Queen, had been a slip of paper bearing Baldwin's signature, which had fallen out of a buff envelope on the previous Thursday morning. What he really couldn't afford to do was annoy this man too much.

'Look,' Richter said, 'I've travelled halfway across England to get here – a very long, irritating and uncomfortable journey thanks to our new cattle-class service – and I face the prospect of doing the same trip in reverse, as soon as I get out of here. The only difference, going back, is that I'll probably have to stand up for most of the way.' He paused. 'As you've already said, I do need a job, but I don't have any readily saleable skills unless, for some bizarre reason, you're looking for a Harrier pilot. If you think you can employ me, I'd very much like to hear about it, but I really would appreciate it if you'd get to the point.'

Baldwin nodded slowly. 'What sort of a job do you think we have on offer?' he asked.

'How should I know?' Richter replied. 'Your letter inviting me to an interview only mentioned – and I quote – "possible employment as a retired officer in a post offering challenging and wide-ranging duties". It also hinted at travel, foreign travel, but it didn't say anything about the nature of the work, nor about the salary. Both of those topics happen to be of considerable interest to me.'

Baldwin appeared to come to a decision. 'Very well,' he said, 'let's look at specifics. First, the salary. This job is based on the normal retired officer scaling, and attracts an initial salary of twenty-eight thousand pounds a year, plus expenses.'

'That amount might attract some people,' Richter said, 'but it certainly doesn't attract me. Why is it so low?'

'I take it you're unfamiliar with the retired officer system,' Baldwin replied. 'All retired officer posts are subject to abated salaries because they take into account the pension that each appointee has already earned from his previous service career.'

Richter looked at him. 'I didn't know that,' he said, 'but it doesn't surprise me. I suppose that's another rule dreamed up by some civil servant at the Treasury.' Baldwin nodded. 'And I suppose,' Richter continued, 'that it was another Treasury civil servant who decreed that most officers should be forced to leave the services between January and the end of March, so as to ensure that they are denied the higher pensions and gratuities they would be entitled to if they continued serving after the first day of April?'

'Probably, yes.' Baldwin looked as if another smile was dangerously close.

'While at the same time,' Richter concluded, 'ensuring that their own substantial and fully index-linked salaries, and eventual index-linked pensions, are completely protected?'

The smile finally appeared. 'Who's pontificating now, Mr Richter? You're perfectly correct, though. But, as they say, there's no point in having power if you can't abuse it.'

Baldwin selected another slim file from the desktop and opened it. 'You're a bachelor, aren't you?' he asked.

'Yes,' Richter replied.

'Would you have any objection to being positively vetted?'

Positive vetting, and an even more rigorous process known as enhanced positive vetting, are the most stringent security checks that are normally applied to anyone working for the British government.

'Two things,' Richter said. 'First, just because I'm thirty-nine years old and not married doesn't necessarily mean that I spend all my spare time interfering with small boys or cruising gay bars.'

'I never implied that—'

'Yes, you did,' Richter snapped. 'Secondly, I've already been PV'd for the last staff job I did in London, at Military Air Traffic Operations Headquarters. That should be somewhere in my file.'

Baldwin looked somewhat embarrassed; not, Richter

suspected, about making a veiled implication of his sexual orientation, but more because he himself had missed the PV clearance.

'Ah, yes,' he said quickly. He flicked on through the file until he found the relevant papers and studied them. Then he closed the file again. 'Now, the job itself,' he continued. 'In simple terms, you'd be a courier.'

'Do you mean a Queen's Messenger?'

'Certainly not.' Baldwin looked slightly shocked. 'Queen's Messengers are very carefully chosen, normally from among senior ex-Army officers.'

'And insubordinate ex-naval officers don't fit the bill, is that it?'

'You said it, Mr Richter, not me.'

Richter nodded. 'So what sort of a courier, then?' He added, 'I hope you're not proposing I join those ranks of pensioners who plod about the Ministry of Defence, pushing trolleys loaded with files.'

Baldwin shook his head in slight irritation. 'Of course I'm not. We'd hardly be headhunting someone for a job like that.'

Now, that was an illuminating remark, Richter thought. He had assumed that the invitation to swell the ranks of retired officers, doing jobs that regular service officers wouldn't usually touch with a ten-foot barge-pole, was simply a normal Ministry of Defence ruse to save on the cost of advertising. If Baldwin was right, it looked as if – despite his service record – someone, for some reason, had actually decided they wanted him to work for them.

Baldwin looked down yet again at the file. 'We have,' he said, 'a need for classified documents and other materials to be transported by hand from place to place, nationally and internationally. That is the job for which we believe you are well suited.'

Baldwin's pedantic speech was beginning to get on Richter's nerves. 'Why and why?' he asked.

'Why and why what?'

'Why don't you send these documents and other bits and pieces by secure mail or by Queen's Messenger, if they're that important? And why do you think I would be any good at acting as a postman?'

'First,' Baldwin said, 'some of these materials are far too sensitive to entrust to the Post Office, under any circumstances. Second, the Queen's Messengers normally travel by regular routes, and their schedule is generally so busy that they cannot be pulled out to do special trips for us.'

'OK,' Richter said. 'So why me?'

Baldwin opened the file again. 'The one thing that all your reporting officers have consistently said about you,' he began, 'with the sole exception of that officer you abused in the Yeovilton Wardroom bar, is that you are totally loyal. Most have also commented on your competence, resourcefulness and stubborn attitude. The man we are looking for will need all those qualities.'

Richter thought about that for a few moments. 'You mentioned a starting salary of twenty-eight thousand pounds a year,' he said. 'What about the annual increments?'

Baldwin smiled slightly. According to the pre-release Resettlement Briefings that Richter had attended, in most recruitment interviews the moment the interviewee starts asking about money, he or she is already mentally committed to taking the job. Richter wasn't actually committed yet, but he was certainly interested.

'Increments will amount to three thousand pounds a year annually for the first six years, then five thousand pounds per year after that. In addition, the basic salary and increments will be index-linked, one year in arrears.'

Richter was surprised. 'That doesn't sound like the niggardly rate one would expect as a retired officer,' he said.

'It isn't,' Baldwin replied. 'I said the initial salary was based on the normal retired officer scales, but the annual increases are not. There is an ulterior motive,' he continued. 'If you accept this offer, we would like to keep you. And the annual increments and index-linking are intended to offer a reasonable incentive for you to stay in the job.' He paused a moment. 'Additionally, you will be allowed a generous expense account, and provided with an unlimited credit card. The only stipulation is that all expenses must necessarily be incurred as part of your duties, and should be reasonable and justified. If you need to hire a car, for example, we would expect you to choose a Ford, not a Porsche.'

'What if I needed to get somewhere very quickly?'

'Then choose a *fast* Ford.'

'I think that's an oxymoron, like military intelligence,' Richter said, and Baldwin looked at him sharply. 'There's no such thing as a fast Ford,' he continued. 'What about a slow Porsche?'

'You just find yourself a fast Ford,' Baldwin said, with a faint smile now. 'And there's definitely no such thing as a slow Porsche.'

'Where will I be based . . . when I'm not playing post-man to some far-flung country, I mean?' Richter asked.

'Here in London. In fact, you will share an office in this building.'

'What about accommodation here in London? I pre-sume you wouldn't expect me to commute every day from Cornwall?'

Baldwin allowed him another brief smile. 'No,' he said, 'we will provide you with service accommodation within a reasonable travelling distance of central London. You will have a senior officer's room at RAF Uxbridge.'

'Handy for the airport?'

'Exactly. In fact, both Heathrow and RAF Northolt are only a few minutes away by car, and Uxbridge also has a large pool of MT vehicles which can be used for deliveries within mainland Britain.'

Richter only had two last questions. 'Who will I be working for?' he asked. 'Who will be my direct superior?'

'Either me or my deputy, Lieutenant Colonel Reese-Jones.'

Richter nodded. 'How many other couriers work in the department?'

Baldwin looked slightly surprised. 'I thought I'd made that clear,' he said. 'This is a brand-new post – in fact, it's something of an experiment. There are no other couriers, or at least, not at present. You, Mr Richter, will be the only one.'

Hammersmith, London

The anonymous seven-storey building was located a little way north of the Hammersmith flyover, amid a tangle of backstreets and parking meters. The faded sign above the entrance door announced it was the premises of Hammersmith Commercial Packers and, in an untidy office suite on the ground floor, a small and very disorganized staff attempted to conduct the business as advertised, usually unsuccessfully.

In fact, the building itself extended for three floors below street level, in addition to the more visible seven above. It also housed the Foreign Operations Executive. The FOE's address and telephone numbers appeared in no directory, classified or otherwise, and no references to it, or its staff, or its considerable budget, were ever to be found in any official publication. There were three good reasons for this.

Firstly, as the FOE was a covert executive arm subordinate to the Secret Intelligence Service, even admitting to the existence of FOE would be tantamount to admitting that SIS itself existed, something that the British government had only ever done with the greatest possible reluctance. This curious failure to acknowledge something that was common knowledge to almost everyone – even London taxi drivers had routinely referred to Century House, the old headquarters building of the SIS, as 'Spook House' – has never been satisfactorily explained, and it led indirectly to the 'Spycatcher' humiliation.

Secondly, all FOE operations were both covert and deniable, which meant that FOE had to be the same.

Thirdly, the FOE's Director, Richard Simpson, was almost chronically paranoid about security, and invariably applied the 'need-to-know' principle as ruthlessly as possible. As far as he was concerned, nobody – apart from the Prime Minister and the Head and Deputy Head of SIS, to whom Simpson was operationally and functionally responsible – needed to know anything at all about FOE.

Even the members of the Joint Intelligence Committee, of which he was a non-speaking member, believed Simpson was simply an assistant to Sir Malcolm Holbeche, the Head of SIS. At an operational level, of course, things had to be somewhat different, as SIS officers frequently had to brief or debrief their FOE counterparts, but Simpson ensured that even these essential meetings were always conducted well away from Hammersmith and, where possible, in safe houses or on neutral ground.

The incoming call from Old Admiralty Building was made just after four in the afternoon. Simpson had been expecting it, and picked up the telephone immediately. 'Yes?'

'Switchboard, sir, with a call from the OAB.'

'Right, put it through,' Simpson said.

There was a click, a pause, and then the slightly nasal voice of Colonel Baldwin could be heard. 'Mr Simpson?'

'Yes. Any problems?'

'No,' Baldwin replied, with a slight hesitation. 'He is somewhat insubordinate, as his reports suggested

– he even inferred, somewhat obliquely, that I was a fool – but I think he has the qualities that you need.'

Simpson grunted. 'Did he take the job?'

'No,' Baldwin said, 'but I'm quite certain that he will. I'm sure he needs the money, for one thing, but I think the idea of the work itself attracted him.'

Simpson, who had ordered a check on Richter's bank account through SIS, and knew exactly how much he needed the money, nodded in silent agreement. 'What's the earliest he could become available?'

'On Monday immediately after he accepts the job,' Baldwin replied.

'So that could be as soon as next week?' Simpson asked.

'Yes, as long as he calls me either tomorrow or Friday,' Baldwin said. He asked, after a brief pause, 'Is there some urgency about this, Mr Simpson?'

'Yes,' Simpson said flatly, and without any elaboration. 'Keep me informed,' he added, and put down the telephone.

Simpson sat in silence for a few moments, then stood up and walked over to the south-facing window. His office was on the building's seventh floor, and he gazed without interest at an uninspiring view across the adjacent rooftops towards the Hammersmith flyover. Simpson was small and pinkish, and as fastidious in matters of dress and appearance as he was professional in his work. His dark grey suit was immaculate, and even the silk handkerchief in his breast pocket looked perfectly pressed.

He walked back to his desk, sat down again, and opened the temporary file bearing the single word

'RICHTER' on the cover. He looked briefly at the photograph attached on the left-hand side, and then scanned the personal details revealed on the printed sheets opposite.

'You'll do,' he muttered. 'You'll have to do.' Then he closed the file, put it to one side of his desk and turned his attention to the pink file he had been studying for most of the afternoon. Its title was 'EGRET SEVEN'.

Southern England

The train journey home was better than Richter had expected, mainly because he had managed to fight his way to a seat immediately. Having picked up a paperback at the station bookstall, he tried to read it as the train headed west, but his mind kept wandering away from the printed word.

Three things bothered him. First, at no time during his career in the service had Richter ever been aware of any requirement for a dedicated courier of the type proposed by Colonel Baldwin. Second, although the salary starting point was about what you might expect for courier duties, the annual increments were far too large. Third, coincidence apart, it seemed more than just providential that this job should have been created at exactly the time when Richter most needed to find employment. It was almost as if this job had been picked for him, rather than the other way around.

The next morning, Richter rang Baldwin and told him he'd take it.

Chapter Two

Monday
Sluzhba Vneshney Razvyedki Rossi Headquarters, Yasenevo,
Tëplyystan, Moscow

There were only seventeen passengers in the pale-yellow chartered coach which turned off the Moscow peripheral highway near the village of Tëplyystan, at just after eight-forty in the morning. Raya Kosov stretched herself comfortably across the two seats she had secured when she had boarded the vehicle, thirty minutes earlier, outside the Davydkovo station to the south-west of central Moscow, and she gazed incuriously out of the window.

The coach bounced and rattled on the uneven road surface as it made its way past the large sign warning 'Halt! No Trespassing! Water Conservation District', and continued slowly down the narrow road leading into the dense forest. About two hundred metres further on, the coach stopped at what looked like a militia post, but was actually a checkpoint manned continuously by armed SVR – Sluzhba Vneshney Razvyedki Rossi, or Russian Foreign Intelligence Service, personnel.

Two of the SVR troopers, wearing the uniforms of militiamen, boarded the coach as soon as it drew to a halt, and proceeded slowly and deliberately down the central aisle, as they carefully checked the identification of each occupant in turn.

Raya was sitting near the back, on the right-hand side of the coach, and she smiled at the young trooper as he reached out his hand for her pass. The trooper smiled back, as he did every time he saw her when he was on duty. Raya wondered how long it would be before he asked her out – or at least said something to her other than, 'Thank you, Captain Kosov.'

'Thank you, Captain Kosov,' the trooper said predictably, and Raya suppressed a chuckle as she replaced her pass in her handbag. The pass was a buff-coloured plastic card bearing her photograph and a series of perforations which formed a code specifying the areas within headquarters that she was authorized to enter.

Once the guards had left the coach, it continued for just over half a kilometre further into the forest, and then skirted a large roundabout bordered by the various car parks used by senior SVR officers. It came to a halt beside the guardroom, which bore an entirely misleading bronze plaque that announced in golden letters, to anyone who penetrated that far, that this building was a designated 'Scientific Research Centre'. The guardroom was the only point of access through a high chain-link fence topped by razor-wire, and it was occupied by armed troops from the SVR Guards Division, who again checked the passes of all the coach passengers as they filed through the turnstiles.

Once she had made it through the guardroom, Raya stepped out briskly along a driveway flanked by lawns and flowerbeds, covering the four hundred yards to SVR Headquarters in just a few minutes. The building was the former headquarters of the First Chief Directorate of the Komitet Gosudarstvennoy Bezopasnosti, better known as the KGB.

As the Soviet Union's all-pervasive Committee for State Security, this organization was the direct linear descendant of the Cheka, the terror organization created in 1917 by Feliks Dzerzhinsky to liquidate any opponents of communism. Over time, it had become one of the three principal forces within the USSR. The other two were the GRU – Glavnoye Razvedyvatelnoye Upravleniye, or Chief Intelligence Directorate of the Soviet General Staff – effectively Russian military intelligence; and, of course, the Communist Party itself. Of the three, the KGB was the largest and arguably the most powerful, but certainly the most feared organization.

The reason for this was simple. Although the KGB had a prime responsibility for any intelligence operations conducted against foreign powers, it was also required to ensure that the various peoples comprising the Soviet Union remained obedient to the directives and instructions of the ruling Communist Party. With such a vast population, the only effective method of achieving this was to enlist the regular assistance of unofficial informers, which the KGB recruited in huge numbers.

The recruitment method employed was as simple and effective as it was ruthless. A Soviet citizen would be told to report to the local KGB headquarters – an invitation that was impossible to ignore. Once there, he would be asked if he wished to assist the Communist Party by acting as an unofficial and unpaid agent of the KGB. To this question, the unfortunate citizen could only answer in the affirmative, because to refuse to act for the

Communist Party could be legally defined as treason, and that was an offence punishable by death.

But, even by agreeing to become an informer, that citizen was not yet out of the wood. If the reports he or she supplied to the KGB officers, about immediate family, friends and acquaintances, did not contain a sufficient amount of compromising material, the informer would be summoned back by the KGB. Its officers would then point out how other informers operating in the same district were producing evidence of the type needed, so the new informer must either be deliberately suppressing information, or not seeking it with sufficient assiduity. Both failings in responsibility were by any definition both anti-Soviet and anti-Communist, and would therefore amount to treason.

In desperation, many informers resorted to inventing stories about mysterious strangers, or reporting snatches of conversation supposedly overheard between unidentified citizens, or else settling grudges by implicating people who had merely annoyed or cheated them.

It was conservatively estimated that, during the KGB's heyday, two out of every five Soviet citizens were operating as full- or part-time informers for the organization. A saying popular in Russia at the time suggested that every time a Soviet citizen farted, the KGB could smell it, and this was not considered to be much of an exaggeration.

When Mikhail Gorbachev, and later Boris Yeltsin, came to power in Russia, the winds of change were already blowing, and the KGB was officially disbanded in 1991. In fact, of course, no such thing happened.

The KGB had always acted as the 'sword and shield'

of the Communist Party, and there was no way that the Party – not to mention the Russian government – would voluntarily disarm itself by destroying its main intelligence service and principal means of support. Besides, it needed the KGB to keep the peoples of the Confederation of Independent States in check, just as the KGB had controlled the actions of the citizens of the Union of Soviet Socialist Republics for over half a century.

What actually took place was little more than a departmental reorganization.

The Border Guards' Chief Directorate, which was charged with maintaining the physical security of all Soviet borders, was transferred to the Russian Army, which should probably have been responsible for that from the start. The Second Chief Directorate, effectively the domestic security service, and the Fifth Chief Directorate, responsible for the control of dissident groups within the Soviet Union, were similiarly reformed and renamed.

But the prestigious First Chief Directorate, with responsibility for foreign espionage and intelligence operations, continued its operations without interruption. Except for two changes of name, that is. The first such change, to Centralnoye Sluzhba Razvyedki, or the Central Intelligence Service of the USSR, occurred in 1991. That designation lasted only until January 1992, when it then became the Sluzhba Vneshney Razvyedki Rossi, the name under which it still operates. The only other significant change at the time was the appointment of Yevgeny Primakov, an experienced professional intelligence officer, as the organization's first head. Neither of these changes had any practical effect upon the ongoing operations at Yasenevo, apart from alterations in section titles and several irritating and largely unnecessary revisions to the internal telephone directory.

The SVR retained control of all agents recruited and run by the KGB, and has been diligently increasing their numbers ever since, not least because the break-up of the former USSR has significantly added to the number of countries from which Russia now requires intelligence data.

The new organization continues to work from the former KGB's sixty-acre complex of offices at Yasenevo – bearing more than a passing resemblance to the headquarters of the Central Intelligence Agency at Langley, Virginia. The main building was designed by Finnish architects and its construction utilized considerable quantities of aluminium and glass. The original seven-storey structure is shaped like three-pointed star, but is now dwarfed by a new twenty-two-floor extension situated at the far end of the western arm of the core building.

Raya Kosov walked towards the extremity of the north-easterly wing, passing on her way the separate entrance reserved for senior officers. She pushed through the glass double doors of the main entrance, stepped into a wide marble foyer, and again showed her pass to further SVR sentries. Striding past the bust of Feliks Dzerzhinsky standing in the middle of the foyer, she crossed to the news-stand to one side, where she bought a magazine. She then passed through a further checkpoint and into the new extension building, before stopping at the main bank of elevators.

As the doors opened, she stepped into the lift, and pressed the button for the fifteenth floor.

Paxton Hall, Felsham, Bury St Edmunds, Suffolk

The land had been a part of the Paxton family estate in Suffolk since 1675, but the proximity of marshy fenland and the difficulty of providing proper drainage had ensured that it remained relatively unproductive. In 1724 Roger Paxton decided to erect a new family seat at the edge of the land, and within eight years the Paxton family had built the Hall and moved in.

Roger Paxton's abiding passion, and his ultimate ruin, was gambling, and in 1742 ownership of the house, and the six acres of woodland that surrounded it, passed to one Giles de Verney in settlement of numerous debts. The new owner took up residence with his family, put up with the damp and cold for just over two years, and then gave the property to his cousin Charles.

Charles de Verney actually liked living in the Hall, and his descendants continued to reside there until the early years of the twentieth century. The last de Verney to own the property was Edith, who survived her husband by the better part of forty years and, after his death in 1876, retreated to the Hall in her widow's weeds.

With the passing years, she became increasingly eccentric and erratic in her behaviour, virtually never leaving the premises and steadily filling each room of the large house with rubbish. Edith finally died in her small single bedroom at one end of the east wing, all alone as she'd been for fifteen years, and her body wasn't found there for nearly three weeks.

William Verney – whose branch of the family had dropped the 'de' in 1863 – became the new owner, but preferred the social life of London and his spacious flat in Knightsbridge. He visited the property, and declared that it was one of the most unattractive houses he had ever seen, and certainly the ugliest property he had ever had the misfortune to own. He had the place cleared out and cleaned up, then secured it against intruders and the winds blowing off the North Sea, and virtually forgot about it.

For no readily discernible reason, the house was requisitioned by the Ministry of Defence in the latter stages of the First World War, but was not actually used for any known purpose. In 1919, with the male line of the Verney family all but exterminated in the carnage of the Somme and in Flanders, the few surviving members decided they had no need of this big, draughty old place on the edge of the fens, and gratefully accepted the ministry's somewhat niggardly offer to purchase it.

Builders were employed to sort out the damp in the extensive cellars, windows and doors were replaced, and the interior was repainted and redecorated. Then, perhaps not knowing quite what else to do with the place, the ministry closed up the Hall and employed a local building firm to visit and inspect the premises on a monthly basis.

With the outbreak of the Second World War, the place was hurriedly opened up again and converted: first into a rest and recuperation centre for injured RAF airmen, and then into a training centre for Special Operations Executive (SOE) personnel. The explosions and noise of small-arms fire that echoed through the surrounding woods were a constant reminder of the difficult and dangerous missions being undertaken by the young men and women that the locals occasionally spotted in the village.

Oddly enough, nobody seemed particularly surprised when those noises continued after hostilities had ended. Locals who thought they knew exactly what was going on – which in Suffolk meant almost everyone – nodded wisely when asked about the Hall, and it soon became common knowledge that Royal Marine Commandos had taken over the estate for training purposes.

When the Special Air Service stormed the Iranian Embassy in London in April 1980, word spread quickly around Felsham that the Hall had been used for the final training before the attack. Many locals claimed to have noticed one or more of the troopers drinking in the local pubs before the assault took place and even to have recognized some of the black-clad figures seen clambering over parapets on *News at Ten*.

All of which, of course, was complete nonsense, but the stories suited the authorities well enough. In fact, neither the Royal Marines nor the SAS had ever been anywhere near Paxton Hall. At the end of the Second World War, ownership of the building had been quietly transferred from the Ministry of Defence to the Foreign Office, and the Secret Intelligence Service had moved in.

Or, to be exact, a caretaker staff moved in, and the Hall became one of two SIS safe houses in Suffolk. The cars and vans occasionally arriving at odd hours of the day and night did not contain SAS troopers eager to improve their shooting skills, although there was a firing range on the property which was still used occasionally. Instead, the vehicles conveyed SIS agents who had to be briefed prior to undertaking missions abroad; or defectors – only a few, but one of the most important sources of foreign intelligence – fetched in for initial debriefing, and intelligence professionals who needed a secure and discreet location for their meetings with members of other services.

The first car to arrive, early that afternoon, was a dark green Jaguar saloon with a single occupant. The vehicle stopped at the guardhouse, just outside the electrically controlled gates, and after a few moments was permitted to proceed up the drive. The second vehicle – also a Jaguar, but black and with three men inside – arrived ten minutes later.

Old Admiralty Building, Spring Gardens, London

The office assigned to Richter, on the first floor of the Old Admiralty Building, was almost exactly what he had been expecting. It was a small room, with yellowish-cream walls that badly needed repainting, preferably in a different colour, and contained two metal desks, with somewhat worn swivel chairs, and four grey filing cabinets. The single window looked out into a light well that extended up to the roof, and the gloom meant that the twin overhead fluorescent lights were switched on all day. Although clearly intended to accommodate two people, there was no sign of any other occupant. The only good thing about it, Richter thought, was that at least he wouldn't be spending all his working hours here.

He had driven up from Cornwall on Sunday, and found his room at RAF Uxbridge without difficulty.

He knew the base well from his previous appointment at Military Air Traffic Operations – MATO – which was then based at Hillingdon House, within the RAF Uxbridge station complex.

That morning he had travelled into London by tube, arriving at the Old Admiralty Building just after nine. He'd been greeted there in a somewhat perfunctory fashion by Colonel Baldwin, before he was shown round the building by a young Royal Navy lieutenant. Getting his photograph taken, and sorting out his building pass and personal identity card – which identified him as a Senior Executive Officer, but did not specify for which organization he worked – had occupied the rest of that morning. Richter had then gone for lunch in a nearby pub with the lieutenant, who was on hold-over pending a posting abroad, and he had returned to his office just after one-thirty.

He had been sitting at his desk for less than five minutes, doing absolutely nothing because there was absolutely nothing for him to do, when Baldwin knocked on the door and walked in.

Richter looked up enquiringly. 'This is somewhat sooner than I expected,' Baldwin announced, 'but it looks as if your first trip will be taking place on Wednesday this week.'

'Where to?' Richter asked.

'France, I think,' Baldwin replied, 'but you're scheduled to attend a formal briefing tomorrow morning. It will take place in Hammersmith, at this address.' The colonel placed a single sheet of paper on the desk top.

Richter barely even glanced at it. 'A formal briefing for a courier delivery?' he asked. 'Isn't that a bit of overkill?'

'Not necessarily,' Baldwin said. 'It may not be completely straightforward.'

Richter looked up and smiled thinly. 'I'd have been very surprised if it was,' he remarked.

Baldwin stared at him silently for a few moments, then turned on his heel and left the office.

Paxton Hall, Felsham, Bury St Edmunds, Suffolk

The main conference room was on the ground floor, but the four men had decided to meet in the first-floor library instead. The chairs were more comfortable for one thing, and Sir Malcolm Holbeche, the current 'C' – the head of the Secret Intelligence Service – preferred an informal atmosphere. And in the library he could smoke.

'Are you sure, absolutely sure, of your facts?' he asked William Moore, the head of Section Nine of the SIS and responsible for Russian affairs, once the pleasantries were out of the way.

Moore shook his head. 'Not one hundred per cent, Sir Malcolm, no. With any data of this sort there is always room for some doubt, some uncertainty. The balance of probability, though, suggests that we have been compromised.'

The man at the other end of the table snorted in disgust. 'Why don't you just come out with it? What you mean is that we've got a high-level mole.'

Holbeche looked pained by the remark. In his opinion, George Arkin – the head of the Security Service, MI5 – was rather too blunt in his opinion, especially where delicate inter-service matters were concerned.

Arkin's background was north-country and police – neither of which endeared him to Holbeche – and both his origins and his career had engendered a fondness for what Arkin liked to call plain speaking and common sense.

One of the tasks with which the Security Service was entrusted was the detection and investigation of traitors within the ranks of the Secret Intelligence Service, and this role had on numerous occasions led to outright hostility between the two organizations.

'Yes,' Holbeche agreed, 'we think we have a mole.'

He had been reluctant to involve Arkin at all, but the data obtained by Moore had left him with little alternative. He just hoped that this whole episode could be wrapped up fairly quickly and quietly.

'Right, then,' Arkin nodded briskly, 'what's your evidence, and what do you want me to do about it? And who's this Mr Simpson, and what's he doing here?' He gestured to the smaller man sitting in the armchair to his right.

'Mr Simpson is here as my assistant and advisor,' Holbeche snapped. 'Now, Moore will outline the data we've so far received.' He sat back in his chair and reached into his jacket pocket for a cigar.

William Moore took a red file from his briefcase and placed it on the table in front of him, but didn't yet open it. He leaned forward and, in unconscious mimicry, Arkin and Simpson did the same. When Moore now spoke, his voice was low and intense.

'Ten days ago,' he said, 'a Russian diplomatic courier was taken suddenly and violently ill at Heathrow Airport. He had already passed through Passport Control, and was sitting in the departure lounge waiting to board the flight to Moscow when he got up and made a dash towards the toilet, but vomited on the floor before he made it, and then passed out.'

Moore paused briefly, then continued. 'The Heathrow medical staff were called immediately, and the Russian, whose name is Sinyavsky, was rushed to the airport medical centre, where the on-call doctor examined him, and from there he was taken to Hillingdon Hospital. Heathrow security staff were notified, because Sinyavsky was carrying a diplomatic passport, and he had a locked briefcase chained to his left wrist. In due course, the Metropolitan Police were notified, and they in turn called the Foreign Office and Special Branch.'

All of them there knew the Security Service had no powers of arrest – in fact, its very existence had only fairly recently been officially acknowledged – and it relied on Special Branch officers to carry out executive actions on its behalf. The Special Branch comprised some four hundred detectives attached to local police forces throughout the country, but with the highest concentration in London, and it was accountable to the Home Secretary through London's Metropolitan Police Commissioner.

'The duty Special Branch Inspector, Charles Wingate, immediately went to Hillingdon and saw Sinyavsky in hospital. The Russian was still unconscious, and the doctors thought he was likely to remain that way. They were treating him, by the way, for salmonella poisoning.'

Arkin interrupted, and tried for a joke. 'Most people get that *after* they've flown with Aeroflot, not before.' He looked at the faces around him, but saw not a trace of a smile. 'And', he added, 'he seems to have suffered a very severe reaction, if it was salmonella. I thought most people just got stomach cramps, the squits, and so on.'

Moore nodded. 'Normally, you'd be right, but there are several strains of salmonella, and subsequent tests showed that Sinyavsky had contracted Salmonella typhi, probably from undercooked poultry. Salmonella typhi is a comparatively rare strain, but it causes typhoid fever, and proves fatal in about thirty per cent of cases. Sinyavsky, I'm pleased to say, is now recovering.'

Moore finally picked up the file and opened it. 'Inspector Wingate instantly ordered Sinyavsky to be kept in isolation – which simply reinforced instructions for what the hospital was already doing – and had an armed police officer posted outside his room. The key for the handcuff on the briefcase was in the pocket of Sinyavsky's jacket, and the doctors had already removed it from his wrist so that they could treat him more easily. The briefcase, of course, was locked, and was considered diplomatic baggage, so Wingate himself took it into safe custody.'

Moore noticed that Arkin had begun to smile. 'Let me guess,' the MI5 man said. 'In order to notify the appropriate authorities, Inspector Wingate had to open the briefcase in order to try to discover the name of Sinyavsky's superior. And, while he was leafing through the contents, he happened to notice – and perhaps even copy – some of the papers it contained?'

Moore shook his head. 'Not exactly,' he replied, 'but close. Wingate knew from Sinyavsky's passport that he was a Russian diplomat, so there was no reason why he should not have contacted the Russian Embassy without even looking at the briefcase. In fact, that's exactly what he did, but he waited until the following morning before taking action.'

Arkin grunted. 'Now I remember,' he said. 'Our people opened an envelope, as I recall, but the contents were passed immediately to SIS.'

'Correct.' Moore nodded briefly, and continued. 'Wingate handed the briefcase over to A Branch of the Security Service – Operations and Resources – for examination. Their technicians opened the briefcase without any particular difficulty, and they examined the contents. Most of it was just routine but, as Mr Arkin has said, there was one thick A4-size envelope that was heavily sealed and gave a destination address of SVR Headquarters at Yasenevo. After consultation with the MI5 and SIS duty officers, it was decided to open the envelope and copy its contents.'

'A "flap and seal" artist?' Simpson asked.

Moore shook his head and smiled. 'No, the march of technology continues unabated. We no longer even have operatives trained to do that. Instead we have a large grey machine that cuts open the envelope, and then reseals it using the actual fibres of the paper itself. Like the brief-case, the envelope was X-rayed first, to ensure that there were no anti-handling or other security devices, but it was found clean, and then the machine proceeded to open it.'

In the pause that followed, Arkin gazed intently at Moore. 'Inside,' Moore continued, 'we found one hundred and thirty-seven sheets of paper. It was a complete listing of the directory structure and all the file names listed on the London Data Centre System-Three computer.'

'Oh, fuck me,' Arkin said very quietly, leaning back in his chair.

Chapter Three

Monday
Sluzhba Vneshney Razvyedki Rossi Headquarters, Yasenevo,
Tëplyystan, Moscow

Raya Kosov got up from her black plastic swivel chair,
picked up her pocket binoculars and walked across to
the window. Working in the new Russian-designed
and built extension at Yasenevo had many disadvan-
tages – including the distance from the staff canteen
located on the first floor of the main building – but it also
offered some compensations.

One of these was certainly the view. From her window on the west side of the extension, she could see a
panorama encompassing most of Moscow, albeit somewhat distant and largely obscured by the ugly tower
blocks of nearby housing estates, and of that splen-
did view she never tired. Most of the offices occupied
by senior officers were situated on the other side of
the building, looking south over a peaceful vista of the
lake and trees, but Raya much preferred her north-
facing room.

The first time she had brought her binoculars to
Yasenevo, she had immediately been suspended, her
superiors duly informed and the binoculars confiscated.
Her explanation, that she simply wanted to look out at
the city of Moscow, had been rejected without comment.

The binoculars had then been examined in detail by the Technical Services staff, who had dismantled them, looking for the camera, tape-recorder or other such device that the SVR guards were certain would be hidden inside. It was with some disappointment that Technical Services, some three weeks later, announced that the binoculars were just binoculars, and therefore of no possible security concern.

A week after that, the binoculars were returned to Raya, and her right of access was restored. Her superior officer gave her a mild reprimand for wasting time – her own time in looking at the view, and Technical Services' time in examining the binoculars – and then she went back to work.

Raya smiled at the recollection as she adjusted the focus. It was a clear day, and she could clearly see the green roof and yellow and white facade of the Great Kremlin Palace. Out of sight from her vantage point, lying slightly beyond and to the right of the palace, lay the Lubyanka. It was the former headquarters of the KGB and for Raya, in many ways, a far more interesting place.

She was still standing at the window, staring northwest, when her office door opened.

Paxton Hall, Felsham, Bury St Edmunds, Suffolk

In the silence that followed Arkin's remark, the sound of approaching footsteps became audible outside the room. The footsteps then terminated with a double knock on the library door.

'Come,' Sir Malcolm Holbeche said, raising his voice slightly.

The door opened and one of the SIS resident staff poked his head around it. 'Mr Willets has arrived, sir.'

'Good,' Holbeche nodded. 'Send him in.'

'Willets?' Arkin looked enquiringly at the head of the Secret Intelligence Service. 'I don't think I recognize that name.'

'I'm glad to hear it, Arkin,' Holbeche replied. 'In fact, I'd have been worried if you did know him. Roger Willets is the Chief Security Officer at the London Data Centre, so he's directly involved in this serious breach.'

The London Data Centre, known as the LDC, was British intelligence's most secret computer centre and occupied three floors underneath Whitehall. The first floor housed the hardware itself, the next one down was the location for the terminals and the system servicing staff, and the lowest and most secure floor held the data disks. Access to the Centre was through the Foreign and Commonwealth Office, since the FCO's entrance was used by so many people that it would be difficult for enemy agents to identify and target the Centre's staff specifically.

'However,' Holbeche continued, 'Willets is also a computer specialist, and I've asked him here because there are some technical factors involved in this problem which need explaining.'

Holbeche stopped speaking as the door opened again and a tall and excessively thin man entered the room. Moore made the introductions, and Willets sat down next to Simpson.

'Right,' Arkin said, ignoring Holbeche. 'Let's have it.'

Willets glanced towards Holbeche, who nodded almost imperceptibly, then he cleared his throat. 'You've heard what was recovered from the Russian courier?' he began, addressing no one in particular.

William Moore nodded, but Arkin butted in before Willets could continue. 'Let's get one thing quite clear,' he said. 'Is there any possibility that this printout the Russian was carrying was not the real thing? It couldn't, for example, have been just a clever fake, part of some deception operation that's being run by SIS without them telling the rest of us?'

Willets opened his mouth to reply, but Holbeche beat him to it. 'Categorically not,' he snapped, 'and that is a wholly improper suggestion. No "deception operations", as you describe them, are run by my organization without my prior knowledge and approval, and I invariably ensure that all interested parties are kept fully informed.'

Willets nodded his agreement. 'There's no possibility that the data was faked,' he said. 'I checked a copy of the printout with the LDC system administrator – without telling him where it had come from, of course – and it is definitely the real thing. I should emphasize,' he went on, 'that the printout is not in itself a serious security breach, as it only lists the computer directory structure and the names of the files, but not the actual contents of those files.'

'Agreed,' Moore said, 'but that rather misses the point. The vital fact is that whoever supplied that listing obviously has access to the computer system, and can presumably supply copies of whatever files the Russians would like to see. Or, at least, those files that his own security clearance allows him to access.'

'In fact,' Richard Simpson interrupted, 'the listing is simply a shopping list for the SVR, to let them pick and choose what they want to see. And that may actually be good news for us.'

'Why?' Holbeche asked.

'Because it's possible that no secrets have so far been betrayed by this unknown source. This looks to me like one of the first steps in a treacherous relationship and, whoever this source is, he's proving to the Russians that he has the necessary access. And by getting them to choose whichever files they want to see, he can avoid copying data which would be of no interest to them. There's also the financial angle, of course.'

'Explain that, please,' Arkin said.

'The only things missing from the shopping list are the prices. My guess is that our source is waiting to see what files the Russians want, before he tells them what it'll cost them.'

Moore nodded. 'Yes, that makes sense, and you might be right. Maybe the leak hasn't started yet, and we can stop it before things go any further. In fact, we might even be able to make capital out of this, by turning it into a disinformation operation.'

Warming to his theme, he leaned forward. 'If we can identify the source, and then intercept the instructions sent to him by the SVR, we can achieve two things. First, we'll find out what particular areas are of interest to the Russians, which will to some extent show what their current objectives are. Second, we can create faked copies of the files they ask for, and thus misdirect them.'

There was a brief silence, then Holbeche spoke. 'There seem to be rather a lot of "ifs" in that scenario,

43

William. Identifying the source won't be easy, which is one reason why Mr Willets is here.'

Holbeche gestured for Willets to speak. 'Perhaps this is the time to discuss the purely technical aspects of this matter?'

Willets nodded. 'For obvious reasons, our security precautions are stringent,' he said. 'We rigidly control access to and from the LDC floors, and all personnel are subject to physical searches of their briefcases and other bags on leaving the section. This volume of paper simply could not therefore have been removed from the LDC.'

'What about someone removing it a few pages at a time, sandwiched inside a newspaper, say?' Arkin asked.

The question was directed at Willets, but it was Moore who answered. 'We looked at that, but it's not possible,' he said. 'The listing we found in the Russian courier's briefcase was printed on continuous stationery, without any breaks. That means it was an original printout.'

'And there's another problem,' Willets went on. 'The printers used in the LDC – apart from the dot-matrix units on the second floor, which are used only by the system support staff – are all lasers. This printout was done on a twenty-four-pin dot-matrix printer.'

'How do you know?' Arkin asked.

'We counted the indentations that the print-head made on the paper,' Willets replied briefly.

'And what about the second-floor staff? From what you've said, they have the right kind of printer, and they also have unrestricted access to the computers. That gives them both the means and the opportunity, and

puts them right in the frame, according to my book.'
Arkin thrust his chin forward, somewhat aggressively.

He had made few friends during his rise through
the ranks, not least because his investigations were
characterized by a thoroughness that bordered on the
obsessive, and he had no objection to treading – or more
accurately stamping – on others' toes.

'You didn't mention motive,' Willets said mildly.

Arkin smiled somewhat sadly. 'Money, perhaps?'
he suggested. 'I don't suppose you pay the staff that
much. Maybe one of them reckoned he could do a little
unofficial overtime for the Russian Embassy, and make
himself enough to retire on.'

Holbeche had turned slightly pink, but Willets
seemed unfazed by Arkin's attack on the integrity of the
LDC staff. 'We think alike,' he said. 'That was my first
reaction, too – but it's impossible. Precisely because of
the access those staff have, and the sensitivity of the data
stored at the LDC, the second floor has a total surveillance system. And I do mean total.'

He leaned forward, tapping his pencil on the table for
emphasis. 'As I've already said, every bag, briefcase or
other package that the staff take in or out is physically
examined. This may include X-raying if the security
personnel think that necessary. Second, the only entry
to or exit from that floor is through specially adapted
turnstiles which include metal detectors, and anyone
triggering the detectors is subject to an immediate and
complete body search. Third, the entire floor is under
video surveillance twenty-four hours a day. And
finally,' Willets concluded, 'every keystroke made on
every computer console on the floor is recorded, and

warnings are automatically generated if certain actions are even attempted. These "certain actions" include directory printouts, file printouts and file copying.'

Willets paused and looked directly across at Arkin. 'About the only thing I am quite certain about here,' he said, 'is that this printout was not made on the second floor of the London Data Centre.'

Sluzhba Vneshney Razvyedki Rossi Headquarters, Yasenevo, Tëplyystan, Moscow

Major Yuri Abramov, the Yasenevo Data-Processing System Network Principal Manager, stood in the office doorway and gazed with ill-concealed appreciation at Captain Raya Kosov's back view. As he did so he reflected how it would have contrasted so sharply with that of his wife had they been placed side by side. Abramov had married early, far too early, and the slim and charming peasant girl with the rosy cheeks had turned within ten years into the shapeless, bulky woman with whom he now shared his life, and his small apartment. The rosy cheeks were still there, but three children and the genes of fifteen generations of farm girls had obliterated almost everything else in her that he had originally found so attractive.

The first time he had met Raya, Abramov had seen in her something of Eugenia as she had been when they got married, and as a result his feelings for his young subordinate had never been entirely dispassionate. Of course, he had never shown Raya any special sign of affection or extended her any special treatment – that would have been considered *nekulturny* or uncultured – but without doubt he enjoyed having her as his senior computer-systems specialist.

Raya had known who her visitor was as soon as the door opened, and she turned very slowly to face him. Like any woman who enjoys the admiration of a man, she was perfectly aware of his feelings for her, and ensured that she looked and acted to please him. She smiled a welcome to Abramov, then stretched, lifting her arms slowly above her head, her fingers interlaced, and elaborately failed to notice the way his eyes widened as her blouse tightened over her breasts.

'Major,' she greeted him deferentially, dropping her arms and moving behind her desk. 'How can I help you?'

Abramov coughed, then walked over to the desk and sat down in the chair facing her, motioning for her to sit also. 'As you know, Raya, I will be constantly in and out of the office during all of next week, so I would like you to do two small jobs for me, because I won't have the time. In fact, you will need to start on one of them almost immediately.'

This was nothing new to Raya. Major Abramov had come to rely on her more and more since she had been appointed to the section some years earlier. As a result, these 'little jobs' had arrived on her desk with increasing frequency as his confidence in her had increased.

At the age of eighteen, Raya had moved to Moscow in order to attend the university. There she had been picked out by her tutors as suitable SVR material, even before the end of her first year. All students at Russian universities were assessed by their tutors for academic progress, but also for their aptitude for employment by either the SVR or GRU – Russian military intelligence.

In Raya's case, her tutors had been favourably impressed by her considerable skills in two areas that were crucial to SVR operations: languages and computer science. Even before she arrived in Moscow to begin her studies, she was virtually fluent in English, French and German.

A background check had revealed no apparent security problems. Her father had died in a road accident when she was still a child, while her mother lived in a small apartment near Minsk, and she had no other close living relatives. Joining the Communist Party as soon as she was old enough, Raya had been a regular attendant at its meetings and an enthusiastic member as a student.

She had been approached by the SVR midway through her second year at university, and had joined them immediately after graduation. After initial general training at one of the organization's numerous establishments on the outskirts of Moscow, Raya had then been selected for a series of advanced computer-systems courses.

Her first posting had been to the Lubyanka, as a junior systems-security officer, and on the strength of her performance, and following a lengthy and exhaustive security check, she had then been transferred to Yasenevo as Abramov's deputy. There she had been cleared for access to documents with classification up to *Sov Sekretno*, Top Secret, and given formal responsibility for computer-system maintenance and document security.

'Of course, Major,' Raya replied, sitting forward.

Abramov leaned across and placed two folders on Raya's desk. She picked them up, glanced briefly at their titles, then put them down again, her full attention focusing on her superior.

'Before we discuss these files, could I ask what progress you've made with the workstation upgrades?'

Like any network manager, Raya was also required to carry out periodic updating of the hardware of all computers on the network. Her current upgrade programme was fairly basic – just adding extra RAM chips to the networked machines. Although the SVR had a substantial budget, computers were still relatively expensive, and the IT section had a policy of upgrading older machines until they became technologically obsolete or simply stopped working.

'I've finished most of them, Major. There's another dozen or so still to do, but I should complete the installation by the end of this week.'

Because of the sensitivity of the data held at Yasenevo, ordinary computer technicians were not permitted to work on machines attached to the network. That meant only she or Major Abramov were allowed to handle the upgrades, which in practice meant Raya always did it.

'Good, and now these files. As you can see, the first one orders a full security check on all files held on the system. You've done one before, I know, but I would like to remind you of the most important checks you should run.'

Abramov began ticking points off on his fingers. 'You must inspect the access history of every file that's classified Top Secret or above since the last full review.

You must make a random check of one hundred files carrying a classification of Secret or lower, and check the access history of at least ten per cent of these files. You should check every officer's password to ensure that it has been changed within the last three months, in accordance with standing orders. And,' Abramov finished, 'you should obviously thoroughly investigate and report on every potential security breach that you detect.'

The Russian officer smiled at Raya. 'I know it's boring and irritating stuff,' he said, 'but that's one of the crosses we must bear. Security never sleeps, and it must be seen to be effective at all times.'

Raya smiled back at him, nodding at the adage that was quoted straight off the front cover of the security section's handbook. In fact, Abramov was both right and wrong. She hadn't carried out just one full security check before; since she had joined Yasenevo she had actually performed *every* scheduled check. Once Abramov had decided she was competent, he had delegated these, and other vital but tedious tasks, to her and then contented himself with simply reading and approving her reports. In fact, Raya was, in all but name, acting as the true Yasenevo network manager.

However, she didn't mind that. In fact, the working relationship she enjoyed with Abramov suited her very well.

'And the second task, Major?' Raya asked gently.

'Purely routine,' Abramov replied. 'You may perhaps remember that, shortly after you arrived here, we began receiving information from a new agent in Britain. We named this source "*Gospodin*" – "Mister" – and one of your first jobs here was to create a restricted-access directory in which all the source *Gospodin* data was stored.'

Abramov paused and looked at Raya questioningly and, as he did so, she felt a sudden chill. She remembered the incident very well, and for more than one reason. Surely not, she thought; not after all this time. Not when she was so close. She cleared her throat and gazed steadily at the officer.

'Yes, Major, I remember it well. Is there some problem there?'

Abramov shook his head vigorously. 'No, no,' he said, 'no problem at all. I just want you to repeat the process.'

'We have a new source, then?'

'No,' Abramov said, 'the new material has also been sent by source *Gospodin*, but it has been obtained from a new location. *Gospodin* is very prolific and has managed to access an entirely new database. In fact, a lot of this material has been received only over the last two months, but the operational staff here have been assessing it to ensure that it is genuine and not disinformation, or some kind of deception operation that's been mounted against us. Yesterday I was told that the assessment is favourable, and now all the material needs to be stored on the database.'

He paused, to let her absorb this, then he continued. 'This information *Gospodin* has sent has the same Top-Secret security classification as his previous material and, like that, will need to be stored in encrypted form in a restricted-access directory. Please create that directory, prepare the encryption routine, and put security protocols in place to allow access by Directorate heads only. This must be done immediately, as those files are already being prepared for uploading.'

Raya didn't comment, other than to ask the obvious question. 'And the name of this directory, sir?'

'*Zakoulok*,' Abramov replied, and, with a final smile, stood up and left her office.

Raya watched the door close behind him, then reached down to open the bottom drawer of her desk. She pulled out a large loose-leaf book and opened it. Abramov's smile, and the way he had said the word *Zakoulok*, had told her that this name was something special or unusual.

If she had served for longer in the SVR, she would probably have recognized the word but, as she was a comparative newcomer, she had never operated out in the field, or even outside Yasenevo and the Lubyanka.

The book she had opened was a directory of old KGB and current SVR slang and code words. The majority of its pages were copied from official SVR publications but, at the back of the book, Raya had begun making entries of her own, as she discovered new words or new implications of code words that she already knew. She didn't even bother with the back pages this time, because she knew she had never encountered *Zakoulok* as a code word. Although she knew its literal meaning: 'the back alley'.

She scanned the printed pages rapidly, then stopped and smiled as she read one particular entry. 'How interesting,' she murmured. 'I wonder . . .' Her voice faded into silence as the implications dawned on her. She closed the book with a snap, and pushed it back into the desk drawer.

For a few moments she sat staring into space, then

swung her chair round to face the computer screen. After entering her supervisor username and password, she began creating the new directory, using the encryption routines and access protocols exactly as ordered.

After she'd finished, she got up and locked her office door. Then she sat down again and created another directory that was both hidden from other users and also password-protected. Then she wrote a single line of code, which she inserted as an additional instruction at the beginning of the *Zakoulok* directory encryption routine.

The unauthorized code contained a single, very simple instruction: the original name and number of every file placed in the *Zakoulok* directory would then be copied into the hidden directory as plaintext. She had done exactly the same thing five years earlier, when Abramov had instructed her to create the *Gospodin* directory.

Raya surveyed what she had done, and nodded in satisfaction. After exiting the program, she unlocked her office door again, and sat back in her chair. She had effectively created a specialized 'back door' into the 'back alley' directory. All she had to do now was wait for the files to be copied onto the system, and the new data would form an important part of her dowry.

Paxton Hall, Felsham, Bury St Edmunds, Suffolk

The silence that followed Willets's last statement was finally broken by William Moore.

'Before we convened this meeting, we had already

established that the printout had to have come from somewhere other than the LDC,' he said. 'If the leak had been from inside the Centre, Willets could have handled it without any external assistance.'

'And that's why you're all here,' Holbeche added.

'Hang on a minute,' Arkin said. Having caught sight of the rabbit, he was unwilling to let it go without a chase. 'If we accept Willets's word that the printout wasn't actually made in the London Data Centre' – and the way he enunciated this phrase made it perfectly clear that he, personally, didn't – 'then there's still another possibility.'

'What?' Moore asked.

'We live in an age of mobile communications,' Arkin said. 'I may be just a simple country policeman' – he looked round the room, as if inviting disagreement, but nobody seemed inclined to dispute what he had just said – 'but even I have a mobile telephone. Suppose one of your precious second-floor staff brought in a mobile phone and modem. Surely he could pull the directory listing off the system, and then send it to his own computer using the mobile phone?'

Willets nodded. 'An excellent suggestion, Mr Arkin,' he replied, sarcasm dripping from every word. 'Unfortunately it ignores just a few facts. I've already told you that every keystroke on every terminal is recorded. I've also already told you that each employee is subject to a search while going in and going out. Do you really think we'd miss something the size of a telephone, not to mention a modem and the cables to link the two together?'

Arkin wasn't going to let it go. 'It could be a wireless modem,' he persisted. 'They're very small these days.'

Willets shook his head. 'No, they're not. The scanners will detect anything even half the size of a card modem, while a mobile telephone would set all of the alarm bells ringing. Besides, there's another excellent reason why your exciting little scenario is rubbish.'

Arkin said nothing, and just stared at him. 'The LDC,' Willets explained, 'is a secure computer centre where extremely sensitive data is processed. That means we take elaborate precautions to ensure that none of the data leaks out, either through the front door or through the ether.' Willets leaned forward. 'The whole section is completely screened against electromagnetic emissions,' he continued, 'and that means no signals can get in or out, from a mobile phone or from anything else.'

He sat back, satisfied, but Arkin was grinning at him. 'You haven't been that successful, though, have you?' he said. 'Despite your Faraday Cage, somebody did manage to walk out with that directory listing.'

'Not,' Willets repeated, his voice rising in irritation, 'out of the London Data Centre.'

Holbeche intervened. 'We're achieving nothing by this bickering,' he said sharply. 'The listing was produced. What we have to work out is how – and from where.' He turned to Willets. 'We'll have to accept your assurances about the physical security at the LDC, so where do we go from there?'

'Right,' Willets replied, 'the principal user of the LDC computer system is the Foreign and Commonwealth Office, so obviously we'll have to investigate the FCO staff thoroughly.' He paused for a moment, and glanced around at the other men sitting there. 'You should also know that the LDC computers are linked by armoured landlines to the secure local-area networks – the intranets – operated by the SIS at Vauxhall Cross and GCHQ at Cheltenham. I can guarantee that these lines haven't been tampered with, because they're gas-filled and any breach releases the gas and sets off alarms at both ends.'

He paused, and again Arkin seized the moment. 'That's a great help,' he said. 'Oh, yes, that's really narrowed it down. At least we don't have to tramp around the streets of London, looking for a man sitting by a manhole cover with a bunch of wires in his hands and a portable computer. Oh, no, we're only looking for a mole at the FCO, or maybe SIS, or perhaps GCHQ. Jesus Christ, that's thousands of people. Even the initial surveillance and elimination could take weeks or months, maybe even years.'

There was a long silence, broken at last by Richard Simpson. 'Not necessarily,' he said. 'There might be another way.'

Chapter Four

'Is all that clear?'

'Yes.' Richter nodded. 'What you've said is very clear. It doesn't make the slightest bit of sense, but it's very clear.'

The briefing officer – a short and stout man who had been introduced to Richter simply as 'Gibson' – coloured slightly and leaned forward on the lectern. 'What, exactly, doesn't make sense?'

'Almost everything,' Richter said. 'You're basically tasking me with flying to Vienna tomorrow to collect a package and then deliver it here.' Richter gestured around the briefing room. 'I'll ignore the fact that I don't actually know anything about the organization you represent, like what it's called or what it does or why I should be playing postman for it, but—'

Gibson interrupted. 'You don't need to know anything more than I've told you,' he said.

Richter looked up at him. 'So you keep saying. Pardon me if I disagree with you. I could just about understand it if, having collected this package in Vienna, I simply climbed back onto the same British Airways aircraft that I arrived on, and then flew back to Heathrow. Why, exactly, can't I do that? Why do you want me to take a week making my way halfway across Europe by road to Toulouse, of all places, and then fly back to Britain from there?'

Gibson was silent for a few moments before he replied. 'That's the predetermined return route,' he said finally, though somewhat lamely.

'Predetermined by who?' Richter asked. 'And why?'

'You don't need to—'

'Yes, yes,' Richter interrupted. 'No doubt that's just something else I don't need to know.'

Gibson studied Richter for a few seconds, then told him to wait, and walked out of the room. Two minutes later he was back, accompanied by a smallish, pinkish man who exuded an unmistakable air of authority.

'You're Richter, right?' the new arrival asked. Richter nodded, but he remained seated. 'I'm Simpson, and Gibson tells me you're unhappy with the return route we've planned for this collection.'

Richter nodded again. 'That, and just about everything else,' he said.

'You served in the Royal Navy, didn't you?' Simpson continued. 'You should be used to taking orders, so why can't you just do what you're told?'

'In the Navy,' Richter replied, 'it was different. There I knew who I was working for, and I knew what was going on. Here I don't, and I'm certainly not going tramping around Europe, lugging some unidentified parcel, until I find out.'

Simpson and Gibson both looked at him in silence for a moment. 'Right,' Simpson said to the other man, 'I'll take care of this.'

After Gibson had left the room, Simpson sat down in

a chair facing Richter. 'You've signed the Official Secrets Act,' he stated.

'Twice, I think,' Richter agreed.

'Right. You are to now consider everything I tell you as being covered by that Act, and never repeat it to anyone. This organization is a part – though a very small part – of the British security establishment.'

'I guessed that,' Richter said. 'It's presumably why you're skulking around the backstreets of Hammersmith.'

'We like to keep a low profile.' Simpson smiled briefly. 'Now, this package collection is very important to us, but to be frank the package itself is almost irrelevant. I can't give you the background, because it's classified at a much higher level than you're cleared to. But this much I can tell you: we need to have someone in place in southern Europe for the next week or so. And before you ask,' he went on, 'for reasons I can't explain, that person has to be somebody totally unconnected to any part of the security establishment – an outsider in other words, with no existing MI5 or SIS connections.'

Richter nodded. 'This is finally beginning to make some kind of sense,' he said. 'You're expecting this person to be contacted, perhaps, by someone who wouldn't trust a professional intelligence officer? A defector, maybe? And the slow return journey has been deliberately chosen to allow plenty of time for that contact to be made?'

This time Simpson nodded and smiled too. 'You may have missed your calling, Richter,' he said. 'You seem to pick things up very quickly. You're quite right.'

'OK,' Richter said, 'accepting all that, why wasn't

Gibson prepared to tell me that, or advise me how to respond if and when I'm contacted by this third party?'

'You would have been properly briefed, but at this stage we know almost nothing about this possible contact. That's why we've chosen a slow route back, so that we could get in touch with you whenever we needed to, and brief you on the fly, as it were.

'Now,' Simpson went on, 'with that cleared up, are you prepared to undertake this collection?'

'Of course, I am,' Richter nodded, 'as long as I know what's going on.'

Simpson suppressed a smile. What he had just explained was almost true, but the real nature of the contact was likely to be very different from what Richter probably assumed.

'Right, then,' Simpson continued. 'Gibson has already supplied you with briefing sheets, your precise itinerary, an airline ticket and details of the pick-up address in Vienna. You'll need some other equipment as well, so we must get that sorted immediately.'

'Equipment?' Richter asked. 'Don't tell me you've got exploding briefcases or sub-machine guns hidden inside shoes?'

'Not exactly,' Simpson grunted. 'Our technical resources are somewhat more modest than those supposedly available to James Bond. We'll be providing you with a diplomatic passport, which will help with the border crossings and any dealings you might have with the continental plods, and a mobile phone so we can reach you wherever you are. Oh, and a briefcase . . . but without extras apart from a handcuff to attach it to your wrist.'

Sluzhba Vneshney Razvyedki Rossi Headquarters, Yasenevo, Tëplyystan, Moscow

Raya checked the new directory immediately after arriving in her office, and was amazed at the number of files it already contained. Even allowing for Abramov's explanation that some of the material had now been held for assessment at Yasenevo for as long as six months, it was still obvious that the *Zakoulok* database was huge, and that the source known as *Gospodin* enjoyed excellent access – perhaps even better than some of the American mercenary traitors, such as Aldrich Ames and the Walker family.

Later that morning, Raya made a call to Major Abramov's office number. She let the phone ring a dozen times before replacing the receiver. She had fully expected him to be out of the building, but was just running a final check.

She opened her office door briefly, to check that the corridor outside was empty, then locked it and walked swiftly back to her desk. Sitting down at the computer, she opened a file-transfer and communication program which automatically dialled a telephone number in a fifth-floor office within the Lubyanka. That telephone didn't actually ring, because a call-diverter, which Raya had installed during a routine security check nine months earlier, intercepted her call as soon as it recognized the prefix.

The prefix was in fact a signal to the diverter to dial another number elsewhere in Moscow, and the only sign of this happening was the small red light on the telephone that illuminated to show that the line was in use. This light stayed on for almost fifteen minutes, but the office itself was deserted, as was always the case in mid-morning.

Once the connection was established, the program transmitted copies of the files contained in both of Raya's hidden directories to the recipient computer. Before the program shut down, it deleted all the files in the two hidden directories, and finally erased any record of this call from her office to the Lubyanka from the internal-communication record file.

During the afternoon, Raya accessed the internal-communication record file herself. After a careful check of the Senior Officers' Diary which was held on the computer system, and the network access log, she inserted nine new and entirely fictitious entries. These showed lengthy calls to a Moscow number made from an office elsewhere in the Yasenevo complex.

Then she opened a directory with a Top-Secret classification, and selected fifteen files dealing with Russian military equipment. She opened each one in turn and added a single extra entry to each file's access record.

As she closed the last file, Raya smiled to herself. It was a smile of satisfaction, but her eyes were hard and bright.

Secret Intelligence Service (SIS) Headquarters, Vauxhall Cross, London

'Mr Stanway?' Mary Bellamy began. A formidable and slightly equine woman, she was personal assistant to

'C', namely Sir Malcolm Holbeche, which entitled her to the official acronym 'PA-C'. Perhaps predictably, she was known in the spacious corridors of Vauxhall Cross as 'The Pack Horse'.

'Yes, Mary?' Gerald Stanway had recognized her voice immediately.

'There's a heads and deputy heads meeting in Conference Room 2 in fifteen minutes.'

Stanway glanced at the wall clock opposite his desk. 'I'll be there,' he replied, then replaced the telephone handset and began clearing his desk. In Vauxhall Cross, the avant-garde headquarters of the Secret Intelligence Service on the south bank of the Thames, all offices operate a 'clear desks' policy. This means that no officer ever leaves his room with papers of any description remaining in view. Everything, including desk diaries, have to be locked away in the officer's personal safe.

Stanway glanced back at his desk for a final check before spinning the combination lock on the safe door. Then he sat down again, in front of the computer terminal, and systematically closed all the open programs. When the display prompted for a username and password, he switched off the screen and left his office.

As Stanway walked in, he found Sir Malcolm Holbeche sitting at the head of the long table in the conference room. Two other heads of department followed him and, once all were seated, Holbeche began.

'This briefing,' he stated, 'is classified Top Secret, and no notes of any sort will be taken. Is that clear?' The men seated around the table nodded agreement, and Holbeche continued. 'This situation is somewhat embarrassing, and has potentially very serious implications for both us and the rest of the security establishment, not to mention our "special relationship" with the American CIA. As Moore here will now explain.'

Holbeche leaned back in his chair, with a gesture to the man sitting on his right. William Moore opened the file in front of him, and glanced quickly round the table.

'Three days ago,' he began, 'a low-level Russian clerk – but one working at Yasenevo – walked into the British Embassy in Moscow and asked for asylum. There was some confusion over who should handle this matter, and the Russian began to get visibly perturbed. It's possible that he was worried that he would be refused asylum, or might even be arrested and handed over to the Russian authorities. Eventually, after half an hour or so, the clerk ran out of the embassy and vanished into the streets of Moscow.'

Moore looked around, at a collection of puzzled faces. 'Nothing much to get excited about? You're quite right. By itself, this episode would be of no real consequence, but what elevates it from the mundane to the significant is what the clerk left behind him at the embassy.'

'Which was?' somebody prompted.

'A small package of papers,' Moore said. 'Most of it apparently was the usual sort of stuff you'd expect a defecting clerk to bring with him, in order to bargain with. We haven't seen this material yet, because our people in Moscow are still going through it, but a copy of it has been sent to us, and should arrive here later today. What alarmed our Head of Station over there involved just one sheet of paper.'

Moore paused significantly. 'It was simply a list of file names with a number handwritten against each one.

Our Head of Station thought he recognized some of the file names, so he signalled us promptly. He was right to do so, because several of the names listed were those of SIS files. More importantly, all are classified as Secret and above, and most relate in some way to Russia or the CIS.'

'And the numbers?' Holbeche prompted.

'Oh, yes,' Moore replied. 'On initial analysis, we deduced that the numbers weren't directly relevant to the files – meaning they weren't, for example, sizes or creation dates or access history or anything like that. What we think is that they indicate sums of money. The Head of Station's interpretation of this – and I have to say we concur – is that this sheet of paper lists files that the SVR has received from somebody within SIS, and what they paid for them.'

'Or perhaps files that the SVR wants from SIS, and what they'd be prepared to pay for them?' one of the other men suggested.

'No.' Moore shook his head. 'The Russian clerk said these files had already been obtained.'

There was an appalled silence.

'You can all appreciate what this means,' Holbeche declared. 'Someone with access to SIS files – and that probably means somebody here in this building – has been selling our secrets to the SVR. What we have to find out urgently is who.'

'And how do we do that?' Stanway asked. 'Call in The Box?'

'The Box' and 'Box 500' were slang terms for the Security Service, MI5, and were derived from its original postal address of PO Box 500, London.

'We hope that won't be necessary.' Moore shook his head. 'We're hoping that the Russian clerk himself might be able to help us out.'

'How?'

'Before he ran off into the Moscow afternoon, he'd talked to the SIS duty officer for about ten minutes. The clerk explained to him that he had a number of other papers, similar to the one bearing the file names, and further information about the individual who had supplied the SVR with those files. Based on what he heard, the duty officer believed the source of the leak could probably be identified from those papers.'

'As the clerk has completely vanished, I don't see how that can help,' Stanway said.

'It helps,' Moore replied, 'because the clerk has now reappeared, in Vienna, along with the rest of the papers.'

Sluzhba Vneshney Razvyedki Rossi Headquarters, Yasenevo, Tëplyystan, Moscow

Raya had always been conscientious in performing her duties, and invariably carried out to the letter all the procedures Abramov had specified for the security checks. One of her tasks was to inspect the access record, since the last full security check, of any files bearing a classification of Top Secret or above.

She looked forward to this task because, as well as inspecting a file's access history, it also gave her – as the network manager in all but name – the absolute right to look at the contents of any file contained in the database. On every security check she'd carried out since she'd arrived at Yasenevo, what she'd done was not merely to inspect the contents of these files, but also to make copies of them within another hidden directory she'd created. She also selected a handful of highly classified files every day, and stored copies of these, too, in the same hidden directory. Most of these files were encrypted but that didn't matter because, as network manager, she also had access to the encryption and decryption routines.

But, despite this unrivalled access, the number of highly classified files was so great that she had never managed to find a real 'gem', though she believed that the *Gospodin* material, and now the new and rapidly filling *Zakoulok* directory, would prove of crucial importance later. This was not because of what the files themselves contained, but because of what they could prove about the person who had sourced them.

During this latest check, she'd decided to carry out a database-wide search for any files containing English words. This produced a huge listing, and included even material dating back to the glorious days of what were known as 'The Apostles' – those ideological traitors whose names were still revered in the corridors of the SVR: George Blake, Anthony Blunt, Anthony Burgess, John Cairncross, Donald Maclean and Kim Philby.

The damage they had done to the British intelligence services had been quite literally incalculable, and the lack of trust engendered by their activities between Britain and America was almost as damaging. While The Apostles were operational, almost no penetration operation mounted by either the British or the Americans against the Soviet Union had been successful, and on several occasions they had even helped the KGB to prevent defections to the West. Possibly the classic example of that had been Constantin Volkhov, and that name was burned permanently into Raya's brain.

Raya studied the listing on the screen and decided to add another filter. Using the listing she'd already generated as a dataset, she eliminated all files that hadn't been accessed over the last six months. That more than halved the number originally displayed. Then she decided to approach the problem from the opposite direction, and she specified only those files, classified Top Secret and above, which had since been accessed by Directorate heads. That reduced the listing to a mere eighteen files, and Raya decided to take a careful look at all of them.

All the file-directory specifications included the directory's size, the number of files it contained, the overall classification and the original creation dates. Studying these, Raya immediately noticed how one of the directories stood out, simply because it was so old.

Having been created over twenty years earlier, it had been classified Secret almost immediately. The security classification had been increased to Top Secret about six months after the directory had been created, but this was not unusual; quite often later material obtained by an agent was more sensitive and important than the earlier information, so the file or directory classification had to be increased accordingly.

But, apart from its age, there were two other unusual features of the *Zagadka* – meaning 'Enigma' – directory. First, its classification had remained Top Secret; and normally, as the information contained became older, it became inevitably less critical, so the security level would be downgraded by at least one or two classifications, sometimes even more.

The second peculiarity was that, although new files had been added to the directory at frequent intervals during the fifteen years after *Zagadka* had been created, no new files had been added for the last five years. This suggested that the source was dead, or had been burned, or for some other reason had ceased acting as an asset for the SVR. But that made a nonsense of the directory's access record, for most of the Directorate heads at Yasenevo looked through the directory at least once every month – but why would a busy SVR desk officer waste time looking at information that must be at least five years out of date?

But then Raya noticed something else. Although no *new* files had been added to the *Zagadka* directory for some years, one file, named 'Appreciation', was still being updated on a regular basis – sometimes as often as once a week. She double-clicked on the file to open it, read through the first page, then closed the file again and sat back in her seat.

Suddenly she knew something that she'd previously only suspected. And she also realized in that instant, that she was going to have to be extremely careful, because what was contained in the 'Appreciation' file changed everything.

Hammersmith, London

Richter emerged from the building in Hammersmith just after two-thirty, grasping a locked and almost empty briefcase in his left hand and with his stomach rumbling. Neither Simpson nor anyone else had offered him lunch, or anything else to eat, and the one cup of coffee provided had been so lukewarm and tasteless that he had had no difficulty at all in refusing a second cup.

He glanced briefly at his watch and immediately rejected any idea of returning to Whitehall and the Old Admiralty Building where there was in any case nothing waiting for him but an empty office. He set off in the general direction of central London, until he found a pub offering all-day food, walked in and ordered a plate of chilli. That was now 'off', according to the blonde barmaid, who was anorexic almost to the point of starvation but still possessed a pair of the largest breasts Richter had ever seen, so he settled for an alleged Cornish pasty – but which had obviously begun its life somewhere well to the east of Slough – and some slightly soggy chips. But the coffee was good enough for him to order a second cup, and his hunger had subsided by the time he finally stepped out onto the pavement and looked hopefully up and down the street.

There were no taxis in sight, but the day was fine, so he decided to walk to the closest tube station. Ninety minutes later found him stepping off the train at Uxbridge station, for a short walk to the local RAF station, which was one of the many non-flying Royal Air Force establishments dotted around Britain. Not for nothing, he reflected, were RAF personnel sometimes known dismissively as 'penguins', because only about one in a million of them actually flew.

Back in his room, Richter put the briefcase on the desk and used the key Simpson had given him to unlock it. Inside was a Nokia GSM mobile phone and charger, plus a two-pin continental adapter, two typewritten pages of briefing notes, and a sealed A4-size manila envelope containing the diplomatic passport Simpson had promised him. Also a single economy-class ticket from Heathrow to Vienna, one thousand euros in cash, split into fifty- and one-hundred euro notes, and a gold Visa card which he'd already signed.

There was also a carbon copy of a sheet of paper signed by Richter and countersigned by Simpson, which listed every item contained in the briefcase, including the Visa card number and the numbers of each of the euro notes, and even details of the briefcase itself. Simpson had also made it clear that Richter was expected to return all of those items except the cash, and he had been instructed to produce receipts for everything he purchased and for every euro and cent he spent. That, in fact, was precisely what Richter would expect, because all government departments and employees worked in more or less the same way, and such an excessive concentration on completely unimportant minutiae was typical of the breed.

He'd already read through the briefing sheets at Hammersmith but before he went downstairs to have an early meal in the dining room he decided to look through them again. He'd given no hint of it while he'd been at Hammersmith, but he was reasonably certain that there must be a lot that both Simpson and Gibson – or whatever his real name was – had so far neglected to tell him.

As he'd informed Gibson, the briefing had been clear enough; but it just didn't make any sense. What Simpson had explained to him subsequently had clarified matters considerably, but Richter hadn't really bought that 'defector running across Europe' story. What was clear was that Simpson's organization needed somebody on the ground in Austria, Switzerland or France, for a week or so, but whether he would actually be contacted by somebody, or whether there was some other reason for his presence there, he had no idea.

What he did know was that he was going to be watching his back carefully, from the moment he climbed out of that British Airways flight in Vienna.

Secret Intelligence Service (SIS) Headquarters, Vauxhall Cross, London

Sir Malcolm Holbeche rang Simpson a little before six-thirty that afternoon.

'How did it go?' Simpson asked him. 'I presume there was no problem getting Moscow to play ball?'

'None at all,' Holbeche replied. 'The origin of any enquiry made to the Holy of Holies there' – he was using the term applied to the section of a British embassy which is occupied by SIS personnel – 'will be logged and the defecting clerk story will be confirmed.'

'And at this end?' Simpson enquired.

'As expected, nobody showed anything other than purely professional interest.'

'What about the other places?' By 'other places', Simpson meant GCHQ and the Foreign and Commonwealth Office, where very similar briefings had been given that afternoon.

'No unusual response received from Cheltenham, and I'm still waiting for the FCO. They're late, as usual.'

'I'm not surprised at that reaction,' Simpson said. 'We're dealing with a professional here, and he's not going to jump up and down in hysterics just because some Russian clerk might be able to finger him.'

'Quite,' Holbeche replied. 'But at least the hare is running.'

'Oh, yes,' Simpson agreed, 'the hare is definitely running.'

Chapter Five

Wednesday
Vienna, Austria

His instructions had been perfectly clear and unambiguous, and the moment he cleared passport control, which was a mere formality thanks to the diplomatic passport he was carrying, Richter began ignoring them.

He had been told to collect a pre-booked hire car from Hertz at the airport, proceed to a street in Vienna, and collect the package from an address there. Instead, Richter checked in his overnight bag at the airport left-luggage section, and walked out of the terminal building carrying just the briefcase. He stood beside the taxi rank for a few minutes, studying a map of Vienna while waiting for the first half dozen cabs to leave, and then took the next available taxi to a location about two streets away from the address he'd been provided with, in the Josefstadt district in west-central Vienna.

Once there, he paid off the driver, made his way on foot to the street where the house was located, and walked a short way along to a cafe. He chose the seat offering the best view of the property, ordered a coffee and a pastry, spread a German-language newspaper out on the table in front of him, then settled down to watch.

Forty-five minutes later, he had learned precisely nothing. Nobody had entered or left the premises, and he'd seen no sign whatsoever of any activity inside. Not for the first time, Richter wondered if he was maybe just being stupid or paranoid, or both. As far as he could see, about all he could do at this stage was exactly what it said in his briefing instructions, which was to walk up to the front door of the house, show his passport, and collect the package.

Richter paid the bill, leaving the newspaper where it was, then stood up and walked away from the cafe. He strode past the house on the opposite side of the road, checking it out as closely as he could without making it too obvious, then crossed the street and headed back towards it. Two minutes later, he was ringing the bell beside the front door.

Sluzhba Vneshney Razvyedki Rossi Headquarters, Yasenevo, Tëplyystan, Moscow

Raya Kosov stood up, pushing her swivel chair back from the desk, and walked over to the window. The view to the north, over the treetops and towards the centre of Moscow, no longer held her interest the way it once had. Her mind was racing as she thought again about what she'd read on the computer screen, and about the implications of the contents of that single file.

But she was committed now. The measures she'd taken already meant that her future course of action was predetermined. She had no choice in that, no choice at all apart from the actual timing. And really, she acknowledged silently, she had few options in that either. She had always known she would have to be careful, but what she'd seen in the file named 'Appreciation' meant she'd now have to take extreme care. And when she moved, she was going to have to move fast.

The other thing Raya realized was that she would have to forget part of her original plan – the bit she had been thinking of as phase two – and work out a completely different approach to that part of the problem. She should have no trouble achieving this, not least because she had the best of all possible motives. For if she failed, she would be killed, and probably killed very slowly and painfully. What she'd read in the Philby file, almost ten years earlier, still haunted her, and ever since then her private, silent mantra had been a simple two-word chant: 'Remember Volkhov'.

But there was something else. She had been playing a complex game virtually ever since she had arrived at Yasenevo, balancing the demands of her work – which were considerable – with her own hidden agenda. That had been difficult but soon, perhaps very soon, it was going to pay off, because Raya Kosov, Deputy Data-Processing System Network Manager at Yasenevo, was quite determined to quit her job, and the SVR, and leave Russia, and she wasn't looking for any kind of severance package.

Vienna, Austria

The door didn't open immediately but Richter knew, as soon as he pressed the buzzer, that he was being watched. After a second or two he spotted the lens of a tiny closed-circuit TV camera, positioned above his head in one corner of the porch. Then a hidden speaker crackled, and a voice asked him something in German.

'My name is Richter, and I have come to collect a packet,' he announced, speaking the words slowly and carefully.

There was a short pause, then the sound of a lock being released, and the door swung slowly open. A swarthy, black-haired man stood in the hallway beyond, and beckoned Richter inside. There didn't seem to be any alternative, so Richter stepped across the threshold and stood waiting, with his back to the open door. The man stepped around him and pushed the door closed, then moved back to face him.

'Your passport, please,' he asked, his English clear and precise but with a distinct German accent.

Richter handed over his diplomatic passport and, for a few seconds, the man studied the document and Richter alternately. Then he closed the passport and handed it back with a slight tilt of his head. Richter almost expected him to click his heels together.

'You're late,' the man observed.

'I know,' Richter replied, but didn't elaborate.

The man, who still hadn't introduced himself, gazed at Richter for a few seconds longer, then shrugged, and headed a few paces further down the hall. Stopping at a low table, he picked up a parcel wrapped in brown paper, returned and handed it over. Richter opened his briefcase, slid the parcel inside, then closed and locked it. The man stepped past him, opened the street door again and gestured.

As the door slammed shut behind him, Richter found

himself standing on the pavement, briefcase in his left hand, and wondering which way to head next.

Sluzhba Vneshney Razvyedki Rossi Headquarters, Yasenevo, Tëplyystan, Moscow

Raya Kosov was planning to defect to the West, as she'd intended to since long before joining the SVR. And one of the things that she knew would sway the British – having no time for the Americans, she hadn't even considered approaching the CIA – was her dowry, so to speak; the information that she would bring out with her.

At the height of the Cold War, she knew, things had been very different. Any file clerk with a couple of secret files in a carrier bag had been welcomed with open arms, because the West was desperate for any information that would reveal what was happening on the other side of the Iron Curtain. But today, after *glasnost* and the rest, and with Russia seeming to a large extent a spent force, the Western intelligence services could afford to be more choosy.

These days, if the information wasn't of a high enough standard, both the British SIS and the American CIA were quite happy to hand a defector back to the Russian authorities. In fact, what they were ideally looking for wasn't some highly placed defector who could bring out a bunch of classified data, but a highly placed mole that they could keep in play for as long as they wanted. For a mole could provide data for years and could also, and just as importantly, be tasked with finding the answer to some specific question.

But the reality was that human moles, living just below the surface of the society they inhabited like their animal counterparts, were loathed by all who knew they were there, and would be killed by anyone who got the chance. Raya wasn't going along that route, though. She wasn't even going to contact the SIS until after she'd got safely out of the Confederation of Independent States, leaving her boats blazing behind her, just to make certain that the 'mole' option would be a non-starter.

The data she could supply, because of her privileged access at Yasenevo, should be enough to ensure her acceptance by the SIS. The rules governing the use of the database at Yasenevo were broadly similar to those applied to any other databases containing classified information. All users had to be authorized by a superior officer, and were then allowed access to only certain areas of the database, and to such files as their duties required. Every time they logged on, each user had to enter a username and password, and then the access record attached to each file they consulted would record their name and rank, the date and time the file was opened and closed, and any additions, amendments or deletions they made to that file. Besides, copying and deletion of any files classified Secret and above required separate and specific authorization.

What all systems of this type required was a network manager; somebody with overall global authority to carry out what are normally termed housekeeping duties. These included such diverse tasks as maintaining lists of authorized users, checking users' passwords to ensure they complied with the system rules, altering the security classification of files, creating directories, moving files from one directory to another, and archiving files that were no longer considered to be current. But the essential point was that the network manager saw everything, knew everything, and could do everything. For if he or she didn't, the system wouldn't work.

That, in one way, was the strength of the system, but it was also, of course, its weakness. As long as the network manager was competent, motivated, and loyal to the organization, everything would be fine. But when a network manager was competent but disloyal, the whole system stood in jeopardy. Raya Kosov herself was extremely competent and highly motivated, but also completely and utterly disloyal.

Most traitors – and Raya Kosov had no illusions about how she would be viewed once her permanent absence was discovered by the SVR – would betray their country for one of three reasons.

The most dangerous were the ideological traitors. These were people motivated by a belief that the system of government in their own country was immoral, corrupt or otherwise flawed and who, rather than trying to change the system openly and legally, instead transmitted intelligence data to another nation that they did approve of. The Apostles were, for many, the classic example.

It was one of the ironies of history that most ideological traitors, like The Apostles themselves, had obtained their perception of the idyllic nature of that chosen country by looking at it through the rose-tinted spectacles of youth. In most cases, they had never even visited the place, to confirm that their perception bore the slightest relation to reality. It was interesting that when Blake,

Philby and others finally escaped to the 'Workers' Paradise', as they saw it, of Russia, all the evidence suggested that they loathed it. Anthony Blunt, of course, didn't even have the courage to move to Russia, but remained in the deeply flawed country of his birth which he had tried so hard to destroy, despite the intellectual pain this must have caused him. Cairncross fled to France.

Such ideological traitors are dangerous mainly because they are so difficult to detect, and conventional counter-espionage techniques are frequently useless against them. There was no point, for example, in checking an individual's past history to determine if he has ever been to Russia or any another Communist state, where he could have been tainted or turned, because many such traitors never experienced any direct contact with the regime they had decided to serve. Recruitment frequently occurred at an early age, usually at university, and the individual might then refrain from engaging in any treacherous activity for years, doing nothing until well established in government service.

In the second category belong the mercenary traitors, who would sell out their country for the proverbial thirty pieces of silver, although with appropriate allowances for inflation. Aldrich Ames, who had worked for the CIA and the SVR simultaneously, received almost five million dollars in return for the secrets he betrayed to the Russians. Ames should have been detected long before he eventually was, because for so many years he and his wife had lived a blatantly opulent lifestyle that his CIA salary was incapable of supporting.

The third category was perhaps the saddest of all: the compromised traitors. These were weak and sad individuals harbouring a secret, very often a secret vice, which they will do anything to keep secret – including betraying their own country. Before it lost some of its stigma, many of these were homosexuals who had suffered entrapment by KGB 'quiet ones' or 'Ravens'. Just like heterosexual Ravens, these men were highly trained in the art of seduction, and lured their victims into specially prepared bedrooms, where KGB officers wielding cameras were waiting behind one-way mirrors to record the encounter. Of these targets, perhaps the best-known example was John Vassal, the Admiralty traitor.

But there was a fourth possible motive for a person's treachery, and it was almost as dangerous as ideology. Raya Kosov was driven by one of the oldest of human emotions, revenge. She had a score to settle with one particular man, and for her the entire organization known as the SVR provided a convenient tool that she was now preparing to use in exacting her long-delayed vengeance.

Vienna, Austria

Ninety minutes after picking up the parcel, Richter was sitting behind the wheel of a left-hand-drive Ford Focus with Austrian number plates which he'd hired from an Avis office, rather than Hertz, in central Vienna. He was currently doing a steady one hundred and twenty kilometres an hour along the A2 autoroute leading south out of the city, and heading in the general direction of Graz.

In the glovebox was an insurance certificate valid for the whole of Europe, and a one-way hire agreement covering a period of two weeks. The car could be left at any branch of Avis throughout Europe, and in the boot was his overnight bag, which he had driven back to the airport to pick up.

Richter was almost disappointed by the ease with which he had collected the parcel and made his way out of the city. He was still consciously watching his back, but so far had spotted absolutely nothing untoward, and nobody appeared to be taking the slightest interest in him or what he was doing. That didn't, he reflected, mean that he was wrong in his wariness. It probably just meant that he hadn't yet got far enough along the route specified by Simpson for his activities to become of interest to anyone.

After putting a reasonable distance behind him, he pulled into a service area just north of Wiener Neustadt. There, he found a quiet corner of the car park, slotted the Ford into a vacant space and switched off the engine. There were two things he wanted to check before driving any further: the first was the route that Simpson had been most insistent he follow, and which Richter was equally determined to avoid, as far as he possibly could; and the second was the sealed package itself.

He snapped open the briefcase and pulled out the typed briefing sheets which, to his slight surprise, Simpson hadn't ordered him to memorize and then destroy. In fact they only contained details of the route and a couple of telephone numbers, so, as far as Richter could see, there was nothing contained in them that could, by any stretch of the imagination, be described as classified information.

The route was simple enough. Richter was instructed to follow the A21 autoroute westwards out of Vienna, then to pick up the A1 near Maria Anzbach and stay on that, crossing into Germany beyond Salzburg. Then he was to proceed via Munich, entering France at Strasbourg, and turn south-west to Lyon and on to Toulouse. But he had followed this route for the shortest distance possible, by deliberately ignoring the A21 turning and continuing along the A2.

He opened the glovebox and hauled out the route map that Avis had supplied him with, then worked out a new route that would take him down to Toulouse via Italy and Switzerland. Unfortunately, the only part of Europe to be shown in any detail was Austria, while the remainder of the continent was shown merely as a planning aid. Richter made a mental note to buy himself a detailed whole-of-Europe route map from the service station before he drove on.

Finally he turned his attention to the sealed package. Totally anonymous, with no markings of any sort and wrapped in thick brown paper, it was reasonably heavy but flexible, like a soft-cover book about one inch thick. The parcel was sealed with red wax in three places, so as to prevent any casual peeking at the contents, but that wasn't what Richter had in mind. He hooked his fingers under the sealed flap at one end, ripped the paper apart, held the package by the other end and shook it briskly, spilling the contents onto the passenger seat beside him.

A wad of paper slid out, secured by two elastic bands fitted criss-cross, which Richter pulled off, before studying the top sheet. It was typewritten in Cyrillic script, which fortunately he could read; for, like many keen young Royal Navy officers hoping for promotion, Richter had taken a course in Russian while he was serving in the Fleet Air Arm. In his case it hadn't helped his career very much, or even at all, but at least he could read the language, and still speak it fairly fluently. His attention was immediately drawn to a single word stamped in red ink at both the top and bottom of the page – *Sekretno* – 'Secret' – and, for a brief few seconds, he wondered if ripping open the package had been a mistake.

Then he looked at the rest of the sheets and relaxed. The first six pages were also typewritten in Cyrillic, and each had the same red *Sekretno* stamps at top and bottom. The text appeared to be an extract from a Russian nuclear submarine's sonar manual – an old submarine, Richter noted, recognizing the vessel as a Victor III, with well-known capabilities. Technically, the Russians might probably still regard details of this boat and its equipment as Secret, but in reality every Western navy now knew just as much about the old Victor as the officers and men who had originally sailed in her. And, apart from a single smaller envelope, also sealed, the rest of the package consisted entirely of blank sheets of A4 size photocopying paper.

'In for a penny,' Richter muttered. He extracted the other envelope and ripped it open.

Its contents were a surprise. They comprised half a dozen sheets of folded A4 size paper, closely typed, and at the top of the first one the title 'SVR Briefing'. He scanned the pages, but didn't bother reading them, deciding that he would do that later. Also in the envelope was a beige-coloured plastic card, one end of which had an apparently random series of holes punched into it. There was nothing else on the card apart from a small black-and-white photograph of a man that Richter recognized immediately – because it was of himself – along with the name 'Anatoli Markov' in Cyrillic script.

It was just as Richter had suspected. Collection of this package was just a ruse, despite Simpson's insistence on its importance, and Richter now knew that he was being set up for something. The only thing in doubt was exactly what Simpson had planned for him.

Hammersmith, London

The call from Vienna had been routed to the Hammersmith building switchboard from the SIS headquarters at Vauxhall Cross, simply because the man in Austria was an SIS asset and that was the only number he had. The message the caller had to pass on was simple enough – just a confirmation that the package had been collected – but he had also received specific instructions not to communicate with anyone except Richard Simpson.

Simpson wasn't worried, but he had been getting slightly concerned as time had passed without receiving news from Austria, so he snatched up the internal phone the moment it rang.

'Simpson,' he said.

'It's Gunther,' the voice replied, using the agreed recognition name. 'Your man was late.'

'How late?'

'An hour or so. He was not driving a car, but arrived on foot. And he then sat in a cafe across the road, watching the house for about half an hour, before he came over and knocked on the door.'

For a few moments Simpson said nothing, thinking

the situation through. 'You confirmed his identity?' he asked.

'Yes, I checked his passport. And he took the package.'

'Thank you. That's what matters,' said Simpson and disconnected. He next made a swift call to a number in Vienna, and listened with obvious dissatisfaction to the reply he received. Three minutes later he dialled the number of Richter's mobile phone.

Austria

Richter was back on the road, again cruising at a steady one hundred and twenty kilometres an hour, when his mobile phone rang. He reached over to the passenger seat, picked up the phone and answered it. 'Richter.'

'Having fun?' Simpson asked.

'Not so's you'd notice,' Richter replied. 'Why?'

'We gave you a number of very specific instructions before you left London. One of the first of those instructions told you to collect a hire car from Hertz at the airport. I've just checked. The car's still there, and you never appeared. Why?'

'I got a better deal from Avis.' Richter swung the Ford off the autoroute and into the next rest area. 'I'm saving you money,' he added as he braked the car and switched off the engine.

'Don't get smart with me,' Simpson snapped. 'Do you think this is some kind of a fucking game?'

'Right now, Simpson, I have no idea what this is. What I do know is that I trust you about as far as I can spit a rat, and that's not a hell of a long way.'

'I told you all you needed to know, Richter, and none of it was difficult or dangerous. Why the hell can't you just follow your orders?'

'I *am* doing what you told me, but I'm also following Frank Sinatra. I'm doing it my way. I'll make it to the rendezvous on the date you specified, with the package, but how I get there is my business. If you need me, you can call me, OK?'

'No, Richter, it's not OK. We expect—'

'So what are you going to do about it?' Richter interrupted. 'Face facts, Simpson. I'm here, I've got the package, I'm in a car somewhere in Austria – and I'm going to get to the rendezvous on time. There's nothing you can do about it, short of flying some other mug out here to take over from me.'

For a few moments Richter assumed Simpson had rung off, but then he heard a snarl through his earpiece. 'Right, Richter, you listen to me. You keep the mobile switched on. You get to Toulouse by the date I told you. You do the job we're paying you to do, because if you don't, I'll find you and I'll make you wish you had.'

'Yeah, yeah, yeah,' Richter said. 'Anything else?'

'Yes, the package you're carrying is sealed, for a good reason. Make sure it stays that way until you hand it over.'

'Why do you think I wouldn't?'

'You've broken every other rule, Richter. Why should I expect you to obey this one?' Simpson rang off. Richter grinned, snapped the phone shut, and glanced over at the passenger seat, where the brown paper wrapping of the package still gaped open. He started the engine, checked his mirrors and accelerated away, heading for the Italian border.

Chapter Six

Wednesday
Sluzhba Vneshney Razvyedki Rossi Headquarters, Yasenevo,
Tëplyystan, Moscow

The call reached Raya Kosov a little after four in the afternoon. Normally calls originating through the civilian telephone system were rejected by the Yasenevo switchboard, but this caller had not only known Raya Kosov's name but her extension number, so it was put through after the operator had checked with the internal security section and switched on the tape-recorder. Raya had been expecting it, expecting it for a long time, but it still gave her quite a shock.

The caller identified herself unnecessarily because Raya had known her since childhood, and her message contained all the code phrases they had arranged between them nearly five years earlier.

'Hello, Raya, it's Valentina. I've got some very bad news, I'm afraid. Your mother's very sick again, and she'll have to go back into hospital, perhaps for the last time. I know you're very busy, but if you could possibly get away for just a few days and come and visit her it would mean the world to her. You know how much she misses you.'

'Oh, Valentina,' Raya replied, her voice suddenly choking with emotion, and it was some seconds before she could form another sentence. She swallowed and

89

tried again. 'Valentina, I'm so sorry to hear that. Look, tell Mama I will try to get some time off. I'll call you about it tonight.'

'Thank you, Raya. It would mean so much to her.'

'Goodbye, Valentina.' Raya waited until she'd put the phone down before she gave way to tears.

A perfectly innocuous, if sad, exchange which the internal-security section played back almost immediately. After confirming that the call had originated in Minsk, where officer Kosov's elderly mother was known to live, the duty security officer transcribed the call, logging its date and time and the originating number, but took no further action.

Secret Intelligence Service (SIS) Headquarters, Vauxhall Cross, London

Gerald Stanway sat at his desk, staring at his computer screen, but his mind was miles away. The briefing that Holbeche had given the previous afternoon had stunned and worried him. Worse, it had frightened him, and he'd suffered a sleepless night because of it.

What was worrying him most was the story about the clerk. It sounded too pat, too convenient, that this unnamed man should have reappeared in Vienna – the town itself was almost a spy-fiction cliché, for God's sake – with some kind of information that might directly implicate him. For Stanway had no doubt at all that, if this clerk really did exist, he – Stanway – was the 'leak that could be identified', as that bumbling old fool Holbeche had put it.

Gerald Stanway had been guilty of passing classified information to anyone who was prepared to pay for it – the Libyans, the Iraqis, the Iranians and, even for one brief period, the IRA; though his principal customer had always been Russia – and he had been doing so for the past dozen years. He regarded himself as a businessman selling a commodity – in this case information – that was in high demand. He had neither morals nor scruples about what he was doing, regarding his employment by the SIS as nothing more than a convenient and un-rivalled source of information.

Two months earlier, he'd managed to gain access to the London Data Centre's System-Three computer system, which had greatly increased the scope and reach, and potential profit, of his activities. He'd already provided his Russian controller with numerous files that he'd managed to copy from the system, and had finally simply taken a snapshot of the entire directory structure, which he'd offered to the Russians as a shopping list, from which to choose the files they wanted to see.

The days when SIS officers were exempt from the payment of income tax were long gone, and nowadays officers receive an index-linked salary based upon the fairly modest scales set by the Treasury. Stanway's lucrative activities as a mole allowed him to enjoy a lifestyle that was opulent rather than comfortable but, unlike Aldrich Ames, he had always been more than happy to explain to anyone curious enough to ask ex-actly how his wealth was earned.

He had realized, right from the start of his information-broking 'career', that the principal danger of his being detected would probably not come from anything as mundane as a spot check as he left Vauxhall Cross, but far more likely from the Inland Revenue. That was possible if he suddenly began spending money he couldn't account for – and Stanway had every intention of spending his money.

The occasional sale of information to minor nations like Libya had been paid for in cash, money that he kept in a safety-deposit box at his bank, to be spent gradually and discreetly, usually in buying readily convertible assets, like paintings, antique furniture, good-quality diamonds, watches and the like.

But his first and best customers were the Russians, and with them he had developed a payment system that seemed foolproof, or at least as foolproof as any system ever could be. With a genuine inheritance of over half a million pounds, after tax, from an aunt some ten years earlier – he'd barely known she was alive, and her death came as a shock mainly because he had been named her sole beneficiary; he had decided to sell his small flat in Islington and buy a larger property in central London. Property prices had been on the rise, as usual, but he'd made an offer on the whole of a large terraced house in South Kensington which had been newly converted into four luxury apartments.

Even after selling his own flat, he had still been three hundred thousand pounds short when his offer was accepted, and so when he'd approached the Russians, he'd simply suggested they might like to underwrite his mortgage for him. He'd taken out the necessary loan with his regular bank and one month after he'd made the first payment, the Russians had begun paying an almost identical amount into an account in his name in the Cayman Islands. Statements of that account, to confirm the payments made, were sent to a post box which Stanway had rented in London. The Russians were, in other words, buying his new property for him.

Stanway moved into the best of the apartments, the one on the top floor, and advertised the other properties for rent. Finding suitable tenants within the month, the rent he received from them was more than twice what he was paying for his mortgage, and he had been able to increase the rent every year while his mortgage payments stayed more or less the same. Suddenly Stanway was a rich man.

Then, after he assessed that the value of the information he was passing to the Russians had increased sufficiently, he suggested a further payment mechanism. As a result, the Russians set up a dummy company in London and took out a ten-year lease on Stanway's personal apartment, at some fifty per cent over the market rate, this extra percentage being in compensation for the inevitable inconvenience that would be caused if and when the lease was executed. Written into the lease was an agreement that Stanway would vacate the premises within twenty-eight days after receipt of a written notice to allow the director of the dummy company – who, of course, didn't actually exist – to occupy the premises on demand.

Within two years of beginning his treacherous activities, Stanway's declared income from his property speculation – and obviously not including the monies steadily accumulating in his account in the Cayman Islands – was more than three times his take-home pay from SIS, and he was able to account for every penny of it to the Inland Revenue.

After returning home the previous evening, Stanway had taken a walk, as he often did. Despite his fondness for good living, considering himself both a gourmet and a wine expert, he had always been careful to keep himself fit. He had even converted the smallest bedroom in his apartment into a gym, where he exercised every morning before his shower or bath, and he frequently walked or jogged along the streets of South Kensington in the evening.

That night, however, he had put on some casual clothes and just walked. His route had taken him into a newsagent's in Gloucester Road, where he browsed for about ten minutes, before emerging with a carrier bag containing a copy of *The Times*, a wine magazine and a small cardboard box, and heading on into Harrington Gardens. At the second crossroad he had turned left into Collingham Road. Outside the church on the west side of the street he had apparently stumbled on an uneven paving slab, dropping the carrier bag, and had to put his right hand against the wall to steady himself as he felt his ankle for damage with his left hand. Then Stanway had retrieved the bag and walked on, limping slightly.

A keen observer might have noticed that, after Stanway had removed his hand from the wall, a small chalk circle was visible on the stonework, which hadn't been there before.

Sluzhba Vneshney Razvyedki Rossi Headquarters, Yasenevo, Tëplyystan, Moscow

'This is not a good time, Raya,' said Major Yuri Abramov, looking across the desk at his deputy, who was standing respectfully at attention in front of him.

'I appreciate that, Major,' Raya said, 'and I am also very aware that you will not be in the office every day next week. But my mother has not been in good health and, if my aunt Valentina is right, she may well be dying.' Raya was very aware that she was addressing her superior officer and, though she'd spent some minutes in the toilet composing herself, she still couldn't stop the tears. She turned away quickly and reached for a tissue.

Major Abramov wasn't a hard man. Like Raya Kosov, he'd been recruited by the SVR for his computer-system management skills, not for any kind of old-style KGB toughness. He stood up, walked round his desk and put an arm around his subordinate, pulling her close to him. 'Sit down, Raya,' he murmured softly, and led her the few paces towards a chair.

In a couple of minutes, she felt able to speak, and to face him again. 'I'm so sorry, sir,' she stammered. 'I don't know—'

'Raya,' Abramov interrupted, 'please don't distress yourself. Your feelings are entirely natural. Look, you're owed a week's leave and, frankly, I wouldn't want you here working on the system in your present emotional state. Is there anything major that you have to get done this week?'

Raya shook her head. 'Nothing that won't wait, sir. I've a few basic housekeeping jobs to do, but I can get those out of the way by Friday.'

'Right,' Abramov said, 'do whatever you feel you need to do by the end of work on Friday. If there's anything you haven't managed to finish, let me know and I'll take care of it on Monday. You can sort out your travel arrangements tomorrow, and then fly to Minsk on Friday evening or Saturday morning. I'll authorize an airline ticket for you. Don't forget to check in at the local SVR office when you get there. I'll call ahead to let them know you'll be in the city.'

'Thank you, Major,' she murmured.

'But what you must do, Raya, is get back here by Friday next week, because I will be away almost all of the following week, and I'll need to do a full handover before I leave at the end of that day. If there's even the slightest possibility of your being delayed, you must let me know immediately.'

'Of course, sir,' Raya said. 'There'll be no problem, I'll make sure of that. And thank you so much.'

Three minutes later she closed Abramov's door behind her and headed back to her own office, with a slight smile brightening her face despite the red-rimmed eyes. She had a lot to do and very little time to do it in.

South Kensington, London

Andrew Lomas had been born Alexei Lomosolov, in Kiev in 1963. After showing considerable promise at school, he had been recruited by the KGB before he was even twenty. He'd then attended language courses, and quickly became fluent in English.

His talents had led to him being selected to undertake lifestyle training at the KGB's Balashikha special-operations school east of Moscow – where Yasser Arafat had been a pupil once, when the Russians had decided to groom him for future leadership of the PLO. Amongst other training included at Balashikha, the KGB provided facilities which precisely duplicated communities in various target countries. In the English facility, to which Lomosolov was sent, only English was ever spoken. Radio and television programmes were the genuine article, recorded and then re-broadcast over the local network; newspapers and books were English; the meals and drinks they were served were exactly what one would expect to find in an English home, pub or restaurant; and even the furniture and fittings had been purchased in London stores. It was the closest the KGB could get to providing an English environment without actually being in England itself.

Lomosolov had spent six months living and working there. The day he arrived the commanding officer had summoned him to his office and addressed him in English. On that occasion, he had explained the purpose of the facility, how it worked and what they expected from him. But he had finished with a warning: the only absolutely unbreakable rule there was that any student heard speaking a language other than English, for whatever reason and in any circumstance, would be instantly dismissed.

Lomosolov had been assessed as one of the top three students in his intake, and was advised by the commanding officer that he would be one of only two students selected to take the final examination. All the others would remain at the facility for a further two months, before being assessed again. When he'd asked what the examination consisted of, Lomosolov had simply been told to wait and see.

Late in May 1985, he was told to report to the facility's English pub. Not knowing what to expect, he pushed open the door and walked in, hailing the barman cheerfully, as he always did, ordering a pint of bitter. Sitting in an armchair at a small round table near the bar was an elderly man, who was clearly frail and not in the best of health. He was nursing a whisky, and smiled as the young man approached him. His face was faintly familiar to Lomosolov and suddenly, with a jolt that was more shock than surprise, Lomosolov recognized him.

Harold Adrian Russell ('Kim') Philby was then seventy-three years old and not merely a major general in the KGB but a living legend whose name and exploits were spoken of in reverent whispers. Suddenly Lomosolov realized that this encounter had to be his final examination. Those thirty minutes or so spent talking to Philby, before the facility commanding officer arrived, had been the most difficult of Lomosolov's short career, and when he was told to return to his quarters, he had no idea whether he had passed the test or failed.

Once Lomosolov departed, Philby had gestured for another Scotch and settled himself back into his seat as the commanding officer sat down opposite him.

'Well, Comrade General?'

Philby had smiled. 'The first student, Nabokov, is

very good. He would pass as an Englishman in any circumstances I can imagine.'

'And the second one, Lomosolov?'

Philby had smiled more broadly, before replying. 'I've been coming here for, what, almost twenty years to assess your students, Colonel, and never before have you tried this stunt. I'm surprised at you.'

'Tried what?'

'You know perfectly well.' Philby wagged a finger. 'Where did you find him? What is he, some English student you've recruited? The son of an English defector? What I do know is that he's not merely a Russian impersonating an Englishman. He is genuinely an Englishman.'

The commanding officer had shaken his head. 'I'm afraid you're wrong there, General, and there's been no trickery. That young man was born Alexei Lomosolov in Kiev twenty-two years ago, the only son of two good Russian citizens named Andrei and Katerina Lomosolov.'

A little over eight months later, following an intensive six-month course in tradecraft and agent-handling, Alexei Lomosolov had arrived in London. He was carrying a genuine Canadian passport in the name of Andrew Lomas, and took out a lease on a small apartment in West London.

If anybody asked him, he explained that he was employed as a 'creative consultant' – which could mean pretty much whatever you wanted it to mean – for a graphic-design company based in Liechtenstein. The company actually existed, and his monthly commission cheques bore the company logo and contact details, but it was simply a KGB front: a device which allowed Lomosolov to receive a regular supply of clean funds to support his lifestyle.

In fact, after a period during which he established himself in London, Lomosolov's – or rather Lomas's – real job was acting as a case officer for a number of other agents in Britain, two of whom were employed within the security establishment. One of these had been operational even before Lomosolov himself arrived in Britain, but the other had been supplying information for a much shorter period of time. This man was code-named *Gospodin*, but Lomas knew, from his pre-departure briefings in Moscow, that his real name was Gerald Stanway.

Their actual meetings were very infrequent, normally never more than once every three months. Lomas's principal task in servicing Stanway was simple enough: he merely cleared one of the current fifteen dead-drops whenever he received notification that Stanway had deposited some material. The routine for that was simple enough as well.

Each evening, Lomas walked from his apartment in Harwood Road, not far from Fulham Broadway Underground station, and through the streets of London, following a variety of routes as he mingled with the homeward-bound commuters, just another face in the thousands. Whichever route he took, he always walked down Collingham Road, and every time he passed the church he looked at the wall.

He also checked five other locations during his walk, but the church wall was always the last one. He frequently found marks at the other five places, too, but he'd never seen one on the church wall. This was because the first five indicated which dead-drop Stanway had filled, but the last one was reserved for emergency use only.

Lomas was so used to passing the wall and seeing nothing there at all that he'd actually taken three steps past before he registered that the chalked circle was even there.

He stopped so abruptly that the woman walking behind him, carrying four bulky carrier bags, cannoned into him. She cursed under her breath as she stepped around him. Lomas muttered apologies before briskly retracing his steps. He checked the street carefully for possible witnesses, before approaching the mark on the wall. As he drew level with it, he reached up and swiftly drew a cross within the circle, then stepped away quickly and carried on down the street, mentally planning the fastest route back to his apartment.

Austria

Richter pulled off the A2 autoroute and into a service area a few miles north of Wolfsberg, and filled up the Ford's petrol tank. It was still well over half full but he always liked to have plenty of fuel, just in case. He was actually stepping through the entrance of the cafeteria in search of something to eat when his mobile phone rang again. He turned round immediately and went back outside, before pressing the button to answer.

'What now, Simpson?'

'How did you know it was me?'

'As far as I know, nobody else has this number.'

'Right,' Simpson snapped, 'where are you?'

'Austria, and about to sample a genuine Austrian motorway sandwich. Where else do you want me to be?'

'Geneva – and as soon as possible. Is that going to be a problem?'

'No,' Richter replied. 'As long as you don't stop the credit card or cancel my passport, I can go anywhere at all. But I won't make it today. It's now gone three, and I reckon I'm still about three hundred kilometres from the Swiss border – and also on the wrong side of the Alps. Whereabouts do you want me to go in Geneva?'

'At the moment,' Simpson said, 'we don't know, so just check into a hotel somewhere near the city. And make sure you leave that mobile switched on.'

'I wouldn't dream of doing anything else,' Richter said.

'Call me when you stop somewhere tonight, and also when you reach Geneva. I'll give you my mobile number.'

Richter noted the number, terminated the call, and turned back towards the cafeteria door.

South Kensington, London

The moment Gerald Stanway reached home he changed into a tracksuit and trainers, then headed down the stairs and out into the street, before jogging off on his usual route around the quieter local streets. He passed the circle which now contained a chalked cross, giving it the briefest possible sidelong glance, and continued on around the block. Fifteen minutes later, he was back in his apartment and standing under a stinging-hot shower.

As he dried himself, he glanced at the wall clock, mentally calculating times and distances. Dressed casually in flannel trousers, open-necked shirt and lightweight jacket, he went into the lounge and called a cab. Like most residents of central London, Stanway had long accepted the fact that owning a car in the city was a complete waste of time and money. He travelled everywhere by tube, bus or cab, and if he had to drive anywhere outside the city, he would call up Hertz or Avis and have them deliver a car to his flat.

Entering his study, he sat down at the computer and opened up Microsoft Word. A fresh empty document appeared automatically, so he typed a few lines of text, read through what he had written twice, and then clicked on the print icon. The laser hummed for a few seconds and then spat out a single sheet. Stanway knew that the output from a laser or ink-jet printer was completely anonymous and untraceable, unlike that produced by any kind of typewriter.

Having once more read the text as hard copy, he nodded and folded the sheet twice. He next clicked the cross in the top right-hand corner of the Word window, and selected 'no' when the program asked if he wanted to save the open document. He definitely wanted no record of what he had just written anywhere on the hard disk.

Outskirts of Verona, Italy

It was seven-thirty local time when Paul Richter pulled the Ford off the A4 autoroute at San Martino Buon Albergo, one of the longest place names he ever recalled coming across. He'd crossed the Italian border at Arnoldstein, where the A2 autoroute transmuted into the A23, and swung south towards a stretch of the Mediterranean that his new road map called the Golfo de Venezia.

Finding a small hotel on the edge of Verona, he parked the car at the rear of the building and climbed out. He plucked his overnight bag from the boot, then recovered the briefcase, which now contained the opened packet he'd collected in Vienna and not much else, from the back seat, before he headed around to the hotel's reception to check in.

As soon as he was settled in his room, he called Simpson.

'It's Richter.'

'Where are you?'

'Two gentlemen.'

'What . . .? Are you drunk?'

'No, I'm perfectly sober – in fact, I'm a teetotaller. I'm now in a hotel on the outskirts of Verona. As in "Two gentlemen of Verona". You've heard of this bloke Shakespeare, have you?'

'Don't try to get clever with me, Richter. When I ask you a question, just give me a straight answer, OK?'

'I'll bet you were the most popular boy in your class at school, weren't you?'

'Don't be impertinent. When do you think you'll reach Geneva?'

'Probably mid-afternoon tomorrow. Any further instructions?'

'Nothing yet. Just call me when you arrive.'

London

The cab arrived twenty minutes later, and Stanway told the driver to take him to Tottenham Court Road, near the Goodge Street Underground station. He paid the driver, then headed towards a nearby side street.

For the briefest of instants he'd toyed with the idea of running various evasion manoeuvres, to shake off any tails he might have acquired, but he immediately realized there was no point. First, he wasn't very experienced in counter-surveillance techniques and had never practised them, and, second, if he was being followed, any such actions on his part would immediately confirm the suspicions of the surveillance personnel. It was far simpler, he'd rationalized, to behave entirely innocently, because all he was apparently doing was going out for a meal in a restaurant, which was something he did three or four evenings every week.

About fifty yards down the street was a small Indian restaurant. Stanway asked for a secluded table for one, and was led towards the back of the room and shown into a tiny booth.

Andrew Lomas was sitting at a table at the front of the restaurant. He was accompanied by his current girlfriend, a thin and somewhat vacuous supposed model named Dawn, who had aspirations towards the theatre and insisted on calling everyone 'dahling'. Lomas privately thought that she was probably on the game, but he didn't care much because she made for good, if temporary, local colour, and besides that she was actually quite good in bed. They had been sitting there for a little over three-quarters of an hour before Stanway walked in. Neither man showed the slightest sign of recognizing the other.

The waiter placed a menu on the table and asked Stanway if he'd like anything to drink. He ordered a half pint of lager, glanced quickly at the menu, and decided on a chicken korma with basmati rice. He disliked Indian food, and had no appetite that evening anyway, but he knew he had to order something as he sat there waiting.

Stanway's lager arrived and he took a cautious sip. It wasn't a drink he particularly enjoyed, but at least it would serve to take away some of the taste of the korma. Five minutes after his meal arrived, Stanway was prodding unenthusiastically at a small number of yellowish chunks of chicken, when he noticed Lomas stand up and walk towards him, obviously heading for the toilets at the rear.

Immediately, Stanway reached into his inside jacket pocket and extracted the folded sheet of paper. As Lomas approached, Stanway placed it at the very edge of his table, with an inch or so jutting out. The Russian's right hand just brushed against the side of the table, as he deftly seized the note and continued towards the toilets. Nobody at any of the other tables could have seen or taken the slightest notice.

Four minutes later, Lomas emerged, passing Stanway again, and continued to his own table while gesturing for the bill. The Russian paid right away, helped his girlfriend into her coat, and nodded briefly to the waiter as the two of them left.

Two other men had used the toilet before Stanway finally stood up and made his way to the rear. There were two urinals and one stall: he stepped into the stall and locked the door behind him. One reason for choosing this restaurant was that the stall had solid walls and a door that fitted its frame completely. They would never have picked one where the door had a sizeable gap at the top or bottom.

Stanway lifted the seat and stepped up onto the bowl. The toilet had an old-fashioned, wall-mounted cistern – another reason for choosing this restaurant – and his probing fingers quickly detected the paper tucked between the back of the cistern and the wall. He retrieved it, stepped back on the floor, lowered the toilet seat and sat down, then unfolded the paper to read what was written there.

His own printed message occupied the top few lines:

Possible I have been compromised by low-level SVR cipher clerk who has fled Russia. According to high-level 6 briefing, clerk approached Moscow UK Embassy but left before asylum granted. Showed intelligence staff papers listing 6 file names and numbers. Claimed he had other data identifying SVR agent in 6. Latest information suggests clerk escaped to Vienna, still seeking asylum. Check veracity and advise.

Below that, Lomas had written a brief reply in block capitals:

NOTHING KNOWN. IF LOW-LEVEL DEFECTOR, LONDON STATION NOT ALWAYS INFORMED. WILL CHECK MOSCOW CENTRE AND ADVISE.

And that, Stanway thought, as he tore the paper into tiny squares and watched the flush carry it out of sight, was encouraging at least. If Lomas had already known about the defection, Stanway would have been forced to take immediate action to protect himself. The fact that Lomas knew nothing about it suggested that either the clerk was flying a kite, or that he was genuinely low-level with nothing of any significance to trade – and the SVR would know exactly what documents such a defector would have had access to – or else that the clerk simply didn't exist.

But that scenario didn't really make sense, for Holbeche – or whoever else had started this particular ball rolling – had to have received some information suggesting that there was a mole inside SIS, otherwise why had he started the witch-hunt? Something or someone had surfaced somewhere, and Stanway just hoped he could rely on Lomas to find out what or who, and quickly.

Chapter Seven

Thursday
Sluzhba Vneshney Razvyedki Rossi Headquarters, Yasenevo,
Tëplyystan, Moscow

Captain Raya Kosov had arrived at work early that morning. The telephone call from Valentina had started the clock, and she knew she had a maximum of two days before she would have to start running.

Her window of opportunity was very small, and for one very simple reason. Raya Kosov had already said her final goodbye to her mother on her last home leave, three months previously. The call from Valentina had actually informed her that Marisa was dead, not sick, and she knew that the hospital authorities in Minsk would be advising her employer, the SVR, as a matter of routine within the next day or two.

Hopefully it would not alarm Major Abramov if he heard about it before end of work on Friday, because Raya had already told him her mother was very sick. It would not be particularly surprising if she had died shortly after the call Raya received, but he would undoubtedly be suspicious if he checked the time of death and found it actually occurred earlier than the time of his conversation with her.

And the SVR, like the KGB before it, liked to have a lever: a way of keeping all its employees in check.

Once Raya's mother was dead, that lever would vanish, and the very least Raya could then expect was greatly increased surveillance and checking of her movements. Once that happened, her chances of getting safely out of Russia were considerably reduced, and she might not be able to manage it at all.

By Friday afternoon she needed to have completed everything she had to do, and early on Saturday morning she would have to leave her apartment and be en route to the airport. Even if Abramov did try and fail to contact her, just to advise her that her mother had died, he would just assume that she had already left for Minsk. But on Monday morning, when she failed to notify the Minsk SVR office that she was in the city, as Abramov had instructed, the alarm bells would start to ring. And she guessed the hunt would be under way no later than Tuesday.

Northern Italy

Richter was up and dressed by seven-thirty, and on the road again an hour later. He picked up the A4 autoroute just south of Verona and turned right for Milan. He planned to avoid Milan itself, but stay on the autoroute circling to the north of the city, then pick up the E62 link running north-east, to join up with the northbound A26.

There were no direct routes from Milan to Geneva, due to the inconvenient obstruction of the Alps, but he had calculated that taking the A26 and then route 33 from Mergozzo would probably be the quickest way.

That would take him northwards to Brig, and west to Sierre, where he would rejoin the autoroute system. Then he would continue through Martigny and around the north side of Lac Leman, passing through Montreux and Lausanne to enter Geneva from the north.

South Kensington, West London

The phone rang just as Stanway was about to leave for work. He strode across the lounge and picked it up. 'Yes?'

'I wonder, sir, if you have ever considered the benefits of installing full double-glazing in your property?' a male voice said. 'If I could just take five minutes of your time, I can—'

'No, thank you,' Stanway snapped, and replaced the telephone handset. He had no idea if his phone line was tapped, though in view of what Holbeche had said it quite probably was, but he was sure that incoming call would have been safe enough. After all, everyone received junk phone calls in the same way everyone received spam emails. He had kept the line open only long enough to hear the actual number the caller had given as part of the spiel: *'five minutes'*.

That was another simple code that Lomas had instructed him to remember, right at the start of their professional relationship. Each of the digits from one to ten had a different meaning. 'Five' was perhaps the simplest, signifying 'no change, no news, or nothing to report', so obviously Lomas hadn't found out anything from Moscow overnight.

In this case, no news, Stanway mused, might well be good news. Moscow knew exactly how valuable he was to the SVR, and he was quite sure that if anything had happened that could threaten his position at Vauxhall Cross, they would very quickly do something about it. Also they would be certain to keep his case officer, Lomas, fully informed.

In any case, Stanway knew Lomas would be getting back to him soon, and that this time they would have to actually talk. It would take more than a brief exchange of written messages in a third-rate Indian restaurant, but Stanway realized the strong possibility that he, and everybody else employed in the higher echelons of SIS, would soon be under physical as well as electronic surveillance, if not already. He felt reasonably certain that he hadn't been followed to the Indian restaurant the previous evening but, until the present situation was resolved, any further direct physical contact between himself and Lomas would be extremely ill-advised.

The best option was the telephone but for obvious reasons not his home landline or his regular mobile. When he had visited the newsagent the previous evening, he had also purchased a cheap pay-as-you-go mobile phone. That was ideal: no name, no address, no contract, just a phone with a number that only he knew. The SIM card inside the phone was good for twenty-five pounds' worth of calls and, once he'd used up that credit, he could top up the card at almost any newsagent. Or he could simply buy another phone.

Lomas had two unlisted contact numbers that Stanway had memorized and, once he knew Lomas had received a reply from Moscow, he would be able to call him without any danger of interception because nobody in the British security establishment had any idea that Lomas even existed. Stanway knew that for a fact, because he himself was in the ideal position to know.

Of course, he wouldn't be so stupid as to call Lomas directly from his apartment. As well as bugging his telephone line, it wouldn't have surprised him if 'The Box' had also managed to sneak an infinity transmitter into his property somewhere, which would relay all his conversations, not just his telephone calls, to a nearby surveillance vehicle. If they had, the last thing he would do was try to find it and remove it, since that, to the suspicious eyes of the Security Service, would be tantamount to an admission of guilt.

He would just wait and act perfectly normally, and obviously for the moment Moscow would have to wait for any further data from him. In fact, Stanway wondered if it might now be time to call a halt to his operations, at least on a temporary basis. He had already ransacked the SIS database, picking out files dealing with any matters Lomas had told him the SVR had an interest in, and his production of the file structure of the London Data Centre System-Three computer had seemed the next logical step.

As a Deputy Head of Department, who was subject to positive vetting every two years, as well as an annual polygraph check, all of which he had invariably sailed through, he enjoyed virtually unrestricted access to all files on the linked databases maintained by GCHQ at Cheltenham, the Foreign and Commonwealth Office, the London Data Centre and, of course, the SIS. He could even access a limited number of files on the Security

Service database, which he did on a regular basis merely to ensure that no hint of Andrew Lomas's existence had been detected.

The actual mechanism he used for copying the files was as simple as it was elegant. Because of his position as a Deputy Head, his personal computer at Vauxhall Cross was not subject to keyboard logging or other forms of detailed surveillance. The machine itself was pretty much a standard IBM. At Vauxhall Cross the electronic security is embedded in the building itself, which is essentially a huge Faraday Cage, allowing no electronic emissions either in or out. The computer was fitted with a DVD-ROM drive – a read-only unit – but not a CD or DVD burner which would facilitate the copying of data, a serial port, one parallel printer port, one Firewire and two USB ports.

When Stanway had first begun copying classified files on behalf of the SVR, he had used a number of different ways of getting the copies out of the building, all of them somewhat risky, but with improvements in technology had come a safer and more reliable method. Stanway only wrote with either a fountain pen or a pencil and, just over three years earlier, Lomas had presented him with a new pen specially created to a most unusual design.

Slightly longer and fatter than most pens, it somewhat resembled a Mont Blanc. Above its 18-carat gold nib was a chamber designed to hold a normal ink cartridge, revealed by unscrewing the nib assembly, and above that was another chamber which was wide enough to accommodate three other ink cartridges at the same time. This was accessed by unscrewing a cap at the top of the pen, which would allow the cartridges to be tipped out. It was of a somewhat eccentric design but still a fully functional pen, though it had one modification not visible to the naked eye.

Stanway had taken the pen with him to Vauxhall Cross, and had walked through the entry and exit scanners every day for two weeks, and the machines had detected nothing unusual. The second day of the third week, he had made one slight alteration to the pen while still at home, but again had found himself able to enter and exit Vauxhall Cross without problems. That evening Stanway had sat at home by himself, as usual, and in celebration had drunk half a bottle of Chateau Lafitte – arguably one of the best red wines that the vineyards of Bordeaux have ever produced, which was not so usual – while the pen sat innocently on the coffee table in front of him.

The invisible modification to the pen was a thin copper sheath positioned underneath the outer plastic, and which enclosed both the internal chambers. This addition effectively screened the inside of the pen from most scanning devices, and the reason Stanway had been celebrating was that he had, that same morning, removed the three spare ink cartridges and replaced them with a single short rod-like object with an oblong socket at one end. It was a tight fit inside the pen, but the two had been designed to slot together. The rod-like object was a specially manufactured solid-state USB drive with a capacity of thirty-two megabytes. To put that into perspective, one full-length novel would occupy only around one megabyte.

That had been three years earlier, but the USB

drive that Stanway had been using for the last six months – and which, as a precaution against discovery during any random search of his apartment, he was going to put in his safe-deposit box at his local bank on his way to Vauxhall Cross – was a device with a capacity of four gigabytes, or *four thousand* megabytes.

To copy files, Stanway merely plugged the drive into one of the vacant USB ports on the back of his system unit. The computer's operating system automatically recognized the drive, and all he then had to do was use Windows Explorer to drag the selected files to the USB drive. And doing everything by using the mouse ensured that there were no keystrokes to be recorded, even if a keystroke logger had been loaded on his machine without his knowledge.

Once the drive was full, he removed it from the port, tucked it away inside his special pen, and left it in one of the dead-letter drops – what the Russians call '*duboks*' – on his way home from Vauxhall Cross. Lomas would collect it later that evening, and leave an identical, but empty, drive in the same location, which Stanway could collect at leisure.

The pen was now back in the pocket of Stanway's suit jacket, but holding three ink cartridges in the second chamber instead of the USB drive.

He picked up his briefcase and his new mobile phone, still in its box, and took the lift down to the ground floor of the building. There was a small utility room there, adjacent to the lift. Stanway put his briefcase on the floor, reached into his pocket and pulled out a bunch of keys. He selected one and unlocked the door.

He stepped inside, put the mobile phone box on

a small workbench that ran along the left side of the room, opened the box and removed the phone and its charger. He plugged the charger into the wall socket, connected the other end of the lead to the phone itself, switched on at the socket and checked that the phone was charging properly. Then he took the box, crushed it beneath his feet to flatten it, and slid it into his briefcase. He would dispose of it somewhere convenient on his way to work.

He was, he realized, perhaps being a little over-cautious. After all, there was nothing illegal in owning a pay-as-you-go mobile phone, but he knew that the Security Service would see that as suspicious, not least because he already possessed a mobile. That was why he had decided to charge the phone here in the utility room, just in case somebody from 'The Box' was planning on visiting this building while he was out at work. They might well decide to search his apartment, but he doubted that they would bother searching the rest of the building.

He would just wait them out, he decided, as he re-locked the utility room door and pocketed the keys. Once Lomas had either confirmed that a clerk had run from Moscow, and could compromise him, or discovered that the whole story was a fiction – simply an operation designed to flush him out by making him panic and run – then Stanway would decide what he had to do next. And if there was some frightened little clerk skulking around Europe clutching a bag of papers that could incriminate him, Stanway knew exactly what he would have to do to eliminate the threat.

Secret Intelligence Service (SIS) Headquarters, Vauxhall Cross, London

Holbeche had reached his office late, having been due to leave Vauxhall Cross for an off-site meeting at nine-thirty that morning, but after he'd taken a look at two classified files, flagged 'Flash', he decided to delay his departure by half an hour and called Simpson just after nine-forty.

'There's been no approach to the Moscow embassy,' he announced, after getting through on the secure line.

'I wasn't expecting one,' Simpson replied. 'Whoever our mole is, he's probably a reasonably experienced intelligence officer, not to mention an experienced spy, and there's no way someone like that is going to ring up the embassy just to ask if the story about the clerk is true. He would be certain that we'd have taps on all the lines out of Vauxhall Cross, and he would hardly try to use his home phone either. You have already placed taps, I presume?'

'Yes,' Holbeche replied. 'Arkin has arranged for taps to be placed on the home phones of all SIS officers, apart from those belonging to the most junior grades, who simply don't have the access needed.'

There was a lot of misinformation in the public domain about telephone tapping in Britain. The official position, trotted out every time anybody asked the question, was that whenever the Security Service MI5 wished to install a telephone tap, the request had to be submitted to the Home Secretary in person, who would read it and then, if he approved, sign the authorizing warrant.

The SIS was required to follow a similar procedure, but their requests were submitted instead to the Foreign Secretary. Each warrant was subject to a monthly review, and a further or extended warrant would only be approved if the requesting organization could manage to convince their particular Secretary that continuing the surveillance could be justified.

The physical installation of telephone taps and other bugging devices was carried out by a security division within British Telecom, and taps would not be installed unless a proper warrant was produced. This rule might be relaxed if it could be demonstrated that the case was extremely urgent or had grave security implications – for example, if the phone is believed to be currently used by active terrorists – but, even then, the authorizing warrant had to be submitted to British Telecom within forty-eight hours of the tap being placed.

Comforting though the above procedures might be to the innocent citizens of Great Britain, the reality of the situation was somewhat different.

First, the Echelon monitoring system – a joint automated-surveillance system operated primarily by the intelligence services of Britain, America, Canada, Australia and New Zealand – monitored every international telephone call that originated in, terminated in, or passed through any of the participating countries. It also monitored emails and faxes within the same broad geographical area.

Second, and rather more worrying to anyone with the slightest interest in personal liberty and freedom of speech, Special Branch, which was the executive arm of the Security Service, had the authority to request the installation of a tap or a bug on a telephone line of a suspected criminal without reference to the Home Secretary, just by applying to a senior British Telecom official. Special Branch officers, even without specific direction from the Security Service, were perfectly capable of interpreting the term 'suspected criminal' in its loosest possible sense. Practically speaking, therefore, MI5 could actually tap the telephone of pretty much anyone they wanted to, for as long as they wanted to, without the Home Secretary or anyone else even being aware of it.

'There has been some other activity here, though,' Holbeche said.

'Oh, yes?'

'Cheltenham has reported some slightly unusual signal traffic between London and Moscow this morning on the usual circuits.'

'A known code?' Simpson asked. 'Or one they can read?'

'No,' Holbeche replied. 'It was a single message in a high-level cipher that has never been broken, but which is frequently used for extended-length transmissions to Moscow.'

'So what was unusual about it, then?'

'As I said, this cipher is normally used for high-volume traffic, long transmissions which GCHQ has always presumed was just the usual diplomatic waffle. But this message was really short, just a few groups, according to Cheltenham.'

Simpson remained silent for a few moments. 'Maybe,' he then said slowly, 'just maybe Cheltenham's take on this is wrong. The short message could have been a simple request for confirmation of the missing-clerk story from Moscow Centre. If it was, that means two things. First, it means that our mole . . . our file on this breach is "Egret Seven", and we've code-named the source of the leak "Gecko" by the way. It means our mole has attended one of the briefings already given, which means he's a very senior officer indeed, and much more dangerous than we thought. Second, it suggests that the previous high-volume traffic might not just have been a bunch of diplomats exchanging off-colour jokes and party invitations. Instead, it might have been stuff that the London SVR *rezident* has already received from the mole, and which he was then transmitting to Moscow. In which case—'

'In which case,' Holbeche finished it for him, 'we're not looking at a new security breach. This bastard could have been sending stuff to Moscow for months, or perhaps years.'

There was a silence on the line as both men absorbed the implications of this suggestion.

Simpson roused himself first. 'It's circumstantial, of course,' he said, 'but it does seem to hold together. And, until something breaks, there's not a great deal we can do. I would suggest tasking GCHQ with tackling that cipher, though if they've had no success so far, that's probably a waste of time. But it might be instructive to find out when this particular cipher was first used because, if our guess is correct, that could give us an indication of the scale of the breach.'

'I'll ask Cheltenham to check the logs and provide us with a breakdown,' Holbeche concurred.

'Good. Perhaps the reason the System-Three directory structure was being sent as hard copy to Yasenevo by courier was because it might have been too difficult to convert it into a format that could be sent in signal form.'

'You could be right and, in that case, we've been incredibly lucky. If that Russian hadn't collapsed, we might never even have known about the mole.'

'Exactly,' Simpson added. 'I would love to find out for sure if that single message this morning was a request to Moscow Centre for confirmation that some SVR clerk actually has skipped.'

'So would I, Simpson. So would I,' Holbeche replied, before ending the call.

West London

Andrew Lomas wasn't worried, but he was definitely concerned, for Stanway was getting decidedly jittery. That was proved by the emergency summons to the meet in the Indian restaurant, one of five emergency rendezvous places and times indicated by different types of chalk mark scribbled on the church wall.

When he had first started working with Stanway, the Englishman had appeared surprised at Lomas suggesting they indicate their meeting places by means of chalk marks or similarly archaic devices. What was wrong, he had asked, with using pagers, mobile phones or even call boxes?

Lomas had been firm, however, since his training in Moscow had been thorough and specific. The problem with using any telephone, whether fixed or mobile, was that with the right equipment the call could be monitored and both the calling and contacted numbers identified. Besides, as a matter of routine, the Security Service monitored all the public telephones located close to Vauxhall Cross and to most of the other buildings occupied by sections of the British intelligence establishment, as well as the phones adjacent to all the foreign embassies.

That was a 'just in case' precaution based on the somewhat tenuous assumption that any British intelligence officer wishing to pass classified information to a foreign power would simply nip out of Vauxhall Cross during his lunch break and call the appropriate embassy from a phone box on the street nearby. And although this blanket surveillance had so far never led to the detection of any serious breach of security, there was some logic to it; for anyone wishing to make a call without being overheard would tend to opt for a public phone, and a phone box that was conveniently located.

But Lomas had firmly refused to let Stanway make any routine contact by telephone, and had insisted that he learn and use the simple codes that Lomas had devised. And, as a result, for years their contact had remained almost entirely impersonal. Stanway would deposit the USB drive, containing the files he had copied, in a dead letter box; Lomas would collect it and replace it with a blank drive. And about once every three or four months the two men would meet, but always briefly and always a long way from home.

Of course, Lomas could understand why his contact was now concerned. If some clerk genuinely *had* run from Yasenevo carrying documents that could identify Stanway, it was a potential disaster. But Lomas was reasonably sure that if such an event had occurred, Moscow Centre would have already told him about it. That left the possibility – or perhaps even the probability – that it was some sort of operation being run by MI5 to flush out a suspected traitor.

He had contacted the Russian Embassy in London as soon as possible after leaving the Indian restaurant, requesting a thorough check. And the response he'd received by encrypted email in the early hours of the morning had puzzled him. The decoded message read:

No defection reported. Assume 'missing clerk' story bogus.
Immediate action: Advise source Gospodin no news. Follow-up
action: none. Await decision on further response
from Moscow Centre.

It was the final sentence that had puzzled Lomas. If there was no defecting clerk and the whole story was just a device, then Stanway was perfectly safe. Of course, he would have to curb his activities for a while, at least until the witch-hunt had died down. So what other possible 'further response' were the wheels at Yasenevo considering?

Bons-en-Chablais, Savoie, France

By mid-afternoon, Richter had reached Geneva. In fact, he'd driven through the city and out the other side on to the A40 autoroute, entering France in the process, but he'd only driven as far as the first junction. There he'd turned north off the autoroute, and had stopped at a small town called Bons-en-Chablais. It was only about fifteen miles outside Geneva, so he knew he could easily reach the city centre within about an hour. That should be close enough for whatever Simpson had in mind.

He'd already filled the Ford's tank at a garage, in preparation for whatever the morrow might bring, and had tried three hotels before settling on a small Logis de France establishment more or less in the centre of the town. It had lockable garages, an attractive dining room and only eight bedrooms.

Once he'd unpacked his meagre possessions, Richter reserved a table for one in the dining room at eight that evening, purchased a *café alongé* – straightforward black coffee – in the bar, and took it outside to one of the tables overlooking the small square where the hotel was located. Only then did he call Simpson on his mobile.

'I'm in Geneva, or near enough,' he said. 'Any news for me?'

'What do you mean by "near enough"?'

'I'm about fifteen miles from the centre of the city, but I'm actually in a small town just over the Swiss border, in France.'

'What's its name?'

'Does that matter?'

'No, I suppose not,' Simpson said, recognizing Richter's reluctance to divulge his exact location. However, as long as his mobile phone was switched on, Simpson knew he'd be able to pinpoint Richter's position to within a few yards by triangulation, using the cells the phone was in contact with. Always assuming, of course, that he could persuade the Frogs to play ball, and that was never a foregone conclusion. 'We've still no news, so leave your mobile switched on, and be prepared to move at very short notice.'

'Right.' Richter ended the call and settled back in his seat to enjoy the coffee and to watch whatever activity there was in the square.

Cahors, Lot, France

'That's it,' David Adamson said, looking up from the map, and pointed to the right just as Colin Redmond Dekker steered the French-plated Renault Laguna over the narrow stone bridge at the southern end of the town of Cahors. The bridge spanned the River Lot, and perhaps a quarter of a mile along it, on the south bank, was a small hotel.

'You're sure?' Dekker asked. Adamson had already called and booked two rooms there while they were still on the road, up in the Dordogne.

'Yes. The directions they gave me were quite clear. There's a roundabout at the end of the bridge. Turn right, and just beyond that there's a narrow road running along the river itself. That leads straight to the hotel, and there's a car park right outside.'

A couple of minutes later, Dekker parked in the closest vacant slot to the main entrance, as he wanted to leave the vehicle in as visible a location as possible. The two men plucked their overnight bags and briefcases from the boot and headed inside. The receptionist's English was workable, though Adamson had been picked by Simpson because he spoke fluent French, and so check-in took no time at all. Dekker spoke hardly a word of the language, but he had other skills that Simpson thought he might need. The two men reserved a table for dinner, in the dining room overlooking the river, then took the lift up to the second floor.

'Let's get unpacked first, then we'll go down and have a drink at the bar,' Adamson suggested. He stepped back and examined the door of his room and the ancient lock on it. 'This isn't the most secure accommodation I've ever stayed in,' he added, 'so I think we'd better keep the weapons with us from now on. I'd hate to come back up here after dinner and find that some French tea leaf had broken in and walked off with the shooters. Simpson would go ballistic. Just make sure nobody can spot the holster under your jacket.'

In their separate rooms, the men unpacked what they might need for the night, then Dekker carried his heavy briefcase into the room opposite. Adamson first checked that the door was securely locked, then snapped open the locks on his own briefcase. Inside were two leather shoulder holsters and two locked pistol cases, each of them containing a Glock 17 semi-automatic pistol with three magazines and a box of fifty rounds of 9-millimetre Parabellum ammunition.

Then the two men performed exactly the same sequence of actions. They first loaded all three magazines, then pulled on a shoulder holster and slid two of the magazines into the specially designed loops. The third magazine went into the weapon itself, which each man secured in his holster. Adamson finally locked the virtually empty briefcase and slid it under the bed.

'What about the rifle?' Dekker asked.

'We'll take it with us.'

'Right.' Dekker picked up his own bulky briefcase and headed for the room door, waiting there for Adamson to unlock it.

In the corridor outside, the two men studied each other for a few seconds, checking that the weapons remained invisible under their jackets. Once satisfied, they walked off towards the lift.

'Order me a beer, will you?' Adamson said, as they stepped out into the lobby. 'I'd better go and tell our esteemed leader that the eagle has landed, so to speak.'

Outside the hotel, Adamson pulled out his mobile phone and dialled an unlisted London number.

A couple of minutes later he walked into the bar and sat down opposite Dekker, who had picked a table up against the wall, with the briefcase jammed into the space beside his chair.

'And how is that poisonous, balding, short, pink bastard?' Dekker asked, sliding a glass of beer across the table.

'How many times have you actually met him?' Adamson asked.

'Just the once,' Dekker replied.

'You seem to have nailed his personality, then, and he's pretty much as you'd expect. He was surprised that we'd only got this far, but I told him that, with the time-scale he's given us, this was as far as we needed to get today – and that seemed to shut him up. And I explained to him that it had taken us a bit longer than anticipated in getting to the Paris embassy to change cars.'

That had been an important component of Simpson's plan, as he'd guessed that a British-plated car would be more instantly noticeable in Ax-les-Thermes than a

French vehicle. So he'd arranged for the pair to leave their British Ford at the Paris embassy, on the Rue du Faubourg St Honoré, and then complete their journey in one of the embassy's own vehicles.

Adamson glanced round the bar, which was still empty at that time of day. 'Anyway, it looks like it's still a go for tomorrow, though there's been nothing from Vauxhall Cross, or anywhere else, to suggest that anyone's swallowed the bait.'

Chapter Eight

Richter got up fairly late, had a shower and shaved, then headed down to the hotel dining room for a typical French breakfast of coffee, bread and pastries.

Once finished there, he walked into the hotel lounge and sat down, placing the briefcase on the low table in front of him. He checked his mobile phone, which he'd left on charge all night. It had a fully charged battery and a good strong signal. Until Simpson called him, he had nowhere to go, nothing to do, and all day to do it in.

He unlocked the briefcase, pulled out one of the three novels he'd bought at Heathrow, and settled down to read.

Hammersmith, London

Almost as soon as he reached Hammersmith, Simpson called Holbeche, but the SIS head had nothing useful to report.

There had been no results so far from their operation to flush out the traitor, and no suspicious telephone calls had been made or received by anybody currently under surveillance. No one had failed to report for work, who wasn't genuinely sick, and no staff member at any of the target establishments had requested taking leave at short notice. It was as if their assumption was wrong, and that the deep-cover mole simply didn't exist. Except that they knew he did.

'Have you briefed Paris?' Simpson asked.

'Yes, I talked to the Head of Station this morning and told him exactly what's going on.'

'And you can trust him?'

'I think so, Simpson, yes. I'm not sure he could even access the System-Three directory listing from the Paris holy of holies, but the reality is that the breach must have occurred on this side of the Channel. If somebody in France had obtained it, a Russian courier would have taken it direct to Moscow from there. It certainly wouldn't have been sent over to London first. No, I'm happy to believe that he's not involved.'

'OK. So what did you ask him to do?'

'I've told him to brief two of his officers – their names are Richard Hughes and David Wallis – to fly down to Toulouse tomorrow afternoon, and then drive on to Ax-les-Thermes. As far as they're concerned, the whole operation is on the level. They'll be told they're being sent down there just to interview this Russian defector, and to assess whatever information he's carrying. Once they've done that, they'll report back to Paris with a straight recommendation of yes or no.'

'They won't be armed?' Simpson asked.

'They can be, if you want, but that might raise eyebrows. This is supposed to be a routine assignment.'

'No, and I'd rather they weren't armed. I just want to

know who's likely to be carrying, so I can brief my own people.'

'Understood. Where's your man now?' Holbeche asked.

'I've sent him to Geneva. He's in a hotel just outside the city, but on the French side of the lake,' Simpson said.

'Why there?'

'No particular reason. It just seemed fairly central, and he can easily get to the rendezvous position in about six hours.'

'When will you send him down? I mean, what's your take on this, bearing in mind we've so far seen no response at all from anyone within the security establishment?'

'That hasn't surprised me,' Simpson replied. 'Whoever Gecko is, he's going to play it cool, and that means no sudden illnesses, dying relatives, or requests for unpaid leave. My guess is that, once he knows where this defector from the SVR has gone to ground, he'll hop on an aircraft – or more likely just get in his car and drive down to the south of France.

'But, to answer your question, I'm going to send this man down there today – his name's Paul Richter, by the way – because I want him in place no later than this evening. That will give Gecko two clear days over this weekend to sort him out, and still let him be back in his office on Monday morning, bright-eyed and bushy-tailed, and eager to hear the latest news about the Russian cipher clerk.'

'What's he like, this Richter?'

'I'm not entirely sure,' Simpson said. 'I've only met him once. We picked him because he matched all the basic criteria we agreed – no immediate family, unemployed, Russian speaker and with a military background. He actually speaks good Russian, which is a bonus – he took an advanced course while he was in the Navy. The other reason I chose him was because, frankly, we couldn't find anybody else suitable in the time available. His service record showed him to be somewhat insubordinate, but also stubborn and resourceful, and I thought he would fit the bill. You'll appreciate that we couldn't do a *full* check on him, simply because of the timescale, but I have to confess he's not the order-following patsy I assumed he would be. In fact, ever since he arrived in Vienna, he's done very little but disobey almost every instruction we've given him.'

'Deliberately?'

'Absolutely. He even told me he trusted me about as far as he could spit a rat – which I presume is an expression they use in the Royal Navy's Fleet Air Arm. He's also deeply suspicious about his tasking, and doesn't believe I've told him anything like the truth about why he's in Europe.'

'It sounds like he's got your number, Richard,' Holbeche chuckled. 'Is that going to be a problem?'

'No. It doesn't matter what he thinks, or even what he does, as long as he eventually goes where I tell him. And once Gecko catches up with him, he'll either live or he'll die, and it really doesn't matter either way. We'll have got our mole, and Richter will have died in a car crash or a climbing accident, or whatever else we decide to arrange in order to get rid of his body. Or maybe he'll walk away from this alive. And if he does walk away, I might even offer him a job. I like the way he thinks.'

'So what do you want from me? To proceed as we agreed?'

'Yes, though I suggest you do it this morning. That will give Gecko plenty of time to make whatever arrangements he needs for the weekend.'

'And what about watchers? You still think they're a waste of time?'

'Definitely. In fact, it would be worse than that. It would be counter-productive. You can't watch every officer, and Sod's Law states that if you do try to put some surveillance in place, either Gecko or somebody else is bound to spot it. Word will get around, and then he'll guess that this whole thing is just a deception operation, and that will then be that. We'll be right back at square one with no idea of Gecko's identity, and no easy way of finding out.'

'If this was a long-term operation, I'd agree with you. But if you're expecting Gecko to act this weekend, within the next two days, I don't see how he could manage to detect any surveillance in such a short time.'

'Would you really want to take that chance?' Simpson asked.

Holbeche paused before replying. 'No, I suppose not. Very well, then, I'll arrange for the information to be released this morning.'

'Another briefing?'

'No, I think we'll keep it low-key. I'll just have it sent round the internal email system, as a routine update. Look, there's a lot riding on this, Richard, so how sure are you that it'll work?'

'I'm not,' Simpson confessed, 'but I still think it offers us our best chance of winkling out this bastard without having Five and Special Branch crawling all over Vaux-hall Cross, and anywhere else he might be employed.'

'And when will your people be in position?'

'By this afternoon. They crossed the Channel yes-terday – couldn't fly because they're carrying weapons – and had reached Cahors by last night. They checked in with me after they'd found a hotel, and they plan on getting to Ax no later than four this afternoon.'

'And Richter? What time will *he* arrive?' Holbeche asked.

In his office in Hammersmith, Simpson glanced at his watch. 'Early this evening, I should think. I'll be giving him his instructions in about an hour, and he's got further to drive than my other two men. That should be time enough, though. It'll take Gecko at least five hours from leaving London to get to the location, even if he flies straight to Toulouse, and my guess is he won't be flying because he'll want to take a weapon with him. I think he'll either drive or go by train, and that means he won't get there until sometime tomorrow.'

'So the timing should work out well,' Holbeche said. 'Let's hope everything else does.'

'Exactly,' Simpson replied.

Sluzhba Vneshney Razvyedki Rossi Headquarters, Yasenevo, Tëplyystan, Moscow

In her fifteenth-floor office, Raya Kosov gazed out of the window towards Moscow for what she guessed would be the last time. She then turned her attention to a hand-written list – each entry apparently innocuous – lying on the desk in front of her. She was being as methodical in her approach to her defection as in everything else she had ever done at Yasenevo.

Beside the list sat an official voucher for a return airline ticket to Minsk, made out in her name. Abramov had organized that for her, and her eyes had again welled with tears when he had handed it to her. Not, in this case, from grief, but simply because she knew exactly how much trouble he was going to be in as soon as her crime was discovered. She just hoped her boss would survive the subsequent purge.

Also on the desk was her passport, obtained nearly five years earlier for a brief holiday on the Black Sea, and which she'd only ever used on that one occasion, and beside it was her SVR identity card. She would need the passport to get onto the aircraft, while the identity card should help smooth her path if she met any obstacles. Like the KGB before it, the SVR was regarded with a mixture of fear and awe by most Russian citizens, and its officers were very rarely impeded.

She had already packed a small case ready for her journey, and that was waiting for her in her tiny Moscow apartment, along with her precious store of euros and American dollars. She'd accumulated those meagre funds as carefully and inconspicuously as she could, buying the hard currency from a handful of black-market traders in exchange for roubles, and paying – she was perfectly certain – well over the odds for it.

As well as clothes, her bag also contained a portable CD player. Somewhat similar to a Sony Walkman in appearance, but much more bulky, it had emerged from the production line of a minor Russian factory about five years earlier, and Raya had immediately seen its potential. She'd bought the unit, which had only worked intermittently from new, and then spent some hours modifying it, with the result that it no longer worked at all. In fact, the only thing that did operate as the manufacturers had intended were the push buttons, and all they did was illuminate. But it was Raya Kosov's prize possession, and would definitely be accompanying her on her final journey out of Russia, together with a few music CDs inside their cases.

Raya looked back at the list and had, she decided, covered almost everything. She'd done a handful of the security checks Abramov had instructed her to perform, and written out a normal report just as if she'd completed all of them. In fact, the report wasn't entirely normal. Under the strictly numerical section – the file-names, numbers and directories she'd checked – she'd added another paragraph headed 'Possible improper access', in which she'd listed a number of files that appeared to have been accessed by somebody here at Yasenevo, identity unknown. She appended a note stating that she was continuing to investigate the matter.

Abramov was out of the office until Monday, and the report, stamped *Sekretno* at the top and bottom of every page, was securely inside his locked safe. He'd given Raya the combination weeks earlier, which broke SVR rules, but Abramov had decided it was worth taking this risk because he was depending more and more on his subordinate, and was out of the office so frequently.

When she'd put the report inside Abramov's safe, Raya had also removed a key. As network manager, the major was required to hold a master key that would open every office door in the building, even those of the most senior staff officers, just in case some kind of a computer problem required one particular workstation to be switched on – or off – when the occupant of that office was away from the building.

She'd also taken another voucher for an airline ticket, applied Abramov's official stamp to it and scrawled a reasonable facsimile of the major's signature across the bottom. But the destination she had inserted on this voucher wasn't Minsk, or indeed anywhere else in the Confederation of Independent States.

Back in her own office, she'd locked the door, opened a small program on her computer – a program she'd written herself – and then used it to dial a Moscow number. The moment the call connected, her program gave her access to the call diverter she'd been using to transfer files to her own computer, a small but quite powerful laptop tucked away in a corner of the bedroom in her own apartment. First, she permanently deleted all the call records held in the diverter, then she looked up a number on the Yasenevo database and copied that to the call diverter. Then she deleted that number as well, but ensured it remained in the diverter's log, and inserted a different Moscow number. She wouldn't be calling the device again, and doubted if anyone else would, but when the call diverter was discovered, as she knew it would be, it wouldn't take an SVR technician long to identify both the number it was set to dial and the previous number as well. In fact that was an essential part of her plan.

When she'd originally worked out how she was going to accumulate her 'dowry' for the defection, she'd decided to keep things as simple as possible. It seemed to her almost poetic to be able to use the same hardware mechanism to both copy the files she wanted, and also to fatally implicate her target.

That had been the easy bit. The next thing would be much more difficult, but she knew she had to do it, and as soon as possible, because the clock was already ticking. She first looked at her watch, then accessed the master workstation record on her computer. That listed the time when every user on the network logged on and off each day. She scrolled through a number of pages, but paused for a few extra moments on one in particular, just long enough to check a single entry, then she returned to her home page.

Raya stood up and opened the top drawer of an unlocked filing cabinet standing against one wall. From there she took a zipped pouch containing an electronic technician's toolkit that included screwdrivers, pliers, chip extractors, earthing wristband, assorted screws and other bits and pieces. She also removed a small cardboard box that held a dozen or so anti-static envelopes containing RAM chips of various types, since there were several different computer models, with different motherboards and memory slots, attached to the SVR network. She put both into a briefcase and moved back to her desk.

Raya opened one of the drawers and took out an unopened box of pencils, another of ballpoint pens, a pair of scissors, and a new reel of clear sticky tape, and slid them all into the pockets inside her briefcase. Then she took out a box of medical plasters, selected two short ones, and stuck one on the end of her right forefinger and the other on her right thumb. The last item she selected was a small rubber bulb with a fine brush attached: it looked almost as if it could be an item of make-up, but it wasn't.

Finally, she reached into her jacket pocket and pulled out two different Yale-type keys, each wrapped in tissue paper. She had prepared these the previous evening by scrubbing them in a strong solution of the most powerful cleaning fluid she could find, and then boiling them in a pan on her stove. She'd repeated the process three times and, at the end of it, she was as sure as she could be that no trace of her fingerprints remained. She checked that the tissue paper still covered them completely, then replaced the keys in her pocket.

She made a final check that she now had everything she needed, opened her office door and stepped out into the corridor, locked the door behind her and strode off, towards the SVR senior officers' floor.

Bons-en-Chablais, Savoie, France

The mobile rang just after Richter had ordered a second coffee.

'Yes?'

'Right,' Simpson said, 'grab a pencil and write this down.'

'Hang on.' Richter opened the briefcase and pulled out a notebook and ballpoint pen. 'OK, fire away.'

'We need you to get to Ax-les-Thermes as soon as possible, and certainly no later than this afternoon.'

'And where is this place, exactly? I presume it's somewhere in France?'

'It's about an hour south of Toulouse, on the N20.'

Richter did some swift mental calculations. It would be a six- or seven-hour drive, he guessed, and offered no problem unless he hit unusually heavy traffic or experienced some kind of mechanical difficulty with the car.

'And when I get there?' he asked.

'The same routine, Richter. Go to the Hostellerie de la Poste and book in there for two nights. This time that is where you're going to be staying because if this is going to work at all, I need to know exactly where you are. Use the name Markov for the booking and, if anyone asks, you're a Russian on holiday in France. So talk to the people at the hotel in schoolboy French, or in Russian. If you have to speak English, make sure you put on a heavy accent. You really do speak Russian, don't you?'

'Yes, and I suppose that's also why the papers I collected in Vienna have *Sekretno* stamped all over them?'

'You opened the packet,' Simpson said flatly.

'Of course I opened the packet. And if it had been full of drugs, or something I didn't like the look of, I'd have dumped it in Austria, orders or no orders. I like to know what I'm carrying, Simpson.'

'Your reporting officers were right, Richter. You are an insubordinate bastard. But I presume you've no scruples about carrying Russian documents classified Secret?'

'No, because I've already read them. Technically, they may be classified at that level, but there's almost nothing we don't already know about the Victor III, and there's certainly nothing contained there that was news to me. Don't forget I was an ASW Sea King pilot until I saw the light and switched to Harriers, and in the Navy we were required to know exactly what the opposition's capabilities were.'

'Right,' Simpson sounded almost resigned, 'apart from the extract from the Victor manual, there should also have been a smaller envelope in that packet. I presume you opened that as well?'

'Of course.'

'Why am I not surprised? Inside it you should have found a briefing paper about the SVR – which is the Russian foreign intelligence service.'

'I do know what the initials stand for,' Richter replied. 'And there was also a small plastic card with my photograph on it. What's that for?'

'You'll find out later. In the meantime, just check in to that hotel at Ax and wait for instructions. While you're there, read the briefing paper. I need you to be reasonably conversant with the structure and functions of the SVR by tomorrow morning, just in case.'

'Just in case what?'

'As I said, Richter, you'll find out later. Somebody might contact you at the hotel tomorrow, or perhaps Sunday. Any other questions?'

Richter had several, but none that couldn't wait. 'No,' he said. 'You want me to call you when I get there?'

'Yes.'

'Right. I'd better get moving, then.'

Finishing the call, he took another sip of coffee and opened the briefcase again. He extracted a route-planning map of France and studied it for a few minutes. It looked like an easy drive, most of it on autoroutes. Richter finished his coffee, picked up the briefcase and walked back into the hotel.

Twenty minutes later, he'd packed his bag, paid the bill and was nosing the Ford out of the hotel car park.

Sluzhba Vneshney Razvyedki Rossi Headquarters, Yasenevo, Tëplyystan, Moscow

Raya glanced at her watch before knocking on the office door.

She'd been studying the routine followed by this particular colonel for several months, simply by looking carefully at his workstation usage records. Every Friday morning that he was in the building, he logged off the network at around ten-thirty, and logged on again about an hour later. This, she knew, was because the Head of the Section convened a weekly meeting in his office. If canteen gossip was to be believed, this meeting first featured briefings from all his subordinates regarding their current projects, followed by the consumption by all concerned of a considerable amount of alcohol, as a kind of a liquid finale to the rigours of the working week.

It was just before ten-forty. So, unless the colonel's routine had changed, there should be no reply. A few seconds later she knocked again, with the same lack of response. Raya glanced up and down the corridor, just in case he was anywhere in sight, perhaps returning to his office to collect something he'd forgotten, but it remained deserted. She took a deep breath, pulled the pass-key out of her pocket, opened the door and stepped inside.

She walked straight over to his desk and looked down at the computer. The screensaver was displayed, and Raya knew this machine would be password-protected. She could of course have accessed her master password list before she left her office, but she had no interest in what was on the hard drive: all she needed to do was shut the computer down. She bent down, eased the computer system unit out of its slot beside the desk, then reached behind it to pull out the power lead.

Immediately the screen went blank, and the fans inside the system unit stopped whirring. Raya opened her briefcase, pulled out the toolkit and selected a cross-head screwdriver. She swiftly removed the six screws that secured the unit's cover, and lifted it off. The next logical step was to insert the new RAM chips, but there were a couple of things Raya needed to do first. The removal of the cover would provide her with an unarguable reason for being in the man's office.

Standing upright again, she gazed down at the desk. There were no papers or files on it, but Raya would have been amazed if there had been. Two telephones flanked a simple desk set comprising vertical pen and pencil holders as well as shallow trays holding paper clips, staples, erasers and other oddments. The only other thing on the desk was a water glass, half full. She looked carefully at the pens and pencils, and smiled in satisfaction.

Raya selected two pencils and a single ballpoint pen from their holders and placed them in a pocket in her briefcase, taking care to only touch them with her plaster-covered finger and thumb. She carefully opened the new packets she'd brought with her, and replaced the two pencils and ballpoint with new ones.

Then she turned her attention to the water glass. She took the rubber bulb, puffed some fine grey powder on to the glass, brushed it gently and looked at it carefully. Three or four slightly smudged fingerprints were revealed. She pulled a length of sticky tape off the roll, taking care to only touch the very ends of it, and carefully applied it to the glass, before lifting off three of the prints.

Raya reached into her pocket and pulled out the two keys contained in tissue paper, unwrapped them and dropped them on the desk. She pushed the keys into position with the plaster-covered tip of her right forefinger, then laid the tape over the keys, sticking them firmly to it. Still holding the tape by the ends, she knelt down beside the desk, rolled over on to her back, and slid underneath. She reached up and stuck the tape at the back of the lowest desk drawer. She wriggled out, reached into her briefcase for the scissors and carefully cut off both ends of the tape where she had touched it.

Only then did she remove the plasters from her finger and thumb and put them in her pocket, and use a tissue to clean the powder off the water glass. She next looked inside the computer system unit, to check the type of RAM chips fitted there. She slipped on the earthing wristband, opened the box of memory chips, selected the correct type and expertly slotted it into place. In less than three minutes, she'd replaced the cover and packed everything she'd brought with her back into the briefcase. She then reconnected the power lead and switched on the computer. As usual, the operating system began a scan of the hard drive, because the computer hadn't been shut down properly. Raya checked to ensure that it had started up, then took a pencil and scribbled a note to advise the colonel that she had upgraded his computer. She left the paper prominently in the middle of the desk, and took a last glance around to ensure she'd left nothing else in the office. Finally she let herself out into the corridor, locked the door behind her and walked away.

Secret Intelligence Service (SIS) Headquarters, Vauxhall Cross, London

The computer on Gerald Stanway's desk emitted a soft double-chime, to indicate receipt of an email message. Normally he ignored such alerts, preferring to check his messages every half-hour or so but, since news of the defecting Russian had reached London, he'd started reading each email as soon as it arrived, just in case it contained any new information.

Opening his email client, he scanned the latest arrival in his in-box. The message was internal, its origin Holbeche's office at Vauxhall Cross, and it was the first communication Stanway had seen that gave him any additional information about the clerk. The email was classified Secret, had a limited distribution – Heads and Deputy Heads of Departments only – and for the most part didn't provide a great deal more information than had already been disseminated. But what it did contain was more or less what Stanway had been expecting, and fearing.

SECRET

LIMDIST – HODs and DHODs only
Subject: Defecting Russian cipher clerk – code name 'Roadrunner'. Update 1.

MANHUNT

Summary
Latest intelligence from Moscow Station, confirmed by technical support services, is that Roadrunner has left Austria and is now in southern France.

Narrative
Roadrunner established telephone contact with Moscow embassy before leaving Vienna and requested a meeting near Toulouse with SIS officers no later than Sunday. If we fail to comply, Roadrunner has stated verbally that he will approach the CIA.

Two Russian-speaking officers will leave Paris Station tomorrow to travel to Toulouse by air with authority to offer Roadrunner asylum in the UK provided they are satisfied with his bona fides. Assuming the defection is sanctioned, Roadrunner will be flown from Toulouse by UKMILAIR (HS-146 on four-hour notice to depart Northolt) to UK, accompanied by SIS handlers, for extended debriefing.

All contact with Roadrunner, apart from his visits to the British Embassies in Moscow and Vienna, has been by mobile telephone. He apparently purchased a pre-paid unit in Austria, and technical services – assisted by France Telecom and the French mobile service providers – have identified his exact location each time he turned on this mobile. As well as the Moscow embassy, Roadrunner also made four other calls to numbers in Russia, the recipients unidentified to date but possibly family or friends.

Continuous tracing action was not possible because Roadrunner switched off the mobile after he'd made each call, and apparently removed the battery, so preventing remote activation and tracking of the unit through the Echelon system. But the calls he made have provided a fragmented record of his route from Vienna to France, and his last known location is at the northern end of the town of Ax-les-Thermes, south of Toulouse.

Conclusion
The probability is that he will remain in this location until the requested meeting with SIS officers. This meeting will take place somewhere in Ax-les-Thermes, precise location to be decided later.

SECRET

'"Roadrunner", for God's sake,' Stanway muttered to himself. Most code names were stupid, but that was just ridiculous. Perhaps almost appropriate in this case, but still ridiculous.

He glanced at his watch. It was early Friday afternoon and, if the update was accurate, he had until Sunday to recover this situation. He knew he'd have to do something about it himself, because it was clear, from what Lomas had told him, that Moscow either knew nothing about this defecting clerk or, more likely, knew exactly who the man was but wasn't planning on doing anything about him.

It was, of course, certainly possible that the defecting clerk knew nothing about Stanway, or might not even exist – for it was conceivable that SIS or The Box, having received intelligence suggesting there was a mole somewhere in the security establishment, were using the story of a defecting clerk as an attempt to flush out the traitor. But Stanway wasn't prepared to take that chance.

He sat silently at his desk for a few moments, working out possible timings and routes. He would have to travel by car, simply because he would definitely need to carry a weapon. Getting a pistol onto an aircraft was possible if you knew what you were doing, especially something like a disassembled Glock because of its mainly non-metallic construction, but it was always dangerous. Driving through one of the channel ports in a car, especially for a traveller leaving the United Kingdom, was as near risk-free as made no difference, the English authorities taking almost no interest and the French less.

Stanway was too cautious to do anything more than read the email. If Holbeche had set some kind of a trap, his keystrokes – and those of every other senior SIS officer – would be scrutinized. If the courier was real, and Stanway's plans for the weekend came to fruition, the same process would be applied *after* the event.

But he had a Filofax at the back of which were several maps, none particularly detailed, but the one covering Western Europe was clear enough to show him where Ax-les-Thermes was located, and the size of the symbol suggested it was a fairly small town. Hopefully, finding the clerk wouldn't be all that difficult: after all, how many renegade Russians could there be hiding out in a small French spa town?

Moscow

Raya Kosov cleared her desk and checked out of Yasenevo as early as she could, catching the first available coach back to Moscow. She got out at her usual stop, near the Davydkovo station in south-west central Moscow, and headed off towards her small apartment, as usual. But the moment the sound of the coach's noisy diesel engine had faded, she retraced her steps, crossed the road and descended into the Moscow underground system.

When the train arrived, Raya entered a half-empty carriage. She ignored the empty seats and stood beside the door, because she didn't have far to go. As the train moved off, accelerating rapidly into the tunnel, she pulled a pair of thin leather gloves from her pocket and slipped them on.

Two stations later she stepped out, climbed back up into the streets of Moscow and walked a few hundred yards down the road to a small apartment building. She glanced around briefly, took out a keyring and unlocked the street door. There was no lift, but the apartment was on the first floor, at the rear, so it was only a single flight of stairs.

Raya unlocked the door and entered. An estate agent would probably have described the flat as furnished, but that was stretching the truth. There were some chairs, a table and a bed, but that was pretty much it. The bed was unmade, and in fact there was no bedding anywhere in the apartment. Or towels, clothes, crockery, or cutlery, for that matter. Absolutely the only thing that suggested occupation was a desktop computer resting on the plain wooden table pushed up against one wall. Incongruously perhaps, bearing in mind the air of desertion in this apartment, the PC was switched on, its system unit humming quietly though the screen was blank. Power cables were connected to a socket on the wall, and a thin cable ran from the modem to an adjacent telephone point.

Raya pulled a chair up to the table, moved the mouse

and pressed a button on the front of the screen. She waited until it had flickered into life, navigated to a particular directory and opened it, checked the names of the files listed, and then switched off the monitor.

She opened her briefcase, laid the pencils and ball-point pen she'd taken from the office at Yasenevo on the desk, and stood up. She glanced carefully around the apartment, checking that she'd not left anything behind, then walked out, locking the door behind her. Less than three minutes had elapsed since she'd first entered the building.

Half an hour later, Raya was sitting in her own apartment, mentally running through her checklist for the very last time. The following morning she'd be leaving Moscow, and she anticipated that, no later than forty-eight hours after that, the dogs would be let loose to find her and haul her back.

Ax-les-Thermes, France

The Hostellerie de la Poste stood at the northern end of the town of Ax-les-Thermes – which was actually more like a big village – where the N20 road runs briefly through the countryside before entering the smaller community of Savignac-les-Ormeaux.

Richter arrived there early in the evening and found the establishment without difficulty, mainly because the road ran right beside it. A comfortable-looking stone building, probably about two hundred years old, the hotel was set back a little way from the road, a terrace running along the front and faded shutters adorning the windows above it. Some kind of plant which Richter thought might be wisteria – but his knowledge of botany was virtually nil – was making a determined effort to reach the roof on the right-hand side.

There was a car park at the rear of the building, accessed through a stone archway guarded by tall steel gates. Their paint flaking and metal rusty, they now stood wide open. He swung the Ford through the entrance and parked it in a vacant space immediately behind the hotel itself.

Richter unlocked the boot, pulled out his bag, headed through to reception and checked in. He first tried out his Russian on the proprietor, to no avail, then switched to very basic schoolboy French. The hotel sleeping accommodation was on two levels, and he chose a room at the rear on the first floor and overlooking the car park. There he dropped his bag on the end of the bed and glanced round. The room could only be found in France, for the wallpaper, in a spectacularly garish floral pattern, covered not only all four walls but also the ceiling, and was also virtually a match for the counterpane on the small double bed. But it was clean, at least, and a quick exploration of the bathroom proved that everything worked there and the water was hot.

Dinner was already being served so, without unpacking his bag, he washed his face and hands, and went downstairs to the dining room. He chose the *menu touristique*, because it offered a cassoulet as one of the main courses, ordered a bottle of still water, and settled back to enjoy it.

After he'd finished eating, he picked up his coffee and found a seat on the terrace outside. After checking that nobody could hear him, he pulled the mobile phone from his pocket and dialled the number Simpson had given him earlier.

'You're in Ax?'

'Yes. What do you want me to do now?'

'Nothing else today, and it's still not clear exactly what's going on. There's been no further contact with the man we were expecting you to meet, so, while we're waiting, we've decided you can assist us in a training exercise. Tomorrow you'll be contacted by two officers from our Paris embassy. I'll call you again in the morning and give you a verbal briefing.'

'A training exercise? I could have *flown* down here if that's all that's going to be happening. And what about afterwards? Do you still want me to carry on driving round Europe like some hopeless tourist?'

'Just do what I tell you, Richter,' Simpson snapped. 'You're not exactly flavour of the month right now, based on your performance to date. Don't do anything else to piss me off.'

Chapter Nine

A little after one in the morning, in French time, Gerald Stanway drove his hired Ford Mondeo off the Euro-tunnel train at the terminal just outside Calais. Within a few minutes he was heading for Paris on the A26 auto-route, driving at a few kilometres per hour above the legal speed limit.

In the boot of the car was a small suitcase containing enough clothes for the weekend, his washing kit and a couple of books. Nobody on either side of the Channel had bothered looking inside the case, or even in the boot. But it wouldn't have mattered if they had, for Stanway's Browning Hi-Power 9-millimetre semi-automatic pistol – which Lomas provided almost five years ago, only after repeated requests – wasn't in the suitcase. Instead, it was wrapped in an old towel, together with two spare and fully loaded magazines, and hidden under the rear-seat squab.

Stanway knew all about documentation and the kinds of tracing action that the British intelligence establishment could and would employ, and had decided that the simplest option was just to be as open as possible about what he was doing, and where he was going.

So when he got home the previous evening, he'd used

his landline phone to call the closest branch of Hertz, quoted his Gold membership number, and told the booking clerk exactly what he wanted. Ninety minutes later, the Mondeo had been delivered to his home address with a full tank of fuel, and valid Green Card insurance cover for continental travel. Stanway had chosen the unlimited mileage option, explaining that he was going off to enjoy a weekend in France, visiting some of the Loire chateaux and also stocking up on wine.

And to substantiate his cover story he would stop somewhere near the Loire later that morning, and use his credit card to buy a dozen or so cases. Once he was actually on the continent, he would simply drop off the British radar screen, because France operated barely a fraction of the surveillance cameras that infest the British Isles, and those they do possess are mainly found on the autoroutes or in major cities. Once he was near Orléans, he'd leave the autoroute and stay off it for the rest of his journey. Then, unless he was unlucky or unobservant enough to be caught speeding, his masters at Vauxhall Cross wouldn't have the slightest idea where he had actually been.

There was virtually no traffic on the autoroute, and probably wouldn't be, at least until he got closer to Paris. Stanway had estimated that he should reach Toulouse after about ten to twelve hours' driving – say about fourteen hours maximum including stops – which would see him in the vicinity of Toulouse by mid afternoon, even after stopping to buy the wine. Then, of course, he had something else to do before he could continue south to Ax-les-Thermes, but he hoped that wouldn't take too long.

He didn't know when the two SIS officers were scheduled to interview the Russian clerk, but they would have to be briefed in Paris before leaving for Toulouse, and so he guessed they wouldn't reach Ax-les-Thermes until Saturday afternoon, at the earliest, which should give him at least an hour or so to find where the clerk was staying. But even if he didn't manage it in that time, Stanway wasn't overly concerned. In fact, it was quite possible that the quickest way to find the Russian was to wait for the two Six officers to pitch up, since they might well be easier to identify, and then follow them. The only downside to that option was that if the clerk handed over the incriminating documents to the SIS men, he might have to take them out as well.

But Stanway wasn't too bothered by the possibility of collateral damage. He was determined not to leave France until he'd resolved the situation, to his personal satisfaction, and if that meant killing three men rather than one, well, so be it.

Moscow

Raya Kosov woke early – in fact, she'd barely slept, or that's what it felt like – and walked out of her tiny flat well before eight, clutching a bulky, black, leather-look overnight case and her handbag. She'd packed the case the previous evening, selecting a few of her favourite clothes as well as the usual toiletries and underwear, and including her precious CD player and a few music discs.

She'd debated about taking her laptop computer, but had decided it simply wasn't worth the risk. The customs or police or perhaps even FSB officers at the airport would be certain to want to inspect it, and not even her SVR credentials would be enough to deter them. And, anyway, she didn't need it, because she already had another storage medium containing everything she wanted to take with her.

So, with regret, she'd left the laptop behind in her flat, after first carefully wiping the contents of one particular directory on the hard drive. She couldn't rely on a simple deletion, though, and used a commercial utility program to perform multiple overwrites of the data, using random characters to ensure that nothing could ever be recovered, even by using a low-level disk sector editor. Then she'd finally switched off the computer and closed the lid, leaving it on the tiny desk in one corner of her living room.

The first part of her long journey that day was also the shortest. Raya simply walked out of the front door of her building and headed towards a bus stop, just as she did every day of her working week. The only difference was that this time she crossed the street to the stop on the other side of the road. For today, her destination lay to the north, at Sheremetievo Airport, rather than southeast of Moscow, at Yasenevo.

Ax-les-Thermes, France

Richter had spent a somewhat disturbed night, despite being tired after his journey. His fundamental problem was not knowing what the hell was going on, and he was acutely conscious that, for the first time since he'd stepped off the aircraft in Vienna, his location was fixed, and therefore known to Simpson and to anyone else he chose to tell. Before he climbed into bed, he'd jammed the back of a chair under the door handle, wondering if he was just being ridiculously paranoid.

The hotel had creaked and groaned as its timbers settled in the cool of the night, with sounds like the occasional pistol shot echoing around the old building. Richter seemed to have woken up almost every time it happened, his eyes wide open and staring into the darkness.

Breakfast, typically French, consisted of a couple of croissants, bread, butter and preserves, with either coffee or hot chocolate. After he'd finished, Richter went back up to his room, picked up the keys of his hired Ford, then headed to the car park. He started up the car, drove through the gateway, and pulled out on to the main road, heading south.

He continued through the town, carefully noting its layout, and followed the road that led eventually upwards to the Principality of Andorra. A mile or so beyond Ax, he turned back and retraced his route, driving up each side street in turn, but this time left the car on a street about a hundred yards from the hotel. The car park at the Hostellerie was certainly convenient but, having a single restricted entrance, Richter had realized immediately that it was also a potential trap. Parked out on the street, at least he couldn't easily be boxed in.

He walked back to the hotel, went up to his room, checked that the unsealed packet of alleged 'Secret' papers was still locked inside his briefcase, then picked up the novel he was ploughing his way through. He left the hotel, waited for a gap in the traffic, crossed the road and walked some seventy yards down the street to the Auberge du Lac. This establishment was somewhat curiously named, as there seemed to be no substantial body of water anywhere nearby. He chose an outside table that offered a clear view of the Hostellerie de la Poste, and sat down. When the waiter appeared, he ordered a *café alongé* and a bottle of still water, laid his mobile phone on the table, and opened the novel. He adjusted the chair slightly to give himself an uninterrupted view along the road and settled down for what he expected would be a long and very boring wait.

Toulouse, France

Gerald Stanway reached Toulouse late that afternoon, feeling surprisingly alert despite having driven through the night. He had stopped for fuel and drinks at regular intervals, twice for snack meals, and once for almost an hour, fairly early that morning, at a vineyard outside Blois, where he had bought his stock of wine.

Toulouse is bordered by two ring roads – known as the interior and exterior *périphériques* – but Stanway ignored both and instead headed towards the centre of the city, looking for two things. He found the first, a small car-hire firm, within about fifteen minutes, but drove on past. Less than a hundred yards down the road, a blue 'P' sign beckoned, and moments later Stanway parked the Ford Mondeo on the third floor of the multi-storey car park. He locked the car and tucked the ticket into his wallet.

Then he removed his overnight bag and a small toolkit from the boot, and took the lift up to the fifth floor, where he investigated the rows of parked cars. Within a couple of minutes, he'd found what he was looking for: an elderly Renault with a thick layer of dust on it. He checked that nobody else was on that floor, and no security cameras either, then bent down behind the chosen vehicle.

Just as he'd expected, the number plates were attached with rivets. From his toolkit he took a small battery drill, a brand-new countersink bit already inserted in the chuck, then pressed the bit against the first rivet and squeezed the trigger. The noise was fairly loud, but it lasted only two or three seconds before the bit cut the rivet away. The second rivet took no longer, and less than two minutes later Stanway was heading back to the lift with both number plates and the toolkit hidden away inside his bag.

The car-hire firm was small, and the cars far from new, which suited him fine. Stanway had no trouble in explaining what he wanted. He needed a car, he said, for only twenty-four hours, and he would be paying the hire charge in cash, although he was happy to leave his credit-card details with the company as security. About half an hour after he'd entered the place, Stanway was driving away in a small five-year-old Peugeot hatchback.

That, he reckoned, should have sanitized his operation well enough. The only obvious link between him and what was about to happen at Ax-les-Thermes was his British-registered hire car, and that was now safely hidden in an anonymous car park in the middle of Toulouse. Even with all the resources available to it, Stanway doubted if MI5 or SIS would have any way of linking him to the French-plated Peugeot, especially once he'd changed the number plates, which he'd do as soon as he got clear of Toulouse and could find a quiet parking area.

Sheremetievo Airport, Moscow

It had gone better, and been easier, than Raya had expected. Her forged travel voucher had been accepted without question by the Aeroflot booking staff, once she'd shown her SVR identity card, and although the customs officers looked inside her case, as anticipated, they didn't fully search it and barely even glanced at her CD player.

One of the Border Guards Directorate officers was rather more thorough, however.

'Why are you flying to Rome?' he asked, as she reached the head of the queue.

'I have been ordered to report to our embassy there.'

'For what reason?'

'That is classified information. You've seen my identification and my travel voucher. If you're not satisfied, you are perfectly at liberty to contact my superiors at Yasenevo.'

That was one reason Raya had wanted to travel at a weekend, for the chances of there being anyone at SVR headquarters who could authenticate her travel orders were slim in the extreme, but the duty staff would certainly be able to confirm her identity from their personnel lists. She'd toyed with the idea of flying somewhere a little closer, like the Czech Republic or Poland, but those states were still subject to influence from Moscow. Although getting to Prague or Warsaw might be easier for her, getting out of those countries would likely prove a lot more difficult, so she'd taken the gamble of choosing Italy as her destination.

The officer looked less than convinced, and Raya wondered if he might even try to contact Yasenevo. That shouldn't create a problem, but she would rather he didn't. The fact that an SVR officer was travelling outside the CIS would certainly raise a flag, official travel voucher or not. She decided to up the ante.

'What's your rank and name?' she demanded, taking out a small notebook and pen.

'Why?'

'So that if I'm delayed here, I can include your name along with the reason I was late reaching Rome, in the report I will have to make to my superiors.'

Stalemate. They stared at each other across the scarred wooden desk, Raya looking cool and confident, her pen poised expectantly, the Border Guards officer openly hostile.

But it was he who dropped his eyes first, and he handed back her voucher and identity card. 'Proceed,' he snapped, and turned his attention to the next passenger waiting in line.

In the departure lounge she settled down in a corner with her book, though she doubted she'd be able to read a single word. The flight didn't leave for another two hours and, despite her outwardly relaxed posture, she was going to be watching every single second for any sign of problems. This was her end-game and, if she was detained in Russia her gamble would fail – and then she had no illusions about the likely outcome. Once her flight landed in Italy, and she was safely outside the airport, then she could start to relax – but not before.

Ax-les-Thermes, France

Colin Dekker pulled the Renault Laguna into a small car park on the right-hand side of the road, just short of the centre of Ax-les-Thermes. They'd decided to walk around the town to get their bearings as soon as they arrived, and then they'd check into their pre-booked hotel to start the waiting game.

'Not very big, is it?' Dekker remarked as they reached the pedestrian area fronting the casino.

'No,' Adamson replied, 'but it's still big enough to miss somebody here. I hope Simpson's right about this place. Come on, let's get to the hotel.'

Toulouse, France

At Blagnac, Richard Hughes and David Wallis stepped off the Paris flight and separated almost as soon as they reached the arrivals hall. Hughes walked straight over to the Hertz desk and joined the end of a substantial and apparently unmoving queue, while Wallis found a seat in arrivals from which he could watch the illuminated flight-information boards. The flight from London that they'd been told to meet looked as if it was going to land a few minutes early, so hopefully they'd be on their way inside an hour.

Forty-five minutes later, Hughes was handed the keys and hire documents for a Renault Megane, and walked back to rejoin Wallis.

'Is he here yet?' he asked, as he sat down.

Wallis pointed at the arrivals board. 'It landed nearly twenty minutes ago, so he ought to be walking through customs any time now. Any problems with the car?'

'Only the queue to get to the desk.'

At that moment, a short, slim man with a balding head and pinkish complexion, and wearing an immaculate light-grey suit, emerged from the customs hall carrying a weekend case and a leather handbag of an aggressively male design. He glanced round a couple of times, then walked directly towards them.

'You Wallis and Hughes?' he demanded, and both men nodded. 'Right, I'm Simpson. Let's get this show on the road. Where's the car?'

'Outside, sir,' Hughes said, stating the obvious, then led the way towards the nearest set of doors.

Within fifteen minutes, the Megane was heading away from Blagnac towards the Toulouse *périphérique* junction. Hughes was driving, Wallis in the front passenger seat studying the local area map Hertz had provided, and Simpson was reclining in the back, with his weekend case on the seat beside him.

Once they'd cleared the city and were heading for Foix along the N20, Simpson leant forward to address Hughes.

'Pull up in the next lay-by,' he ordered, his tone making it quite clear this wasn't a request.

'What briefing were you given in Paris?' Simpson asked, after Hughes had switched off the engine.

'We're to drive down to Ax-les-Thermes, interview this defecting Russian cipher clerk and, if we're satisfied with his dowry and what he can offer us, whistle up the RAF and then take him to London for interrogation. We were told that you'd be accompanying us, and would have all the contact details.'

'That's good. Right, the Russian's name is Anatoli Markov, and he's staying at the Hostellerie de la Poste at the northern end of the town. Our information is that he's carrying a packet of documents extracted from the SVR archives. He probably won't want to hand these over to you at the first meeting, but that doesn't matter. I'm just as interested in what he can tell you about his job in Moscow. Concentrate on finding out exactly where he worked, who he worked with, the names of his superiors, his security clearance – that kind of thing. That's all useful background that should help establish his bona fides.'

He drummed his fingers on the seat back. 'But don't push him too hard. Remember that he ran out of the embassy in Vienna when the Six people didn't react quickly enough for him, and he's been running ever since. That means treat him gently. If he doesn't want to tell you something, just leave it. I'm more interested in what you feel about him, whether you think he's the real deal or not. You've done this before?'

'Once.' Hughes nodded. 'About five years ago with a Romanian who pitched up in Munich. We threw him back.'

'We might do the same with Markov. It all depends

on what he's offering. The most important thing about this man is that he claims to know the identity of a high-level mole in the British intelligence apparatus, who's been supplying information to the SVR, and that's what I'm really interested in. So, I say again, treat him gently, and above all don't frighten him off.' Simpson passed a small piece of card to Wallis. 'That's my mobile number. Call me as soon as you've talked to the Russian.'

'You're not going to sit in on the interview?' Hughes sounded surprised.

'No,' Simpson replied shortly. 'I've got other things to do.'

Sluzhba Vneshney Razvyedki Rossi Headquarters, Yasenevo, Tëplyystan, Moscow

The Border Guards Directorate officer had taken his time in making a decision, but had eventually realized that he had nothing to lose by running a routine check on the attractive young SVR officer. He'd noted her name and department and, when he was able to do so, he left the departure gate and headed to his office. He checked the number of the SVR switchboard, and was eventually connected to the duty officer.

'Who are you?' the man demanded.

'Border Guards Directorate, at Sheremetievo. This is a routine enquiry about one of your officers. Can you confirm that a Captain Raya Kosov is employed there at Yasenevo?'

'Wait.'

The officer at Sheremetievo could hear the clicking

of a keyboard in the background, while he waited for a response.

'Yes, she is. Why do you want to know?'

'She's just been checked onto a flight to Rome. I just wanted to confirm that she's been authorized to leave Moscow.'

There was another short pause as the SVR officer accessed another list. 'Yes, she's booked for a week's compassionate leave, and has been issued with a travel warrant. Anything else?'

'No, thank you.'

At Yasenevo, the duty officer put down the phone with an irritated expression on his face. The SVR and the Border Guards Directorate had never exactly seen eye to eye, a hangover from the old days when both organizations had been part of the KGB, where they frequently tried to score points off each other.

He looked down at the notes he'd made during their brief conversation, then one word seemed to leap off the page at him. *Rome?* That didn't sound right, somehow, for compassionate leave, unless this officer had close relatives living outside the Confederation of Independent States. That wasn't unheard of, but it certainly wasn't very common.

Perhaps, he thought, he should check that he'd heard the man at Sheremetievo correctly. Then he realized he hadn't made a note of his name or even his rank. And he wasn't prepared to now ring the Directorate office at the airport, and end up looking like an idiot while he tried to identify the officer who'd called him.

Instead, he turned back to his computer and accessed the personnel records. The information available to him was strictly limited, so about all he was able to confirm was Raya Kosov's name, rank, date of birth, her Moscow address, and her department and superior officer. There was no information about family members except for her mother in Minsk. So it was at least possible that she had some other relative living in Italy?

The duty officer leant back in his chair. He was very junior and comparatively inexperienced, but something about this business didn't seem right. Would another junior officer – she was only a captain, after all – be allowed a week's compassionate leave for anyone not a member of her immediate family?

For several minutes he sat in thought, considering his options. Then he looked up a number in his database, and reached for the telephone.

Ax-les-Thermes, France

Stanway slowed down as he entered Ax, thereby irritating two French drivers who were tailgating him. Both of them swept out and roared past the Peugeot, hooting derisively as they overtook. Stanway ignored them, concentrating on checking the layout of the town. He passed the Hostellerie de la Poste and the Auberge du Lac, but only glanced at them, for the moment identifying them as nothing more than possible locations for his quarry. He carried on down the main street, realizing that Ax-les-Thermes consisted primarily of buildings erected along both sides of the N20, and noted relatively few hotels.

The route he took almost mirrored the one Richter had followed earlier that morning. Stanway drove a short distance beyond Ax, towards Mérens-les-Vals, l'Hospitalet and Andorra, then returned and headed back through the town. As far as he could see, there were only about half a dozen hotels, so if Holbeche's information was accurate, the clerk would be in hiding somewhere at the northern end of the town. That meant the most likely location for him was either the Hostellerie de la Poste or the Auberge du Lac.

While he decided what to do next, he pulled the Peugeot into a parking space opposite the casino, which was the second of the town's main attractions, after the thermal springs that gave its name, and attracted visitors seeking relief from rheumatism and similar disorders.

He stuck money in the machine and placed the ticket on the dashboard – not wanting to attract attention by disobeying the parking restrictions – then made for a cafe beside the casino and ordered himself a *grande café crème*. He'd had a couple of tours in France and Stanway's French was fluent and colloquial enough for him to easily pass as a native.

Maybe the obvious way to proceed was to check in to one of the two most likely hotels, and just use his eyes and ears to try to identify his quarry. The downside of that plan was that when one of the hotel guests turned up dead – the most likely outcome of this weekend – the French police would be bound to check all the local hotels, and then possibly detain all their guests for questioning. And that would be disastrous for Stanway, so he'd have to just wait and watch, identify his target, do the job and get out.

He finished his coffee, left three euros on the table, and headed back to his car. Four minutes later, he slotted the

Peugeot into a vacant space in the unsurfaced car park beside the Auberge du Lac, and strolled towards it and into the bar.

Richard Simpson leant forward between the seats, as the Renault Megane entered the northern outskirts of the town.

'Over there.' He was pointing towards a hotel on the left-hand side of the road. 'That's the Hostellerie de la Poste, where Markov is staying. My information says he'll remain in the hotel all this afternoon. He'll be expecting you to approach him, and he should be easy enough to identify.'

'Do you want us to book in there, as well?' Wallis asked.

But that was the last thing Simpson wanted. To allow Gecko a clear run, he needed the minimum number of friendlies hovering around Richter.

'No,' he said, 'you can book yourselves in to one of the more central hotels. Keep going now, and drop me off first.'

Without slackening speed, Hughes drove on, heading for the middle of Ax, where Simpson had a room reserved in one of the bigger spa hotels.

As soon as he'd taken his bags up to his room, Simpson left the hotel and made his way across the road to the open area in front of the casino, where he sat down on one of the benches. As he pulled out his mobile, it started ringing.

'We're in position,' David Adamson said.

'Where?' Simpson demanded.

'At the northern end of the town, covering the main road.'

'OK, stay there for the moment, but I think you'll probably be wasting your time. Gecko might well be here already and, if he isn't, he could come in from a different direction, from the Andorra road, say. And he might well have swapped cars, so that he's now using a Frog-mobile, not something on British number plates. Any sign of Richter – or a car on Austrian plates?'

'I thought he was supposed to be here already?'

'He *is* here. I just wondered if you'd seen him driving about, or anything. Or if you'd recognized him from the stuff I gave you.'

'We've not seen him,' Adamson reported, 'but there's an Austrian registered Ford Focus parked on a street not far from the hotel. Reckon that could be his?'

'Probably,' Simpson agreed. 'Now, as soon as I know what time the two guys from Paris are going meet Richter at the hotel, I'll call you in. You do know which hotel, don't you?'

'Yes, we scoped it out earlier. We can be there in around three minutes from the go signal.'

Simpson snorted. 'Do at least *try* to be literate when you're talking to me, Adamson. You're starting to sound like an American cop in a bad B-movie.'

He ended the call, then dialled another number.

When his Nokia rang, Richter was sitting at a table by himself at one end of the terrace of the Auberge du

Lac, the novel open in front of him, though he'd so far read barely a couple of chapters. There were several men inside the bar behind him, and a handful of people had appeared on the terrace since he'd taken his seat. There were three couples, one of them with two young children, and at the far end sat a single middle-aged man drinking coffee and reading a French newspaper. Richter had pegged him as a commercial traveller or businessman. All of them were well out of earshot.

'Simpson. Where are you now?'

'Ax-les-Thermes.'

'Don't try and get funny with me, Richter. Where are you *exactly*? At the hotel?'

'No. I'm watching the hotel from along the road, just in case I don't like the look of the people you're sending to meet me.'

'This is a training exercise, for God's sake. We're all on the same side here.' Even as he said the words, Simpson smiled slightly. 'Now, keep your eyes open, because they'll probably be arriving any time now. They're driving a silver Renault Megane with a local number – a thirty-one plate.'

'They're here already and arrived a couple of minutes ago. The Renault's in the car park at the back of the hotel, and I can see it from here. So what now?'

'Listen carefully. I'm not giving you a detailed briefing,' he began, 'simply because although you and I know that this is a training exercise the two men you'll be meeting think it's a genuine operation, and it'll be interesting to see if you can fool them. So these are the ground rules. First, everything you say to these two men must be in Russian or in really poor English.'

'And I presume one of these men will be wired for sound?' Richter asked.

'You presume correctly. Now, your name is Anatoli Markov, and you're a defecting clerk on the run from your masters in the SVR, and currently seeking asylum in the West. Your dowry, so to speak, is the packet of papers you're carrying. Keep that with you at all times, but don't hand it over. The most you can do is show the men the first page, but don't let them handle it. Just let them see the *Sekretno* stamps on it, and tell them you've got other papers squirrelled away somewhere. Your ace in the hole is that you know the identity of a traitor somewhere within British intelligence, who's been copying files from Vauxhall Cross and selling them to the SVR. But, obviously, don't tell them anything at all about this business, apart from the fact that you know who the person is.'

Richter snorted. 'You've been reading too much John le Carré, Simpson. That scenario's a total spy-fiction cliché.'

'It may be, Richter, but that's the way we're playing it. Keep the meeting short – no more than about thirty or forty minutes. Talk only in general terms about where you work: you're employed as a clerk at SVR headquarters at Yasenevo, in the south-east area of Moscow, which is why I needed you to be familiar with the contents of that briefing paper. I hope you've read it?'

'Yes,' Richter replied. 'I wouldn't want to try going on *Mastermind* with the Russian Foreign Intelligence Service as my specialist subject, but I think I've retained enough to bluff my way through a conversation.'

'Good,' Simpson said. 'Invent some people you work

with there, and a few superior officers. The people you'll be talking to won't know any better. You've still got that perforated plastic card, I hope. That's something we knocked up here in London, but it's an exact replica of a Yasenevo building pass. About the only way to tell it's a fake would be to try to use it to actually get inside SVR headquarters. If you have to, show it to the SIS men, but don't let them handle it or take it off you. It's a part of your dowry, and you have to hang on to it.'

'When do you want me to do this?'

'I'll call you in a few minutes. I just have to brief the SIS guys, so make sure you can get back to your hotel within about fifteen minutes. I'll tell them to approach you, so go and sit in the lounge or the bar, somewhere public. When you've finished talking to them, arrange to have a second meeting sometime tomorrow, but not later today. As soon as you've finished, call me on this mobile number to let me know how it went, but ensure you're well away from the hotel, so you can't be overheard. Take a drive out somewhere, or go down into Ax proper and have a drink, something like that.'

'Do I get to ask you any questions?'

'You can ask, but there's a limit to what I can tell you.'

'Where are these two SIS officers from?'

'Paris station, and they've been given the other half of the briefing.'

'Very convenient for you that I just happened to be in the area with that packet of papers, isn't it?'

'Not really, no. It was always possible that the man we were expecting to pitch up in France wouldn't make it, so your journey was always planned to include an exercise scenario as well.'

'And now you don't think this anonymous man is going to turn up, is that it?'

'Right now, Richter, we don't know. All I can tell you is that we've passed on your name and location to him, but the last time we heard from him he was still in Vienna. He could be in Ax right now, or on his way here, or still in Vienna. We just don't know. We've been tracking him using the signal from his mobile phone, but he knows what he's doing, and only switches it on whenever he wants to make a call.'

'And the last time he did that was in Vienna, right?'

'Exactly,' Simpson said. 'About two days ago.'

'And *if* he turns up, what do I do about it?'

'We've told him that you're a Russian-speaking British military officer, which is approximately true, and that you're using the name Anatoli Markov.'

'Why, though? I mean, why am I pretending to be Russian for this guy? I'd have thought he'd be expecting to meet a Brit.'

'Local colour, that's all. He asked that we send out somebody who spoke his own language, and we decided that if you used a Russian name you both could appear more casual at the meeting itself. Two Russian tourists running into each other away from home, that kind of thing.'

'Sounds like bullshit to me,' Richter muttered.

It sounded like bullshit to Simpson, as well, but he didn't say so.

Chapter Ten

'What was his name and rank?' Major Yuri Abramov
demanded.

He was wearing civilian clothes, and was far from
pleased at being summoned to the duty office at Yasenevo on a Saturday morning, on what he knew was a
wild-goose chase.

'I don't know, sir.'

'You don't know very much, do you? Somebody called
you to verify the identity of an SVR officer. You have no
idea of the man's name or rank, and you don't even know
for sure if he *was* calling from Sheremetievo. And you *think*
he said my officer was flying to Rome, which is ridiculous.
Her travel warrant is for Minsk, and nowhere else.'

But the duty officer stood his ground. 'No, sir. He
definitely said she was flying to Rome. That much I am
sure about. And if he *wasn't* calling from Sheremetievo,
how did he get the number here? It's unlisted.'

Abramov stared at him for a few seconds.

'Right, call the Border Guards Directorate at the
airport, and we'll sort this business out once and for all.
While you try to track down the man who called you, I'll
collect the book of travel warrants.'

In the small suite of offices where they worked, Abramov unlocked the door of Raya Kosov's room, and nodded. Everything was neat and tidy, exactly as it had been on every other occasion he'd looked in there. In his own office, he quickly unlocked his safe, pulled out the book he needed, locked up carefully, and returned to the duty office.

The duty officer sat at his desk, with the telephone in his hand. 'Just a moment,' he spoke into it, as Abramov entered. 'The Border Guards' office at Sheremetievo, sir,' he informed Abramov, gesturing to the handset.

The senior officer took it and sat down. 'This is Major Abramov,' he began. 'I gather you've been enquiring about my colleague Captain Kosov.' As he spoke, he was flicking through the pages of the book of travel warrants, searching for the one he'd issued to his subordinate. When he found the counterfoil, he noted the number and the details he'd written there.

'She was issued with a warrant to travel to Minsk,' he began firmly, but then his voice tailed off as he noticed another counterfoil, from which the warrant had been detached. But, in this case, the counterfoil was blank, and Abramov had always been as meticulous in processing travel warrants as he was with every other accountable item in his charge. He would never have removed one without completing all the details.

In fact, the counterfoil wasn't entirely blank. There was something written there, in a hand he was entirely familiar with. It was the single word 'сожалеюший' – 'sorry'.

Until that moment, he was convinced it had all been a mistake – probably nothing more than something misheard over the telephone. But the missing warrant, and that one word written by Raya, now suggested a very different possibility.

The Border Guards officer continued saying something, his voice an irritating twitter in Abramov's ear, but the SVR officer was no longer listening.

'Wait,' he interrupted, and turned back to the duty officer. 'Get onto Minsk,' he ordered, 'and tell them to check which hospital Kosov's mother is in.' He lifted the telephone to his ear again. 'Give me the flight details,' he instructed, and listened for a few moments. 'Where is the aircraft now? Can you recall it? Right, what time does it land in Rome?'

Less than ten minutes later, Abramov realized he was standing at the epicentre of a disaster in the making. The travel warrant he'd issued for a flight to Minsk hadn't been used by Raya, or anyone else, but the other warrant from his book had been used for a flight to Rome. The Minsk SVR office had made two phone calls and confirmed that Raya Kosov's mother was already dead, but what chilled Abramov was that she'd died the very day Raya had told him she was terminally ill, so he now knew, beyond any reasonable doubt, that his subordinate had intended to defect.

And the flight had already left Russian airspace. In fact, it had crossed the Italian border at about the time he was talking to the Border Guards Directorate officer at Sheremetievo, so there was now no way of recalling it.

All he'd been able to do was issue the most specific instructions to the SVR office in Rome, backed up by a full description and photograph of Raya Kosov. Abramov just hoped that would prove enough, because it would take time for their officers in Rome to get themselves out to the airport. And, even then, Raya probably wouldn't be that easy to spot in the milling crowds of people there.

Ax-les-Thermes, France

Simpson ended the call and for a couple of minutes sat in thought, running over the sequence of actions in his head, mentally checking to see if there was anything he'd forgotten.

Then he dialled Adamson's mobile.

'It's Simpson,' he said. 'Richter will be appearing at the hotel in about twenty minutes, so get yourselves into position now. Orders as stated, objective unchanged.'

'Copied. We'll be mobile in two, and in position in ten.'

In the Renault Laguna parked beside the road to the north of the town, Adamson started the engine and shot a glance at Dekker.

The two men were dressed very differently, for Adamson looked like a businessman, in an outfit of slacks, shirt and tie, and a lightweight jacket concealing his pistol and shoulder holster, whereas Dekker wore a pair of thorn-proof olive-green trousers and a camouflage-pattern jacket. Also, in contrast to Adamson's polished loafers, Dekker's feet were encased in tough boots with thick rubber soles.

'It's a go?' he asked.

'Yup, it's a go. You got everything?'

Dekker nodded and gestured to the bulky briefcase lying on the back seat. 'Drop me where we agreed.'

Adamson checked the road in both directions, then pulled the Renault out of the wide lay-by and turned south, back towards Ax-les-Thermes. About three hundred yards short of the Hostellerie de la Poste, he indicated and pulled the car in to the side of the road.

'Wait,' Adamson ordered, checking the road ahead of them, then glancing in his mirrors to see behind them. 'All clear,' he said. 'Go now.'

Dekker slid out of the passenger door, opened the rear door to grab the briefcase, looked both ways and then crossed the road swiftly, to disappear through a scrubby hedge and into the field beyond.

Adamson checked that Dekker was well out of sight before driving back onto the road. He indicated when he reached a lay-by about seventy yards from the hotel, and pulled the car off the road again. He lowered the windows, took out his mobile phone and placed it on the dashboard, then picked up a cardboard folder from the back seat and opened it. Inside were printed pages covered in pie charts and diagrams, together with several sheets of text, all of it in French. It was exactly the kind of stuff a commercial traveller would be expected to carry and, as Adamson spread it out on the seat beside him, he hoped this would provide him with a plausible reason for sitting there in the car by the roadside for an hour or so, with a mobile phone constantly pressed against his ear.

The moment he was through the hedge, and out of sight of the road, Dekker crouched low and hurried away up the gentle slope leading towards a small copse of trees some fifty yards ahead of him. He was shielded from the road behind by the hedge bordering that section of the N20, and from the hotel by another, rather lower, hedge that extended across the southern edge of the field.

Reaching the trees, he straightened up and eased his way into their sun-dappled gloom. He had already selected this as being the best – and realistically the only – spot from which he could watch the rear of the hotel from cover. Dekker chose a position on the perimeter of the copse which offered a clear downhill view of the target, and crouched down beside a large shrub with fleshy green leaves. He clicked open the briefcase, studied the component parts of the sniper rifle lying in their custom-shaped recesses and then, with the ease that only comes with long practice, began the assembly process.

The weapon was one of the variants of the standard SAS sniper rifle, the British-made Accuracy International PM – Precision Marksman – or L96A1. Designed for covert operations, the rifle Dekker had chosen was the AWS, or Arctic Warfare Suppressed, model. The name was a hangover from the days when the manufacturer produced a modified version for the Swedish armed forces, a move which spawned several different models generically known as the AW range. The stainless-steel barrel was fitted with an integrated suppressor which reduced the sound of a shot to about that of a standard .22 rifle. It was a comparatively short-range weapon, because of the subsonic ammunition, effective only to about three hundred yards in contrast to other versions and calibres of the rifle, some of which were accurate at up to a mile.

Both the stock, its green polymer side panels already

attached, and the barrel were a tight fit in the case, each lying diagonally across its interior. He pulled them both out, fitted and secured the barrel, and lowered the bipod legs mounted at the fore-end of the machined-aluminium chassis to support it, while he completed the assembly. Then he took a five-round magazine out of the recess in the briefcase, along with an oblong cardboard box containing twenty rounds of 7.62 x 51-millimetre rifle ammunition. Before leaving Hammersmith, Dekker and Simpson had discussed what type of bullet should be used.

'It all depends,' Dekker had said, 'on whether you want me to stop this guy *dead*, literally, or just stop him. If I use a hollow-point or a dumdum bullet, at the ranges you're talking about, a hit anywhere on the torso is going to kill him pretty much instantly.'

Simpson had shaken his head. 'If we need him dead, you can put a bullet through his head, right? No, just use standard copper-jacketed rounds, and hopefully there'll be enough left of him to talk to us afterwards.'

Dekker took five rounds out of the box and loaded the magazine, then pressed it into the slot in front of the trigger guard.

The last item was the scope. The normal sight used on the AW rifle was from the Schmidt and Bender PMII range, but Dekker preferred something slightly different. He'd chosen a huge Zeiss telescopic sight that offered variable magnification, and incorporated a laser sighting attachment which would project a spot of red laser light directly onto the target, but he probably wouldn't need to use that, not at this range. Once he'd clipped that to the Picatinny rails mounted on top of the receiver, Dekker removed one last piece of equipment, a two-way radio comprising an earpiece and clip-on microphone which were attached to a flat black battery-cum-transceiver. He clipped the microphone to the lapel of his jacket, slid the earphone into his right ear, then attached the battery pack to his waist belt and switched it on. Finally, he closed the briefcase and slid it to one side, and out of sight.

Dekker laid himself full-length beside and under the bush, settled the butt of the rifle into his right shoulder, drew back the bolt, and then slid it forward to load the first round. Only then did he peer through the sight at the target building, which was some one hundred and fifty yards away.

Dekker was a captain in the SAS and a sniper-team commander, and had been 'borrowed' from Hereford for this particular mission. He was a professional sniper who was competent enough, behind a good rifle, to guarantee accurate shot placement on a man-sized target at anything up to a thousand yards' range. At only one hundred and fifty, he would barely need the telescopic sight at all.

In his earpiece he heard a series of clicks and bursts of static, then Adamson's voice.

'Sierra, this is Whisky. Radio check.'

The code was simple enough, and they'd devised it before they left their hotel in Cahors that morning. Sierra was the 'sniper', namely Dekker, and Whisky was the 'watcher', or Adamson. The radio system they were using included a scrambler circuit so that if any of their transmissions were detected they would sound like meaningless static. The units were, in any case, deliberately very short-range, and the FOE techies had estimated that none of their transmissions would reach more than about two miles.

'Roger,' Dekker replied, a military response normally meaning 'received and understood' or, as in this case, 'loud and clear'. Only amateurs resorted to hack phrases like 'wall to wall' or 'five by five'.

'Sitrep,' Adamson continued. 'I'm now in front of the building, with a clear view of the entrance. No activity. Confirm your position and status.'

'Position as briefed,' Dekker muttered. There was nobody behind him in the copse of trees as far as he knew, but a loud voice apparently emanating from a bush was the kind of thing that could attract attention. 'I'm locked and loaded. Clear view of the target.'

In the centre of Ax-les-Thermes, Richard Simpson consulted his watch, and opened his mobile phone again.

'Richter, this is Simpson. Get yourself back to the hotel now.'

'I'm on my way. Oh, one last question. Are these two pointy-heads from Paris carrying weapons?'

'Of course not,' Simpson snapped. 'For them, this is just a routine initial debriefing of a potential source. Neither of them will be armed. Why do you ask?'

'The usual, Simpson. You know, a matter of mutual trust, spitting a rat, that kind of thing. I just like to know what I'm up against. If they *are* carrying, I might feel the need to borrow whatever it is. Just in case.'

'They're not carrying pistols or anything else, Richter. You have my word on that. But, even if they were, remember there are two of them, both highly trained professionals, and only one of you. So how, exactly, would you "borrow" one of their weapons?'

'I'm a professional too, Simpson, just in a different field. And don't worry – I'd find a way.'

Simpson lowered the phone from his ear and looked at it thoughtfully. Not for the first time since this operation began, he wondered if he was underestimating Richter, and he wished the timescale had permitted a thorough background check on this man on whom the success or failure of his plan now very largely depended.

Richter picked up his book, paid the bill for the drinks, and headed away from the Auberge du Lac, along the road leading to his own hotel. He then glanced both ways, checking for oncoming traffic, but the road was fairly quiet and he was able to cross immediately.

He strode through the front entrance of the Hostellerie de la Poste, took the stairs two at a time to his room, and tossed the book on the bed. He rinsed his face in cold water at the sink, and for a few moments just looked at his reflection in the mirror.

'You're a fucking idiot, Richter,' he muttered. 'You just know this is all going to end in tears.'

'Sierra, this is Whisky.'

'Go ahead.'

'Target Romeo has just entered the hotel. No other movement.'

'Roger.'

*

In the copse, Dekker altered the position of the sniper rifle slightly, and scanned the bedroom windows at the rear of the hotel. He saw movement in one of the windows on the first floor, above the car park, and increased the magnification on the scope a couple of clicks. Through the high-quality Zeiss optics, the face of the fair-haired man in the hotel room sprang into view.

'Contact,' Dekker radioed. 'First floor, second window from the left. Identity confirmed.'

Inside the Hostellerie de la Poste, Richter picked up the packet of 'Secret' papers, tucked the faked SVR pass into his jacket pocket, locked the room door and headed along the landing and down the stairs. He crossed the hall and entered the empty lounge, sitting down at a round table in one corner, which offered a clear view of the room. He ordered a Coke in halting and guttural French from the barman, since he seemed to have been drinking coffee all day and thought he could do with a change.

As the Coke arrived, so did two other men, and Richter immediately knew who they were. They were similar in appearance – about six feet tall, dark hair, solidly built, and wearing black shoes and grey suits – and ordered drinks at the bar before turning round to face Richter.

Then they walked over to stand side by side in front of his table.

'Are you Mr Markov?' one asked, in English.

Richter inclined his head slightly. 'Markov, da. Anatoli Markov.'

'Do you speak any English?' the same man continued, very slowly and clearly.

Richter shook his head. 'No English, no,' he said. Let
the buggers work for it, he thought.

'No problem,' the man said, switching smoothly into
Russian with, Richter thought, just a hint of a Georgian
accent. 'My name is Richard Hughes and my colleague
here is David Wallis. Do you have any identification on
you? A passport, perhaps?'

Richter shook his head. 'I was stationed in Moscow,'
he said. 'So I had only my internal passport, and I left
that in Russia.'

'So how did you get out of the country?' Wallis asked.

'Friends,' Richter said. 'Few borders present a problem if you have friends.'

'You worked at Yasenevo,' Hughes said, 'so do you
still have your building pass?'

'Yes.' Richter reached into the inside pocket of his
jacket and held up the buff-coloured plastic card. 'You
can look,' he said, 'but not touch.'

'Can we take a picture of it?'

'Of course.'

'Good.' The two men sat down at the table, and
Hughes gestured to Wallis, who produced a small digital camera from his pocket. Richter obligingly placed the
card on the table and waited while Wallis took two pictures of it, the camera flashing each time. Then Richter
turned it over to allow the SIS officer to photograph the
reverse side.

'Right,' said Hughes, pointing at the envelope on
the seat beside Richter. 'We understand you have some
papers with you. Are they in that envelope, perhaps?'

'Some are, but some I have elsewhere, in safe keeping.'

'May we see them?' Wallis asked.

'No, not yet. I was expecting to be contacted here by somebody from British intelligence. I have shown you my identification, but I still do not know exactly who you two are. I will offer you nothing else until I am satisfied with your credentials.'

Wallis glanced at Hughes, then shrugged his shoulders.

'Very well.' Both men produced small leather wallets and placed them on the table in front of Richter, who studied them with genuine interest, never having seen an SIS officer's identification before. He took out a pen and notebook and carefully copied down the two names. Then he slid the wallets back towards their owners, and sat back in his chair.

'So, *Gospodin* Wallis and *Gospodin* Hughes, that tells me your names and who you work for, but I still do not know what authority you have. If you are satisfied with who I am, is either of you senior enough to offer me asylum?'

Again Wallis and Hughes exchanged glances.

'That's not the way it works, Anatoli,' Hughes said. 'I think we're satisfied with your identity, but there's a long way to go before we even start talking about asylum. We need to be certain that the information you have brought out with you is important enough to make it worth our while sending you to Britain, then setting up a new identity for you, teaching you English, providing enough money for you to live on – and all the rest of it. And that means we have to see the product, in order to assess it.'

'The product?' Richter asked, a puzzled frown appearing.

'The papers you brought with you from Yasenevo.'

Richter looked from one to the other, then nodded in understanding.

'I will show you the first page only,' he said, 'and that is all. No touching, no pictures, OK?'

The two SIS officers signified their agreement, and Richter slowly slid the first page of the Victor manual out of the envelope, and held it up.

'This is secret information,' Richter continued, 'about one of our submarines.' He pointed to the *Sekretno* stamps, at the top and bottom of the page, then quickly replaced the sheet in the envelope.

'We're not very interested in submarines these days, Anatoli. What else have you got for us?'

Richter smiled. 'I have a lot of good hard data, including the name of the man who sent us copies of some files from your Vauxhall Cross.'

Both Wallis and Hughes leant forward. 'That's more like it, Anatoli,' Hughes said eagerly. 'Tell us about that.'

Rome, Italy

Raya Kosov cleared passport control without any problems and headed into the baggage-reclaim hall at Rome's Fiumicino Airport. She stood for a moment and watched the couple of hundred people surrounding two of the luggage carousels, which had just started moving, and above which the incoming flight numbers were displayed. Beyond this mass of jostling humanity, three other carousels were also rotating, each carrying a few pieces of orphaned luggage on endless and pointless journeys into and then out of the terminal building.

If the SVR had sent anyone to intercept her, she was reasonably certain they wouldn't have involved any of the Italian agencies, at least not at this stage. That was partly because it would be embarrassing to admit one of their own officers had flown the coop, but mainly because, if she was picked up by the Italian police or customs officers, she could try to claim political asylum, and the resulting media storm would do nothing to help Russia's new international image as an emerging democracy.

But Raya had no intention of being caught, and she'd already planned to do something about it. Her two most distinctive features were probably her short blonde hair – she'd had it cut in this new style the previous week – and her light blue eyes. That gave her an almost Nordic appearance, and she hoped this was what any watchers now positioned on the other side of the customs' channels or outside the airport building would be looking for.

Raya looked around, till she spotted a ladies' lavatory, and walked quickly across to it. She had to wait a couple of minutes for a vacant cubicle, the airport being very busy, then she stepped inside and locked the door. She took off her jacket and blouse, hung them on the hook behind the door, then sat on the toilet bowl and opened her carry-on bag, taking out a small folding compact, a make-up kit, and a tiny plastic case. Resting the bag on her knees, she opened the compact and positioned the mirror so she could see her face, before she snapped open the case and took out a coloured contact lens. Swiftly, she slipped the lens into her left eye, and repeated the process with her right eye. She then smiled at the result: her blue eyes had vanished behind the dark-brown plastic lenses.

They were completely at odds with her very fair skin, however, so she set about doing something about that as well. From her make-up case she took a tube of instant tan, squeezed some into her palm and began massaging it into the skin of her face and neck. Within a few minutes, she'd achieved an even colour, making sure she'd covered her hands and wrists, and the back of her neck, as well. She wasn't so worried about her legs, as she'd deliberately chosen dark-coloured tights. Now, when she put her blouse back on, she was satisfied that her appearance would seem Mediterranean.

Next, Raya opened a plastic bag and took out a long, dark wig. She tucked her own newly cropped hair neatly under it and settled the wig on her head, making sure that not a single blonde strand was visible underneath.

Finally, she took out a bright-red lipstick, much brighter than she normally wore, and applied it carefully.

Raya put her blouse back on, held the compact at arm's length, and looked critically at her image in the small round mirror. She almost didn't recognize herself, so she hoped there was little chance any of the Rome SVR officers would either.

The very last thing she did was pull the jacket inside-out. She'd spent a long time searching for exactly the right garment to wear on this journey, and had finally chosen a lightweight reversible jacket, one side a dark blue, the other a creamy off-white. When she'd arrived at Rome, she'd been a blue-eyed blonde wearing a dark jacket. Now, leaving the Ladies, she'd be a brown-eyed brunette in a light-coloured one. A complete transformation, she hoped.

After a few more minutes in the cubicle, checking her appearance, she pulled her coat back on, opened the door and stepped out. She crossed to the washbasins and stared at her reflection for a few moments longer, then left the Ladies.

Raya had no luggage to collect, since everything she now possessed in the world was crammed into the black carry-on bag in her left hand, but she didn't want to leave the baggage reclaim hall walking by herself. So she waited until thirty or forty new arrivals had fought their way through the scrum to the carousel and retrieved their cases, before she began making her way towards the exit.

Like almost everyone in front of her, she headed for the green channel, *nothing to declare*, and strode purposefully through it, at the tail-end of what seemed to be a large Italian family group. A handful of Italian customs officers in dark-coloured uniforms watched the departing passengers, their eyes flicking over each in turn with a relative lack of interest. None attempted to stop her, or even speak to her, but she could almost *feel* them watching her as she walked past.

Outside, the arrivals hall was an apparent chaos of crowds milling about, and with loud and, to her, incomprehensibly garbled announcements echoing from loudspeakers in rapid-fire Italian. Everyone appeared to be talking at the same time, while those unencumbered with bags were making their points in the way only Italians can, through wide and expansive gestures that had passers-by ducking and dodging to avoid their swinging arms.

And Raya walked silently through it all, her eyes darting in all directions as she constantly looked out for danger. She hoped she was home free, but if that officious little shit of a Border Guards officer had decided to run a check on her at Yasenevo, she knew that there could already be a snatch squad waiting, somewhere at Fiumicino, with orders to grab her. And if that happened, she knew she'd be on the next available flight back to Moscow, probably heavily sedated, and that she would then spend the last few days, or weeks, of her short life screaming her lungs out as she waited for death in the torture chambers under the Lubyanka.

The Russian intelligence organs implement a simple policy with regard to any employees who betray the motherland. They are almost never tried for their crimes, but simply disappear. Shortly after joining the SVR, Raya had been shown a graphic example of the way such 'disappearances' happened.

It was an old and scratchy film, shot possibly with an 8-millimetre hand-held camera, and it had been taken in the basement of the 'Aquarium' – the headquarters building of the GRU, Russian Military Intelligence, at Khodinka Airfield in Moscow.

The film showed a man wired, rather than strapped, to a metal stretcher. Within seconds of the film starting, the reason for the steel wire became obvious. For the man was being fed feet-first into a working incinerator, in which straps of any usual kind would have disintegrated quickly in the intense heat. The victim was struggling violently, his screams the more disturbing to her because of the absolute silence of the film. The two men lifting the stretcher onto the rails that led into the furnace wore body protectors, heavy gloves and heat-resistant face shields. And they appeared to be following specific orders, for the lower half of the stretcher was fed into the furnace first and then, after half a minute, deliberately pulled out again.

At that point, Raya was forced to look away, unable to bear watching the man's agony any longer. His trousers had already vanished, burnt away to nothing, and the bones of his feet and lower legs glistened in the reddish light from the flames, the flesh on them already consumed. The stretcher was dumped on the floor, where it was left for a few minutes while some rubbish bags were fed next through the furnace door. Meanwhile the camera panned the length of the condemned man's body, zooming in for several close-ups.

Then the stretcher was hoisted up onto the rails again and slid slowly – terribly, terribly slowly – back into the furnace, the victim screaming in agony throughout. Finally, the top end of the stretcher vanished inside, and the furnace door slammed shut behind it. The image darkened, and after a few seconds a legend appeared somewhat shakily on the screen. It read simply: 'Death of a traitor'.

So now Raya looked everywhere – and at everyone.

Chapter Eleven

Saturday
Rome, Italy

Nobody stopped her. As far as Raya could tell, nobody even looked at her as she fought her way through the crowds and stepped out of the airport building. The sunshine was dazzling, its glare compounded by the reflection from vehicle windows, and the heat hit her like a muggy blanket, the air so heavy and humid that she felt she could almost grab a handful and squeeze the moisture out of it. She slipped on a pair of wraparound sunglasses with a 'DG' logo on the frame – a Dolce & Gabbana knock-off she'd picked up for a few roubles from a street market in Moscow a couple of months earlier.

The chaos, she saw at once, extended outside the airport as well, but here a cacophony of car horns now added an even sharper and more discordant note. The Italians, she noticed, didn't queue for taxis the way people in Russia did, always lining up so obediently. In Rome, it was a no-holds-barred free-for-all, as men and women shouted and elbowed their way forward to get to the vehicles first.

This was such an unusual – such a *foreign* – sight, that she stood and watched it for a few seconds. But, even as she stood there, staring at the crowds of people milling about her, three black Alfa Romeo saloon cars drove up, their tyres squealing as they stopped just beyond the taxi rank. Six men climbed out, and three of them began walking quickly towards the terminal building, while the remaining trio fanned out, two of them checking groups of people waiting for taxis, the other one heading across to the stops where the hotel buses picked up their passengers.

For a few seconds Raya didn't move, just remained standing beside a group of Italians who were arguing loudly over something. Just watching the six men, she didn't need telling who they were.

She was stunned that the hunt for her had started so quickly, having hoped that she would have at least the weekend to put some distance between herself and her pursuers. This meant the Border Guards officer must have raised the alarm at Yasenevo.

At this stage in her escape, Raya didn't care where she went as long as it was somewhere well away from the airport. She had originally planned to take one of the small buses that ran to various hotels in the centre of Rome, but now immediately ditched that idea. And she'd never even considered taking a taxi, since their drivers sometimes remembered faces, and might even recall exactly where they had taken an individual customer. The only other possible method of transport from Fiumicino was by rail, and the train station was actually inside the terminal building.

Raya silently gave thanks that she'd taken the time to apply her rudimentary but hopefully effective disguise, as she turned round and headed back into the terminal.

MANHUNT

Sluzhba Vneshney Razvyedki Rossi Headquarters, Yasenevo, Tëplyystan, Moscow

Major Abramov sat, with his head in his hands, at the table in a small interview room in the security section of the Yasenevo complex.

As soon as he'd known for certain that Raya Kosov had defected, he'd done what he hoped were all the right things. He'd issued immediate instructions to the SVR duty officer in Rome, once the Sheremetievo Border Guards had definitely confirmed that the city was Raya's destination, and given orders that she was to be apprehended and held for questioning, pending further instructions.

And only then had he told his direct superior what had happened, telephoning the colonel at his small dacha on the outskirts of Moscow. The officer had listened in silence to Abramov's halting explanation, then ordered the major to remain at Yasenevo until further notice, while he, in turn, informed the higher echelons of the SVR.

Within two hours of Abramov's arrival at Yasenevo, a full-scale operation had begun, and almost the first thing the SVR senior officers did was to open a sealed red file classified *Sov Sekretno* – Top Secret – that possessed a distribution list so restricted that only one of the officers summoned to Yasenevo even knew the document existed. And he only knew about it because he'd been involved in preparing some of the contents.

Specialist officers had immediately been summoned to Yasenevo and briefed, and they were now already either en route to the Moscow airports or actually there, awaiting flights that would take them to France, Austria and Switzerland, with the largest number flying to Italy, for obvious reasons. Photographs of Raya – taken from her personnel file as well as a couple transferred from the security cameras at Sheremetievo – had been sent to the Rome embassy, and also those embassies located in other cities to which the SVR officers were travelling, together with an accurate written description of her.

In parallel with what could be termed this recovery operation, a damage-control analysis had been ordered to assess what she might have taken with her. They weren't expecting that she walked out of Yasenevo with any classified documents, since the elaborate security protocols in place at the SVR headquarters would have prevented that, but her position as Deputy Computer Network Manager would have obviously given her almost unparalleled access to virtually all of the data held on the Yasenevo computer system. And that was what worried them most.

A search team had already entered her small apartment and removed everything that wasn't nailed or screwed down, and this haul was now being picked over by a group of specialists at Yasenevo, looking for clues to where she might have gone, or any other evidence of her guilt.

Abramov had already faced one interrogation by a hawk-faced colonel named Yevgeni Zharkov, who had simply introduced himself as a member of the security staff. It was a session that left the major white and shaking, after which he'd been instructed to wait in the interview room.

Abramov looked up, his eyes staring sightlessly at the blank white wall opposite, and muttered the same mantra he'd been repeating for the last hour: 'Why, Raya, why?' But, again, no answer was forthcoming.

At that moment, the door swung open and Colonel Zharkov strode in, two SVR guards following him.

Abramov stood up automatically.

'Hand over your building pass,' Zharkov snapped, and the major hastened to obey. 'Now we'll go to your office.'

'Why?' Abramov asked.

'Because, from this moment onwards, your security clearance is revoked. You will give me all your keys and passwords, and open your safe. You are to hand over every classified document in your charge, and your office will then be sealed until this investigation has been completed.'

'But I—'

'But what, Major? Did you expect that you'd be able to continue working here as if nothing had happened, despite the fact that your direct subordinate is now apparently trying to defect to the West?'

Twenty minutes later, Abramov was escorted back to the interview room by the two guards, pushed inside and the door locked. Zharkov hadn't accompanied him back, but had remained in the network manager's office suite, inspecting the rooms occupied by Abramov and Raya Kosov.

This time the major had a longer wait. Nearly an hour passed before Zharkov returned, clutching a bulky file in his hand. He slammed it down on the table, pulled out a chair and sat down opposite Abramov.

For several seconds he just stared at the major, his mouth compressed into a straight, hard line and his expression unblinkingly hostile.

Abramov dropped his own gaze, unable to face such blatant aggression. He looked down at the folder and recognized it immediately as a personnel file. The name printed on its front cover was 'Kosov, Raya'.

'Was it your plan?' Zharkov began.

'What?'

'Was it your plan – or was it all Kosov's idea?'

'I have no idea what you're talking about.'

Zharkov lifted the cover of the file and pulled out a slim red folder. He opened it and glanced at the first page, taking his time. Finally, he looked up again.

'Then let me explain it to you. Kosov used a travel warrant taken from your safe to escape from Russia. She cannot possibly have known the combination of your safe, because that would be in direct contravention of Yasenevo standing orders. So obviously you yourself must have supplied her with the warrant, and therefore you must have known that she intended to defect. Or am I wrong, Major?'

Abramov held the colonel's gaze for less than a second this time, then dropped his eyes. He had already guessed the direction Zharkov's questioning was likely to take, and he knew that the only possible chance he had of getting out of this mess was to make a clean breast of everything, while trying as far as possible to exonerate himself. If he attempted to obstruct the investigation, or conceal anything, he knew he could face the same fate that was being planned for Raya.

'Please believe me, Colonel,' he replied. 'I had no knowledge, no knowledge at all, of what Kosov planned to do. I didn't know she had the combination of my safe, nor did I ever tell her what it was. I can only assume that she must have watched me open the door and noted the numbers I was using.'

That was the first lie Abramov had told, and he mentally crossed his fingers as he spoke the words. Zharkov's next words chilled him.

'Perhaps,' the colonel said, his eyes never leaving Abramov's face. 'Or perhaps not. When we get her strapped down on a table in the cellars at the Lubyanka, we'll find out the truth. And,' he added, leaning forward for emphasis, 'if I even begin to suspect that you're not cooperating fully with this investigation, that's where we'll continue your questioning, too.' Zharkov sat back. 'Now,' he said, 'why did she run?'

'I have absolutely no idea,' Abramov replied truthfully. 'I thought she was happy here and enjoyed her work. Her mother—'

'Her mother,' Zharkov interrupted, 'was dead even before Kosov requested compassionate leave, you fucking idiot.'

'I know,' Abramov said miserably. 'I know that now,' he amended.

'Precisely. Didn't it ever occur to you – didn't you even think – to check on what she was telling you? One telephone call, that's all it would have taken. One call to Minsk and we wouldn't be sitting here now, having to mount a recovery operation that's going to cost us millions of roubles.'

'I trusted her,' Abramov muttered. 'I know I—'

'Trust is for idiots. I trust no one, and nothing I can't prove. So you've no idea why she ran?'

Abramov shook his head, but didn't reply.

'I haven't had time to read her personnel file. Did she have any relatives outside Russia – outside the Federation?'

'None that I knew of.'

'So why did she choose to go to Italy?'

Again, Abramov shook his head. 'I've no idea.'

'We're just lucky that a border guard at Sheremetievo wasn't satisfied with her explanation, and decided to check her story. Otherwise we might not have even known she'd run until Monday, and by then she could have got to almost anywhere in Europe. It's just a shame he didn't call us *before* she got on that flight.'

'But you *will* find her?'

Zharkov smiled unpleasantly. 'Don't worry, Major, we'll track her down. And I'll make sure we get all the answers from her, before I order someone to put a bullet in the back of her head.'

For a few seconds Abramov just stared down at the surface of the table in front of him, weighing up his options, few though they now were. He knew he'd be lucky to survive the purge that would inevitably follow Raya Kosov's defection, but maybe, just maybe, if he could show that he was fully committed to helping find her, he might at least escape with his life. He murmured a silent apology to his subordinate, then looked up at Zharkov.

'There is something,' he began.

The colonel looked interested. 'Yes, Major?'

'Well, two things, actually,' Abramov said. 'I know Kosov, and you don't, and I don't think she'll be easy to find. She's obviously been planning this for a long time, and I know the way her mind works. She must have had some good reason for choosing to fly to Rome.'

'To defect. We already know that,' Zharkov snapped.

'No, that's not what I meant. Why did she pick Rome? Why not Paris or London or Madrid? What was her reason for choosing Italy?'

'That's a good point.' Zharkov nodded slowly. 'So why did she select *that* city?'

'I don't know, but it might be worth somebody going through her personnel record to see if she's ever had any connection with anyone in Italy. I'm not aware of any relevant association, but I've never fully checked.'

'Perhaps you should have done, Major.'

'Perhaps,' Abramov snapped, 'but I was under the impression that investigating the background of Yase-nevo staff was the responsibility of the SVR security staff, not its line officers. The responsibility of your department, in fact, Colonel.'

Zharkov's cold eyes bored into him, though Abramov met his stare levelly. 'I'm not responsible for internal security, Abramov,' he snapped back. 'I just have to solve the problem once it's arisen. I'm the senior colonel in the Zontik Directorate. Perhaps you know what that means?'

Abramov nodded and dropped his gaze. He knew exactly what Zharkov was talking about.

In 1988, a specialist and ultra-secret unit had been created within the SVR itself. The Spetsgruppa Zaslon – special operations or *spetsnaz* team 'Barrier' or

'Shield' – was formed ostensibly to provide armed back-up for SVR operations. But in fact its remit was more wide-ranging, and it was given a virtually unlimited budget. It was also known as the *Zontik* or 'Umbrella' Directorate, or sometimes just as the 'Z Directorate', by those few people within the corridors of Yasenevo who even knew about it.

Spetsgruppa Zaslon had been involved in a variety of different types of operations since its first creation. These included a clandestine mission deep into Iraq, at the time Saddam Hussein still held the reins of power, when the operatives successfully located and removed a large quantity of highly sensitive and secret documents from the dictator's palaces. Those were documents that would have severely embarrassed Moscow, had they been found by the invading American forces.

Some three hundred very experienced officers were selected for Spetsgruppa Zaslon, all characterized by two criteria: all had extensive experience in special operations and also in working outside the borders of the Russian Federation. Many of the officers selected had a further qualification that wouldn't normally be on their CVs. For, during some of their special operations, they'd been involved in what the old KGB used to refer to euphemistically as *mokrie dela*, 'wet affairs', meaning that blood had been spilt.

The reality was that, despite its somewhat vague and deliberately ill-defined operating brief, the principal job of Zaslon operatives was, ever since the unit's inception, to act as a highly professional assassination squad.

'Was that it, then? We should spend our time finding out why she chose to run to Italy?'

Abramov shook his head. 'No, not just that – and, in any case, I might be wrong about it. Maybe she just stuck a pin in a map, though I doubt it. No, there are two things that I think you need to bear in mind during your search for her.'

The major leant forward then, and spoke earnestly to the Zaslon colonel for a couple of minutes, before he sat back in his seat.

Zharkov nodded. 'I confess I hadn't thought of that,' he said. 'Good, Major. You might have just bought your life with that. As long as we *do* find Kosov, of course.'

Ax-les-Thermes, France

On the terrace of the Auberge du Lac, Gerald Stanway gazed up the road towards the Hostellerie de la Poste, and wondered if he'd missed anything.

He'd watched a tall blond man, who'd been sitting at the far end of the terrace, receive a phone call on his mobile and leave the hotel. But there was nothing un-usual about that, of course. What *was* odd was that the same man had then walked down the road, crossed to the other hotel and gone inside.

Then there was the Renault Laguna. The vehicle had pulled up in a lay-by a short distance down the road, and it had been standing there ever since, nearly half an hour. It could, of course, just be that the driver was making a long phone call, or was completely lost and trying to find out where he was on a map. But the sim-pler explanation, Stanway guessed, was that the man in the Renault was watching the Hostellerie de la Poste.

Putting these two things together, it seemed to him most likely that the blond man was the Russian cipher clerk he'd come to find, and that the man in the car was covering the hotel to ensure that the clerk's initial debriefing wasn't interrupted. And that, in turn, meant that there was at least one or possibly two SIS officers inside the building as well.

Stanway wasn't concerned that the Russian would betray him at this stage in the questioning. The man would obviously realize that the identity of a traitor within the British establishment must be the crown jewel in his dowry, and he wouldn't release that piece of information until he was safely tucked away in a safe house somewhere in the Home Counties, in possession of a new identity, a British passport and a decent bank balance.

No, Stanway had read enough reports regarding the debriefing of various defectors to have no worries on that score. In this first – he assumed it was the first – meeting, all the interrogators would be doing was establishing the man's identity and asking him a lot of background questions. They'd be trying to find out where he'd been employed at Yasenevo, what his job description was, what grade and classification of files he had been allowed to work on. All of these were questions intended to confirm that he was who he claimed to be, and that he might have access to the kind of information he was supposedly peddling.

So far, Stanway reckoned, he'd done quite a good day's work. He'd possibly identified the renegade Russian as well as the vehicle being used by one of the surveillance officers. All he needed to do now was confirm his suspicions, and he thought he'd worked out an easy, if slightly risky, way to do so.

He stood up, put enough money on the table to cover the cost of his drinks, and picked up the copy of *Le Monde* that he'd bought in the centre of Ax. He walked out to the car park, climbed into his Peugeot, and started the engine to let the air-conditioning cool the interior. He pulled out his Browning, extracted the magazine and checked that it was loaded, then replaced it in the butt of the pistol. He racked back the slide to cock the weapon, then set the safety catch and tucked it into the waistband of his trousers, resting in the small of his back, and out of sight.

The one thing he hadn't been able to establish, from his vantage point on the hotel terrace, was whether or not the watcher in the Renault was using binoculars. That meant he had to be careful, so it would all be a matter of timing.

Stanway drove the Peugeot over the uneven ground to the entrance of the car park, which lay on the south side of the hotel and was at least one hundred yards from where the Laguna was parked. If the watcher had binoculars, the Peugeot's number plate would be readable at that distance, but not with the naked eye. So what he had to do was make sure that, when he made the turn onto the main road, he was effectively invisible. He didn't want the man in the Laguna to realize that the car had also been at the Auberge du Lac, because that would immediately raise a flag.

He stopped the car at the side of the road and checked the oncoming traffic heading south towards the centre of Ax-les-Thermes, picking his moment. An elderly Citroën van, painted brown, perhaps to hide the rust, was just coming around the bend towards him. Stanway waited until the van was directly between him and the Renault, then pulled out, accelerating hard and turning right. Behind him, the van driver noisily expressed his displeasure at this manoeuvre with a blast from his horn, but Stanway ignored him. He would have preferred to have driven away from the hotel in a less obtrusive manner, but he was certain that all the watcher in the Renault would know about him now was the make, model and colour of the car, and Peugeots were common enough for that not to be a problem. His registration plate would have been completely invisible, and that was all that mattered.

Stanway drove on through the town until he reached the small roundabout just outside the casino, where the main road forked. Then he swung the Peugeot left, right around the roundabout, to head back the way he'd come. There were several parking spaces in front of the casino itself, and he pulled into one of them and waited for a few minutes. After about fifty cars had driven past him, heading north, he waited for a convenient gap in the traffic, then backed out and joined the northbound flow himself.

He drove steadily back through the town and as he reached the Hostellerie de la Poste he pulled off the road and stopped the vehicle in one of the handful of vacant parking spaces directly in front of the hotel.

Stanway turned off the Peugeot's engine and unbuckled his seat belt, but his eyes never left the interior mirror, in which the parked Renault Laguna and its driver were clearly visible – the man's face staring directly towards the hotel. As Stanway watched, he saw the seated figure briefly move his lips, apparently just uttering a sentence or two. The man could easily have been mouthing the words to a song playing on the radio, or talking into a hands-free mobile phone, but Stanway frankly doubted either explanation. His guess was that he was using a short-range, two-way radio to tell one of the men inside the hotel that a car had just drawn up outside. Well, in that case, he'd soon find out.

This was, Stanway knew, probably the most risky part of the entire operation, the time when he would literally have to show himself to the enemy, but he couldn't think of any other way of confirming his suspicions about that tall blond man. He picked up his copy of *Le Monde*, checked that his Browning was securely in place but still invisible, opened the car door and walked into the hotel.

'Sierra, this is Whisky. That Peugeot outside is on French plates, registered in this *département*, and it has a single male occupant. I've noted the number. Stand by.'

Adamson didn't take his eyes off the car newly parked outside the hotel, till the door opened and the driver climbed out.

'Confirmed. Single male carrying a newspaper. He's heading for the front entrance.'

'Copied,' Dekker radioed. 'Nothing seen to the rear of the building.'

Stanway stood for a couple of seconds in the small lobby of the Hostellerie de la Poste and looked around. There was a small reception desk, currently unmanned, directly in front of him, and to the right of that a wide curving staircase leading up to the first-floor bedrooms. To his left was the dining room, where he could see several tables already laid with plates, napkins and cutlery, but what he was primarily interested in was the bar and lounge over to his right-hand side.

He could hear the soft murmur of voices from behind the half-closed door, too faint for him to decide what language was being used, much less decipher what was actually being said.

Stanway pushed open the bar door and walked in. The sound of the voices immediately ceased. Seated at a circular table in one corner were three men: one was the fair-haired man he'd seen crossing the road from the Auberge du Lac about three-quarters of an hour earlier, but the other two were unfamiliar to him. All three had turned to look as he entered the room.

He nodded in their direction, murmuring a polite 'Bonjour', then carried on over towards the bar. He pulled up a stool, opened up *Le Monde*, and started reading an article. A few seconds later, one of the hotel staff appeared from a back room and asked what he wanted to drink. Stanway ordered a small beer, and for a couple of minutes he and the barman chatted about one of the stories in the newspaper.

They'd barely begun this exchange of views before the three men at the corner table started talking again. And, within ten seconds, Stanway knew his guess had been right. For although their murmured conversation was too quiet for him to catch more than the odd word, the language spoken was definitely Russian.

*

Wallis and Hughes had exchanged glances as the new-comer walked into the room but, after he continued across to the bar and started a conversation in French with the barman, they'd more or less dismissed him. Richter watched him for a few seconds longer, then turned his attention back to the lies he was busy telling the two SIS officers.

As the barman retreated into the back room again, Stan-way bent his head over the newspaper and appeared to completely ignore the other three occupants of the bar, but actually he was straining his ears, to pick up any recognizable snippet of their conversation. Though his spoken Russian was poor, he did have a reasonable vocabulary, but unfortunately those few words and phrases he managed to overhear didn't help him much. Twice the blond-haired man mentioned 'papers', and once each 'Moscow' and 'Yasenevo', the latter word confirming to Stanway that he'd identified his quarry correctly. Because they had their backs to the bar, the voices of the other two men were much less clear and from them he could gather nothing useful.

The question now, Stanway mused, was not *what* he should do about it but *when*.

He had no idea if the men wearing grey suits were armed – he presumed they were SIS officers, probably from the Paris station – but he knew he would have the element of surprise on his side if he just pulled out the Browning and started blasting away, right now.

But there were two obvious problems attending that course of action. Quite apart from the fact that it would involve shooting three men in cold blood, the barman who'd served him might remember Stanway's face well enough to provide an accurate photofit picture, and by now the watcher in the Renault Laguna might have taken down the number of the Peugeot. Not that it would help him or anyone else, of course, because they were stolen plates. But, after a triple murder, the French police would obviously be keen to follow up every lead, and Stanway didn't want a photofit image of his face in circulation after the event.

Nor did he think he'd be able to get across the road and take out the man in the Renault as well, for good measure. He'd just have to wait and bide his time, but at least he now felt certain of his target.

Five minutes later, Stanway drained the last of his beer, tucked the newspaper under his arm and walked out of the bar, wishing the three other men *bonne journée* as he passed them. None of them replied to him, or even looked up as he left.

On his way past the empty reception desk, Stanway reached over to grab one of the room keys, then continued on his way.

Rome, Italy

Raya kept hoping the odds were in her favour. As far as she knew, none of the SVR personnel stationed in Italy had ever seen her in person, so all they could be using in their search were whatever photograph and description Yasenevo would have sent electronically to the embassy in Rome. And she knew perfectly well that she now looked nothing like the person appearing in any of those pictures.

She pushed her way through the crowds, and back into the terminal, her glance flicking left and right as she searched urgently for the three men who'd already entered the building.

She spotted them almost immediately. They'd positioned themselves widely apart, so as to cover the maximum area and number of passengers. And, no doubt, once the three men outside had satisfied themselves that Raya wasn't waiting for a taxi or a hotel bus, two or maybe all three of them would join their companions inside the terminal. She knew she had to move quickly.

But Raya didn't want to risk just heading straight for the train station because no matter how effective her rudimentary disguise, she knew that the SVR men would be looking out for a single woman.

Several Italians were heading in the same direction. Raya checked them out as she walked along, looking for a suitable cover. She really needed to make herself part of a group, or at least one half of a couple, and quickly.

An elderly lady, carrying a heavy suitcase as well as a carry-on bag, was making her way slowly towards the train station. Raya crossed swiftly towards her and tried out a little of the Italian she'd tried to learn in Moscow.

'*Mi scusi, Signora, posso aiutarla?*' she said, pointing to the obviously heavy suitcase.

The old woman turned and looked her up and down carefully, but apparently approved of what she saw.

'*Grazie molto, Signorita,*' she replied, and waited while Raya seized the handle of the suitcase and began heading steadily on towards the railway station.

'Quale è il suo nome?'

'Mi chiamo Maria,' Raya replied, giving the woman the first name that popped into her head.

'Di dove è?'

'Sono Americana, Signora, e imparo l'italiano da un mese.'

Claiming to be American seemed safe enough, because she doubted the woman spoke a word of English, though Raya was fluent in it.

'Bene.'

They continued swapping pleasantries all the way to the platform, and actually passed within fifteen feet of one of the men who'd climbed out of the three black Alfas. He looked at the elderly Italian lady chattering away to a young dark-haired woman who could be her granddaughter, then shifted his glance to inspect the mass of people approaching behind them.

Raya helped her new-found friend to a seat on the platform, bought for herself the cheapest ticket she could from a machine, had it validated and then sat down next to her to wait. Within a couple of minutes a train arrived, and with a smile she helped the elderly Italian lady on board and then followed her, lugging the heavy suitcase. She had not the slightest idea where the train was going and cared less. All she was interested in was getting away from the airport as quickly as possible.

Raya glanced out of the window, back towards the terminal itself, and what she saw made her realize she was still a long way from safety.

Ax-les-Thermes, France

Outside the Hostellerie de la Poste, Stanway climbed back into the Peugeot, started the engine and drove away, heading north and away from the town. This manoeuvre allowed him a second opportunity to take a look at the Renault Laguna, still parked in the lay-by.

The fact that the car was still there was confirmation of his suspicions that the man sitting inside it was a surveillance officer. Stanway decided to drive a few miles up the road, find somewhere for an early dinner or just buy a snack, and then return to the town in a couple of hours. Then he'd have to find a suitable vantage point from which he could see the Hostellerie de la Poste clearly. Ideally, he hoped he'd be able to spot the fair-haired man leaving the hotel, because then he could follow him and take him down. But, realistically, he knew he'd probably have to tackle him in his hotel room.

'Sierra, Whisky. The unidentified male who arrived in the Peugeot has just left, going north.'

'Copied. No change at the rear of the building. No sightings of anyone.'

In the driving seat of the Renault Laguna, Adamson stretched his cramped limbs and shuffled the papers on the seat beside him. Whatever was going on inside the target hotel, he hoped *somebody* would appear soon, because he was getting extremely bored, and God knows what Dekker felt like, lying motionless under some bush up in the copse, staring at an unchanging scene through the telescopic sight attached to his rifle.

'We will have to talk again, and soon,' Hughes said, as the three men stood up. 'Later this evening, perhaps? Or over dinner here?'

'No.' Richter shook his head. 'Tomorrow, please.'

'Very well, then. We'll see you here, in this room, at ten tomorrow morning, agreed?'

'Agreed.' Richter shook hands with the two men and walked out of the bar and up to his bedroom.

The discussion had been quite draining, partly because he hadn't spoken Russian very much over the last couple of years, and had found it quite hard work just to keep up with Hughes. But the more difficult task – despite the SVR crib sheet Simpson had supplied, and Richter had memorized – was that the SIS man's questioning had forced him to invent more and more detailed stories about his work in Moscow. He'd been approaching the point where he was likely to trip himself up because he'd forgotten the answer he'd given to an earlier question. And Wallis and Hughes would certainly pick up any errors he made, because both had been making copious notes throughout the interview.

He just hoped Simpson would be satisfied with what he'd done and now call a halt to the whole pointless charade.

'What do you think?' Wallis asked, as he and Hughes ordered drinks from the bar.

'I'm not convinced. He looks the part – I've met quite a few blond-haired blue-eyed Russian men – but there's something about that man that doesn't quite ring true. A couple of times he gave slightly different answers to the questions I asked him, but that could be just a minor misinterpretation.'

'He also refused to give us any information at all about this mole he claims to know about in London.'

'Yes,' Hughes agreed, 'but that didn't really surprise me. He'd know that data would be the clincher, so I wouldn't expect him to even talk about it until we'd lifted him. No, it's more his whole manner. I've debriefed half a dozen defectors over the years, and every one of them spent most of his time looking over his shoulder, metaphorically speaking. Markov just sat there, looking perfectly comfortable with the situation, and quite calm. That's what bothers me: his whole demeanour is wrong.'

'And that's what you'll tell Simpson?'

'That's my assessment, so that's what I'm going to tell him,' Hughes confirmed, taking his mobile out of his pocket.

'Not over the phone,' Simpson warned, as soon as he answered the call. 'Meet me outside the casino in ten.'

'I think he's a plant,' Hughes said, once he and Wallis sat down opposite Simpson at a table outside a cafe situated on the west side of the main road that ran through the centre of the town.

'Why, precisely? Justify that.'

'He's giving the right answers, but he seems too comfortable. He's not worried enough. The data he's supplying is superficial, and just sufficiently detailed to be believable. So I think he could be part of a deception operation being run by the SVR. I recommend we either assume he's SVR and sweat him, subject him to some hostile interrogation, or just throw him back.'

'Good deduction,' Simpson observed. 'In fact, Anatoli Markov is as English as you are. His real name's Paul Richter, he's ex-Royal Navy, and he's never even been to Russia.'

Hughes stared at him. 'Then what the hell are we doing wasting our time like this?'

'This is important, so shut up and listen. There's a hell of a lot you're not aware of. You're right, this *is* a deception operation, but we're running it, not the Russians.' In brief sentences he then explained how Richter was just a decoy playing the part of a defecting Russian cipher clerk.

'Why choose us?' Wallis asked.

'Because neither of you has the level of access needed to obtain the kind of data Gecko is trying to sell to the Russians. Also you're based in Paris, not London, so for both reasons I'm satisfied you're clean.'

Hughes nodded. 'So what happens now?'

'Richter has a packet of papers with him, which you probably saw – and that's the real bait.'

'What's in it?' Wallis asked.

'Most of the sheets in the packet are blank, but the first few pages are copies of an extract from a Russian maintenance manual for the Victor III submarine. Technically, they're classified Secret, but in fact there's nothing in them that we haven't known for years. The papers are just a decoy, something we could safely give Richter to carry, and something that the target, Gecko, can focus on. I hope Gecko will believe that those documents contain enough evidence to identify him, because that's the story we've disseminated. I told you not to take the packet, because that would mean Gecko would come after you, and not Richter. In fact, he'd probably come after you *and* Richter.'

'So all we've really been doing here is fingering Richter.'

'Exactly. That's why you've been speaking Russian. I want Gecko to be certain that Richter is the defecting clerk, so that he'll act.'

'And if he decides to do that while we're with Richter tomorrow?'

'Trust me, he won't. He'll want to eliminate Richter sometime when he's alone.'

'Do we know who this target is?' Wallis asked.

Simpson stopped and stared at him. 'Of course we don't know who the fucking target is,' he snapped. 'If we did, none of this charade would be necessary. We'd just have picked him up and shoved him in the slammer.'

'Sorry, I meant do you know which division Gecko works for, anything like that? SIS or GCHQ, maybe?'

'No, not yet. We've no idea who he is except that he's someone highly placed in the security establishment. Now, what you did today was start talking to Richter, the kind of initial meeting we'd do for real in the case of a defection, and I didn't brief you about it beforehand because I wanted you to handle it as realistically as possible. And it needed to be realistic in case anyone was watching you. Was there anyone else in the hotel when you talked to him?'

'Richter's good,' Hughes said grudgingly. 'I thought he was a plant, but it never occurred to me that he wasn't Russian. No, there was nobody in the lounge apart from the barman – and I presume you'd exclude him – and the only other person who turned up was some French guy who walked in and ordered a beer. He was there for about five minutes.'

'You're quite certain he was French?'

'Yes, he chatted to the barman for a few minutes, about some story in the newspaper. He was a local, I'm sure.'

'Right,' Simpson said, nodding, 'so it looks like Gecko hasn't shown yet. Richter will be staying at the hotel tonight, and you'll be seeing him again tomorrow. Carry on exactly as you'd do if this was for real. I'll brief him tonight so that he, too, knows what he's supposed to do.'

'And then?'

'And then you pack your bags and head for the hills. If Gecko doesn't appear here tomorrow either, we'll know he hasn't taken the bait. And if he does, I've got people waiting ready to take him down.'

'Take him down as in kill him?'

'If it comes to that, yes, but I'd rather keep the bastard alive so we can sweat him for a while. We need to identify his case officer or handler, and he'll have some other useful information, no doubt. We'll kill him only if we've got no other options.'

'And if your decoy, this man Richter, is threatened?'

'Different rules apply. Richter's expendable.'

Chapter Twelve

As she stared through the window of the train, trying to avoid eye contact with the two men she could see searching for her in the crowds, Raya realized that something had changed.

Another man had approached one of the watchers, and was now speaking to him urgently, grasping a couple of sheets of paper in his hand. Raya possessed no lip-reading skills, but felt sure that the new arrival uttered the name 'Kosov' at least twice. That didn't bother her so much, as she already knew these men were searching for her, but what was on those sheets of paper was a matter of increased concern. They had to contain some kind of new information, some extra details they could use to try to track her down.

Then the second man turned round, and Raya caught a brief glimpse of the pages he was holding. Both were clearly photographs, but not merely copies taken from the personnel files at Yasenevo. One looked more like a surveillance shot of a group of people, and the other showed a dark oblong shape, that was apparently a magnified section of a larger image.

But that didn't make sense. Why would they need a photograph showing her among other people, instead of just a full-face image that would be much more detailed?

And then it dawned on her. They already had obvious pictures of her, but somebody must have guessed she might attempt to change her appearance after arriving in Rome. She'd attended to her hair and eyes, and her jacket was now a different colour, but there'd been nothing she could do about her bag. She had thought about ditching it and buying another one on arrival in Italy, but had decided not to bother. That decision now looked as if it might have been a dangerously false economy.

The images the man held had almost certainly been taken by one of the surveillance cameras back at Sheremetievo. One would show how she was dressed before she boarded the aircraft for Rome, and the other showed a close-up of the bag she'd then been carrying.

Even as that unpleasant thought surfaced, Raya saw one of the men point at the train she was sitting in, and for the briefest of instants their eyes met. She glanced away immediately, then quickly she looked back.

But it was too late. Already two of the men were moving, heading swiftly towards the carriage doors.

Raya stood up and grabbed the back of her seat. She knew she'd never be able to tackle the two of them, but she wasn't going to go down without a fight. And, if she made enough fuss, perhaps some of the other passengers would come to her aid.

At that moment the train lurched and, a second or two later, it began to move, gathering speed quickly. Her last sight of her pursuers was of the furious expressions on their faces as they ran along the platform, impotently trying to climb on board.

Raya sat down again quickly and smiled for the first time since she'd left Moscow that morning.

Ax-les-Thermes, France

Thirty minutes after the Peugeot hatchback had driven away from the hotel, and ten minutes after a silver Renault Megane with two men inside it had left the car park and headed towards the centre of town, Adamson tensed suddenly in his seat. Then he depressed the transmit button on his two-way radio.

'This is Whisky. Target Richter has just come out of the front door of the hotel. It looks like he intends walking into the town, or maybe he's just going off to get his hire car. I'll follow him. Are you OK there?'

'Affirmative,' Dekker replied. 'I'll stay here covering the building. Keep in touch.'

'Roger that.'

Richter crossed the road, climbed into the Ford Focus, did a U-turn and drove north, through the adjacent town of Savignac-les-Ormeaux. He checked his mirror as he cleared the northern edge of the town, saw only a Renault Laguna following some distance behind him, spotted a piece of waste ground, pulled off the road and parked. He stayed inside the car, fetched the mobile from his pocket and dialled Simpson's phone number.

'It's Richter. I finished a few minutes ago,' he said, 'and that wasn't the most entertaining afternoon I've ever spent. Ninety minutes talking Russian and thinking up convincing lies to tell the Chuckle Brothers.'

'Do you think they bought it?'

'I don't know. My Russian's a little rusty, though I don't know if Hughes noticed it. The biggest problem was remembering what I'd already told them whenever we went over the same ground again. They were both taking notes, but obviously I couldn't do the same, so I was relying only on my memory.'

'OK. Did you arrange a second meeting?'

'Yes. Tomorrow morning at ten – but, before you dream up some cunning plan for it, I've not the slightest intention of being there. Wallis and Hughes are both pretty sharp, and I can't keep this up any longer.'

'No, you *will* be there, but there's no need to worry. I've just briefed the two SIS men that this is just a training exercise. In fact, Hughes did suss you out, but it wasn't your Russian that let you down.'

'What was it?'

'A combination of things, but mainly the fact that you didn't look hunted enough. Hughes reckoned you were just too calm and comfortable, so he guessed you were probably a plant sent over by the SVR.' Simpson finished, 'And that's good.'

'So now what?' Richter demanded.

'Go back to the hotel, have a coffee, take a bath, get drunk, read a book. Do whatever you want, I don't care. But make sure you stay in the building this evening, and I'll call you tomorrow morning.'

'Right.' Richter glanced up and down the road. 'How many people have you got in the surveillance team?' he asked.

'What are you talking about?'

'This guy in the Renault Laguna, on Paris plates, he was parked on the other side of the N20 when I came out of the hotel. Then he followed me up this road, and I've just seen him stop about a hundred yards behind me. If he isn't one of your men, you'd better tell me right now.'

'OK, Richter. You're better at this than I thought you'd be. Yes, he's one of mine.'

'What a surprise. And he's doing what, exactly?'

'He's also taking part in the exercise.'

'And where's his sidekick? Covering the back of the hotel, I suppose?'

'How do you know there's another one?'

'I don't know a lot about surveillance, but I do know that you never deploy a single watcher. You'd have had at least two outside the hotel: one in the car in front and the other somewhere behind it – and on foot, in case I decided to walk instead of drive. And maybe two more in reserve, in a car somewhere nearby.'

'There are just two of them, Richter,' Simpson snapped.

'Right, and your bright idea is that I should go back to the hotel and just wait for something to happen?'

'Yes, that *is* what I want you to do. And if you don't, I'll know.'

'I'm sure you will,' Richter said, and ended the call.

Rome, Italy

Raya leant back in her futuristic, padded, blue seat on the Ferrovie Regionali carriage, her mind racing. She was safe for the moment, because neither of her pursuers had managed to get on board the train before it left Fiumicino Airport. But she also knew she was only safe until it stopped again. And that, according to a station map prominently displayed inside the carriage, would be soon, at Ponte Galeria.

Before that happened, she knew she had a life-or-death decision to make: whether to get off at that first stop and try to vanish there, or stay on the train until it reached one of the stations closer to central Rome, where she'd have more choice of finding transport links and, of course, much bigger crowds in which to lose herself.

She scanned the station map, looking for inspiration. She'd obviously never visited Rome before but, as part of her preparations for her escape from Russia, she'd thoroughly familiarized herself with the layout of the city. But Fiumicino was quite a long way outside central Rome, in fact right down on the coast, and she didn't know much about the districts the railway line ran through until it reached the outskirts of the city. All she was certain of was that Ponte Galeria was about halfway between the airport and Rome itself, so she guessed that it, Muratella, and the other two stops before Trastevere, would be no more than minor stations serving the south-eastern suburbs. She had no idea what alternative transport links might be available if she got off at one of them.

There was also the time factor. Clearly SVR and other Russian Embassy staff had been scrambled to intercept her, and had been sent out to the airport where her flight from Sheremetievo was due to land. What she didn't know was exactly how many people the embassy might have at its disposal, but she was fairly sure that they couldn't adequately cover every railway station exit in Rome.

In fact, one reason Raya had chosen Italy was because she knew that the SVR maintained only a relatively small number of operatives in that country. The downside was that Italy was a potential trap simply because of its elongated shape, and if the SVR didn't track her down quickly themselves, she feared Moscow would swiftly concoct some story to justify involving the Italian police and other agencies in the hunt for her. She also knew that Moscow would already have several snatch teams on their way to Italy, to supplement the embassy staff.

While planning her escape, Raya had realized that she had exactly two options, and that only one of them genuinely worked. She could try remaining in the city, going to ground somewhere until the heat died down. The problem there was that if Moscow did manage to get the Italian police involved she could be found fairly quickly, simply by undertaking routine checks on hotels and boarding houses. In short, if she tried to hide, she'd inevitably be caught so, however she did it and whatever happened, Raya knew she had to get out of this country as quickly as possible.

Her fastest way of leaving Italy would obviously be by air, but that would leave a paper trail because she'd have to show her passport – and remove her disguise – so that option had been out of the question from the start. And, of course, SVR surveillance was likely to be far more intense at the airports.

Her original thought had been to buy a Eurail pass, allowing her to travel freely around most of Europe, but checking on the Internet she'd found the cost prohibitive. At the moment she had only a few hundred euros in cash, and no guarantee of obtaining more.

But whatever route or method of transport she opted for, she had been counting on getting into central Rome immediately she arrived, becoming just one more anonymous face among the tens of thousands of tourists thronging the city every summer. If she could still achieve that, the SVR's chances of ever finding her were remarkably slim. But doing so was now her biggest problem.

Raya studied the station map again, then shook her head. The SVR knew, she was certain, that she'd changed her appearance and what she now looked like: also that she was a passenger on a train that went all the way to Rome's main railway station, Termini. But they couldn't possibly have enough officers to cover every one of the stations between Fiumicino and Termini, even if they could reach those stations ahead of the train itself, which was unlikely given what she knew about Italian traffic conditions.

She now had to gamble, and take a chance with her life. Staying aboard all the way to Termini wouldn't be a good idea because, no matter how fast the train, it couldn't outrun a phone call, and other SVR officers would already be on their way to Termini to intercept her. She would just have to get off somewhere before.

Decision made, Raya nodded. She'd stay on the train only as far as Trastevere, then get off and take her chances. There were bound to be buses and taxis there – or maybe she could hop onto the other line that ran through the station, taking the FR3 around to Stazione San Pietro, and then switch to the FR5 route running out towards the north-west, heading for the coastal town of Ladispoli, or maybe Cerveteri, well outside the city itself. Or just take a coach or bus out of Rome – anywhere away from Rome would do. That might be a better idea, she decided, and it would certainly be a whole lot cheaper.

Chapter Thirteen

Saturday
Ax-les-Thermes, France

Back in his hotel room, Richter was in something of a quandary. He *really* didn't like the idea of being stuck in one place, one known to Simpson and very likely others as well, when he had no idea what was actually going on. And there was an analogous situation that kept on popping unpleasantly into the forefront of his mind. In India, during the good old days of the Raj, when they were trying to get rid of a man-eating tiger, the hunters would first tether a goat to a tree in order to attract it, then somebody would shoot the beast while it was busy enjoying a couple of goat steaks, extra rare.

Ever since he'd arrived in this small French town, Richter had been feeling increasingly like some form of tethered animal, set up as bait or target, and he didn't like the experience at all. He couldn't just leave Ax, because the surveillance team would know it, so he was committed to following Simpson's orders and staying inside the hotel for that evening and throughout the night. So what he needed to do now was find some way of evening up the odds, so that when the tiger eventually turned up for dinner, he'd find a goat with very sharp teeth and a nasty attitude.

And there was one way he might do that, but first he

needed to check out two things. One was the layout of the hotel rooms, and the other to establish what the floor of his room was made from.

Ten minutes later, Richter stepped outside the hotel again and started up the Ford. Waiting until the road was clear in both directions, he swung the car around in a U-turn, and headed back towards Ax-les-Thermes. As he passed the Renault Laguna, he gave its driver a pleasant wave. The man gave him a hostile glare, and Richter grinned as he drove on.

He parked near the casino at the southern end of the town centre, and wandered off into the side streets situated on the west side of the main road. He was looking for a particular kind of shop, and soon he found just what he was looking for. He made two inexpensive purchases there, both of which he tucked into a large plastic bag. Then he walked back towards his car, but stopped off at a small supermarket to buy the final item he needed.

Back outside the casino, he glanced around for the Renault Laguna, but saw neither the car nor its driver, though he felt sure he was still under surveillance from some quarter. After that he drove back to the Hostellerie de la Poste, to begin his own preparations for whatever the night might have in store.

Stazione Trastevere, Rome, Italy

The moment the doors slid open at Stazione Trastevere, Raya stood up and moved towards them. But she didn't immediately alight, and for several seconds just stared up and down the platform, looking out for any sign of danger. But all she saw was the bustle of passengers leaving the train, pushing their way through equally large crowds of people who were trying to get on it. Nobody stood out as a potential threat, but then, she realized, stepping down onto the platform, if the SVR were covering this station they'd most likely be waiting for her outside.

She paused at the station entrance, trying to check the street beyond, but she saw nothing to worry her, apart from the sheer volume of urban traffic. Cars were everywhere, as well as countless scooters and mopeds weaving in and out of the dense traffic, the sound of their buzz-saw exhausts ripping through the air as a counterpoint to the deep bass rumble of the diesel engines of trucks.

What she needed now was a bus or something else to get her away quickly from the station. Raya shot a final look in both directions, then stepped warily out into the street. A short distance away she spotted a *tabacchi*, or tobacconist, where she knew she could buy a bus ticket. Her rudimentary Italian proved unnecessary, as the proprietor spoke enough English to understand exactly what she wanted. A couple of minutes later she emerged clutching a comprehensive ticket that was good for all-day unlimited travel on buses, trams and the Rome metro. All she had to do then was find a bus or a tram or a metro station.

But, before she could make a move, a dark-coloured saloon car swept past her and squealed to a halt directly outside the station. Two burly looking men got out and hurried over to the entrance, their heads swivelling left and right as they scanned the passengers emerging.

Raya didn't need telling who they might be or who they were looking for.

Her heart thundering in her chest, she paused deliberately for a few seconds outside the *tabacchi*, peering in the window and using the reflection in the glass to watch what was happening in the station opposite.

One man had stopped directly in front, where he would be able to see everyone who used the main exit. The second man forced his way through the crowds and vanished inside the station itself. The reflection in the *tabacchi* window was slightly distorted, and nothing like as clear as a real mirror, so Raya couldn't see what the driver of the car was up to: whether he was focusing his attention on the station, or scanning the people moving along the street.

Forcing herself to move slowly, Raya turned away to walk in the opposite direction, her senses preternaturally alert for the first shouted order that would mean one of them had spotted her. After several paces, she risked a quick glance over her shoulder.

Just then the driver, who had now climbed out of the vehicle and was standing beside it, with his door wide open, suddenly turned in her direction. Their eyes met, and in that instant Raya knew she'd been spotted.

A sudden yell followed immediately by an insistent blast on the car's horn was all the confirmation she needed. She turned and ran, clutching the bag to her side, desperate to put some distance between herself and her pursuers.

Outside the station, the driver dropped back into his seat and slammed the car door shut. The engine was still running, and he immediately pulled the gear lever into reverse and began driving the car backwards up the street, into the teeth of oncoming traffic and weaving around cars and scooters as he went.

Even for Italian drivers, who generally seemed to regard any road signs as just part of the scenery, and tended to drive wherever and however they liked, this was too much. A frantic cacophony of blaring horns greeted his erratic progress, which then came to an abrupt halt when the rear of his vehicle encountered the front of an approaching cement lorry. The truck driver had no room to avoid the reversing car even if he'd wanted to, which he probably didn't. So he just let the truck roll on until it struck the back of the reversing car with a satisfying crash. Then finally he applied the brakes.

Raya registered all this briefly as she ran, but it wasn't the car that now bothered her. The man previously standing outside Stazione Trastevere had responded immediately to the yells of the car driver, and was now sprinting down the street towards her.

She risked another glance behind her. He was perhaps fifty yards back, and gaining steadily. Raya was no runner at the best of times, and her footwear – a pair of soft black leather shoes with kitten heels – would have been sufficient handicap even for a decent sprinter. She knew there was no chance of outrunning him, so she'd have to do something else.

Ax-les-Thermes, France

Adamson's mobile suddenly shrilled, almost startling him, and he reached over to retrieve it.

'You don't seem to be very good at this,' Simpson declared, without preamble.

'What does that mean?'

'It means that Richter made you, and he even guessed you were here two-handed. The only thing he didn't know was where exactly Dekker was positioned, but he assumed he'd be somewhere behind the hotel.'

'I thought you told us Richter wasn't a professional?'

'He isn't, and neither are you by the sound of it. Anyway, if Richter's spotted you, it's not too big a stretch of imagination to guess that Gecko might have as well. So stop pissing about and get the hell out of there, right now.'

'What about Dekker, sir?'

'He stays where he is,' Simpson said. 'I may be throwing Richter to the wolves, but I want Dekker out there to cover his back, and to take Gecko down if he gets the chance.'

'I don't think Dekker's got any food or drink up there.'

'That's his problem, then. He's SAS, isn't he? Perhaps he can nibble on a few blades of grass or something, drink his own urine, that kind of thing. And it'll only be for tonight, anyway, because if Gecko *is* here, that's when he'll have to strike.'

'And where do you want *me* to go?'

'Don't tempt me.' Simpson sounded extremely irritated. 'Somewhere well away from the Hostellerie de la Poste, obviously. But if you can find a vantage point where you can still cover the building without erecting a large sign on the car announcing "This is a surveillance operation", that would be good. Right, brief Dekker, then off you go.'

Rome, Italy

Raya took a deep breath and screamed as loudly as she could, and simultaneously angled herself slightly to one side of the pavement, a route that would take her close to the front of a cafe with several tables sitting outside.

Half a dozen young Italian men were already standing, their eyes fixed on the incomprehensible accident that had happened almost right in front of them. At the sound of distress they all spun round, taking in the scene in an instant. A young and pretty girl running for her life, pursued by a heavily built dark-suited man probably intent on rape or worse.

Raya's breath erupted in short, ragged gasps as she neared them, and she realized she couldn't carry on much further. As she reached the young men, they parted to let her through, as if coordinated by a silent signal, then immediately closed ranks as the running man approached.

Seeing the human obstacle blocking the pavement, he didn't hesitate. He swung out into the roadway, obviously intending to run around the Italians. As he swerved, one of the young men grabbed for him, but missed. A second one didn't and this man, the biggest of the half-dozen Italians there, timed his move to perfection.

As the runner reached about six feet from him, he simply extended his left arm at a right angle to his body, directly in front of his target, and braced himself, a move known in close-combat as 'the clothes line'.

The dark-suited man had no chance. He was going too fast to swerve or avoid the outstretched arm, so caught the Italian's forearm squarely in his throat. His momentum drove his legs on for a couple of feet before he tumbled backwards, retching and choking, to the ground. Two of the other young men immediately leapt forward and sat on him, pinning him down. He was going nowhere any time soon, even without the injury to his throat.

Raya registered all this in another backward glance, but knew she still daren't slow down. Because the driver of the car was now out of his vehicle and running as well, angling his way towards her from the road and obviously intending to intercept her.

But, actually, that wasn't going to happen either. A crowd of passers-by had already assembled, and when they saw the man who'd just caused the accident trying to escape from the scene, several of them grabbed him and wrestled him to a halt, shouting and gesticulating in fast and very angry Italian.

As Raya kept on running, but now a little more slowly, she saw the SVR officer struggling violently and trying to fight his way free of the men holding him. A road junction loomed, and she swung left to run down the side street.

But, as she did so, she heard a sudden gunshot from behind her, and turned to look. The SVR man had wriggled free of his captors and had pulled out a pistol, which she could clearly see in his hand, and one of the men who'd been holding him now lay on the ground, clutching his stomach and screaming in agony.

Raya didn't wait to see what would happen next: she just took to her heels again, finding new energy and additional speed from somewhere. She pounded along the street, dodged across the road, weaving through the traffic and down another side street, hoping she'd managed to get out of sight before the man wielding the pistol saw where she'd gone.

But that faint hope evaporated seconds later, when another shot rang out from behind and a bullet smashed into the wall only a few feet in front of her. She glanced back.

The man had just swung round the corner and was at least seventy yards back, still a slim enough margin. 'Kosov, stop now!' he yelled in Russian.

Raya ignored him, and ran. Ran for her life.

She dodged around the next corner, putting solid stone between herself and her pursuer, then turned left again, and almost immediately right, anything to try to confuse the SVR pursuer, to try to slow him down by making him stop at each junction to work out which way she might have gone.

And then, at the far end of the road, an unlikely source of salvation beckoned. A young Italian girl was just buckling on a crash helmet as she prepared to ride off on a Vespa scooter. Raya summoned her last reserves of strength and tried to speed up, desperate to reach the Vespa before the girl rode away.

Raya knew her safety margin was only seconds, maybe even fractions of seconds. As she approached, the girl glanced round curiously, then took a step closer to her scooter.

Another shot cracked out, the bullet ricocheting off a wall somewhere nearby.

The girl whirled round in panic, just as Raya reached her.

Raya knew she had no choice. She grabbed the girl by the arm, spun her round and pushed her away from the Vespa. The girl tumbled backwards, stumbled against the kerb and fell flat on her back.

Raya leapt onto the seat of the scooter, her eyes already flickering over the unfamiliar controls. She guessed the throttle was on the right of the handlebar, while the numbers on the left-hand side were the gear change and clutch.

The engine was already running, with a reassuring throb that she could feel through the seat. She pulled in the clutch lever, rotated the handlebar control to the number '1', then simultaneously twisted the throttle and released the clutch.

It was a long way from being the smoothest start ever. The Vespa leapt forward, its engine screaming in protest, the front wheel almost lifting off the road, but Raya didn't care. She was moving, already moving faster than any man could run, and right then that was the only thing that mattered.

She accelerated as hard as she could down the street, which continued straight for perhaps a hundred yards. Halfway along it, she risked changing up into second gear, then braked hard for the T-junction at the end. Only then did she risk a glance down the street.

The scooter's owner had scrambled to her feet, and was staring straight along the street towards her. Raya could guess what the girl was thinking but, right then, pissing off an Italian teenager was frankly the least of her worries.

The SVR officer stood in the middle of the street, eighty-odd yards away from her, now well out of effective pistol range. He was talking into a mobile phone, no doubt calling for help and providing a description of the scooter Raya was riding. The Vespa had got her out of trouble, but she couldn't stay with it long. She'd be altogether too exposed, and there was a good chance a policeman might stop her for not wearing a helmet.

What she had to do was get well clear of this district before any other SVR men turned up, then ditch the Vespa and lose herself somewhere in the sprawling city of Rome.

Ax-les-Thermes, France

He had to do it that same night, Stanway knew, because he needed to be back at his desk on Monday morning. As he'd have to drive all day on Sunday to achieve that, the Russian clerk would have to die tonight.

He'd found a cafe a few miles up the road, and stopped there to eat a very early and very average dinner, and now he was on his way back to Ax-les-Thermes, heading south down the N20. As soon as he entered the village, he noticed that the Renault Laguna was no longer parked opposite the Hostellerie de la Poste.

That could simply mean that the SIS officers sent to debrief the Russian defector had checked out of the hotel, that continued surveillance wasn't considered necessary. Or it could mean that they were already satisfied with what the defector had told them, and had decided to move him elsewhere, in order to start processing him. Stanway had no way of knowing which. If they'd moved the Russian, Stanway would have to abandon his plans and try again the following week, after he'd found out where the man was being held. But that would probably be both difficult and messy.

As he drove past the front of the hotel, he shot a glance to his left. The dining-room windows were wide open, it was a warm evening, and he could see, perfectly clearly, the fair-haired man sitting eating a meal by himself in the corner.

'Excellent,' Stanway breathed, and continued down the road without stopping, the Peugeot becoming just one more vehicle in a long line of cars heading south.

Palazzo Margherita, Via Vittorio Veneto, Rome, Italy

'So what in hell's got our Russian friends so riled up? Any ideas?'

Clayton Richards III laced his hands behind his head, leant back in his leather swivel chair, and stared across his desk at the junior CIA officer who had just brought in the surveillance report.

Richards was the Central Intelligence Agency's Chief of Station in Rome, and he headed up the covert CIA section that resided in the big, square-cornered building on the Via Vittorio Veneto, which housed the Embassy of the United States of America to the Italian Republic.

'They're obviously looking for someone, sir,' George Edwards said, 'but right now we've no idea who. A little under an hour ago they scrambled a whole bunch of personnel. The first team went out to Fiumicino, and a second group headed to Termini. Others positioned themselves outside various railway stations situated between the airport and the city. That much we do know.'

Before Edwards could continue, there was a brief double-knock on the door.

'Come,' Richards ordered, and it swung open.

A tall, slim, dark-haired man stepped into the room. 'Mind if I sit in on this?' he asked politely.

Richards got to his feet and nodded. He might be the most senior CIA officer stationed within Italy, but this new arrival was John Westwood, the Company's Head of Espionage, a Langley big wheel, currently over in Rome for a liaison visit.

'Of course, sir,' Richards said. 'Please take a seat.'

Westwood strode across the room and sat down in one of the leather easy chairs positioned against the wall opposite Richards's desk.

'Edwards has just been telling me about the recent activity noticed from the Russian Embassy,' Richards explained.

Westwood nodded. 'I'm curious about that, so please continue.'

'Yes, sir. We noticed that they sent men out only to Fiumicino, not to Ciampino, so we assume whoever they're looking for was known to be on a flight due to land there. And the fact that they were also covering the railway stations suggests that the aircraft was already on the ground. So if their target had already landed and they missed him at the airport, they'd try to pick him up as he walked out of one of the railway stations. The further implication is that their target is either hostile or a fugitive, and most likely the latter, because if they were looking for a criminal, they surely would have asked the *carabinieri* for help, but the Italian police have not so far been contacted. So increasingly it looks as if Moscow may have a defector.'

Edwards paused to glance at both men in turn, and Richards nodded for him to continue.

'We checked all today's inbound flights, and one of them stood out immediately. An Aeroflot from Sheremetievo landed at Fiumicino just a few minutes after the Russkies scrambled their teams, but *before* any of them could reach the airport. That's obviously why they've been covering the railway stations as well. We're trying to get a passenger list for that same Aeroflot flight, but it's not going to be easy – and might even be impossible if the SVR have already sealed it. That's what we'd do, too, in the same circumstances. Our guys have been tailing the Russian teams, but they've been keeping well back for obvious reasons. The Russians have been issued with identification details of their target, because our guys have noticed the pages of details in their hands. They don't seem to amount to more than a few lines of text and a photograph. We've got people out there with high-resolution cameras, but trying to get a decent shot of the paper has so far been near impossible. Now, the next—'

He was interrupted by a knock on the door, and strode across to open it. Edwards held a brief conversation with the man outside, then closed the door and walked back over to Richards's desk, looking slightly puzzled.

'There's been a development,' he said, 'but I'm not sure about the reliability of this information. We've just received reports about a disturbance outside the Stazione Trastevere. That's on the main Ferrovie Regionali route between Fiumicino and the main station at Termini,' he added, for Westwood's benefit.

'What kind of a disturbance?' Richards asked.

'Apparently a car was in a collision with a lorry, but that's common enough in Rome. What's rung bells is that at least one pistol shot was fired at the scene, and a man was injured.'

'The putative defector, maybe?' Westwood asked.

'No, sir. Or, at least, it doesn't sound like it. According to what I've been told, the injured man was a bystander who tried to intervene to stop a pursuit. The odd thing,' he finished, 'is that, according to this report, the fugitive was a woman.'

Rome, Italy

A little under an hour later, Raya was standing at the counter of a small cafe in a narrow side street just off the Via del Corso, and not far from the Piazza del Popolo on the old northern edge of the city, and taking her first sip of a *cappuccino*. She preferred standing inside rather than sitting at one of the tables outside, for two good reasons. First, she had read enough about Rome to know that the price of a cup of coffee depended on where you drank it, and by standing at the counter she would pay about a quarter of the amount charged for sitting at an outside table. But the second reason was perhaps more obvious: she needed to keep out of sight.

She'd driven the Vespa about halfway across the

city, before pulling it to a stop by the roadside and abandoning it. She'd tucked the keys under the seat, and hoped the young Italian girl would eventually recover it. Though she felt bad about stealing it, the vehicle had undoubtedly saved her life.

From then on, she'd stuck with public transport, solely buses, in fact, ending up at the northern end of the Via del Corso about fifteen minutes earlier. In a public toilet, she removed the dark make-up, the contact lenses and finally the black wig, which was now itching like crazy.

Standing there in the cafe, Raya felt herself truly starting to relax for the first time since she'd left her Moscow apartment that morning – even though it now seemed like weeks ago. There was no way at all that those Rome embassy men could still be tracking her. For the moment, at least, she was safe.

What had surprised her was the degree of surveillance she'd witnessed, and how quickly the SVR had moved once the alarm was raised. And to have nearly caught her twice, they must have deployed virtually every agent available. This was a clear and unequivocal measure of their determination to find her before she could contact any Western intelligence service.

She'd picked up a bus and railway timetable, as well as a tourist map of Italy, which she'd put down on the counter beside her cup. She began studying routes and timings and costs, and trying to work out exactly what to do next, while simultaneously trying to avoid the gaze of two young Italian men standing a little further down the bar. They'd stared at her intermittently ever since she walked in, but at least their interest was obviously carnal rather than homicidal, so she was cheerfully unconcerned. The attention of over-eager young men she was well used to dealing with; what she couldn't handle so easily were the thugs from the SVR.

One thing was for sure, if she was going to get out of Rome alive, she'd have to avoid all the railway stations, and obviously the airports as well. But at least there was another option. The SVR might have the manpower to cover every railway station and airport in and around Rome, but there was no way that they could also mount surveillance on all the bus stops. There were literally hundreds of them, served by over two hundred separate bus companies, so that had to be by far her best choice unless . . .

Another thought struck her, and she stood for a few moments, considering. She realized that she'd barely escaped death twice already that day, and it really would be bad luck if the SVR managed to spot her trying to get out of Rome on a coach. Even so, a private car would obviously provide the best option of all, since she'd be completely undetectable amidst the sheer volume of traffic.

But if she was going to attempt that route, she had to do it quickly, because the SVR might soon enlist the aid of the Italian police after painting her as a fugitive from justice on some really serious charge, resulting in roadblocks and increased surveillance on all modes of traffic attempting to exit the city.

It all depended, she decided, on what such a strategy would cost her – and not necessarily in purely monetary terms. She glanced over at the two young Italian men and gave them a half-smile. Perhaps, she mused, eyeing them critically, it wouldn't be too high a price to pay.

A few minutes later, her mind made up, she walked over to stand close to them.

'Do either of you speak English?' she asked sweetly, not trusting her rudimentary Italian for this encounter. If neither of them did, there would be other men in other bars and cafes. Somewhere, soon, she would find what she was looking for.

The one standing closest to her nodded. He looked about twenty-five, and the other one slightly younger.

'Yes, I work as a tour guide,' he said. 'My name is Mario Villani and I speak English and French.' He added, 'My friend here just speaks Italian.'

Raya smiled at him again. 'And do you have a car, Mario?' she asked.

Again the young man nodded.

'Are you doing anything tonight? I need to get to Civitavecchia as quickly as possible. I can pay you for the petrol or . . . perhaps we can come to some other arrangement?'

'What kind of arrangement?'

'I'll tell you when we're in the car,' Raya said briskly. 'Let's go.'

Chapter Fourteen

'It looks as if the trail's gone cold,' George Edwards reported, as he re-entered the room.

Richards and Westwood were still sitting in the Chief of Station's office, relaxing in easy chairs with a coffee pot and the remains of a plate of sandwiches littering the table in front of them.

'Our guys are still keeping a close eye on the Russians, but they now seem to have split up their teams. They've kept watchers outside some of the larger railway stations, but most of them are just driving around the major streets, concentrating on the bus routes. We reckon they must have lost sight of their target, and now they're just driving around, hoping to spot her.'

'So you do think it's the woman who was being chased near the Stazione Trastevere?' Richards asked.

'Yes, we're now reasonably sure the Russians are looking for a woman. One of our surveillance teams managed to get a couple of good shots of the briefing pages they're waving about, and the photograph's definitely of a woman. We've tried enhancing the images as much as we can, but we can't get a picture clear enough to resolve her features. So we still don't know who she is.'

'Is there anything else you can do about that?' Westwood asked. 'Maybe it's time we stopped just following the Russians about and started doing something for ourselves. Like getting proactive?'

Richards stared at him. 'You got a suggestion?'

Westwood nodded. 'If we *are* assuming the Russians have a defector on their hands, this woman is presumably hoping to make contact with either us or the Brits. And since, as far as I know, there's been no approach to us here or back at Langley, that could mean she's already talking to the British SIS.'

'And you think we should interfere, sir?'

Westwood grinned at him. 'Maybe "interfere" is the wrong word. But if we can assist our British friends in handling this defector, it might turn out to our mutual benefit. And, of course, if we managed to find the woman first, and get her safely into the embassy, or on a flight to Washington, then we'd get a chance to talk to her, and maybe make her a better offer.'

'The Brits wouldn't like that,' Richards said, grinning, 'but it'd be a hell of a coup to pull off. But how could we go about it?'

'OK,' Westwood said, all business, 'the first thing would be to identify the target, and find out who she is. I'm thinking maybe one of our guys runs across one of the Russian watchers, and relieves him of that data sheet with her picture on it. Like a mugging, maybe? Then maybe one of the databases at Langley can help us identify her – and tell us why she's so important to Moscow.'

'You still here, George?' Richards looked up at Edwards. 'Why don't you go and organize a mugging?'

'A pleasure, sir. I know just the man to do it.'

As the door closed behind Edwards, Richards swung round to face Westwood again. 'You sure this is a good idea, sir?' he asked.

'It's worth looking at,' Westwood replied. 'If one of your guys can get us the description sheet the Russians are using, we might know if it's worth going any further. There'll just be one Russian wandering about with a sore head, which is the only downside. If the girl's just some low-level clerk or a runaway we can just walk and forget it. But if she's important, and the Russians' reaction so far suggests that she is, then we can get ourselves a bit more involved.'

Outskirts of Rome, Italy

Raya Kosov leant back in the passenger seat of the Fiat Punto and closed her eyes, the hum of the engine and the sound of the tyres on the tarmac road surface providing a comforting lullaby. She wouldn't relax properly, though, until she reached somewhere she felt truly safe, which meant out of Italy altogether, and somewhere like France or Germany instead, where she'd have more freedom to manoeuvre. At the very least, she knew she had to get herself further up to the north of Italy, to somewhere like Genoa or at least Livorno. Maybe she could even persuade Mario to take her that far, but anywhere more than about fifty miles from Rome would do, because it would expand their area of search exponentially.

Mario had said goodbye to his friend as they'd left the bar, for Raya was not prepared to make an 'arrangement' with both of these men, and then the pair of them had walked a couple of hundred yards to where the young Italian had parked his car.

Mario chatted away as they pulled into the stream of traffic and started heading out of the city, but Raya managed to tune him out as she scanned their surroundings. She checked the crowds of pedestrians, tried to peer into every passing car, scanned the people waiting at bus stops. She saw nothing to arouse her suspicions except for a dark-coloured saloon car, with a couple of shadowy figures inside, parked a short distance from each railway station they passed. Clearly her trail had now gone cold, and the SVR officers had gone back to covering all the most obvious exit routes from the city.

Raya sank a little lower in her seat, though she knew the chances of her being noticed were slim indeed. The Punto was just another car, in an unending succession of them, with two anonymous seated figures inside it.

Mario had glanced at her curiously at this reaction, but hadn't commented, just continued pointing out various places of interest as they passed them. However interesting they might seem to any one of Rome's annual influx of hundreds of thousands of tourists, at the moment Raya didn't care a jot about the Aurelian Walls or the Appian Way or the Coliseum, or anything else. All she was interested in was getting out of this city as quickly as she could. To her the only good news was that there couldn't be enough Russian Embassy staff to cover all the roads leading out of the city.

But only when the Fiat Punto crossed the Grande Raccordo Anulare, Rome's ring road, known simply as the GRA, and continued westbound on the Via Aurelia, heading for Civitavecchia, the port of Rome, did she finally begin to feel safe. For a few delicious seconds, she lay back in the seat with her eyes closed.

'Thank you, Mario,' she murmured on opening them again.

The young Italian turned to face her. 'For what?' he asked. 'I've driven you about a dozen kilometres, that's all.'

'That's enough,' said Raya. 'You've helped me more than you can ever know.'

He eased his foot slightly off the accelerator. 'Are you . . . I mean, do you want me to stop and let you out somewhere here? Not at Civitavecchia?'

'Absolutely not.' Raya shook her head. 'We have a deal . . . an arrangement, you and I, and I always keep my promises.' She reached over and squeezed his thigh gently. 'Actually, I'm looking forward to it.'

'Good, so am I,' Mario said, grinning. 'You're beautiful, Raya, and I feel so lucky to have you here with me.'

'How lucky?' Raya asked. 'I was just wondering if we could change our arrangement slightly. How about making a weekend of it and going a bit further north? I'd love to visit the Ligurian coast, for instance.'

For a moment Mario paused, then he smiled again. 'I don't have to even think about it. One night with you would be fantastic, Raya. Two nights would just be twice as fantastic. You're on.'

She settled back in her seat, feeling finally at ease.

A few minutes later she suddenly sat forward and glanced around.

'Something wrong?' Mario asked.

'No,' Raya assured him. 'It's just that there are a

couple of things I have to do. Can you stop somewhere that might have a shop selling mobile phones, and at an Internet cafe?'

'You can use my mobile and laptop when we get to a hotel, if you like?'

Raya shook her head firmly, as she felt in one of her pockets for the slim shape of a USB memory stick.

'Thank you, but I need a mobile of my own – and I must use an Internet cafe. I have to send off a couple of emails, but they won't take long. And wherever we stop for tonight, there must be a cyber cafe nearby. That's because I'll have to send another email first thing in the morning.'

Ax-les-Thermes, France

Adamson had managed to find a vantage point from which he could clearly see the front of the Hostellerie de la Poste. It was an area of rough ground lying about three hundred metres down the road, and was surrounded by bushes and undergrowth in which he'd been able to conceal the Renault Laguna so that it was now completely invisible from the road. The disadvantage was that it would take him a few minutes to get the car back onto the road along a rough track.

He had already spent an almost terminally boring evening, sitting motionless in the car with all the lights off, staring out at the front of the hotel through a pair of binoculars. But at least he'd had the foresight to buy some sandwiches and half a dozen cans of soft drink in the town, before finding somewhere to park. He felt guilty about Colin Dekker with each mouthful he took, but not guilty enough not to eat and drink.

The SAS officer was still in the same position, hidden up on the slope and covering the rear of the hotel with his rifle, and if Adamson was bored sitting in a comfortable car with food and drink to sustain him, God knows how Dekker was feeling.

The Hostellerie de la Poste seemed to be doing reasonable trade that Saturday night. In the early evening, about a dozen cars had turned up there to disgorge couples or families, but by nine-thirty all but one of the vehicles had departed, since the French tended to eat early. Just after ten, a couple walked out of the hotel and soon the lights of the final vehicle were switched on, and Adamson heard the engine start. Two minutes later the hotel car park was empty – apart from a small white Renault van, parked well over to one side. It had been in the same spot all day, so Adamson guessed it belonged to the owner of the hotel.

'Sierra, this is Whisky.'

'Go.' Dekker still sounded bright and alert, despite his circumstances.

'The last vehicle's just left. The front door's now closed, and the lights in the bar and dining room are out. Where's target Romeo?'

'The same place he was the last time you called. He's up in his room. The light's on but the curtains are still open.'

'Is he in bed?'

'I can't see the bed from here,' Dekker replied, 'but I don't think so. He went into the bathroom wearing just his underwear, a few minutes ago. Then he came out, but the last time I saw him he was wearing a shirt and trousers.'

'You think he's intending to go out somewhere?'

'No chance. I'm sure that pink bastard Simpson's ordered him to stay put there tonight, just to give Gecko the best chance of finding him. I doubt if Romeo knows what's really going on, but I think he's probably expecting trouble, and doesn't want to get into a fight while he's still half-naked. Wait one . . .'

There was silence on their radio link for a few seconds, then Dekker spoke again.

'I'm beginning to like this guy,' he said. 'Now he's dressed himself all in black – black jeans and a black polo-neck sweater – so he's definitely prepping for trouble. And he's just come to the window, opened it wide and had a look out. He stared straight towards me, waved, and then gave me a thumbs-up.'

'He knows where you are?' Adamson was incredulous.

'He can't possibly know for sure,' Dekker replied. 'I guess he's just taken a good look at the terrain behind the hotel, and worked out more or less where I would have to be hidden. He may be only an amateur at this, but he's got talent, that's for sure.'

'You're still OK up there?' Adamson asked, not that there was much he could do about it if Dekker wasn't.

'A piece of piss, this, compared to what we have to do at Hereford.'

'Food and drink?'

'Don't worry about me. I've got water and chocolate, so I'll survive. Right, the window of the room is still open, but he's just switched off the main bedroom light.

There's a dimmer light still on – maybe the bedside lamp. He's left the curtains open so I can still see inside the room. And the open window means that, if I do have to take a shot, the glass won't deflect it. And I think our friend Romeo knows that, too.'

'So now we wait,' Adamson said.

'Exactly. Now all we do is wait.'

Palazzo Margherita, Via Vittorio Veneto, Rome, Italy

George Edwards returned to Richards's office just over an hour later, this time with a broad smile on his face and a sheet of paper in his hand. He strode across to the desk and laid the paper in front of his superior officer. It was creased and crumpled, but the text and photograph were clear enough.

'Our guys mugged one of them?' Richards asked.

'No, sir, we used a dip – a pickpocket. The Russian never even knew he was there.'

'So who is she?' asked Westwood, moving over to the desk to stand beside Richards.

'According to this, her name's Raya Kosov,' Richards explained, studying the photograph of a pretty, blonde-haired woman of about thirty. 'The rest of it's all about her physical description, but nothing about who exactly she is or where she works. Not that I would have expected there to be, of course.'

'OK,' Westwood said, 'put her name on the wire over to Langley. Mark it "Flash" on my authorization, and let's see if we know anything about her.'

The answer came back to them in under ten minutes,

when Edwards returned to the office with a database printout that had just been transmitted to Rome from CIA headquarters at Langley, Virginia. A total of eight women named 'Kosov' having a first name beginning with the letter 'R' were listed on the CIA's database as possibly working in the Russian government and intelligence organizations. The information had been culled from numerous sources, many of them in the public domain, and was just a small part of the regular background information every intelligence organization collects about both hostile and friendly states. Three of these women were called 'Raya', but the first names of the other five were unknown.

The problem, Westwood saw immediately, was that none of those eight women appeared to occupy a position of even the slightest importance intelligence-wise. Most of them were clerks or low-level administrators, and none of them worked for either the SVR or the GRU, which was the information Westwood had been hoping to find.

'No way they'd do all this for a runaway filing clerk,' he muttered. 'She must be somebody else, someone who's never popped up on our radar before.'

'Hang on a minute,' Richards said. 'There's something about the dates that doesn't fit.'

Westwood examined the printout again, and immediately saw what Richards meant. Beside the details for each woman – essentially a mini-biography containing everything known about her – were inscribed two dates. The first recorded when she had initially been identified, and the second the last time any additional information about her had been added to the file.

Beside one of the three identified as 'Raya Kosov', the date of the last amendment was over ten years earlier, while the details for all the others had been updated within the last two or three years.

'Check her age,' Westwood instructed. 'What does it say on that sheet your man took off the Russian?'

'Here.' Richards passed it over.

Westwood compared the age cited there – no date of birth was given – with the details on the printout. 'That could be her,' he said. 'The age is about right. So what was she up to ten years ago, when she dropped off our radar?'

'She was a loyal Communist Party member and still at the university in Moscow,' Richards replied. 'Studying modern languages and computer science.'

'That's her,' Westwood said decisively. 'The reason we've heard nothing about her since is that she was recruited by either the SVR or GRU around that time, and they made sure she vanished from all public records. A modern languages specialist who's also competent on a computer – that's pretty much a definition of the ideal SVR recruit.'

'So now what do we do? We know her name and what she looks like, but we don't have the slightest idea where she is, or where she's aiming to go.'

'I know,' Westwood admitted. 'Let's assume she *was* nearly caught by the Russians at Stazione Trastevere. Just remind me again what those eyewitnesses actually said.'

Richards picked up a couple of sheets of text and rapidly scanned them. 'This is the statement that the Italian police reckon is the most accurate. The witness describes seeing a dark-haired woman running away from some-one along a street near the Stazione Trastevere. OK, the Moscow description says she's got blonde hair, but she could have easily dyed it, or have been wearing a wig. And Kosov would be a fool *not* to change her hair colour, knowing that Russian security personnel might be looking out for her in Rome.'

'Which does raise an obvious question,' Westwood interjected. 'Presumably the description issued by Moscow was accurate, regarding the way she looked when last seen there, so how did their embassy men know that she now had dark hair?'

'There must have been an earlier sighting some-where,' Richards said, 'since she arrived in Rome. Somehow they discovered that she'd altered her appear-ance, and found out what she looks like now.'

'Makes sense, I suppose. Now, I want to think again about what happened back at the Stazione Trastevere. According to that same eyewitness, the pursuer was closing fast on the girl. Most men can run faster than most women, especially when you consider their choice in footwear, but the fact that they're still out searching for her means she must have managed to get away. How did she do it?'

'That's a very good question,' Richards said. 'I doubt if she'd have any accomplices over here in Italy. If she had, they would have arranged to meet her at the air-port, and then the Russians would never have caught sight of her.'

'Agreed. I don't think anyone was waiting for her here. So about the only way she could have got away from that Russian was to use some form of transport. I don't mean she hopped on a bus, though a taxi is still a possibility. Why not approach your police contacts and get them to canvas the taxi firms to see if any of their drivers recall picking up a female in that immediate area at the same time the incident happened?'

'No problem.'

'And there's another question you can ask them. Were any vehicles reported stolen locally within the same time frame? If so, what type of vehicle, and if it's been recovered, where was it found?'

'You think she stole a car? Would she have had time to manage that, with some Russian thug breathing down her neck?'

'No,' Westwood replied, 'but if some driver happened to stop his car with the engine running, she might have dragged him out and jumped in. Remember, she must have been desperate, running for her life, and a desperate woman is capable of astonishing things. Anyway, just ask the questions.'

Five minutes later, Richards ended a call to his contact in the local *carabinieri* and glanced across at Westwood. 'That was a good call, sir,' he announced. 'A young Italian girl had her scooter stolen near the Stazione Trastevere, by a dark-haired woman who simply pushed her aside and grabbed it. The girl said a man was chasing the woman, and even fired a pistol at her. So far, nobody's reported finding the scooter anywhere.'

'So now we know how she got away from the Russian, but the real trick's going to be finding out where she's gone now.' Westwood paused for a few moments, as if considering, then he nodded. 'Maybe it's time to start tackling this problem from the opposite perspective. Perhaps I should call up a few people I know in London, and try to find out what's going on from their end.'

For the next twenty minutes, Westwood made some calls, and got absolutely nowhere.

'That's it,' he said grimly, hanging up the phone at last. 'I've called in every favour I'm owed, but nobody in London seems to know anything. Or, if they do, they're not prepared to tell me.'

'So now all we can do is sit here and wait?'

'Exactly. But just let your *carabinieri* contact know that we're particularly interested in that missing woman, or anything else that might relate to her.'

Piombino, Italy

They'd been making good time, passing Civitavecchia less than an hour after leaving Rome. Having witnessed some examples of Italian driving in the city, Raya was pleasantly surprised to discover that Mario was pretty competent behind the wheel. They'd stayed on the coast road for at least one hundred and fifty kilometres, catching glimpses of the Mediterranean to the left side as they headed north. Finally they abandoned the main road, and followed the signs to Golfo di Follonica.

As they'd approached the tiny coastal town of Piombino, Mario pointed to an island a short distance offshore.

'That's Elba,' he'd said, and explained how Napoleon had been exiled there after his abdication in 1814, but had stayed on the island for only three hundred days.

As a sop to his vanity, he'd been allowed to retain his title of Emperor and given sovereignty over the island, accompanied by his personal bodyguard of six hundred men. But that hadn't been enough, of course, and he'd escaped back to France the following year. Rallying his forces, he was soundly defeated at the Battle of Waterloo, and this time exiled yet again, to a barren island in the South Atlantic.

This history lesson had helped pass the time, but Raya was still totally exhausted when they finally arrived at a small hotel on the outskirts of Piombino. She perked up a bit when they entered the dining room and started eating two large plates of pasta, a dish with which she was totally unfamiliar.

And then they'd gone to bed in a room overlooking the sea, and made love to the sound of the waves breaking gently on the beach below. It had been a long time for Raya, but Mario was careful and cautious and he took his time, till they finally fell asleep in each other's arms.

Chapter Fifteen

Sunday
Ax-les-Thermes, France

Gerald Stanway reached up to make sure that the interior light in the Peugeot was switched off, so that he wouldn't be illuminated when he opened the car door. He then checked his Browning pistol again. His car was parked about a quarter of a mile from the Hostellerie de la Poste, an easy and level walk. It was a little after two in the morning, and time he made his move.

He slipped out of the vehicle and pushed the door closed as quietly as he could, the catch making barely a click. He wouldn't lock it, as he didn't want the hazard warning lights to flash. That would be a dead giveaway, if there was anybody watching.

Stanway glanced in both directions before he stepped away from the car, but the road was completely deserted and he couldn't even hear the sound of traffic nearby. He made sure he'd still got the room key he'd grabbed from the hotel reception earlier, again checked the Browning, then started walking slowly northwards along the side of the road, heading towards the Hostellerie de la Poste.

'Sierra, Whisky, heads up. Single figure, probably male, walking northbound and approaching target.'

'Roger. Keep me posted.'

In the parked Renault, Adamson kept his binoculars focused through the open window. But the distance and the lack of ambient light – the moon, high in the sky, casting only a faint glow over the landscape – meant he could do little more than tentatively identify the approaching figure as male.

'Still walking slowly, direction unchanged,' he radioed, more for something to say than because it provided useful information for Dekker. 'He's a possible target, so I'm allocating him the code name Tango One.'

'Roger that.'

At the edge of the gravelled driveway that led off the N20 road and into the forecourt of the Hostellerie de la Poste, Stanway paused and again looked all around him. He'd neither seen nor heard anything since he'd stepped away from his car. It was as if the entire town was asleep – which, on reflection, it probably was.

Then he turned right and stepped off the road. The hotel lay directly in front of him, dark and silent.

'Sierra, Whisky. Tango One now approaching the hotel. Is Romeo's room light still on?'

'Negative. Extinguished about an hour ago. No lights showing anywhere else in the building.'

'Tango One has stopped in front of the hotel. He's just looking at the building.'

*

On the hillside rising behind the hotel, Dekker clicked his transmit button twice to acknowledge. He couldn't see the man Adamson was watching, because he was still on the opposite side of the building, but for the moment he wasn't concerned about him. Dekker had never met the man named Paul Richter, but he already felt a kind of kinship with him.

He knew Richter had been set up by Simpson, knew that there was a very good chance that, within the next few minutes, Gecko would get inside the building and do his best to kill him – assuming it was Gecko who'd just appeared at the front of the hotel. He knew all that because Simpson had given both him and Adamson a very comprehensive briefing back in London. Richter was merely a stalking-horse, a target intended to entice Gecko out of hiding, and Dekker had been ordered to do nothing at all to interfere with events at the hotel, until after the traitor had made his move.

But, a couple of times during his career in the British Army, Dekker had also been treated like a mushroom – kept in the dark and fed on shit – and he hadn't much enjoyed the experience. And he couldn't think of a single good reason why he shouldn't do whatever he could to help Richter survive.

In fact, there wasn't a huge amount of help he could give right then, but there was one action he could take that might just give Richter an edge. That assumed he was still awake, and Dekker was prepared to bet a substantial sum that, despite the darkened room, Richter was sitting over to one side of it, and wide awake.

He altered his grip on the sniper rifle very slightly,

carefully aimed the rifle at the exact centre of Richter's open window, and switched on the laser sight.

Through the Zeiss telescopic sight, a pinprick of red light appeared on the wall inside the bedroom, and Dekker knew that if he pulled the trigger right then, the bullet would end up within half an inch of that tiny dot. He switched the laser sight off, then on again, repeating this three times. If Richter was awake, that should be all the hint he'd need that something was about to happen.

Dekker switched off the laser sight, for the last time, and settled down to watch.

In front of the hotel, Stanway turned to his right and headed towards the rear of the building. He intended walking right around it, just to make sure no lights were burning, and that everyone inside was asleep. Then he'd walk through the front door, do the job and walk out again.

'Tango One moving right. I'm losing him.'

'Roger,' Dekker muttered.

A little later, a dark shape appeared at the side of the building, and for a moment Dekker wondered if it would be worth switching over to his night-vision glasses, but he decided not to. The chances were that the action would take place inside Richter's room, and there the lights would probably go on before anything happened, simply because Gecko would want to be certain of hitting the correct target before he pulled the trigger. And then the Zeiss scope would be all Dekker would need.

'Contact. He's checking the back of the hotel. Moving around it anticlockwise.'

'Roger,' Adamson said. 'I'll call Simpson and give him a heads-up.'

'Enjoy,' Dekker muttered, still watching the slowly moving figure.

Stanway neither saw nor heard anything to suggest that anyone was still awake inside the Hostellerie de la Poste, so he moved back to the front door of the building, fishing in his pocket for the stolen key. As in many French hotels that Stanway had used in the past, next to the room key on the keyring was one that opened the main door, so that guests returning late could let themselves into the building without ringing the bell and disturbing others.

And Stanway was particularly keen not to disturb anyone that night.

He slid the key into the lock, turned it carefully and pushed on the door. A moment later, he vanished into the building.

'Sierra, Whisky, he's inside. Through the front door, and it looked as if he simply used a key. You don't think we've just been watching the barman creeping back after a night out somewhere?'

'No chance,' Dekker said. 'This guy's either Gecko or some tea leaf who's really good with locks. And I guess we'll find out which of those pretty soon.'

*

Stanway walked across to the reception desk and replaced the room key he'd taken earlier. Then he used the slim beam of a pencil torch to check all the other keys, and nodded in satisfaction. The only key not hanging on a hook behind the desk was for room 11, on the first floor, so that had to be where he'd find the blond-haired Russian clerk.

He took out the Browning, slipped across to the staircase rising in one corner of the entrance hall, and began ascending it cautiously, keeping right over to one side, where he hoped the wooden treads might not creak too much. In under half a minute, he'd reached the first-floor landing, and twenty seconds after that he was standing outside a wooden door with the number '11'.

Stanway found himself sweating slightly under the stress of what he was planning to do. For a few seconds he just stood there, wiping his hands on his trousers before reaching out for the door handle.

He turned it slowly, and the door swung inwards easily, without even a creak. For an instant, Stanway was puzzled. He'd expected to find the door locked at the very least, and possibly jammed with a chair or something. He looked again at the room number, confirming he'd got it right, then, flicking on his torch, opened the door wide enough to see further into the room. The beam moved across clothes hung over the back of a chair, then a briefcase standing nearby, next over to the bed. It just had to be the right room.

Reaching back, Stanway flicked on the main light and stepped fully into the room, his pistol extended in front of him, as he aimed the barrel at a hunched shape he could see lying under the bedcovers.

Chapter Sixteen

Sunday
Sluzhba Vneshney Razvyedki Rossi Headquarters, Yasenevo,
Tëplyystan, Moscow

Major Abramov was still imprisoned in the darkened interview room. Sitting on a hard chair, he slumped forward over the table, sleeping fitfully. He felt uncomfortable, exhausted, hungry and thirsty, because he'd had nothing to eat or drink since Zharkov had left him there several hours earlier. That, he guessed, was deliberate, for nobody had entered the room since, or responded to his knocks on the locked door.

Suddenly the silence was broken by the sound of brisk footsteps approaching along the corridor outside. Then the door swung open, the main lights snapped on, and Colonel Yevgeni Zharkov strode back in.

Abramov lurched upright, his aching joints protesting, and leant back again in his chair. Strictly speaking, he should have stood up when the senior officer entered, but he was too far gone to care any more. He still guessed Zharkov would order his execution when all this was over, just because Raya Kosov had worked for him.

'So have you arrested her?' Abramov asked, as Zharkov sat down opposite him, looking pleased with himself.

'Not yet, but we know where she is.'

Abramov immediately doubted the truth of that assertion. If Zharkov's assassins really had located her, by now she'd either be dead or strapped heavily sedated to a stretcher on her way back to Moscow. Despite his own problems, a tiny part of him still hoped Raya would make it to the West and elude the pursuit. But Zharkov's next words simply stunned him.

'And now we know for sure that you're working with her, because last night she sent you an email.'

'What?' Abramov stared at the man. 'She did what?'

'I said she sent you an email, but it's encrypted. So you will now decrypt it for me.'

'But I—'

Zharkov smiled wolfishly. 'You're not refusing to assist us, I hope, Major? After all, if you really are as innocent as you claim, then perhaps this email will prove it and you can go home.'

Abramov knew there was virtually no chance of that happening, no matter what the contents of this message that Raya had apparently sent.

'No,' he said, 'I meant that I might not be able to decrypt it, because I don't know what code she used. Where did she send it from?'

Zharkov hesitated for a moment, apparently deciding whether or not Abramov could derive some advantage from this piece of information. Then he shrugged and gave his answer.

'She used a cyber cafe on the outskirts of Rome,' he said. 'Now, Major, we will go to your office and see if you are able to decipher this email. But mark my words, Abramov, if you cannot produce the plaintext, there will be only one conclusion we can reasonably draw.'

And that would be confirmation of his guilt, Abramov thought.

As he preceded Zharkov down the corridor, he wondered about two things. First, what cipher Raya had employed, which probably wouldn't be that difficult to work out, given that there was only a handful in use in the section, email being inherently unreliable and insecure. Second, and far more importantly, what on earth had Raya got to say to him after her flagrant betrayal of both him – and indeed the entire SVR? Was she gloating? Or apologizing? Or was there some other dimension to this entire affair that he had so far entirely missed?

West London

Andrew Lomas was wakened by the ringing of his mobile. He muttered in irritation as he switched on the bedside light, grimaced at the time indicated on his alarm clock, and snatched up the phone.

'Yes?' he snapped.

'Is that Mr Weaver?' The voice was high-pitched, almost nasal.

'No, you've got the wrong number, you idiot.'

'Isn't that seven-five-three-nine-eight-two?'

'No, it bloody isn't.'

Lomas punched the button to end the call and then sat upright in bed. There was a pad and pencil beside the clock, and within a couple of seconds he'd written down both the name and number the caller had used: 'Weaver' and '753982'. The call wasn't a wrong number.

It was a coded message, and it meant he needed to take immediate action.

The name 'Weaver' meant there had been a leak of some sort from Moscow Centre – for instance a breach of security, a lost file or a defector – which Lomas thought might well relate to the story of the Russian clerk that had so alarmed Gerald Stanway. Or it might be something completely different, something new. To find out anything more he needed to decode the rest of the message.

Lomas strode out of his bedroom and into the lounge, pressed the button to power up his laptop, then went into the kitchen to make himself some coffee. By the time he got back to the computer, the operating system had finished loading.

He first ran a program that generated spurious information resulting in a false IP address. That was necessary to conceal his physical location from any type of surveillance method in use. He had no idea whether any intelligence service was taking the slightest notice of him, but running this IP program was a sensible precaution. He ran his Internet browser, checking that his apparent location was outside the United Kingdom, and then input a website address from memory. The site was apparently located in Australia, but was actually based in Russia itself. Lomas accessed this site regularly, but usually from a cyber cafe, and only ever visiting that establishment once.

When the homepage appeared on his screen, the site appeared to be very badly designed, and was purportedly intended for hobbyists interested in the manufacture of aboriginal musical instruments. Lomas clicked the centre of the top border twice. Nothing happened for twenty seconds – which was about four times the attention span of the average browser. Then a new page appeared, which simply contained a dialogue box, and nothing else. Lomas copied the six numbers the caller had given him into the box and then pressed the Enter key. There was another delay, this time for only about five seconds, and then the screen cleared.

Lomas leant forward to read the text very carefully. Immediately he could understand why he had received the call. An important officer in the SVR had defected and, through her position at Yasenevo, was ideally placed to reveal the identity, not only of Gerald Stanway, but also of a second penetration agent working inside the SIS – an agent for whom Lomas also acted as a handler.

Lomas was instructed to warn and assist Stanway in any way he could, the message from Moscow stated, but ultimately the British agent was considered expendable. The greater prize was the other agent, the more senior and much more important man, and Lomas was instructed to contact him as soon as possible, and brief him fully on the defection. Moscow Centre would keep Lomas fully informed about the SVR's pursuit of the traitor Raya Kosov, and it was hoped they would have her in custody within days or even hours, in which case the crisis would be over.

The final paragraph contained explicit instructions regarding what Lomas must do should Kosov somehow manage to make contact with any British intelligence organization or, even worse, actually arrive on British shores. He smiled when he read that section. That might prove to be the most entertaining part of the entire operation.

Ax-les-Thermes, France

'The light's been switched on,' Dekker said urgently into his microphone, though there was nothing Adamson could do from where he was. And little enough that Dekker could do either, since his orders were perfectly clear.

He watched a figure enter the room, some kind of semi-automatic pistol in his right hand, then move to one side, out of sight of the open window.

'Tango One's in the room, but now out of sight. Standby. And there's somebody else there as well.'

As Stanway levelled the pistol, and took a couple of cautious steps across the room, he suddenly became aware of a presence behind him. He half turned, swinging the pistol towards the man who seemed to have materialized from nowhere. But he was too late . . . far, far too late.

The fair-haired man raised some kind of tube towards Stanway's face, and suddenly he was enveloped in an eye-stinging spray that threatened to choke him. And then the agony was compounded when some brutally hard object smashed down on his right forearm. He could actually hear the crack of the bones breaking.

In a reflex action, he squeezed the trigger, and the pistol bucked once and tumbled from his hand. Then the sudden sharp pain of his injury overwhelmed him, and he screamed in a long, blubbering wail of utter and total agony.

Half-blinded and staggering, Stanway felt a sudden hard shove into his stomach and he stumbled backwards, tripped over the carpet, and landed with a crash on the floor. But his suffering wasn't over, even then. He heard a click from somewhere nearby, a powerful hand seized his left wrist firmly, and then a blade of some kind was driven clean through his hand, pinning it to the wooden floor.

'What the hell's going on?' Adamson demanded. 'I heard a shot and a scream. Was that Richter or Gecko?'

In his agitation, he'd forgotten to use both code words.

'I heard it, too, but didn't see what happened,' Dekker replied. 'My view through that window is very restricted . . . Wait, just hang on.'

Through the telescopic sight, Dekker saw a figure move back into view at the window. Even though the man was back-lit, he could still tell that it was Richter. The figure waved, then dangled what appeared to be a set of keys out of the window.

Dekker grinned to himself and stood up. The show was over.

'Get mobile, Whisky,' he said. 'Target Romeo is fine. Call Simpson again and tell him that the trap is sprung. It's time to go down there and see what sort of a rat he managed to catch. If you get there before me, go around to the back of the hotel. Romeo'll throw you down a set of keys, so you can let yourself in.'

*

Ten minutes later, Dekker and Adamson were both standing in Richter's hotel room, looking down at the moaning figure lying on the floor. His right arm was badly broken, and his left hand pinned to the bare floorboards by the five-inch blade of the flick knife Richter had bought that same afternoon in Ax. The man was still conscious and obviously in pain, a rough gag thrust into his mouth and held in place with a binding of adhesive tape around his head.

Richter himself was lying comfortably on the bed, with Stanway's Browning resting on the bedside table right next to him.

'What did you use?' Colin Dekker asked. 'Was it mace or something?'

'Nothing so exotic,' Richter replied. 'Just good old-fashioned hairspray. It has much the same effect, or at least for a few seconds, and that's normally all you need. Oh, thanks for the warning, by the way – the laser, I mean. That was a big help. Once I knew this comedian was on his way, I stood by the window listening, so I heard him on the gravel outside. I'm not sure I would have detected it, if I'd still been lying on the bed.'

'You were waiting somewhere outside the room for him?'

Richter nodded. 'As soon as it got quiet in the hotel tonight, I walked down to reception, borrowed the key for the room opposite and unlocked the door. Then I put the key back so he'd know where to find me. Once I was sure he was coming in, I walked across the hall and waited inside.'

Dekker nodded. Richter's other improvisation in

weaponry was a crowbar leaning against the wall beside the door.

'You don't fuck about, do you?' the SAS officer suggested, with a slight smile. He pointed at the flick knife, and the blood still welling from the savage wound and pooling around the man's hand.

Richter shook his head. 'No, not when people are trying to kill me. You got a problem with that?'

Dekker smiled again. 'Hell, no,' he said, 'I'm on your side. As far as I'm concerned you could have used a couple of flick knives and a nail gun, too, and just crucified the bastard. And if I'd been in here myself, I'd have helped you do it.'

'It doesn't sound as if you fuck about either,' Richter said. 'But it'll be interesting to hear what Simpson has to say about all this.'

'He should be on his way now,' Adamson said, sticking his head out of the door as they heard footsteps on the landing. 'No, it's the hotel proprietor. I'll go and talk to him, and head him off. I've left the front door open, by the way.'

'What was your brief?' Richter asked, as Adamson headed away along the corridor.

'Simple,' Dekker replied. 'Observation of the target room, meaning your hotel room, then I was supposed to take this guy down if he managed to get away safely from the hotel. Preferably leaving him in a fit state to talk, of course. But you seem to have achieved that all on your own, so you've saved the Queen the price of a rifle bullet.'

'I hope she'll be pleased,' Richter muttered. 'You people from Hereford?'

'Good guess,' Dekker nodded. 'I'm Regiment, but the

other bloke, Adamson, he's SIS, a spook, sent along just to hold my hand and smooth the way with the Frogs because I don't speak French. My job's simple – I just shoot the bad guys.'

Footsteps again approached along the corridor, this time brisk and purposeful.

'That sounds like our esteemed leader,' Dekker said, 'so you'd better mind your manners.'

Three seconds later, Richard Simpson strode into the room, looking as fresh and immaculate as ever. He glanced at Dekker, then at the figure moaning on the floor, and finally at Richter.

'Dear God,' he said. 'What the fuck happened here?'

'I'd have thought that was obvious,' Richter said, the tone of his voice low and dangerous. 'You set me up as a Judas goat . . . No, in fact that's wrong. A Judas goat is trained to lead other animals to slaughter, but is the one animal that's always spared. In this case you didn't give a flying fuck whether I lived or died. You just used me as bait, as an unarmed target for this comedian. Then I suppose, once he'd shot my head off, you'd have called the French plods and had him arrested? Devious little pink bastard, aren't you?'

Simpson turned slightly pinker. 'It was necessary. You don't have any idea of the bigger picture.'

'Of course I don't,' Richter snapped, 'because you didn't fucking well tell me, did you? And you didn't even give me a weapon.'

'No,' Simpson admitted curtly. 'And I'll take that Browning now, thank you,' he added, pointing to the pistol on the table beside Richter and holding out his hand.

'No fucking chance.' Richter snatched up the weapon and aimed it at the floor, just in front of Simpson. 'You want this pistol, you come over here and try to take it off me.'

'Disarm him,' Simpson snapped at Dekker.

The SAS officer shook his head. 'I've fulfilled my brief and I'm not getting involved in your domestic, thanks very much. This is your mess, Simpson, so you clean it up.'

For a few seconds, Simpson alternated his gaze between Richter and Dekker, then it settled on Dekker. 'I'll be talking to your superior as soon as I get back,' he snarled.

'Help yourself,' Dekker said. 'He's not a great fan of your secret squirrel outfit, so he'll probably tell you to go screw yourself. I'll even give you his phone number, if you want.'

Simpson stood in silence for another few moments, then again studied the wounded man pinned to the floor.

'You broke his arm,' he remarked flatly. 'And what you've done to his hand with that flick knife is just plain sadistic. That's overkill and unnecessary violence.'

'What do you mean "unnecessary violence"?' Richter replied, then leant forward and kicked Stanway sharply in the thigh. 'This bastard came here to kill me, so what should I have done? Made him a coffee and then helped him point his pistol at me? I don't fuck about in this kind of situation, Simpson – anyone who points a gun at me can face the consequences. And he can still talk, can't he, which I presume was the point of this whole bloody charade?'

'What do you mean?'

'It's obvious, isn't it? You were trying to flush some rodent out of the woodwork. You had a traitor somewhere within British intelligence but you didn't know exactly where. So you spread some story about me, or whoever I was supposed to be, so that he would come after me just to shut me up.' He kicked Stanway again, and the wounded man moaned in pain. 'I presume that was the point of all the fannying about with the sealed packet of papers, and my debriefing in Russian with the Chuckle Brothers downstairs.'

For a long moment Simpson didn't reply. 'That's a remarkably accurate assessment,' he said at last, eyeing Richter appraisingly. 'You're not what I expected. When we recruited you, I assumed you'd just do what you were told.'

'I do follow orders, when they make sense, but this whole set-up stank from day one. I've told you before that I trust you about as far as I can spit a rat.'

'Good,' Simpson nodded, 'very good. I have a feeling you might have a future in my organization, after all.'

'You can dream on. I'll be handing in my resignation as soon as I get back to London. I'll go off and sell insurance or something. At least I wouldn't have to spend all my time watching my back and trying to work out what the hell's really going on, as opposed to what other people tell me is going on. And, most of the time nobody'll be trying to kill me.'

Simpson smiled for the first time since entering the hotel room. 'Your resignation might not be accepted,' he said, 'because I seriously think I might be able to use your talents. Anyway, we'll talk about that later. Now, who exactly is this man?' He bent forward to look more closely at the injured man on the floor.

'His name's Gerald Stanway,' Richter said, 'and he lives in South Kensington, in London.'

Simpson looked surprised. 'You know him?'

Richter shook his head. 'Of course I don't know him. I simply checked his pockets once I'd sort of immobilized him.'

Dekker smiled at Richter's choice of verb.

Richter picked up a wallet from the bedside table and tossed it to Simpson. 'I found that in his jacket pocket.'

Simpson flicked rapidly through the contents, before sliding it into his own pocket. He bent over to lift up Stanway's head by the hair, staring at the man's flushed and pain-racked face for a few seconds.

Then Simpson shook his head. 'Never seen him before in my life.'

'I have, though,' Richter explained. 'He came into the hotel bar earlier today, while I was trying to think up convincing lies for your two blokes about my work at the SVR headquarters in Moscow. He spoke fluent French to the barman, read a French newspaper, had a drink, and then buggered off. I presume that was his idea of reconnaissance: to eyeball me and check out any possible opposition. That's before he came back tonight to make sure I'd never collect my pension.'

'OK,' Simpson rubbed his hands together briskly, 'it looks to me as if we've got the result we wanted. Stanway here presumably works for SIS, or maybe GCHQ – but we'll soon find out which. I'll make a couple of calls to sort out a compliant Frog doctor who'll patch him up enough so that he can travel, then we'll freight him back to London and put the screws on him.'

'I think if you just stepped on his broken arm right now, he'd probably tell you anything you need to know,' Richter suggested. 'I'll do it myself, if you like.'

Simpson shook his head. 'I'm sure you'd enjoy it, but I don't know what questions to ask. The interrogation will have to be done by someone from SIS, and we won't necessarily have to resort to physical persuasion. We have an interesting selection of chemical compounds that can loosen any tongue.'

'And afterwards?'

'There won't be any afterwards. The days when former traitors could live out their days in genteel retirement are long gone. Mr Stanway will either die after a short and tragic illness, or he'll be involved in a motor accident. Either way, he's dead as of right now. He just hasn't stopped breathing yet.'

Simpson's cool and matter-of-fact tone sent a chill up Richter's back, and in that moment he realized that he would never, ever, underestimate this man.

'So what about me?' Richter asked.

'Your part of this job is over. Get yourself back to London, back to the office, and then we'll talk further. Make sure you bring those briefing papers with you. I know the Victor manual isn't exactly top secret, but I don't want to leave a paper trail over here in case the Frogs start getting interested in what's going on. I suggest you lose the Browning before you try to cross the Channel, because if you get caught carrying it, I won't feel any particular inclination to haul you out of the slammer.' Simpson glanced at the SAS man. 'You, too,

Dekker, you can head for home as well. Thanks for your help.'

'I didn't actually do anything,' Dekker pointed out. 'Richter here did it all by himself.'

'Whatever,' Simpson said, pulling a mobile phone out of his pocket. But, before he could dial a number, the phone suddenly rang. The conversation between Simpson and the caller lasted less than three minutes. What unnerved Richter was that Simpson switched his gaze directly towards him about half a minute after they'd started talking, and his eyes didn't leave him until the call finally ended.

'What?' Richter demanded.

'You'll be keeping the Browning, Richter,' Simpson declared, 'at least for the moment. I'll see you get a couple of spare magazines and a box of 9-millimetre ammunition, too. Everything's changed, and right now you're the only asset I've got here that I can use. And this time,' he added, 'it's for real, so I expect you to do exactly what I tell you.'

Chapter Seventeen

The mobile phone rang insistently in John Westwood's hotel room, his brain first weaving the sound seamlessly into a dream before it finally penetrated his consciousness. Then he grabbed the unit, pressed the green button, and put it to his ear.

'Westwood,' he said.

'This is Richards, sir, and it's an open line.'

'Understood. What is it?'

'We now know how our colleagues from the other side of the street are going to try to find our mutual friend,' Richards said. 'And they're real serious about it.'

Westwood's brain did an immediate translation. The Russians had obviously come up with some way of tracking down Raya Kosov.

'How?' he asked.

'You're familiar with the old expression "button man"?' Richards asked.

'Yes. I haven't heard it for a while, but I know what it means.'

In the days of Al Capone, a 'button man' was a hit man, or assassin, employed by the Mob.

'Well, they're now claiming that our friend is a professional in that field, and that while she was in Moscow

284

she used her talents on a senior official there. They want to talk to her real bad, so they've asked the locals to give them a hand. There'll be pictures of her plastered everywhere, and teams at every airport, ferry terminal and railway station in the whole area, plus search teams covering bus routes and talking to taxi firms. Every registered hotel and rooming house in Italy will be receiving a visit, real soon. Other officers will be stationed at the toll-booths on all the autostradas in the country, and they'll be watching or even blocking the main roads. The locals have already made this a priority one task, and they're sewing the place up as tight as a drum. If she's not out of Italy by now, I don't think she's ever going to get out.'

'Understood,' Westwood said again. 'I'll come in later this morning. Keep your ear to the ground. The first sign of our friend, I want to know about it.'

'You got it.'

Westwood sat on the edge of the bed for a few moments, considering. Then he switched on his laptop, entered the twelve-digit password that gave him access to his files, and looked up a London phone number. He dialled it and waited a few seconds for it to be answered.

'This is John Westwood,' he began. 'We discussed a certain matter yesterday, if you recall.'

'And I told you then that we had no idea what you were talking about,' snapped the man at the other end of the line.

'I know,' Westwood's tone was mild, 'but now I have some information that may be relevant.'

'I'm listening.'

'In case you haven't already been told, our friends from the north have virtually shut down the country, with the assistance of the local people. They're watching airports, ferries, buses and taxis, plus checking the hotels and the main roads. You might want to pass that on to somebody.'

'Thank you. I've noted that, and I'll pass it up the line. Anything else?'

'No. But if I hear anything more, I'll let you know.'

Piombino, Italy

Raya woke early, her eyes snapping open as the first rays of the morning sun lanced through a gap in the curtains. For a moment she had no idea where she was – the room was completely unfamiliar to her – till she glanced at the shape that lay beside her, snoring gently, and the memories flooded back.

Raya looked at her watch on the bedside table, then slid out of bed and walked into the bathroom. She emerged a few minutes later, her hair still damp from the shower, and dressed quickly. When she left the room, Mario still lay dead to the world, one arm dangling out of the bed.

Raya smiled at him, remembering the previous night, then walked out of the bedroom. She needed two things: a cup of coffee and then the cyber cafe, in that order.

Ax-les-Thermes, France

'Just tell me again why it has to be me,' Richter demanded.

He sat facing Simpson at an outdoor cafe near the casino in Ax-les-Thermes, with the remains of a breakfast of coffee and croissants on the table in front of them. Adamson was sitting at a table slightly to one side, taking no part in the conversation but just scanning the surrounding area to ensure that nobody was trying to listen in to what was being said. Hughes and Wallis were sitting in Richter's hotel room, babysitting a semi-conscious Gerald Stanway, who'd been dosed with drugs to ease the pain and, more importantly, to keep him subdued until a specialist team arrived from London to take him back for interrogation.

'Didn't you understand what I told you?'

Richter smiled at him. 'Oh, yes,' he said, 'I understand it completely, but I just like hearing you say it.'

Simpson nodded resignedly. 'Very well, that call last night – or, rather, early this morning – was from the duty officer at SIS headquarters, Vauxhall Cross. They'd received an email yesterday evening from a cyber cafe on the outskirts of Rome, with a rather large attachment. The attachment contained a complete listing of every person employed by SIS, their names and dates of birth, and a short extract detailing the service records and thumbnail photographs of about a dozen of them.'

'Stanway really screwed you, didn't he?' Richter suggested with a grin.

'This is no laughing matter. I don't know how long that bastard has been selling our secrets to the Russians, but he's going to suffer for this. We'll wring him dry and then I'll personally ensure he dies as painful a death as we can arrange.'

'You never explained to me why they contacted *you*,'

Richter pointed out. 'I didn't think your outfit was a part of the Secret Intelligence Service.'

'It isn't . . . that's the whole point,' Simpson said. He paused for a few moments, gazing at Richter as if deciding how much to tell him. Then he spoke again. 'I think I need to explain a few things to you. First, have you ever heard of "The Increment"?'

'No,' Richter replied.

'OK, every now and then, the SIS gets wind of something going on inside Britain that they have particular interest in, but which they can't investigate directly because they only have a remit to operate *outside* the UK.'

'I thought that was what MI5 was supposed to cover?'

'It is, but the two services don't have a particularly good working relationship. And often there's some question about sources or procedures or something and, for whatever reason, SIS don't want MI5 sticking their oar in. Or maybe the situation is somewhere abroad, but there's a good chance it'll all go tits-up at some point, which would embarrass SIS and, by extension, the British government.

'So, a while ago, some desk officer at Vauxhall Cross came up with the idea of The Increment. For jobs like these, the SIS would recruit ex-military personnel, usually former SAS soldiers because they're used to thinking on their feet. They'd assemble a team, brief them, and send them off. Then, if the shit hit the fan later, and those guys were caught or killed, SIS could simply deny all knowledge of them, and there'd be no provable link to the men involved. It would be a totally deniable operation.

'My section is called the Foreign Operations Executive, a nicely meaningless name, and we essentially function in exactly the same way as The Increment. We take care of those jobs that the SIS thinks might turn round and bite them. If you like, FOE is a secret, and unacknowledged, covert section of the SIS – a covert outfit working for another covert outfit – and there are no direct, or at least no provable, links between the two of them. In other words, FOE is a kind of formalized and established version of The Increment.'

'So that's why you skulk around in the backstreets of Hammersmith instead of enjoying extensive views along the Thames from that bloody-awful-looking building by Vauxhall Bridge.'

'Exactly. Now, a short time ago, evidence was found that confirmed there had been a penetration of the British security establishment, most likely in the SIS or possibly GCHQ, and I was tasked with coming up with a plan to unmask the source. FOE was trusted because we have no access to at least one of the computer data-bases known to have been compromised, so that proved that we had to be clean. If we couldn't ourselves access the information, we obviously couldn't have leaked it. The result, as you now know, was this deception operation you've got involved in. We needed you because the identities of a lot of the FOE staff are already known to SIS officers, for obvious reasons, so whoever got to impersonate the mythical defecting Russian clerk had to be a complete outsider, and not somebody the traitor could possibly recognize.

'That worked out quite well, I think, but we now have the bizarre scenario of life imitating art. There's a real Russian clerk on the run, and he has access to the

SIS personnel files, so he, too, might be able to recognize any SIS officer we send to bring him in. And the reason he doesn't trust us over this is that he knows the identity of the traitor who's been leaking data to the SVR. If that traitor – obviously that was Stanway – happened to be assigned to the operation, Yuri – which is the name the clerk is using – knows that he'd never make it to first base. Stanway would simply contact Yasenevo, and a hit team would be waiting at the rendezvous to pick Yuri up.'

'That sounds bloody far-fetched to me.'

Simpson looked over at Richter. 'How's your history?' he asked.

'Average to poor, I suppose. Why?'

'Let me take you back to the years just after the end of the last war, and tell you a story about a man named Constantin Volkhov. He was a low-level Russian diplomat, stationed in Turkey, who wanted out of the Soviet Union and assembled a dowry he thought we'd be interested in. He talked to the British vice-consul in Istanbul, and requested asylum in the West. In return for this, he would give us information about a couple of deep-penetration Soviet agents working at the Foreign Office, and another who was a senior officer in MI5.

'We now know, of course, that the MI5 officer was Kim Philby. What beggars belief is that, despite Volkhov's claim that there was a traitor in MI5, it was MI5 that was given the file to investigate. That would have been bad enough, but the officer tasked with handling and interviewing Volkhov was Philby himself. It was agreed that he'd fly out to Istanbul and interrogate the Russian there. Philby took as long as he possibly could before heading out to Turkey, but of course he informed Moscow Centre immediately.

'A KGB snatch squad was sent to Istanbul and had grabbed Volkhov before Philby even arrived there. The Russian was never seen alive again. And there's a rumour, never confirmed, that, after Volkhov had been questioned in the cellars of the Lubyanka, his body was cremated. In stages. While he was still alive.'

Richter grimaced.

'These are not nice people we're dealing with here,' Simpson said. 'The KGB was vicious, brutal and very efficient, and nothing we've learnt so far about the SVR suggests that it's any different.'

'So you need me,' Richter said, 'because this Russian clerk – this *real* Russian clerk – who's on the run from Moscow will only deal with somebody not included on that list of SIS personnel?'

'Exactly,' Simpson agreed. 'I've no doubt that Yuri will be thoroughly checking out the rendezvous before he shows himself, making absolutely sure he doesn't recognize you from the SIS personnel files. We daren't risk trying to use any of the SIS staff because if Yuri even suspects we're doing that, he'll run straight to the Americans.'

'And that would be a bad thing?' Richter suggested.

'Of course it would be a bad thing. It'd be fucking disastrous. If Yuri checks out – and the mere fact he can supply that personnel listing means he's had pretty much unrestricted access to the SVR's computer system – this could be the biggest intelligence coup of the decade. The last thing we want is to have the Yanks blundering in and buggering everything up, or Yuri handing them everything he knows about SIS.'

'No last name, then? He's just calling himself "Yuri"?'

Simpson nodded. 'It's obviously not his real name, but that doesn't matter. It's what he knows that we're interested in, nothing else.' He paused and stared at Richter for a few seconds. 'Look, I know we've pulled you in off the streets, as it were, and you probably haven't much enjoyed the last few days, but this is *really* important. You're literally the only person I can use to bring this clerk in. I'm devious, yes – as I have to be, in my job – but right here, right now, I'm being completely honest with you. I'll answer any questions you ask as fully as I can, and you'll also have whatever resources you need to complete this tasking. Will you do it? Will you go and meet this clerk and bring him back to London?'

Richter took another sip of his cooling coffee. 'Bring him in from the cold, you mean?'

'Don't go all le Carré on me, Richter. It's the wrong style and it doesn't suit you.'

Richter grinned at him. 'You're wrong about one thing, Simpson,' he said.

'What?'

'Oddly enough, I *have* enjoyed the last few days – driving round Europe, trying to figure out what the hell was really going on. I just wish you'd been straight with me from the start.'

'I couldn't, and I've explained why. So will you do it?'

'Yes,' Richter nodded, 'or I'll try to, anyway. Where am I supposed to meet him? In Italy?'

'Probably, but we don't know yet. The email only stated that Yuri wanted to be escorted to London by somebody with no connection with SIS. He even suggested we send out a policeman – as if we'd trust some bloody woodentop with something like this. You're here, you don't work for SIS and, apart from Adamson here and the two guys from Paris, nobody at SIS has any idea you even exist. Plus, you speak Russian.'

'You told me the email was written in English?'

'It was, but we don't know for sure how fluent Yuri is in the language, so your linguistic ability might be a big help. Anyway, hopefully we'll hear sometime today when and where this Russian wants to meet.'

As if on cue, Simpson's phone rang.

Piombino, Italy

Raya Kosov walked back to the hotel from the cyber cafe that Mario had driven past the previous evening. She strolled into the bar, ordered a Coke, and took it to a window seat overlooking the bay. That last email she'd sent would have set the wheels in motion, she was sure, and although she was certain the SVR snatch-teams couldn't possibly have traced her to Piombino yet, she knew she had to get as far north as she could, because every kilometre she put between herself and Rome would increase her chances of survival.

As soon as Mario surfaced, they needed to get back on the road. And, she realized, with sudden clarity, that there was one way she could wake him and more or less keep her side of their bargain, because she doubted that she'd still be with him that night.

She put down the half-drunk Coke and headed for the stairs, with a slight smile on her lips.

Sluzhba Vneshney Razvyedki Rossi Headquarters, Yasenevo, Tëplyystan, Moscow

Major Yuri Abramov stared at the monitor screen for a few seconds, then sat back and rubbed his eyes. He'd attempted unscrambling the text of the encrypted email using every decryption code that he and Raya had used together, but none of them had worked. Each attempt had simply changed one flavour of gobbledegook into a different type of gobbledegook.

Zharkov sneered at him from across the desk. 'And have you succeeded yet, Major?' he asked.

Abramov shook his head. 'She hasn't used any of the standard codes we're authorized to use. It must be one she's developed herself.'

'So you say, Major. So you say. Or maybe there's a much simpler explanation? Perhaps you don't want to decipher the message because you already know what it will say. It will tell you that your treacherous colleague has evaded capture in Italy, and that the way is now clear for you to join her.'

'Look, Colonel,' Abramov said, his voice cracking under the fear and stress, 'I have no idea why Raya Kosov fled from Russia but, whatever her reasons, it was nothing to do with me. I have no idea, either, why she sent me this email, and I'm as keen to see the contents of it as you are. But she hasn't used a code that I recognize, so she must have left something on her desk, or in her office – some clue that would allow me to decrypt it.'

'Like what?' Zharkov demanded.

'I don't know. Maybe a memory stick, a CD or DVD disk, or even a handwritten note – something like that.'

'Wait here.' Zharkov crossed to the door and walked out into the corridor, locking Abramov's office door behind him. He was back in less than ten minutes, holding a plastic bag in his hand.

'This was everything I could find,' he explained, dropping the bag on the desk in front of the major.

Abramov upended it and picked through the contents. There were several notepads, half a dozen CDs, and one memory stick labelled 'utilities'. All but two of the CDs could be ignored, because they were genuine program-installation disks, meaning no additional data could be burnt onto them. Abramov inserted the first of the other two CDs into his desktop computer and checked the contents, but could spot nothing that looked unusual. The second CD contained a handful of utility programs. However, as soon as he inserted the memory stick, he saw that there was only a single file on it, entitled 'decrypt'.

Abramov gestured to Zharkov and pointed out the file.

'I'm guessing that could be it,' he said, some of his normal confidence returning now that he felt there might be some explanation, some reason for what had happened, contained in the encrypted email. 'Could you witness what I'm about to do?'

Zharkov pulled his chair around to the other side of the desk, and sat down beside him.

Abramov next opened the file and inspected the contents. It was a plaintext file, headed by a couple of lines of writing which Abramov read out loud.

'"Yuri. I'm really sorry for what's happened, but I had my reasons for doing it. When you decrypt that email, I promise you'll understand. Raya."'

Abramov paused and gazed at Zharkov. 'I don't think that makes me sound like her accomplice, does it?' he asked.

Zharkov shrugged. 'Just camouflage, perhaps. Now sort out that email.'

Abramov studied the remaining text of the message. The second part consisted merely of the name of one of the standard encryption/decryption programs that the section used, plus a random string of characters.

'That must be the code she used,' Abramov said, copying it and opening the correct program. He pasted the character string into the 'decode string' field, and then ran the email through the opened program.

This time the result was very different because, instead of the routine generating a stream of random characters, some clear text appeared on the screen, and both men leant forward eagerly to read it.

Ax-les-Thermes, France

'Is all that clear?' Richard Simpson asked.

Richter nodded. 'Yuri wants the pick-up to take place somewhere in or near Genoa tonight, so I need to get on the road soonest,' he said. 'He's given us his mobile number, and I'm to text him on that once I've crossed the Italian border. He'll then text me the location for the meet itself.'

'Right,' Simpson nodded agreement. 'The techies at

Vauxhall Cross have checked the number, and discovered it's a cheap pay-as-you-go mobile, bought in Rome yesterday. It's also switched off at the moment, and has been ever since Yuri's email arrived at Legoland.'

'Legoland? What are you talking about?'

'Vauxhall Cross, SIS headquarters. If you'd ever been inside the building, you'd know exactly why some wit bestowed that nickname on the place. It's got a lot of other names as well.'

'I'll bet it has. And you're sure that this guy is for real, are you? I mean, it's not just the Russians yanking your chain for some reason, maybe running some kind of deception operation against the SIS? Or maybe even the Italian secret service, whatever it's called, having a go at you?'

'Absolutely not.' Simpson shook his head. 'The Italians don't have either the balls or the ability to mount something like this. The data that Yuri sent us had to have been culled direct from the SIS personnel files, and that means there's been a deep and serious penetration of the Service. I've already checked with Vauxhall Cross, and Stanway was in an ideal position to supply that kind of data, so – at least at this stage of investigating his treachery – we're quite satisfied that he was the source of the leak. And we also believe Yuri is exactly who he says he is.'

'Which is what?'

'He's one of the network managers at SVR headquarters at Yasenevo, where you were pretending to have worked. That means he's had unrivalled access to virtually the entire database of the SVR.'

'And that's why you want him?'

Simpson nodded again. 'That's why we want him.'

'Anything else?'

Simpson paused a few seconds before he replied. 'Yes,' he said slowly, 'I told you to hang on to that Browning pistol you took off Stanway, because I think you're going to need it. The moment Vauxhall Cross received Yuri's first email from a cyber cafe in Rome, the SIS staff in the embassy there were ordered to a higher alert state and instructed to start watching the Russian Embassy and its staff. They weren't told why, only that a "person of interest" had arrived in Rome, and that the Russians would be trying to find him.'

He paused again for a moment, apparently considering his next words. 'Let me explain something about the way intelligence services operate. Every service watches its rivals very closely, so in London every person who enters the Russian Embassy is photographed by a team of watchers, low-level surveillance specialists, employed by MI5. That's just in case some brainless British politician, and that means most of them, or a member of the SIS, or anyone else with access to sensitive information, decides it's a good time to visit the Russians to offer his or her services to the opposition in exchange for large handfuls of folding money.

'And we do exactly the same everywhere else. The only difference is that in Rome the Russian Embassy has to be watched by SIS surveillance officers, not people from MI5, because the Security Service has no remit to operate outside the United Kingdom. Besides, in Rome they're likely to find their cameras being jostled by watchers employed by the Italian government and the

Americans and the Germans and the Israelis, and God knows who else.

'Anyway, the point is that a couple of hours before Yuri sent his email, our people in Rome had already noticed a sudden flurry of activity at the Russian Embassy. Just about every car they have was suddenly sent out of the place, each one with two or three on board. The SIS people were caught slightly on the hop, and only had a couple of mobile units immediately available. Each of these units latched on to one of the Russian cars, and followed it. One went to the airport and the other to Rome's main railway station, and in both cases the occupants jumped out to start watching the arriving passengers. Each was carrying a sheet of paper with a photograph on it, but none of our watchers could get close enough to take a satisfactory look.'

Simpson shot a glance at a passing waiter, and the man instantly appeared beside their table – a trick Richter found quite impressive, from his personal experience of French waiters. Simpson ordered two more coffees, plus one for Adamson, and then continued with his explanation once the waiter had moved out of earshot.

'Now, at that time nobody at SIS Rome had any idea what had happened to stir up the Russians so badly. However, the inference was fairly obvious: clearly they were looking for somebody. It wasn't until that email from the cyber cafe arrived at Legoland that we knew exactly what was going on. Somehow, the SVR had not only already discovered that Yuri had done a bunk, but also that he'd been on his way to Rome. And we also knew that he'd slipped through the net they'd cast, simply because of the time the message was sent to us.'

'So it's likely that the Russian Embassy people will still be out there looking for him?' Richter said.

'Yes, but it's worse than that, because SIS Moscow has since reported witnessing a lot of arguments and disputes at Sheremetievo Airport. Angry passengers were confronting airline officials about being bumped off their booked flights. Within a couple of hours, we knew that those flights were all heading to Rome and other destinations in Italy – and to some parts of France as well. So the Russians obviously weren't relying just on their local staff to find Yuri; but were sending out specialist teams from Moscow as well. SIS Rome now estimates they've sent out at least fifty men to Italy.'

'And in this context the word "specialist" means what, exactly?' Richter asked, sitting back in his seat as the waiter reappeared with the drinks Simpson had ordered.

'You can call them what you like,' Simpson said a few moments later, stirring his coffee thoughtfully. 'Snatch teams, hit squads, whatever. But their orders will be simple enough. They'll be tasked with finding Yuri and hauling him back to Moscow, probably unconscious and strapped to a stretcher. When they get him back to Russia, they'll stick him in a nice quiet interrogation room somewhere, then they'll pull out his fingernails and apply other interesting techniques to ensure that he tells them what they want to know, before they finally kill him. And if there's some reason why they can't actually capture him, they'll do their best to eliminate him in Italy, or wherever else they find him. The one thing we do know for certain is that the Russians are desperate to plug this leak.'

Richter stared at Simpson for a long moment. 'And you really think there's some chance that I can slip past all these highly trained assassins, find this Yuri and simply take him to London?'

'Yes,' Simpson nodded. 'Because nobody knows who you are. You're not a known face to the Russians, so you'll have no trouble at all until you actually meet Yuri. Once you're together, of course, then the risks will multiply because the Russian teams know exactly what he looks like.'

'And then you expect me to fight my way out of trouble with just a Browning nine-mil and fifty rounds of ammunition? Fight my way past fifty-odd heavily armed Russian assassins with shoot-to-kill orders? All by myself?'

Simpson shook his head briefly. 'Not quite by yourself. I've talked to Hereford, and Dekker's been reassigned. He's going to be your shadow, your guardian angel watching you from a distance. He'll cover whatever meeting point Yuri chooses, and he'll take out any opposition players he notices. Dekker's a specialist sniper.'

'Oh, that makes me feel much better,' Richter snapped. 'So now the odds are twenty-five to one instead of fifty to one. That's a hell of an improvement.'

'If you move carefully,' Simpson said soothingly, 'there's absolutely no reason why you should even encounter any of the Russians. Italy's a big country and, once you've made contact with Yuri, you should be able to just drive straight over the border into France. And once you're here, there's almost no chance anybody would be able to follow you. France is huge and it offers dozens of possible routes you could take back to Britain.'

Simpson leaned forward and continued. 'You can do this, Richter. I know you can. You're stubborn and resourceful, and you obviously think on your feet. You'll be carrying a weapon, and you'll have Dekker watching your back. As of now, the opposition have no idea who either of you are. I'll give you some contact numbers for me back in Hammersmith, and I absolutely guarantee you'll get whatever help I can provide you. Make no mistake, bringing in Yuri is vitally important, and we'll do everything we can to make sure it happens.'

Richter grunted. 'There's one other thing you need to think about doing right now.'

'What?'

'Yuri must have a passport to get out of Russia in the first place, but that'll be no good now because the Russians will have blocked it for every border crossing. So you'll have to arrange a diplomatic passport for him. As soon as I meet him, I'll email you his picture and the name he wants to use, then you'll need to send it out here somewhere so we can pick it up. Otherwise getting him to London's going to be difficult.'

Simpson nodded. 'That's already in hand. But don't think you have to rely only on commercial transport. If it makes better sense, I can have a private plane or an RAF aircraft, something like that, on standby, ready to fly down here to pick you up, which will avoid the passport problem altogether.'

'OK,' Richter replied, 'I'll let you know.'

Simpson's phone rang again, and he answered immediately.

Richter listened with interest to one side of the conversation.

'What? No, I've heard his name. I mean, I know who he is but I've never met him . . . he said what? . . . how did he find out? . . . right. I'll pass that on.'

Simpson snapped his mobile closed with an irritated expression.

'What?' Richter asked.

'I don't know exactly how it happened, but now the Americans have decided to stick their oar in the water as well. Just a short while ago, the SIS duty officer was called by a man named John Westwood. He's CIA, and a big wheel at Langley, in fact their Head of Espionage. He's in Rome at the moment and he called SIS yesterday to see if we knew anything about a Russian defector. Obviously the SIS officer there denied all knowledge of it, because actually only one man at Vauxhall Cross *does* know what's going on, and he won't tell anybody.'

'So what did this Westwood guy want?'

'To give us a warning,' Simpson said. 'Apparently the Russians have upped the ante and got the Italian police involved. According to Westwood, the hunt for Yuri is now overt, and the Eyeties will be watching everywhere for him – checking the hotels, the whole nine yards. You've got Yuri's mobile number, so you need to send him a text message. I'll dictate it now.'

Richter pulled out his mobile, opened up a blank SMS page, input the number he'd been given for Yuri's mobile phone, and waited.

'Right, here goes,' Simpson said. 'Tell him: "Airports, ferries, trains, buses, taxis watched. Hotels slash guest houses checked. Autoroute toll-booths watched slash main roads blocked or watched." That's it. I don't know how Yuri's travelling, but if he checks his phone for messages, at least he'll now know what he's up against. There's nothing else we can do for him at the moment.'

Richter pressed the button to send the text, then

looked up at Simpson. 'I presume I'm still heading for Italy?'

Simpson nodded. 'Yes, proceed as we discussed. It doesn't look good for Yuri, but if he makes it out, you'll need to be right there ready to pick him up. And there is one hopeful sign.'

'What?'

'The last email Yuri sent to Vauxhall Cross originated in a cyber cafe in a place called Piombino. It's a small town on the west coast of Italy, almost opposite Elba, so that means Yuri's already well clear of Rome. And the further out he gets, the thinner the search net will become, obviously.'

'OK,' Richter said, 'I hope you're right. Now I'd better get going. And Dekker will be following me?'

'He should be on the road within the next half-hour. We put him on a train up to Toulouse earlier and told him to pick up a hire car there. He's got your mobile number, and you've already got his. Meet him somewhere near Genoa before you rendezvous with Yuri, and then sort out how you're going to play it.'

Simpson stood up and extended his hand.

Richter stood as well, and shook it. 'Right, then,' he said. 'I've got a long way to drive, so I'd better hit the road.'

He strode across to the parking bays fronting the casino, climbed into his hired Ford, backed out and drove away, heading north towards Toulouse.

Tuscany, Italy

At almost the same moment Richter was driving north out of Ax-les-Thermes on the N20, Raya Kosov sat in the passenger seat of Mario's Fiat Punto, waiting for him to follow her out of the hotel, after he had paid the bill for their overnight stay. She knew it was still too soon for the man the British would be sending out to meet her to have arrived in Italy, but she switched on her phone just in case. Almost immediately it emitted the double-tone that indicated receipt of a message.

As she read it, Raya paled. She hadn't expected that level of surveillance, that quickly. She just thanked her lucky stars that she'd found Mario and managed to get out of Rome the previous night, because if she'd still been there the Russians and the Italian *carabinieri* would almost certainly have been able to find her. But she'd still have to be very careful, and Mario would now have to stick to the back roads.

She switched off the mobile, reached over, took a slightly dog-eared road atlas from the glovebox and started studying it.

A few moments later, Mario sat down beside her and started the engine. He drove out of the car park, and then threaded his way through the streets of Piombino, heading towards the main road which ran northbound along the west coast of Italy. Livorno, which had been the port for the Renaissance cities of Pisa and Florence, lay about fifty miles ahead of them, and Genoa over a hundred miles beyond that.

'It's quite a long way,' Raya remarked, as she calculated the distances in her head.

'Yes, but the roads are good,' Mario replied, 'so it shouldn't take us too long to get there. We can take the autostrada.'

'Actually,' Raya said, 'would you mind if we didn't? This is such a beautiful part of Italy that I'd like to follow the country roads and see a bit more of the countryside.'

'The autostrada's much quicker,' Mario pointed out.

'I know, Mario, but it's soulless and boring. Please, let's take the prettier route.'

'Whatever you like.' He grinned at her. 'But I don't really know this area, so you'll have to navigate, OK?'

'No problem.'

The obvious route up to Livorno was to follow the coast road, so Raya immediately directed Mario onto a spider's web of country roads that lay between the coast and the autostrada running right past Sienna.

They drove through tiny villages whose picturesque names evoked the spirit of Tuscany, like Frassine, Serrazzano and Fatagliano. Some were little more than hamlets, strung along roads so narrow that in some stretches the only way two vehicles could get by each other was to use special passing places.

It was a slow and sometimes irritating route because of the condition of the roads, but they didn't see a single police officer or anything else that might give Raya any concern, and that was far more important to her than their speed of progress.

By midday they'd reached a place called Calamecca, near the town of Pistoia and north-west of Florence. There they stopped for a bite of lunch at a small cafe.

'It's certainly pretty, going this way,' Mario admitted, digging his fork into a plate of *tagliatelle carbonara*, 'but we could have been in Genoa by now if we'd taken the autostrada.'

Raya nodded. 'But I'm really enjoying the journey,' she said, 'and I'm in no hurry.'

'And who is he, this man you're going to meet in Genoa?' he probed.

'He's only a business associate,' Raya said, which she thought probably sounded rather vague, but nevertheless contained an element of truth.

'And will you want me to wait for you there, in case he doesn't show up?'

Raya shook her head. 'Thank you, Mario, but no. He will definitely be there.' At least she could be sure about that. Whoever the British had decided to send would certainly turn up at their rendezvous. 'All I ask is that you get me to Genoa, or at least to somewhere fairly close by. Then I'll be fine, and thank you again.'

'I just wish we could have one more night together.' Mario gave a wistful smile.

'So am I, and I'm sorry, but I explained all that this morning. We've had a great time together, and we'll part as good friends.'

'Will you ever come back to Italy?'

'Maybe,' Raya said, with a slight smile of her own. 'Who knows?'

They were back in the car twenty minutes later, Raya planning the next part of their route north.

Sluzhba Vneshney Razvyedki Rossi Headquarters, Yasenevo, Tëplyystan, Moscow

Major Yuri Abramov leant back in his seat, still staring at the computer screen. What he'd just read – and what Zharkov, still sitting beside him, had read – was simply unbelievable.

He'd guessed that Raya's message might contain a list of excuses, of reasons, or her personal justification for deciding to betray the SVR's – and thus his own – trust in her, and to flee to the West. But that wasn't what he'd read here, for her message claimed that she hadn't actually defected at all. When Zharkov read that passage he'd snorted in total disbelief. But when he looked at the next section his brows furrowed with concern.

What Raya Kosov was claiming was that she'd fled for her life, not for asylum. She had, she said, detected the presence of a traitor within the SVR data system: somebody in a senior position who was accessing highly classified files and illegally copying them, presumably to sell the contents to Western intelligence agencies. And she believed that this unknown traitor now knew that she'd discovered what he was doing, and had already tried to kill her.

She claimed she'd been crossing the street near her apartment, when a man in a car had quite deliberately tried to run her down. The vehicle had suddenly mounted the pavement and she'd only jumped to safety at the last possible moment. She'd been far too shocked to note its registration number, only that it was a small dark-grey car – a description fitting most of the vehicles in Moscow – with a single occupant.

'Treacherous bitch,' Zharkov muttered.

'You don't believe her claim?' Abramov asked.

'Of course not.' Zharkov looked at him sharply. 'She's just offering a lame excuse for her own defection. You'll note that nowhere in this message does she ever mention returning to Russia. That bitch knows exactly what she's guilty of, and she's just trying to muddy the waters with this ridiculous and spurious claim of hers.'

'But she's very specific about what she claims to have found,' Abramov gestured to the text of the email still on the screen. 'Surely it wouldn't hurt to at least investigate what she's saying?'

The bulk of her message, in fact, was an extract from the security report Raya had been instructed to carry out by Abramov, and which she had placed in his safe before leaving Yasenevo for the last time. The major had instructed her to check a random-selection of a hundred files classified Secret or below, and then to inspect the access records of at least ten per cent of them. That had revealed no anomalies. But she'd also checked the access history, since the last full review, of every file classified Top Secret or above and that had thrown up an oddity which Raya claimed she'd started to investigate.

A total of fifteen Top Secret files had clearly been accessed, but all record of that access had then apparently been removed, so she had no idea which officer was responsible. She had only detected this intrusion because, on each of the files she'd checked, the date and time of the last access was recorded, and on those particular files the time stamp didn't match the last time actually recorded in the access record – which had to mean somebody had tampered with it.

That, Raya explained in her email, didn't really make sense, because whoever had looked at the file clearly possessed the correct security clearance, otherwise he wouldn't have been able to open it. And if he had the right clearance, why did he then try to cover his tracks? The evidence only made sense in one context: the perpetrator didn't want anyone to know he'd looked at the files, because he was doing something with the information they contained, and that suggested some form of espionage.

Then Raya claimed to have inspected the communication records, purely as another obvious check she could carry out, and had found an anomaly there as well. Several lengthy calls had been made over the last three months from an office in Yasenevo to a Moscow number. The problem was that the office in question was unlocked, unoccupied and not assigned to anyone, so she had no idea who had been responsible for these calls. And when she then tried to run a check on the Moscow number, it was unlisted.

She'd gone into the vacant office to look around, but found nothing. As Raya had emerged, she noticed a figure at the far end of the corridor, apparently watching her, but too far away to identify. And it was that same evening, just before she got home, that the attempt on her life had taken place. Whoever was driving the car had clearly had access to her personnel records at Yasenevo, in order to have discovered her address, and that meant the treachery must reach into the highest levels of the SVR, and this was what Raya claimed had made her decide to run.

'There's a lot of information here,' Abramov repeated. 'Prudence dictates that we at least check what she's saying.'

'That would be a complete waste of time and effort,' Zharkov snapped. 'And it would also divert our attention from the main task, which is finding Kosov and dragging her back here. In this matter, "prudence", as you put it, is whatever *I* decide to do.' He jabbed a finger at the computer screen. 'This is pure fiction, none of it ever happened. Look at the inconsistencies. She decides to look in the empty office, and the supposed traitor just happens to be in a position to see her? Rubbish. And if there really was an attempt to run her down outside her apartment, the driver obviously had to know where she lived, so why didn't he enter the building and finish the job?

'No, none of this is real. It's just Kosov trying to sow doubts in our minds over her own treachery. But I promise you this. When we've got her strapped naked on a table in the basement of the Lubyanka, with electrodes hitched to her nipples and vagina, if she's still able to claim that all this really took place, then I might have some further checks run.'

Abramov felt a chill run down his spine as he listened, because he knew Zharkov was absolutely serious. If his minions did manage to find her, and brought her back to Moscow alive, Raya would end her short life in one of the sound-proof cellars in the Lubyanka, begging for a quick death.

Nervi, Italy

'This will be fine,' said Raya, as Mario pulled the Fiat to a stop close to the centre of a small seaside resort.

They'd driven through the place once already, Raya keeping a sharp lookout for signs of hostile activity, but the village appeared totally normal and unthreatening, It was simply a typical Italian seaside community, and she just hoped that, thanks to Mario and their 'arrangement', she'd managed to travel further and faster than the Russian security personnel would have expected.

The large piazza situated near the centre would be ideal as a rendezvous, and all around there were plenty of cafes, bars and shops she could duck into, if she needed to.

'Are you sure, Raya?'

'Absolutely.' She leant across to him and kissed him firmly on the lips. 'Thank you for everything, Mario. It's been a great weekend, and I'm really glad we met up. Now, please go.'

The Italian still looked unhappy as Raya grabbed her bag and opened the passenger door.

'You'll be OK?' he asked. 'This is the right place?'

'I'll be fine.' Raya nodded. 'I've two small final favours to ask you, though,' she said.

'Anything. Just name it.'

'First, don't believe everything you read in the papers or see on television. Second, don't tell anyone you saw me.'

'What?' Mario's face clouded. 'I don't understand.'

'You will, Mario, you will. Just remember what I said. Now, goodbye, and thanks again for everything.' She closed the door firmly and stepped back onto the pavement.

The Italian stared at her for a few more seconds, his expression troubled, then he gave her a smile and a wave. As he drove away slowly down the street, Raya gave him a final wave, then she turned away, choking back a sob. Mario was a decent human being, and she just hoped that this fleeting contact wouldn't land him in trouble with the *carabinieri* or, much worse, with the Russians.

She checked behind her once more, but the Fiat had disappeared. Now she had her own preparations to make. There were numerous tourist shops nearby, and she picked the largest one she could find, relying on the number of people milling about inside. As she rummaged around the racks of clothing and accessories, she was very conscious that she had extremely limited funds. But she bought a cavernous white shoulder bag to replace the one she was carrying – the same overnight bag that must have given her away at the airport.

Then she picked out a large floppy-brimmed hat that would completely overshadow her face, and the biggest and darkest pair of sunglasses on the rack. After checking the prices of the items she'd selected, she decided she could just about afford a light jacket as well. Together, these purchases would radically change her appearance – to the extent, she hoped, that nobody would be able to recognize her.

After that she walked around the town until she found a crowded cafe, realizing that safety lay in numbers. She ordered a *caffè latte* and took just a few sips, then headed for the toilets at the rear. A few minutes later she emerged, in a change of jacket, and with her overnight bag wadded up inside the new shoulder bag. As expected, nobody at the bar gave her transformation a second look.

When she'd finished the coffee, she opened the bag, pulled out the new hat and sunglasses and, with a muttered *grazie* to the barman, walked outside. On a quiet side street, she tossed her overnight bag into a rubbish bin, then walked slowly on through the neighbouring Piazza Centrale, working out the details of the crucial rendezvous.

A few minutes later she turned on her mobile and nodded when she saw a message from the British man who'd been sent to meet her. Immediately she composed her reply and pressed the Send button. When that was done, she turned off the phone, well aware that, as long as it was switched on, her position would be announced to anyone with access to the cellular service provider. With the power off, on the other hand, she was invisible.

Then there was nothing else she could do until the rendezvous time arrived, so she continued to wander the streets like a window-shopper. But all the while she was looking out for any possible problems, like a car full of *carabinieri* with copies of her photograph, while making sure she learned the layout of the town as accurately as possible. For her life might depend on knowing the fastest way out of it.

Chapter Eighteen

Sunday
Southern France

The shortest route to Genoa would have taken Richter due east from Ax-les-Thermes over to the Mediterranean coast, but he'd never even considered that route. It would have meant keeping on minor roads, with numerous climbs and descents, and Richter needed speed now if he was going to make the rendezvous. So he had headed north out of Ax, and through Foix, taking the tunnel there to avoid the town centre, and then picked up the new autoroute spur near Pamiers. That took him north-east to the Autoroute du Sud, the main route east from Toulouse to the Mediterranean coast near Narbonne.

He passed the impressively massive walls of the fortress of Carcassonne, and vowed that one day he'd come back there and take a look around – when he wasn't carrying a pistol in a shoulder holster on his way to meet a Russian defector, and possibly about to tangle with numerous SVR-sanctioned assassins.

At Narbonne he turned left, and settled down to covering the remaining distance as quickly as he could. He kept the Ford at between one hundred and forty and one hundred and fifty kilometres per hour – round about ninety miles an hour – which was above the posted speed limit, but not enormously so. The French helpfully placed large warning signs before every static radar trap, so he was able to ease off the accelerator as he went past, but he still kept his eyes open for the mobile units. They had a tendency to hide their vehicles off to the side of the autoroute and place only a tiny tripod-mounted radar gun on the hard shoulder. Those devices took some spotting.

Richter wasn't worried about getting stopped by the gendarmes, because his diplomatic passport would ensure his being able to drive on within minutes, but he didn't need even that amount of delay. And he particularly didn't want some French police officer spotting the pistol he was carrying. Diplomatic passport or not, it would require some explaining, so he kept his eyes open.

Somewhere near Montpellier, he pulled into a service area, filled up the Ford's tank, then ate a pre-packed chicken sandwich and swallowed a cup of instant coffee bought from a machine near the toilets. That was to be his lunch, consumed in under ten minutes. Then he got back on the road again.

He passed Nîmes, Arles and Aix-en-Provence, and bypassed Marseilles, the autoroute continuing east through spectacular hills and valleys lying north of Toulon, before dropping back down almost to sea level near Fréjus. By mid-afternoon, Richter was following the autoroute that ran to the north of the playgrounds of Cannes and Antibes, and then on through Nice and Monaco.

Just after three-thirty he entered Italy east of Menton, barely slowing down even as he crossed the border. He was now into the province of Liguria, which gave its name to the sea lying immediately to the south. A quick glance at the map showed him how the autoroute – now an autostrada – hugged the coast all the way to Genoa, still about one hundred miles ahead. It was time to make contact with Yuri, and also with Colin Dekker, who should be somewhere behind him.

Richter pulled into the next service area, topped up the Ford's tank yet again, and took the opportunity for another coffee. Then he prepared a text for Yuri, telling the renegade Russian that he was currently near San Remo, and only about an hour from Genoa itself. He had no idea when Yuri would read this message, but it would remain in cyberspace until the Russian next decided to turn on his phone. Richter explained that he would stop somewhere near the outskirts of Genoa and wait there for a text containing details of the meeting place and time.

Next he called Dekker's mobile, which rang about half a dozen times before it was answered, so Richter guessed the SAS officer must be on the road somewhere.

'Yup?'

'It's Richter. Where are you?'

'About five miles west of Cannes. Where are you?'

'I've just crossed the Italian border, so I guess I'm about thirty miles ahead of you. I've stopped in a service area and just sent a text to our mutual friend.'

'You want to hang on there until I reach you, then we can sort everything out?'

Richter glanced at his watch. 'Yeah, why not? I'll be in the cafe, checking if Italian coffee is any better than the muck they serve in France.'

*

Just under half an hour later, Colin Dekker entered the service area cafe, bought himself a drink and a sandwich, then walked over to Richter's table and sat down opposite him.

'Apart from one fill-up, I've not stopped since leaving Toulouse,' Dekker explained, ripping open the plastic to get at the sandwich inside. 'So I really need this: an Italian sarnie and a cup of hot brown whatever.'

'What's it supposed to be?' Richter was peering at the cup Dekker had placed on their table.

'I think I asked for coffee, but my Italian is pretty non-existent, so for all I know it could be oxtail soup.'

Dekker chewed contentedly for a couple of minutes, then brushed some crumbs off the table and tried a sip.

'Yup, coffee, and not that bad, either. Right, what's the plan, boss?'

Richter shook his head. 'Until we know what Yuri's got planned, I don't have any real idea. And, anyway, I wouldn't like to think I'm in charge of this little shindig. It's really more your area of expertise than mine.'

Dekker grinned at him. 'Maybe,' he replied, 'maybe not. You've done OK so far, I reckon, but whatever may happen in Genoa, we can already make some assumptions. Yuri will want to check you out, just to make sure you're not one of the spooks on that list he got from Legoland. That means the meet will take place in the open, probably somewhere very public – lots of people, lots of traffic. My guess is that he'll want to get you sitting on a bench or, better still, at an outside table of a cafe, so that he'll be able to watch you, first from a distance, or maybe walk past two or three times to inspect you real close.'

Dekker glanced round, checking that no one else was within earshot. 'Now that's both a help and a hindrance. An open urban space means I should be able to find somewhere high up, maybe a rooftop or a balcony, where I can cover the whole area around you. The weapon's fitted with a suppressor, so if I do have to get involved, nobody will know I'm there except you and whoever takes the bullet. Until the blood starts spreading, it'll look like he's just fainted or something, so you and Yuri will be able to thin out without anyone being any the wiser.'

He paused, then continued. 'That's the good news, then. The bad news is that, if the area's really crowded, my biggest problem's going to be identifying the bad guys. You and I can't be linked by radio, because that would only worry Yuri. You're supposed to be meeting him solo, so an earpiece and lapel mike would definitely cause problems. In a crowded place my big problem would be trying to decide which of the couple of hundred people wandering about below me is a Russian hit-man.'

'The picture you're painting doesn't exactly fill me with confidence,' Richter remarked.

'Facts of life time. That's the reality of the situation, or it might be, depending on whatever plan Yuri's busy cooking up. Otherwise, what's your intention, in general terms? Identify Yuri and then head for the hills with him?'

'Pretty much, yes.' Richter nodded. 'All Simpson's interested in is getting Yuri off the streets and safely over to the UK. He's prepared to lay on an RAF jet or just about anything else that I ask for, just to make sure that happens.'

'He must want Yuri very badly, so really this whole thing should be pretty simple. Yuri isn't going to show at all unless he's managed to avoid the Russian wet brigade. On the other hand, nobody can be following you or me, because nobody knows who the hell we are. So once Yuri's happy that you're not a spook, and that you're on your own – I'll be out of sight, of course – he should just identify himself to you, and then we're out of there.'

'Sounds like a plan,' Richter agreed.

Five minutes later, his phone emitted a muted double-tone, then repeated it.

'Yuri?' Dekker asked.

'Probably.' Richter took the phone from his jacket pocket and peered at the screen. 'No, actually, it's Simpson.' He scanned the few lines of text. 'He wants to know where we are, and what's happening.'

'You can let him wait. You've got nothing to tell him anyway.'

Richter put the phone on the table, but almost immediately its message tone sounded again.

This time, it was indeed Yuri. Richter read the message, then slid the phone across the table to Dekker. The text was fairly short and very much to the point.

Nervi. 1823. Cafe Belvedere. Piazza Centrale.
Outside. Red umbrella.1839. Fallback +60.
C: Is there a good hotel in this town? R: You
could try the Consul. I'm staying there.

'This guy sounds good,' Dekker remarked. 'Professional, too. He's telling you all the right things, and he's not making silly mistakes like arranging a meet on the hour or the half hour. You probably know what he means anyway, but let me just talk you through it. The rendezvous will be in a town or village called Nervi, which I guess is somewhere near Genoa. The meet will take place at the Café Belvedere, and you're to sit down at a table outside at exactly twenty-three minutes past six. If for any reason you don't make the RV by the first time suggested, the fallback time will be exactly one hour later. The exact timing is so that Yuri will be able to recognize you. Your confirming ident feature will be that you'll be carrying a red umbrella. There are some in the motorists' shop over there: I noticed them on the way in. At twenty-one minutes to seven, Yuri will sit down at your table, or maybe at the one next to it. That will obviously depend on how busy the cafe is. He may well say a few words to you: "Is this seat taken?" or something like that, but the challenge phrase will be "Is there a good hotel in this town?" so that's what you have to listen for. And once he says that, you reply "You could try the Consul. I'm staying there". That completes the challenge and response. If all that works, you get up, put Yuri in your car, and drive away.

'Now this bit's important, so listen carefully. As long as you're satisfied that Yuri's the real deal, and that it's all clear and nobody's watching you, take the umbrella with you when you stand up. If not, just leave it on the table, and I'll take out anyone I see following you. I won't try to follow you myself, because it might spook him if he spots my car, but I'll be on the end of my mobile if you need help. It's probably best, though, if you don't call me or Simpson until Yuri's sitting in a

Hercules or something en route to Northolt – just in case he thinks you're trying to set up an ambush somewhere. Are you clear on all that?'

'Pretty much.' Richter nodded, and glanced at his watch. 'Now we need to get moving, find out where the hell this place Nervi is. And I've got a red umbrella to buy.'

'I'll head off.' Dekker stood up and thrust out his hand. 'It'll take me a while to scope out the place, check the angles, and set up my perch. Good luck, Paul.'

Five minutes later, Richter tossed a red compact umbrella onto the passenger seat of his hired Ford, and pulled out the road atlas. He opened it at the page that showed Genoa, and quickly scanned the area around the city. He spotted Nervi almost immediately, a small town or maybe just a village situated on the coast just to the south-east of Genoa itself. He'd have to get through Genoa first, and he'd probably be reaching the city at about the time of the evening rush hour, but he guessed it would still only take him just over an hour to get to the destination Yuri had specified. And there was always a fallback rendezvous time, if he didn't manage it quickly enough.

Palazzo Margherita, Via Vittorio Veneto, Rome, Italy

'There've been no other sightings of this woman?' John Westwood asked.

Clayton Richards shook his head. 'None that we're aware of. The last time anyone saw her for sure is when someone, presumably Kosov, boosted that scooter from the Italian girl.'

'So what are the Russians doing?'

'They still have teams covering the airports and railway stations, but with a much reduced presence now. I think they know she's slipped through the net, and they're just covering their asses in case she surfaces again in Rome. But I'm pretty sure she's long gone. She probably took a coach out of Rome that first day, before the Russkies could deploy the extra manpower Moscow sent over here.'

'Have your watchers been able to identify any of the new faces?'

'A couple,' Richards said. 'The two we made positively were middle seniority SVR officers, and one of them is believed to be a part of Spetsgruppa Zaslon, though we have no way of confirming that without access to the personnel files at Yasenevo.'

'And maybe not even then,' Westwood remarked. 'We're not even sure that the officers seconded to Zaslon have that fact recorded anywhere, because it's a real covert operation, even within the SVR. But your analysis is that they're kill teams?'

Richards nodded. 'If they can't find her and take her alive, they'll just kill her, yes. There's not much doubt about that. Our watchers suggest that almost a hundred men have now been sent out from Moscow, and they sure haven't come here for the coffee or the ice cream.'

'Agreed.'

Westwood got up and walked over to the large map of Italy that dominated one wall of Richards's office. For a few moments he just stared at it, his fingers tracing the northern borders of the country.

'She won't try to get out at any seaport or airport,' he

mused. 'That'd be real stupid, especially after the Brits passed on our warning.'

'You told them what we found out?' Richards sounded surprised.

'Yes. They probably still don't know her name, because I didn't tell them, but I passed on what we discovered about the Russians' search tactics.'

'And they've told Kosov? How?'

'I don't know but, if we've guessed this right, they have to be in contact with her somehow. A mobile, maybe, or emails – something like that. The point is, I told them what we knew, and if there's anybody competent at SIS – and there will be – they'll have got the information to her somehow. So the real question is: how's she going to get out of Italy? It's got to be in a car or on a motorbike and I don't think she'd risk public transport, so I guess she's either stolen or hired something.'

Westwood turned back to the map and again studied the northern border. Then he tapped the area to the west of Ljubljana, the capital of Croatia.

'I'm pretty sure she won't run that way, and I also doubt if she'll try crossing the Swiss border, because there she'd have to produce her passport, and the Russians will have notified the Swiss that she's a wanted fugitive.'

'So it must be France or Austria,' said Richards, walking over to stand beside him and examine the map. 'Those are the only two countries left, so which one do you reckon she'll choose?'

'It could be either, but my guess is France. It's a huge country, and she'd find it real easy to lose herself there. And she'd only have one border to get over, too – apart from the Channel crossing to Britain.'

'So what can we do?' Richards asked. 'It's a border, about a hundred and fifty miles long, and she could decide to cross it pretty much anywhere. On any available roads, I mean. Otherwise, a lot of the terrain is really mountainous, because of the Alps, and those areas wouldn't be easily passable.'

'I think we need some help from above,' Westwood decided, 'and I'm not talking about God. Get me a line to Langley.'

Sluzhba Vneshney Razvyedki Rossi Headquarters, Yasenevo, Tëplyystan, Moscow

Major Yuri Abramov had made a decision. He still wasn't exactly sure of the game Raya had been playing, or how seriously he – or the higher echelons of the SVR – should be taking her claim to have discovered a potential traitor at Yasenevo. But he was certain that there must be an investigation, which was something that Colonel Zharkov seemed peculiarly reluctant to agree to.

He also knew that the only way to start the ball rolling was to go over Zharkov's head, and he had little doubt how the colonel would react if he did. But he felt he owed Raya that much and, being network manager, he did have a channel he could use. Because of the crucial importance of database security on the Yasenevo computer system, he was authorized to contact the most senior security officer directly, bypassing all the normal bureaucratic channels of communication.

All he needed was access to a computer, and now

Zharkov had left the office for a few minutes, he had the chance he needed.

Quickly, Abramov opened his internal email account, selected the correct address, security classification and routing priority, and typed a five-line message. When he'd finished, he paused for a few seconds to check what he'd written. Then, just as he heard footsteps approaching down the corridor, he pressed the Send button, and watched as the message vanished from his screen.

Palazzo Margherita, Via Vittorio Veneto, Rome, Italy

Just over half an hour later, Westwood replaced the phone.

'Success?' Richards asked.

'Yes.' Westwood nodded. 'Langley will be making a formal request to the NRO for all of the "Advanced Crystal" birds – the KH-12 satellites – to concentrate on northern Italy during their next passes, and until further notice.'

Located in Chantilly, Virginia, the National Reconnaissance Office was responsible for designing, building, and operating all the spy satellites sanctioned by the United States government. The designation 'KH-12' given to the Advanced Crystal vehicles – also known as 'Ikon', 'Improved Kennan' or 'Key Hole' – was unofficial. Paranoid about security, the NRO now allocated a random-number designation to the satellites it controlled, following repeated press and media references to earlier vehicles in the 'KH' series. The final known official use of the 'KH' designation was the KH-11 Kennan satellite series, the last one of which, KH-11/10, was launched on 1 March 1990 as part of the STS-36 mission of the Space Shuttle *Atlantis*. The very first KH-12 launch was by Titan IV rocket from Vandenberg Air Force Base on 28 November 1992, and the last known vehicle in the series, still in orbit, was KH-12/6, launched on 19 October 2005 from the same location.

'So we have a handful of birds in orbit,' Richards observed, doubt evident in his voice. 'I'm not sure how much use a bunch of satellites a couple of hundred miles up is going to be if we're looking for one woman on the ground somewhere in Italy.'

'It won't be,' Westwood said, 'but what they *will* do is allow us to see any incidents that take place on the border without having to rely on your contacts in the *carabinieri* to tell us about them. That's only as long as one of the Ikon birds is within range, obviously. And if we do see anything happening that looks interesting, I've got a U2 sitting on the ground at Aviano ready to launch at fifteen minutes' notice. It's a NASA cab that's over here to do high-level atmospheric sampling, but it's still got all its cameras installed, and they're dry rather than wet, so it can send the images direct into the TDRSS network. That means Langley will receive them within minutes, and can then squirt them straight over here.'

The Tracking and Data Relay Satellite System network was a system of communication satellites designed to transfer data from surveillance vehicles – which might currently be on the opposite side of the planet to the United States – to American ground stations as quickly as possible.

'Pretty impressive stuff, bearing in mind that Kosov is clearly defecting to the British rather than to us. Just glad I'm not picking up the tab for that lot. But you really think she's important enough to justify all this?'

Westwood grinned at him. 'If she can give us an inside line into Yasenevo, then definitely. The British must be satisfied with her dowry, otherwise they wouldn't even be trying to get her out of Italy.'

'But I thought you said they'd denied all knowledge of her?'

'They did, and that's why I'm sure they're doing whatever they can to find her before the Russian hit squads do. Just in case we can pick her up before the Brits get their act together, I've also got a Lear 60 on its way over here. That'll land at Fiumicino this evening, and it'll wait there until further notice.'

He picked up the phone. 'I think it's time to talk to the Brits again – just to register our interest, as it were.'

Chapter Nineteen

Sunday
Nervi, Italy

The Café Belvedere was located in the Piazza Centrale, a reasonably large open space with a street running through the middle. Close to the centre of the small town, it was more or less surrounded by three- and four-storey buildings, which were a mix of commercial and residential properties. Colin Dekker had parked his car in a side street about a hundred yards away from the square, and then carried out a quick surveillance as he checked possible firing angles.

The buildings around the square were too close together for his liking, but a street that opened up on one side of the piazza offered quite a clear view of the Café Belvedere itself. He strolled along it and quickly picked out one building that looked the most promising. It was an old and somewhat battered three-storey residential block, containing probably four apartments per floor, and with an open roof where the residents could hang out their washing. As he eyed the top of the building, he could see the edge of a blue sheet flapping in the light wind that was blowing off the Gulf of Genoa.

It was probably his best option, so Dekker strode confidently along the pavement and entered the building through its unlocked main door. There was no lift, so he took the stairs. Behind another door, on the top landing, he found a narrow flight of stairs leading upwards to the roof.

Half a dozen washing lines were strung between upright steel posts, and a low parapet extended around the edge of the roof, about three feet high. In one corner stood a small stone-built shed with a steel door and two windows. Peering through one of the windows, Dekker could see ladders, scaffold poles, paint pots and other equipment, so presumably it was used for storing materials for maintenance of the building.

More importantly, the space between one side of the shed and the parapet offered an excellent view of most of the piazza at the far end of the street. He could see the whole of the Café Belvedere, and for a reasonable distance to either side of it. It was probably as good a vantage point as he was likely to find.

Dekker took the stairs down to the street, and returned to his car. He glanced at his watch and found he had almost an hour before the time specified for the rendezvous, and there was no point in getting into position too early, because that meant there was more chance of somebody spotting him.

He looked round, saw another cafe about fifty yards down the road, walked across to it and ordered something to eat by pointing at a colour picture on the wall behind the bar. Then he picked a table allowing him a view of his car, and with one eye on his watch settled down to eat his early dinner.

*

Paul Richter entered Nervi at just after six that evening, and spotted the Café Belvedere as he drove through the Piazza Centrale. There were parking places on the street, but he didn't stop immediately. Instead he drove on for another hundred yards, until he was able to turn round and retrace his route. Then he pulled in about fifty yards away from the piazza, with the vehicle facing in the same direction he'd come from, which was the best way to get out of the town in a hurry.

He checked his watch: 6.17 p.m. Six minutes to go. He hoped Dekker was already in position, and watching his back, because pretty much all he could achieve in six minutes was get his bearings. He glanced round, making sure that he was unobserved, pulled out the Browning Hi-Power and checked that it was loaded with a full magazine, a bullet in the chamber and with the safety catch on, then replaced it in the shoulder holster.

He got out of the car, locked it and walked back to the Piazza Centrale, and past the Café Belvedere, trying to spot anything that might suggest trouble.

At 6.20, he turned back. The cafe seemed to be doing quite good business, but there were still a couple of vacant tables outside. He strolled along the pavement towards it, and at exactly 6.23 he pulled back one of the plastic chairs and sat down. As he did so, he reached into his jacket pocket and pulled out the red umbrella he'd bought earlier and placed it on the table in front of him. And then there was nothing more he could do except wait for Yuri to turn up – assuming he hadn't already been grabbed by the Russians or the Italians, of course.

After about five minutes a waiter appeared beside him. Richter ordered a *caffè latte* and a glass of water, having memorized the correct phrases from a guidebook he'd bought. When the waiter returned, he paid him immediately, which would allow him to leave as soon as he wanted.

Richter kept his eyes open, looking all around the piazza for anyone who might be observing him, but saw nothing. Nobody appeared to have the slightest interest in him or what he was doing there. He wondered inconsequentially just how accurate Yuri's watch was. Would the Russian really bail out if Richter had been a minute or two early or late? Then he dismissed the thought. As long as he stuck to the recognition signals, this should work. Yuri *needed* him to be there.

Richter pulled back his jacket cuff and glanced at his watch: 6.38. If Yuri was going to make it to the rendezvous, he needed to appear within the next minute. Richter glanced casually around the piazza. There was a girl – rather, a young woman – standing beside a shop over on one side, peering in the window, and a couple of men talking together in loud Italian perhaps twenty yards away. But he saw nobody who looked even slightly like a renegade Russian clerk.

He shifted focus, glancing up at the buildings that surrounded the piazza, wondering exactly which of them Colin Dekker had picked as his vantage point. He was still looking the other way when he heard a chair scraping across the cobbles by his table, and he glanced back.

The young woman who'd been window-shopping was now standing beside the table, one hand resting on the back of the chair she'd pulled out from under it.

'Is this seat taken?' she asked him, in slightly accented English.

'No, but—' Richter started to say, but she interrupted him.

'Good,' she said. 'I hate drinking alone, even if it's just a coffee.'

Richter looked up at her and shrugged, then checked his watch again: 6.40. It looked as if Yuri was a no-show, but at least the girl looked as if she might be pleasant enough company for a few minutes – before he called Simpson to let him know the operation was a bust.

'How did you know I was English?' he asked.

The girl gazed at him, her eyes all but invisible behind her huge sunglasses, and smiled.

'Somehow, you just looked English,' she replied, 'and who but an Englishman would carry an umbrella on such a beautiful day?' She indicated the compact red umbrella lying on the table in front of him. 'Though I wouldn't have thought red was exactly your colour.'

'Good deduction.' He smiled back at her. 'But that umbrella was the only one I could find.'

The girl nodded, then glanced up as a waiter materialized. She ordered a coffee, then turned back to Richter. 'I rather like this place,' she said. 'So I wonder if you can help me. Do you know, is there a good hotel in this town?'

To his credit, Richter didn't react. He just lowered his glass of *caffè latte* to its saucer and glanced round casually before replying. 'You could try the Consul,' he said. 'I'm staying there.'

The girl's smile widened. 'I'm glad that's over,' she said.

Richter leaned forward and spoke in a low voice. 'If your name really is Yuri, and you're a man, I'm going to have to make some fundamental changes to my sex life.'

The girl laughed. 'No, Yuri was just a convenience, and a way of adding another layer of anonymity. My name is Raya. Raya Kosov.'

'Pleased to meet you, Raya. I'm Paul Richter.'

'Richter? Like a judge in German?'

Richter nodded. 'Same spelling, but I'm English, as you guessed.'

'Who do you work for?'

'Right now,' he said, 'I'm not entirely sure. I'm ex-military. I was a Sea Harrier pilot in the Royal Navy, and then I was recruited as a kind of international courier. But right now I'm sort of on loan to an outfit that works with the Secret Intelligence Service.'

Raya visibly tensed, and Richter guessed that, under her calm and friendly exterior, she was almost frantic with concern. He raised his hand reassuringly. 'But you don't need to worry,' he went on. 'I'm not, and never have been, a part of the SIS. That explains why I'm here.'

'Are you alone?'

'No, we're being watched by an officer from the Special Air Service, which is part of our special forces. He's been sent to make sure nobody interrupts this meeting, or tries to follow us.'

'Where is he?' Raya asked.

'I've no idea. Probably high up, maybe on the roof of one of these buildings, and armed with a sniper rifle. And I'm armed as well, so I reckon you're quite safe now. You got my message about the extreme measures the Russians have put in place to find you?'

'Yes, and thank you for that. I was lucky I got out of Rome as quickly as I did. That way I think I was ahead of the pursuit. So what now? What are your orders regarding us?'

'Simple. I've been told to get you to London by whatever route and method I choose. And, the way things are looking at the moment, that means by car, at least until we get out of Italy, because every possible form of public transport is being watched. There might also be a problem at whatever border we cross, but we'll tackle that one when we get to it.'

'So who else will know how we are travelling, and what route we're taking?'

'Just you and me,' Richter said, 'and the SAS officer if we think we need him along as well, for protection and another pair of eyes. Nobody else.'

'And he's good, is he, this man from Hereford?' Raya asked.

Richter was slightly surprised that she knew where the SAS Regiment was based, but then realized Raya would probably have had access to files containing exhaustive information about all branches of the British armed forces.

'I think so, yes,' he said. 'I trust him, anyway.'

'That's good,' Raya said, her voice suddenly sounding concerned, 'because I think we're going to need him. Where's your car now? Don't point, just tell me.'

'In the street directly behind me,' Richter said, renewed worry flooding through him. Something was clearly wrong, and he didn't know what. 'It's a Ford Focus, on Austrian plates.'

Raya leaned forward, in the action of a lover rather than a conspirator, placed her face against his and whispered in his ear. 'There are two men watching us from the far side of the square, right behind you. Side by side, with dark suits and black hair. I'm sure they didn't follow me here, so they must have been tailing you. Unless you already know who they are.'

'Not me,' Richter said. 'And, as far as I know, nobody followed me either. Are you sure they're watching *us*?'

'It definitely looks like it. Somehow they've found us, but at the moment they're just looking, so maybe they're waiting for orders – or waiting for us to set off down a quiet street, where they can snatch us. Perhaps this place is a bit too public for them to grab us. Give me the car keys, and we'll leave separately. I'll go first and wait by the car, then you follow in about half a minute.'

Raya pulled back, looked Richter in the eyes, and gave a slight smile. 'It's been nice knowing you,' she said, 'and here's something to remember me by.' She kissed him full on the lips, then took the keys he'd pulled from his pocket. She stepped back and walked away, heading for the parked Ford.

Richter turned his chair slightly so that he could now see the other side of the piazza, immediately spotting the two men Raya had described. They'd both stepped forward and were heading across the square, obviously to follow her. Their jackets were unbuttoned, which suggested both of them were carrying weapons in shoulder holsters.

He made an immediate decision, and just hoped Dekker could clearly see what he was now doing. He picked up the red umbrella, then very deliberately replaced it on the table, then turned on his heel and walked briskly after Raya.

*

Colin Dekker had watched Richter's encounter with the unknown woman with a wry smile. Either 'Yuri' was a girl, he decided, or the Russian defector had already been picked up somewhere and Richter had just got lucky.

But after the girl left, and Richter picked up the umbrella and then put it down again, Dekker knew something was wrong. He widened his field of view, trying to see what had apparently alarmed them. He focused on the two men in dark suits almost immediately. They seemed to be heading after the girl, and as Richter, too, walked away from the cafe, they both broke into a run.

That was all Dekker needed to know. He lowered the stainless-steel barrel of the AWS rifle slightly, took careful aim and squeezed the trigger. The weapon kicked against his shoulder, but the crack of the shot was barely audible against the background noise of the town.

In the piazza, one of the running men stumbled and fell to the ground, both hands clutching his leg. His companion stopped immediately, pulled out a heavy-calibre semi-automatic pistol and spun round, looking for a target, while apparently talking to himself. Dekker realized he had a hidden lapel mike, and was either summoning help or just reporting in.

On the far side of the square, a dark-coloured saloon suddenly appeared, one occupant visible behind the wheel, and it raced across to the fallen man. As it stopped, the car was directly broadside on to Dekker's position, offering too good an opportunity to miss. He sighted again, the AWS sniper rifle cracked twice more, and both the tyres on the near side of the car blew in quick succession.

'Now get going, Paul,' he muttered, and quickly started to disassemble his weapon and pack it away.

Richter heard a scream of pain behind him as he reached the edge of the piazza and quickly glanced back to see one of the two men writhing in agony on the ground. Obviously Dekker had identified the danger and had done what he claimed to do best – shooting the bad guys.

When Richter reached the Ford Focus, the engine was running and the driver's door open. Raya had already moved to the passenger seat. He jumped in, slammed the door and pulled away from the kerb.

'I almost expected you to drive off before I got here,' he said, accelerating hard down the street.

'I can't drive,' Raya said simply, 'otherwise I might have done. But it looks like your friend did his job.'

'I told you I trusted him. Now, how did they find us? Are you *sure* nobody could have followed you?'

Raya shook her head. 'Obviously I can't be sure, but I don't think so. If they did manage to trace me here, to this town, why didn't they pick me up straight away? They've got no interest in you or your friend – or, at least, they didn't until he crippled one of them – so why did they wait until the two of us were sitting together in that square?'

For a few moments neither of them spoke, as Richter drove under the autostrada, staying on the minor roads.

'Where are you going?' Raya asked.

'Right now, I don't know,' Richter replied. 'Just getting away from Nervi, I suppose, and trying to make it as unpredictable as possible. If even *I* don't know where I'm going, nobody else can guess my destination.'

Raya glanced at him, her face still clouded with worry. 'Let's try and work it out,' she insisted. 'Who knew you were heading to Genoa to find me?'

'The SAS man, his name is Colin Dekker, me, obviously, and the senior guy who tasked me with this job. He's called Richard Simpson, and he's not an SIS officer. He heads his own separate operation.'

'Nobody else?'

Richter thought for a moment, recalling the circumstances of the moment when Simpson had briefed him, back in Ax-les-Thermes. Absolutely the only other person within earshot had been David Adamson, and he was one of Simpson's own men.

'One of Simpson's people was there as well,' he said finally, 'a man called Adamson. But I'm not even sure he could have heard Simpson while he was briefing me. Even so,' he continued, 'it couldn't have been Adamson, or in fact Simpson either, because all they knew was that the rendezvous would take place in Genoa or thereabouts. They didn't know specifically about Nervi, because I was already over the Italian border by the time you sent me that text message that specified the RV. The only people who knew *exactly* where and when I would meet you were Colin Dekker and me.'

'You didn't tell this Simpson man?'

'No.' Richter shook his head firmly. 'Just before you sent your text, Simpson sent me a message asking where I was, but I didn't reply to it. In fact, I still haven't.'

'That's it, then. There's only one possible explanation.'

'What?'

'It's your mobile. Somebody has to be tracking your mobile. Those men knew you were somewhere in Nervi. Triangulation from the cells would have located you somewhere in the piazza, but they wouldn't know exactly where. So they were probably watching all the single men, and waited until a woman approached one of them. That would have identified you – and therefore me too.'

Richter was silent, appreciating the grim and inescapable logic of what Raya had just said. And, so far, it was the only explanation that made sense.

'So who exactly knows your mobile phone number, Paul?'

Richter took the phone out of his pocket, quickly switched it off and tossed it on the back seat. Then he glanced back at Raya. 'Simpson gave it to me, so he obviously knows it, and Colin Dekker, because I used it to call him this afternoon. But I have no idea who else might know that number.'

Raya reached behind her to grab the phone, then she fiddled with the catch and removed the battery.

'Just in case there's a tracking chip or something inside,' she explained, examining the main circuit board that was now exposed.

'If there is, it might be worth hanging on to it,' Richter suggested. 'We can send the phone one way while we go the other. And I know what you're going to say next, how the two names that seem to keep on cropping up are Richard Simpson and Colin Dekker. Dekker is the man who's just shot someone back in Nervi, and then disabled their car, which is exactly why there's nobody following us right now. I've known him only a very short time, but his actions seem to me to speak for themselves.'

'And what about Simpson?'

'Richard Simpson is one of the most devious men I've ever met, and he's lied to me almost from the first moment I met him. But the strange thing is, that I think he's being straight, at least, over this.'

'But you can't be totally sure?' Raya persisted.

'No, I can't. And also Simpson told me he would personally arrange whatever transportation we needed – like an aircraft or something.'

'So we won't be travelling to Britain that way,' Raya said firmly.

'Absolutely not. We'll make our own way back. And I've got another idea that might help muddy the waters a bit, too.'

Dekker drove slowly out of Nervi, avoiding passing through the Piazza Centrale, now a scene of apparent chaos, and drove on through the outskirts of Genoa, retracing his previous route but avoiding the main roads. He concentrated on the traffic, watching his rear-view mirror for any signs of pursuit, while watching out for police or roadblocks on the road ahead. It would be a very bad idea to be stopped and have this car searched, because explaining away the Accuracy International AWS sniper rifle would be difficult, especially if somebody linked the presence of the rifle to the shooting in Nervi, then decided to carry out a ballistics test.

But most of all, he kept listening out for the sound of

his mobile phone because, until Richter called him, he had no idea where to go next or what to do. A couple of times, as the traffic slowed him to a halt, he tried ringing Richter's mobile, but each time the system reported that the other man's phone was switched off. And that worried Dekker, because he couldn't think of a single reason why Richter would want to remain incommunicado. The only other explanation was one he wasn't yet prepared to accept: that Richter and the woman had been captured, or worse.

Chapter Twenty

'How are we going to get out of Italy?' Raya asked again.

'I think the best option is the most obvious route: we go over the border and into France,' Richter said. 'And we'll need to cross soon, before the opposition can get their act together again. They can't possibly cover the whole border, not now that controls have been virtually abolished under Schengen, so I think a little bit of disinformation might help us as well.'

'What do you mean?'

Richter didn't answer directly. 'You still think that somebody's been tracking my phone?'

'That's the only explanation I can think of for what happened there, yes.'

'Right, so we'll take advantage of that. We'll head inland for a while, keeping off the main roads, then I'll turn the phone on again and make a call . . . But first I need to talk to Colin Dekker.'

He drove on along the minor road till he spotted what he was looking for in a small town called Torriglia.

When he'd pulled in earlier at a service area just over the Italian border, Richter had picked up a route map and an accommodation guidebook. Now, as he stopped the car on the side of the street, he pulled them both out of the door pocket and studied them carefully for a few minutes.

'Right,' he muttered, 'that should work. Then he stepped out of the car, strode across to the public phone he'd spotted, and called Dekker's mobile number.

'I was getting worried about you,' the SAS officer said, as soon as Richter identified himself.

'Join the club,' Richter replied. 'I'll make this quick. It's possible my mobile's being tracked, and I'd like to confirm that, and also try throwing the opposition off the scent. But to do that I'll need your help.'

'You've got it. You've already switched the phone off and pulled the battery?'

'Yes. Now, what I'm planning is this.'

For a couple of minutes Richter outlined exactly what he wanted Dekker to do.

'Got all that, and none of it should be a problem. How do you want to communicate? You'll use a public phone – like you are now?'

'Yes, that's safest.'

'OK, Paul. I'll head that way right now. Take care of yourself, and keep your eyes open. Very tasty totty, by the way. I was hoping Yuri would be some hairy-arsed heavyweight with a face like a brick shithouse. Some people', Dekker finished, 'have all the luck.'

'Tell me that again once we're back in London.'

Just under two hours later, as the evening light started to fade, Richter pulled the car into an open parking area on the outskirts of Piacenza, where it would be just another anonymous saloon in a car park full of similar vehicles.

'Are you sure about this?' Raya looked worried.

'It's worth a try, and if it doesn't work, we're no worse off than we were before.'

He picked up his mobile, reinserted the battery and switched it on. As soon as he had a signal, he dialled the number Simpson had given him.

'Where the hell are you, Richter?' Simpson demanded, the moment he answered the call, 'and what the hell's going on? I've been trying to get hold of you for hours.'

'And good evening to you, too. I forgot to charge the phone. That's why it's been off, and it'll probably only last a few minutes now.'

'Do you have the package?'

'If you mean Yuri, yes.'

'Is she OK?'

Richter paused for a second before he replied. 'How do you know Yuri's a woman?' he asked.

'Because I'm bloody well informed, Richter,' Simpson snapped. 'In this case, we aren't the only people who know about her defection. As I told you before, our cousins across the Atlantic are also trying to get in on the act. I've been talking to a man named John Westwood who – unusually for an American – actually seems to know what he's doing. He's a Company man, and some-how managed to get hold of one of the briefing sheets the Russian watchers were using in Rome. So unless Yuri's a real master of disguise, the person sitting next to you should be a girl named Raya Kosov.'

Richter nodded. 'OK, you're quite right. And, yes, she's fine. Now, we had a problem at the rendezvous, and our friend from Hereford had to intervene. It looks like somehow they tracked Raya to the RV, which means they've got an accurate starting point for a search. We need to get out of Italy, but I'm not going to risk trying to get into France.'

'So where will you cross?'

Richter glanced down at the route map open on his lap. 'Switzerland is out of the question because there'll be border checks there, so we're heading for Austria. We'll try to cross just to the south of a place called Vinaders, on the main road between Bolzano and Innsbruck. If we get over OK, can you organize an aircraft for us at Innsbruck? Say at about one o'clock tomorrow afternoon?'

'Leave it with me. Where are you now?'

'Just south of Piacenza, which is about sixty miles north-east of Genoa. We're going to stay the night in the Hotel San Pietro in Lodi – that's about halfway between Piacenza and Milan. Then we'll head for the Austrian border first thing tomorrow morning.'

'So you should be back in London by tomorrow evening?' Simpson asked.

'With any luck, yes. We should—'

In the middle of his sentence, Richter pulled out the battery again.

'Oops,' he said, 'it seems to have gone flat again. But if somebody in British intelligence *is* tracking my phone, at least they'll know I was telling the truth about where we were when we made that call.'

Raya smiled at him. 'So what are we *actually* going to do?'

Richter took another look at the route map, then started up the Ford and headed for the car-park exit.

'Well, we wouldn't be able to make the French border until about midnight from here, at a guess, and it's much easier for the police or anyone else to inspect vehicles and their occupants when it's quiet, like at night. So we'll be better placed to cross in daylight, when the crossing point is busy, and when we'll also be able to see if anyone's checking the vehicles. And if there is still a problem there, you might be able to cross the border on foot, up in the hills somewhere. Again, that would be a lot easier in daylight.'

Raya frowned at this suggestion. 'I'm not sure I like the idea of doing that by myself,' she said. 'Suppose there was a police patrol up there or something?'

'You wouldn't be alone,' Richter said. 'If we had to do that, either I would go along with you, or more likely Colin Dekker. And, I promise you, he's perfectly capable of taking on a bunch of *carabinieri* or any of your Russian pals.'

'I'd still rather not do it. But where are we going now?'

'We're going to find somewhere where we can sleep tonight, but nowhere near Lodi, of course. Not a hotel, either, because by now I'm sure the *carabinieri* will have circulated your description. And if my phone is being tracked, the Italians will probably have listed my name, too, and maybe even my passport details, and requested hotels to report to them if I take a room.'

Richter drove on in silence for a couple of minutes, then glanced at Raya again.

'There's something I should tell you,' he said, 'because I think we need to discuss the implications. I was sent to France to act as bait for a traitor we knew was working somewhere within British intelligence. I was supposed to be a defecting Russian cipher clerk who'd been working at Yasenevo. Anyway, the plan worked, and the man who'd been selling stuff to your masters was caught. He's in custody and on his way back to England right now.'

Raya nodded.

'The man who recruited me – or conned me, to be exact – for this operation is pretty sure he's now plugged the leak,' Richter went on. 'So if he's right, and our traitor is sitting handcuffed in the back of a car somewhere, who's tracking my phone?'

'There were two of them,' Raya replied quietly. 'We had *two* sources in Britain that I knew of.'

'Oh, bugger,' Richter muttered. 'Can you identify them?'

'Their names were never recorded in any of the files. But I know most of the information they passed to Yasenevo, so your security people might be able to identify them from that. They can easily cross-reference the information.'

'How did you find out about it?'

'It was part of my job. I had access to almost every file held at Yasenevo.'

Richter whistled softly. He didn't know a hell of a lot about the world of intelligence, but even he could see that Raya Kosov was an asset potentially worth her weight in gold – as long as she did actually have the data she claimed.

'But the files are still in Russia,' he objected.

'Yes, but I've been planning this for a long time, and I made enough preparations.' And, with that, she lapsed into silence.

Richter drove around the outskirts of Piacenza heading to the west, and stopped at a large garage to fill the car with fuel. As he paid for it, using his credit card because

Simpson already knew where he was, he also drew five hundred euros from an ATM and bought four packets of sandwiches, some soft drinks, biscuits and chocolate bars.

Raya glanced at the bag as he sat down again in the car.

'Dinner,' Richter said shortly. 'We really can't risk going into a restaurant or cafe, just in case some off-duty *carabinieri* officer is sitting there and spots us.'

Next he picked up the road that ran south of the autostrada, past Alessandria and Asti towards Turin. He followed this route as far as Asti itself, then turned north-west. And every time he saw another car or a motorcycle, he watched it closely, checking for any signs of hostile intent, supremely conscious that not only were Russian hit squads looking for them, but also the Italian authorities – and, by now, probably agents from the American CIA as well.

He finally stopped in the countryside near a small town called Piea, and indicated a sign over to one side of the road. Painted on it were the words 'San Frediano' and below that 'B&B', which was an almost universal shorthand. The sign indicated a narrow lane that wound up a gentle slope towards a sprawling house set on the side of a hill. It was perhaps seventy yards off the road itself, with lights blazing from several windows.

'That'll do,' he decided, and swung the car into the lane.

'What is this place?' Raya asked anxiously, as the Ford bumped along the track.

Richter explained the concept of bed and breakfast, something Raya had never encountered before.

'No passports, no credit cards, and probably no records for the taxman,' he finished. 'Mainly passing trade, paying cash only. Just what we need. Now, we'll go in together, and you wear that floppy hat,' he instructed, stopping the car just outside the house and turning to her, 'and keep the sunglasses on. Just pretend you're a celebrity – somebody famous.'

'I suppose I am now a celebrity of sorts,' Raya replied. 'Or at least a lot of people are very keen to see me.'

The house was obviously old, but had ample parking space on a gravel drive beside the property itself. It was big enough for about half a dozen cars, and the Ford would be well out of sight of the road.

Richter knocked at the door, and a man in late middle age opened it a few seconds later.

'Do you speak English?' Richter asked.

'Yes, a little.'

'You have a room? My wife and I need a room for the night.'

The Italian opened the door wide and gestured for them to step inside the house. He had one double room left, with a view of the countryside in front of the house and back towards the road. Richter wasn't bothered about the vista, but a decent vantage point was important.

Telling the proprietor they'd take it, he left Raya inside the room, and walked back out to the car to collect their bags.

'There's only one bed,' Raya pointed out when he returned.

'We'll work around it,' Richter replied.

'What does that mean?'

'It means you'll sleep in it, and I'll sleep on it, so it won't be a problem.'

In fact, it didn't quite work out that way.

Chapter Twenty-One

Monday
Piemonte, Italy

'Where are you?' Richter asked. 'And what happened last night?'

He was using a public phone by the side of the road on the outskirts of Chieri, about fifteen miles west of Piea and ten miles south-east of Turin. Raya sat in the front passenger seat of the Ford he'd parked a few yards away watching him as his eyes ceaselessly scanned the surrounding area.

'At a service area on the autostrada north-east of Chivasso,' Dekker said. 'That's about fifteen or twenty miles from Turin. You were right about the hotel, but we need to talk face to face, just in case anyone's listening in. Walls have ears, Echelon, and all that. So where do you want to meet?'

Richter looked at the road map he held in his left hand. 'There's a town named Roure about halfway between Turin and the French border. We'll be at the first cafe on the right-hand side of the road after you enter the place from the east.'

'You've been there before?' Dekker asked.

'No, never. But this is Italy, so there will be a lot of cafes there, and there's bound to be one on that side of the road. We've got about the same distance to go as you have, so we should arrive at about the same time.'

'Got it. I'll see you there.'

Richter climbed back into the Ford, started the engine and pulled away from the kerb.

Raya eyed him from the passenger seat. 'Now what?' she asked.

'Not good news, but I'll let Colin Dekker explain when we meet him.'

'You *do* trust this man Dekker?' Raya sounded uncertain.

'As much as I trust anyone else in this business, yes. He's SAS, and nothing to do with British intelligence. He was only sent out here because he's an expert sniper, and Simpson, who recruited me, wanted to make sure that the rat we were trying to trap wouldn't be able to walk away. Don't forget, he's also the reason we're still free. If he hadn't stopped that man in the square in Nervi, you'd now be on a flight back to Moscow, and I'd probably be dead. So, yes, I do trust him.'

A little over an hour later, Richter stopped the Ford about fifty yards from a small cafe that lay just off the street, on the right-hand side. The paved area in front of it was crowded with round plastic tables and matching chairs, and a small thicket of 'Martini' umbrellas had already been unfurled to provide some shade from the bright morning sunshine.

As Richter and Raya approached, a stocky man wearing a light jacket stood up and waved to them. Richter angled across to join him at his table.

'Raya, meet Colin Dekker, our watchful shadow. Colin, this is Raya Kosov – or "Yuri", if you prefer.'

Dekker grinned at her. 'No, I definitely prefer "Raya",' he said.

'Are we safe meeting here?' Richter asked.

'Probably. It's a public place and we're both carrying personal weapons. More importantly, you used a public call box and I never gave Simpson, or anyone else, the number of my mobile phone. Though I suppose they could find it out from Hereford, but in that case my boss would call to give me a heads-up. And he hasn't rung me yet, but keep your eyes open anyway.'

They all sat down and, after a few seconds, a waiter wandered over to take their order.

As soon as he was out of earshot again, Dekker leaned forward. 'You were right, Paul,' he said.

'What happened?'

'I got to Lodi just after eight-thirty, and found a spot where I could park the car and watch the Hotel San Pietro. Just before ten, two black Alfa saloons appeared in the street, and drove past the place twice. Then they parked up, one either side of the building, and two men got out of one of them. They headed down the street running to one side of the hotel, presumably to cover the rear of the building. A minute or so later, another four men climbed out of the cars. Two of them went inside the hotel, while the other two remained to cover the front.'

'Presumably they then checked the register and found we weren't there?'

'Something simpler and more effective than that, be-cause obviously you might have registered under false names. They needed the building totally cleared, so about thirty seconds later one of them set off the fire alarm. Everyone, guests and staff alike, piled out onto the pavement outside. Those guys checked every woman under forty, and also every man. They each held a sheet of paper, which I guess had Raya's photograph on it. If you'd actually been there, they'd have found you for sure.'

'Who were they?' Richter asked, though he already knew the answer.

'They certainly weren't your friendly Italian *carabinieri*,' Dekker said. 'None of them was wearing a uniform, and they really hustled the people around, obviously in a big hurry to get things done. A couple of men tried arguing, and they just flattened them with a single blow each time. Very competent. Those guys were obviously really experienced at close combat, so I'm guessing they weren't local thugs. More likely some of the professional hoods Moscow Centre flew out to find Raya and drag her back to Yasenevo.'

Raya shivered on hearing his words.

'Anyway,' Dekker went on, 'they got everyone out of that place, checked their identities, realized that you and Yuri weren't there, and buggered off just ahead of the local fire brigade and the police. OK, that's the good news. Now the bad news is that you were right: the only person who knew where you were supposed to be staying in Lodi last night was that pink bastard Richard Simpson. Either he passed the information on to Moscow himself or he told somebody, and they did. Either way, you have to assume that Simpson's organization or the SIS, or maybe both, has been penetrated by the Russians.'

Richter nodded. 'That ties up with what Raya's already told me. She says the SIS has been compromised by two people. Stanway was obviously one of them, but it sounds as if the other one is still in place, and still active. And, you're right, it could be Richard Simpson, but I personally doubt that. Apart from anything else, he isn't actually a part of SIS.'

'Well, somebody told Moscow, that's for sure, and Simpson or his secret squirrel outfit had to be the conduit, at the very least. Unless there's a tap on that number you called him on, of course.'

Richter shrugged. 'I remember reading somewhere that the world of espionage and counter-espionage was known as the "wilderness of mirrors", and I'm beginning to see exactly what the author meant. If you look at it a certain way, any truth can also be a lie, and each reflection shows something slightly different from the original. So who the hell can you trust?'

'That's a bloody good question,' Dekker said, 'but you'll have to work out the answer for yourself. Personally, I don't think Richard Simpson should be anywhere near the top of your list, but that's your decision. More importantly, we need to decide what to do next – though I guess that getting out of Italy is pretty high on your agenda.'

'Definitely.' Raya nodded. 'I won't feel safe until we're in France, and maybe not even then.' She glanced round the cafe nervously, but saw nothing there to alarm her.

'Yes, we need to get over the border,' Richter agreed, 'but I don't want to just drive towards it along an ordinary road, because the Italians will have probably mounted watchers on most of the border crossings, and once we get stuck in a queue of vehicles, there's no way out. I know European borders are supposed to be open these days, but because the Russians have involved the Eyeties, there are almost certainly some kind of checks now in place.'

'So what can we do?' Raya asked.

'We lose one of the cars, and then we split up,' Richter said, opening a road map on the table in front of him. 'We're here.' He pointed out Roure. 'The road we're sitting beside follows the course of the River Chisone and runs in a semicircle northwards, and finishes up here' – he pointed to a spot further to the west – 'just beyond Sestriere, where it joins the main road. That road then becomes the Route Nationale 94 where it crosses the border into France, just east of Briançon.'

Richter paused and glanced at his two companions. Dekker nodded for him to continue.

'That's a fairly obvious crossing point for the Italians to be covering, because it's the main route from Turin to Grenoble, so I'm almost certain they'll have manned the border there, looking for Raya of course, and possibly me now as well. We're probably listed as escaped convicts or murderers, something like that, and they'll have orders to check every single car leaving Italy. So that's why I think we need to split up. As far as I know, they won't be looking for you, Colin, so there's no reason why you can't just drive across the border in your hire car, though it would be a good idea to lose the sniper rifle and your pistol before you do.'

Dekker didn't look at all happy with this suggestion. 'I've signed for them,' he said, 'and I can't just dump them.'

'Sorry, wrong choice of word. We'll be hanging on to the weapons, but we'll get them over the border by another route.'

'How?'

'See just here,' Richter pointed, 'beside this peak called Roche Bernaud? There's a small place called Bardonecchia, near the tunnel that runs north–south through the mountain and across the border. There's a minor road that runs roughly south from that point, across the French border and down to Névache. Then it turns east and south to join the N94 just east of Briançon. I'm hoping that will be our route out of Italy.'

'So I drive you two up to Bardonecchia, drop you both there and then drive across the border east of Briançon and pick you up on the other side?' Dekker asked.

'Maybe, but I was rather hoping you might be able to take us a bit beyond that, perhaps a little way further up the minor road that crosses the border, but that will depend on what we find when we get to Bardonecchia. But I certainly think we should leave our car here, and ride in yours from now on, just in case Simpson or somebody has flagged my vehicle, too.'

'OK,' Dekker said. 'That sounds like a plan. And when I drop you two off, you'll take the rifle and my short with you?'

'Short?' Raya asked. 'What's a short?'

'He means his pistol,' Richter explained, then turned back to Dekker. 'Exactly. So you should have no trouble at the border, even if the *carabinieri*, or whoever, stop you and search the car.'

Three minutes later they were on the move. Richter had left the locked Ford on a side street in Roure, with the keys tossed underneath the car, and the three of them were now riding in Dekker's hired Peugeot – the car he'd picked up in Toulouse. Richter was in the front, while Raya sat in the back, trying to keep her head low, just in case the Italians had stationed any *carabinieri* in the area immediately to the east of the border.

Their route took them out of Roure, around the north slopes of Monte Albergian, and then south-west to Sestriere. Leaving the village, the road began twisting and turning its way down hairpin bends traversing the fairly steep side of the valley, until they finally reached the village of Cesana Torinese, and the junction there with the main road.

'Beautiful scenery,' Dekker muttered, as he approached the roundabout.

All around them rose mountain peaks: an artist's palette of shades of green and brown, grass and trees and rocks, framed by the silver streamers of mountain rivers that tumbled down the sheer slopes below the white teeth of the mountain tops. It was, by any standards, spectacular.

'Keep down,' Dekker ordered, a couple of seconds later, after a glance to his left. 'Reception committee.'

Raya ducked down in her seat, keeping herself below the level of the windows.

Dekker kept up the commentary as he turned right, and accelerated up the road heading north.

'Half a dozen *carabinieri* just beyond the roundabout, with two blue and whites. Plus a couple of suits just observing. They've pulled over three cars that were obviously heading for the border, and they're checking the boots and also the identification of the drivers and passengers. Could be a routine check, of course, but I doubt it.'

'Just as well you didn't turn left, then,' Richter muttered.

'You got that right.'

As Dekker accelerated, Richter peered cautiously out of the rear window. The Italian police were clearly taking their task seriously. Two of them stood on opposite sides of the road, sub-machine guns cradled in their arms, and covering the scene, while their colleagues, also armed but with riot shotguns and regulation pistols, carried out the inspections of the vehicles and their occupants. He glanced at the route map, then made a quick decision.

'Change of plan now, Colin. I was expecting them to be checking people a lot closer to the border. But, looking at this map, I reckon they'll have a roadblock on this side of Bardonecchia, because that way they can cover both the tunnel and the road over the col. I think we need to try to cross somewhere here, before we get too far away from the border. Can you pull over soon?'

They found a small pull-in on the right-hand side of the road, temporarily empty of other vehicles, and Dekker swung the Peugeot into it and switched off the engine. All three of them climbed out of the car and stared around.

'Nice and quiet,' Dekker remarked.

'Good.' Richter looked to the west, in the direction they had to proceed. The mountain rose quite steeply in front of them, riven with deep and inhospitable-looking valleys that also rose steeply towards the west. He had hoped they'd be able to follow a curving route around the mountain, keeping to more or less at the same level, until they started the descent towards the minor road on the French side of the border. But now clearly that wasn't an option, for it would be a long, exhausting slog over very uneven ground, and climbing for most of the way.

'How far is it?' Dekker asked.

'If this map's accurate, about seven or eight miles. That's in a straight line, so maybe ten miles actually walking.'

'Ten miles?' Raya echoed. 'Over that sort of ground? That's going to take us hours.'

'Most of the day,' Richter agreed, 'but I don't think we've got much option.'

'We can't crash through the border, that's for sure,' Dekker said, 'if every crossing point's got the same sort of police presence. Two pistols and a sniper rifle aren't much use at close quarters against sub-machine guns and shotguns. They'd cut us to pieces. And if, by some lucky chance, we did manage to shoot our way through, they'd put out a Europe-wide watch order for us, because we would be bound to have wounded or even killed some of the *carabinieri*.'

'What about hiring an off-road vehicle?' Raya suggested.

Richter shook his head. 'A good idea, but we'd probably have to drive back to Turin to get one, and that's about sixty miles away. Getting there, finding one and getting back here could easily take three or four hours. But the bigger problem is that we're trying not to be noticed, and if the Italians have any sense they'll be flying helicopter patrols along the border on the lookout for us. If we're on foot, we can just lie flat and hide. But you can't hide a Jeep.'

'On the other hand,' Dekker said, 'you're a pilot, aren't you?'

Richter nodded.

'So how about flying over?'

'Good plan, apart from the fact that we don't have an aircraft.'

'Ah,' Dekker said, 'but I think I know where you can find one. On the way up to Roure I passed a windsock on the right-hand side of the road, and there was a kind of cleared area in a field beyond that, and a barn. Five gets you ten, one of the local farmers has a Cessna or something parked there.'

Richter considered this suggestion for maybe two seconds. Then he nodded. 'Sounds good to me,' he said. 'Let's go.'

'Of course,' Dekker pointed out, settling in the driver's seat and starting the engine again, 'I don't know if there actually *is* an aircraft inside that barn. It's always possible the farmer's popped over to Milan or somewhere, so we'll find the nest is empty.'

'It's still worth taking the chance. It's a better option than a six-hour walk, that's for sure.'

Dekker drove back down the N94 towards the roadblock but, as he approached the roundabout that marked the junction with the road to Sestriere and on to Roure, he tensed.

'One of the *carabinieri* is staring at me,' he muttered to Richter, who was now crouching down in the back of the car, with Raya beside him.

'Maybe he fancies you,' Richter muttered, in a weak attempt at humour.

There were about half a dozen cars halted on the

right-hand side of the road, waiting to pass through the checkpoint, with *carabinieri* inspecting the contents of their boots and also the identification of the occupants. Other Italian police officers were scanning the approaching traffic – which at that moment consisted only of the car Dekker was driving.

As Dekker watched, the officer called out something to a colleague, then stepped forwards, raising his arm.

'He's waving a hand at me. I think he wants us to stop.'

'Don't for Christ's sake do that,' Richter muttered.

'Don't worry, I won't. Now hang on. This could get bumpy and noisy.'

Dekker didn't have a lot of options, so he did about the only thing he could. As the Italian police officer headed down the road towards him, Dekker completely ignored both him and his signals, simply indicated left and accelerated around the tail end of the short line of waiting cars, then swung east, around the roundabout and into the other road.

Whistles shrilled behind him as he floored the accelerator pedal, and powered his car into the centre of Cesana Torinese.

Chapter Twenty-Two

Monday
Piemonte, Italy

'That was subtle,' Richter said, sitting up in his seat and staring out of the rear window.

Behind the accelerating Peugeot, he could see uniformed figures running towards the blue and white official *carabinieri* cars.

'No bloody option. You any good with a rifle?'

'Not as good as you are. But I can drive.'

'You might have to, then,' Dekker said tightly. 'Let's put some distance between us and them. While I do that, get that rifle assembled, just in case we have to shoot our way out of this.'

Richter unsnapped the catches on the case Dekker had laid on the floor in front of the rear seats, and took out the weapons' component parts. He'd never seen this particular model before, but he was familiar with rifles from his military career. Within a couple of minutes he'd assembled the rifle, attached the telescopic sight, and loaded a full magazine of subsonic 7.62-millimetre ammunition.

'Mean piece of kit,' he remarked.

'Ideal tool for the job,' Dekker said, 'and that's the point.'

Richter again looked through the rear window.

They'd almost cleared the edge of Cesana Torinese and were starting the climb up the slope, but the road behind them appeared to be empty. 'Where are they?' he wondered. 'And how many?'

'Two cars,' Dekker said, 'and each at least two-up. They're about five hundred yards behind us.'

'We need to stop them now,' Richter said. 'I remember that the road's pretty straight beyond Sestriere, so our best chance is on this twisty section.'

'Are you going to kill them?' Raya asked. She hadn't spoken since Dekker had avoided the roadblock.

'I bloody hope not. We just have to stop them, or at least slow them down for long enough to get away.'

'That'll do,' Dekker said, pointing ahead. He slewed the car off the road and onto a patch of rough ground to the right, sliding the gear lever into neutral and pulling the Peugeot to a stop in a cloud of dust. He left the engine running and jumped out.

Richter was just as fast, pushing open the rear door and immediately handing Dekker the sniper rifle.

'You drive,' Dekker instructed, then dropped to the ground, beside the front of the car. He rested the AWS rifle on its bipod and, through the telescopic sight, stared back along the road, waiting for a target to appear. The road was more or less straight until a bend perhaps a hundred yards away. Any pursuing vehicles would have to drive around that corner, and doing so would bring them directly into his sights.

'I can hear an engine,' Richter said, climbing into the driver's seat and strapping himself in. By changing places with Dekker, they'd be able to drive away as quickly as possible, and that would leave the SAS officer able to use the rifle while the vehicle was moving, though hopefully it wouldn't be necessary.

Seconds later, the first *carabinieri* car raced around the corner and headed straight towards them, a second vehicle following close behind it.

Dekker peered through the telescopic sight, adjusted his aim slightly, and then squeezed the trigger of the rifle.

There was a crack – sounding to Richter no louder than the report of a .22 hunting rifle – as the subsonic round fired, and instantly the leading car slammed to a halt as its right-hand front tyre exploded with a bang that was clearly audible even from where they were watching.

Dekker worked the rifle's bolt, chambering another round, and fired again almost immediately. The second car pursuing them also lurched sideways, as its left front tyre received similar treatment.

'That'll do,' Dekker said, standing up. 'Now let's get the hell out of here before they call in the cavalry.'

The moment Dekker sat down in the passenger seat, Richter lifted his foot off the clutch and accelerated away, the car bouncing over the rough ground before he reached the tarmac and headed down the road towards Sestriere.

'I think that's called burning our boats,' he said, keeping one eye on both rear-view mirrors.

From behind came the sudden crackle of sub-machine-gun fire, as one of the *carabinieri* opened fire at the speeding Peugeot, but none of the bullets reached them.

'We're pretty much out of range already,' Dekker said. 'Just keep going.'

Seconds later, as a second automatic weapon opened up behind them, Richter drove around a bend that placed the side of a hill between them and their pursuers. For the moment, they were safe.

Richter barely slowed down as they drove through Sestriere, whose streets were largely empty, and as soon as they'd cleared the edge of the village, he accelerated hard along the straighter and more level stretch of road that ran along the side of the mountain, towards Pragelato.

'We must be clear of them by now,' Raya said. 'Can't we slow down?'

'No.' Richter shook his head firmly. 'It's not the Italian police behind us that I'm worried about, but the roadblocks they might be setting up somewhere in front, if those *carabinieri* have radioed ahead.'

'And they will have,' Dekker added.

'I'm just hoping most of their people will be concentrated fairly close to the Italian side of the border, so we might be keeping ahead of them.' Richter glanced across at Dekker. 'And I'm not quite sure what we're going to do if you were wrong, and that wasn't a hangar you saw. Or even if you were right, but there's no aircraft there.'

Dekker shrugged. 'I know what I saw,' he said, 'but I've no idea what's inside that building.'

It took them over half an hour to reach Roure, checking out for *carabinieri* all the way, but without seeing a sign of any. Once they'd cleared the southern end of the village Dekker started peering over to his left.

'How close was it, exactly?' Richter asked, still driving as fast as he could.

'I can't remember. It was just something I noticed as I drove along this stretch of road.'

They passed through another village, named Perosa Argentina, and then another called Pinasca, and about a mile beyond it Dekker suddenly pointed.

'There you go,' he said.

On the opposite side of the road stood a wooden pole from which a windsock hung down limply, and beyond that a well-mowed area running along the centre of a field. To Richter, it looked about five or six hundred yards long, which suggested it was used by quite a small aircraft. And he hadn't flown off a grass airfield since the days when he'd been at the Royal Naval College in Dartmouth, doing his flying grading in a Chipmunk at Roborough Airfield near Plymouth.

'Right,' he said. 'Let's take a look inside that barn over there. At least that'll get us off the road.'

A narrow track ran down one side of the field, past the barn, presumably leading to other farm buildings or maybe even the farmhouse itself. Richter swung the car across the road and bounced along the track's uneven and heavily rutted surface, which was more suitable for a four-by-four or a tractor than a saloon car. There was a turn-off behind the barn, and he pulled into it and stopped the Peugeot close to the building. It wasn't completely hidden from view of the road, but wouldn't easily be noticed.

The barn was partly brick, the masonry extending about halfway up the sides and rear of the building, with wooden panelling above that. There was a side door secured with a padlock, but the double front doors had no visible locks at all, so they were presumably secured by internal bolts. The padlock looked strong and new, but the wood that the hasp was screwed into was soft, and within five minutes Dekker's pocket knife had loosened it enough to free the screws. He glanced round, pulled open the door, and the three of them stepped inside the building.

The only light penetrating the interior came from the now open side door, and the sudden contrast with the bright daylight outside made it difficult to see. But, through the gloom, Richter had no trouble identifying a light aircraft parked in the middle of the floor.

It was a single-engined, low-wing monoplane, basically white with a stripe running down the side of the fuselage, in three different shades of blue. The engine drove a three-bladed propeller, and it had a retractable tricycle undercarriage, a single door on the right-hand side, and four seats.

'It looks almost new,' Dekker observed. 'Is it?'

'Far from it.' Richter laughed shortly. 'That's a Piper Arrow, and it's probably at least twenty-five years old – maybe as much as forty. Don't forget, aircraft don't show their age the ways cars do. Piper have been making light aircraft that look pretty much the same as this for half a century, and most of them are still flying.'

'So how do you know it's that old?' Raya asked.

'One big clue. The Arrow changed from a conventional rudder and tailplane to a T-tail in the late seventies – in 1978 or 1979, I think – but this aircraft still has the original layout, which means it had to have been made before 1980. In fact, this model's been around since about '67, so it could be as old as that.

'Bit of a flying antique, then. Is it safe?'

'Yes. All aircraft have to be checked on a regular basis, and that includes stuff like compulsory engine overhauls, at specified intervals, so they're much better maintained than cars or trucks.'

'And they'd need to be,' Dekker remarked, 'because if your car engine blows up, you don't fall ten thousand feet out of the sky and crash to the ground in a ball of flame.'

'Not a fan of light aircraft, then, Colin?'

'Not really, no. The more wings and engines and pilots the better, as far as I'm concerned.'

'This was your idea,' Richter reminded him, 'not mine.'

'Yeah, and I'm beginning to have second thoughts about it. Have you ever flown something like this before?'

'Not for a few years,' Richter said, 'but yes, I have. Until a few weeks ago I was tooling around the sky in a Harrier, and I promise you this will be a hell of a lot easier to fly. And, right now, I don't think we have much choice.'

He strode across to the aircraft's door, pulled it open, climbed inside, and sat down in the left-hand seat.

'No ignition switch?' Dekker asked.

'As a matter of fact there is, but the key's still in it. The hangar's supposed to provide the security, not what's inside it. And not everyone can steal an aircraft. It's not like nicking some Ford parked on the street.'

Richter checked the instruments, particularly the fuel gauge, then climbed out again.

'What're you doing?' Dekker asked.

'Basic airmanship,' Richter replied. 'External checks first, then pre-start checks, then all the rest of them.'

'We don't have time for that. We need to get out of here.'

'Then we *make* time. I'd rather spend the rest of my days in an Italian prison than end up as a red smear on the side of some mountain because I forgot to remove all the control locks.'

But, even so, it didn't take long, because it wasn't a big aircraft and there wasn't a lot to check. Within a couple of minutes, Richter was back in the pilot's seat and busy checking the flying controls for full and free movement. He noted that the altimeter was showing an altitude of around 2,100 metres, which probably indicated the height above sea level of the grass strip outside. He didn't touch the sub-scale to alter it, because he knew he would need some indication of his altitude in case they ran into cloud or bad weather.

'OK,' he said, after a few moments, 'we're ready. Raya, get in the back, please. Colin, those doors at the front of the building should slide sideways on runners. You open them up, while I start the engine.'

'About time,' Dekker muttered, then trotted over to the double doors. He pulled open the bolts securing them at top and bottom, then pushed sideways on the left-hand door. Just as it started to move, he stepped back into the hangar and pointed silently over towards the roadway outside.

Richter peered through the windscreen and the open door and cursed silently. Two *carabinieri* cars, their blue and white colour scheme making them quite unmistakable, had stopped near the entrance to the track that led down to the small hangar, and a handful of officers were standing beside them, some talking on mobile phones, others just gazing around. They weren't actually focusing on the hangar, as far as he could tell, but that situation would change as soon as he started the Piper's engine. It all depended on whether they would associate the departing aircraft with the fugitives they were looking for. And Richter guessed they probably would.

Dekker pushed open the other door. Both moved almost silently on well-oiled tracks, and his actions so far didn't seem to have attracted the attention of the Italian police officers.

'There are chocks around the main wheels, Colin,' Richter called out. 'Pull them clear, then get on board.'

The moment Dekker had closed the single door of the aircraft, Richter started the ignition sequence. The Lycoming engine turned over noisily, coughed twice and then caught, settling down to a reassuringly steady roar, the sound grossly magnified by the walls of the hangar.

The effect of the sudden noise was immediate. Half of the *carabinieri* jumped into one of the cars, switched on the lights and sirens, and turned it down the lane leading towards the hangar.

'Cat and pigeons,' Dekker muttered. 'You want me to slow them down a bit?'

'Not unless you have to,' Richter said. 'Belt in, both of you, and if you know any good gods, this would be an excellent time to pick one and start praying.'

He pushed the throttle forward gently, in order to start the Piper moving. As soon as the wing tips cleared the hangar doors, he increased the power setting and sent the little aircraft skidding across the grass towards the nearer end of the basic runway.

'Aren't you supposed to take off into wind?' Dekker asked, gesturing towards the windsock, which was now moving lazily, but pointing in the general direction Richter was heading.

'You just concentrate on the shooting and let me do the flying.'

The *carabinieri* vehicle had almost reached the hangar, and the turn-off beside it, when the Piper reached the near edge of the short-cropped grass. Dekker watched as the officers piled out of it. He couldn't hear what they were saying, but their gestures were quite unmistakable.

'I think they know we're in this aircraft,' he said urgently. 'They're going to start shooting any time now, so getting ourselves airborne is probably a good idea.'

'I'm doing it,' Richter snapped, engaging full flap and lining up the Piper along the grass strip ahead of them.

The *carabiniere* driver was now sounding his horn in a long, continuous blare of sound, easily audible even over the roar of the Piper's Lycoming engine.

'Now they've spotted the Peugeot,' Dekker said, looking back through the side window of the aircraft.

The other car lurched to a halt beside the hangar and its doors swung open. Grey-clad officers spilled out, weapons in hand.

Palazzo Margherita, Via Vittorio Veneto, Rome, Italy

'There's just been an incident near the border,' Clayton Richards said, putting down his desk phone and standing up.

'Whereabouts? And what sort of incident?' Westwood asked.

Richards strode over to the map. 'Near Sestriere, just here.' He pointed at a curving minor road that lay to the west of Turin. 'Our contact in the *carabinieri* has reported that shots were fired at police vehicles, but we've no reports of casualties at the moment. It happened about fifty minutes ago, and apparently the *carabinieri* are now in pursuit of a vehicle with at least two people in it.'

'That could be it,' Westwood said, after a moment. 'At least, it's the first report of anything happening that sounds likely. I'll scramble the U2 out of Aviano and see what that can detect. And I'll also check with Langley and find out if any of the KH-12 birds were within range at the time this happened.'

Piemonte, Italy

The Piper was now accelerating quickly along the grass strip, with the throttle fully open. Richter was controlling the direction with the rudder pedals, and starting to ease back on the control yoke as the aircraft's speed increased. The little aircraft banged and crashed around on the uneven surface, as the wheels hit humps and dips, and the cabin shook uncomfortably.

Behind them, there was a sudden rattle of submachine-gun fire as the Italian officers opened up. If the *carabinieri* had been armed with rifles, it would have been a different story, but the weapons they were carrying were intended for close-quarter fighting against soft targets – human beings, in fact – and the Piper was already nearly a hundred yards away from them before they started firing. A couple of stray rounds hit the roof of the cabin, drilling harmlessly through its thin aluminium skin. Out of the corner of his eye, Richter saw another round hit the port wing, near the tip.

But he was ignoring everything except getting the aircraft into the sky. The Piper was feeling lighter, that almost indefinable sensation felt through the controls as the aircraft approached sixty knots – which he guessed was about take-off speed. Moments later, he eased back gently on the yoke. The nose lifted, and the bouncing and juddering ceased, as the Piper lifted smoothly into the air, about a hundred yards from the far end of the grass strip.

Richter kept the throttle fully open and continued climbing as quickly as he could – which wasn't that fast. He was used to a Harrier's 50,000 feet-per-minute rate of climb, and the Piper felt more like it was going up at only fifty feet a minute.

'Thank God for that,' Raya murmured, both hands firmly clutching her seat belt.

'Can we get to England in this thing?' Dekker asked.

'No,' Richter said shortly, raising the undercarriage as the Piper picked up speed. 'With full tanks it can cover about eight or nine hundred miles, but we'd never make anything like that distance. We've just shot our way out of Italy, and there's absolutely no reason why the Italians shouldn't ask the French to force us down somewhere. If we tried going all the way, we'd find a couple of Mirages or something on either side of us really soon. And if we didn't land where and when they told us, they'd probably just shoot us down.'

'So what's the plan?'

'Simple. We're out of reach of the Italians now, so we use this aircraft simply to hop over the border into France, pick our own landing spot, and then vanish.'

Richter checked the altimeter. They had climbed to an indicated altitude of just over 3,000 metres, and were probably already five or six miles from the grass strip, but still heading east, towards Turin. He continued the climb. Attached to the dashboard of the Piper was a plastic plate with radio frequencies, various speeds and other information written on it. In fact, the kind of stuff that a pilot flying in this area would need to have immediately available. At the bottom of the plate were two heights indicated in metres.

The first number was 2,160, which was probably the elevation of the grass landing strip, so the pilot would know what his altimeter should be telling him when he reached the touch-down point. The second was just over 5,000 metres, which Richter guessed was the safety altitude for this area, which would guarantee clearance above even the highest peaks in all weather conditions. That was the altitude he was going to aim for, as long as the Piper could reach it – and it was probably pretty close to the plane's maximum ceiling.

But, first, it was time he altered course.

Palazzo Margherita, Via Vittorio Veneto, Rome, Italy

Clayton Richards looked up as somebody knocked at the door of his office, before stepping inside. It was a junior officer clutching a sheaf of photographs.

'From Langley, sir,' he said. 'The latest downloads from the last Ikon satellite pass.'

'Thanks,' Richards growled, then cleared a space on his desk and spread out the pictures so that he and Westwood could look at them together.

The definition was high and the images were amazingly clear, but there was nothing the designers of the satellite cameras could do about the laws of physics, so there was a limit to what could be seen from even a state-of-the-art, high-speed platform travelling some two hundred miles above the ground.

Helpfully, one of the analysts at the NRO had annotated the photographs before sending them to CIA Headquarters, so the Franco-Italian border was clearly marked, as was Turin and several of the larger towns in the area. In response to Westwood's specific request, they'd also indicated two apparently abandoned *carabinieri* cars on the road outside the town of Cesana Torinese. That was interesting, and served to confirm the report Richards had already received about an 'incident' near the border.

But what was even more interesting was another pair of Italian police cars to be seen just east of Pinasca. One was stationary on the road, but the other was clearly in motion, driving down a narrow track towards a building located in a field. And beyond that building was the unmistakable white shape of a small civilian aircraft.

'That's them,' Westwood muttered. 'Five gets you ten, whoever the Brits sent out to pick up Raya Kosov is a pilot, and he's going to fly her out of Italy.'

'That's a hell of a leap of logic, sir,' Richards said.

'No, it makes sense,' Westwood insisted. 'The first incident occurred on the same road, near Cesana Torinese, so they had to be driving east. They spotted the hangar, took a chance there'd be an aircraft in it, and they've stolen it. Gotta admire that kind of thinking.'

'But they can't make it to England in that little thing, can they?'

'No. That's why I've got the Lear here. Get me a car and driver to take me to Fiumicino right now. Then contact the U2 through Aviano Operations, and tell the pilot to get airborne asap, and concentrate on the area around Pinasca. I need to know where that civil aircraft is heading. Tell him I'll call Aviano from the Lear, once we're in the air, so they can patch me straight through to the pilot.'

Above Piemonte, Italy

There were various maps and charts to be found in the aircraft cabin, but Richter didn't think he'd need to use most of them. As long as they headed more or less west, and he managed to avoid flying into the top of a mountain, they'd eventually end up where they wanted to go. And Richter figured it was more important, at that moment, for him to keep looking out of the window rather than bury his head in an aviation chart. They'd been only about thirty miles from the Italian border when they took off, so within the hour, and with a modicum of luck, they should be on the ground again, but this time in France.

'We'll head north,' he decided.

'North?' Dekker and Raya replied, almost simultaneously.

'Only so as to try to mislead the Eyeties on the ground,' Richter explained. 'They can still see us, remember. If we simply reverse direction and head straight for Briançon, that's where they'll tell the French to start looking for us. And they'll definitely be talking to the gendarmes any time now. If they think we're heading north, trying to get to Switzerland, or even Germany or Austria, that will widen the search area, and right now that's very important for us.'

'Yeah, makes sense,' Dekker said. 'And I take back what I said before. You *can* fly an aircraft – even one you've not flown before.'

'The Queen seemed to think so too. That's why she paid me for years.'

Richter looked ahead, mentally planning his route. Directly in front, he could see a couple of small lakes and, beyond them, the urban sprawl of Turin. To his left, ranges of mountains extended in all directions and, perhaps ten miles away, the black ribbon of the A32 autostrada snaking along the base of the Val di Susa.

'Right,' he said, pressing the left rudder pedal and turning the yoke to the left, then starting the Piper in a left-hand bank. 'We'll start tracking north.'

He stabilized the aircraft on a northerly heading, then reached down and pulled out the navigation charts. He flipped through them until he found a topographical chart, and opened it up.

'I'll hold it for you,' Dekker suggested, and took hold of one side of it.

'Thanks.'

With the tip of his finger, Richter traced a route running north, and across the autostrada.

'We'll turn west about here,' he said, 'between Pointe de Charbonnel and L'Albaron. That's actually on the French border. Then I want to head west over open country, not fly over towns where people might see us, or even over major roads, and that route seems to be about the best option.'

'Not a bad choice.' Dekker nodded. 'We'll have to fly over that minor road there, the D902, but after that there's nothing much on the ground until we reach some of these small Alpine villages. And most of them seem to be located at the limits of dead-end roads, so I guess they're mainly ski resorts. And that means they should be pretty much deserted at this time of year. Where will you land?'

'Buggered if I know,' Richter said. 'We'll need to get clear of these mountains first, then I'll start looking. All I'll need is a reasonably level piece of ground, about five hundred yards long, preferably grass, that's not too far out in the sticks – because, once we abandon this aircraft, we'll be walking.'

'We'll find a car,' Dekker promised, 'one way or the other.'

They'd just crossed the autostrada a couple of miles east of Borgone Susa, when Dekker pointed ahead.

'What?'

'A glint of something just over there. Something moving,' Dekker replied.

Then Richter saw it too. A sudden oval shimmer of light, in view for just a bare second or two, then disappearing again. But, unlike Dekker, he knew exactly what it was, and it wasn't good news.

'That's a helicopter rotor disc,' he said. 'I thought

the Italians might have a chopper or two patrolling this area, searching for us, and it looks to me like that one's following the line of the border fairly closely.'

'But we're OK up here, aren't we?' Dekker asked. 'I mean, we're well above it, and this plane must be faster than a chopper, surely?'

'We are above it, yes, and most light, fixed-wing aircraft are quicker than most helicopters, yes. If that's just a surveillance bird, it shouldn't be a problem. But if it's a gunship, and the crew manage to spot us, we're in trouble.'

'And the Italians have helicopter gunships, do they?' Dekker asked.

Richter nodded grimly. 'They even build one of their own: it's called a Mangusta, and it's a bit like an Apache with attitude. It's got a twenty-millimetre cannon, and it can carry quite a bouquet of missiles – Stingers, TOWs, Mistrals and Hellfires. This Arrow could just about out-distance the chopper in a straight line, but we'd never be able to outrun its missiles.'

'Oh, shit.'

'That about sums it up.'

For the moment, Richter did nothing. It was just possible that the helicopter was a private aircraft that simply happened to be in the area, in which case it was no threat to them. Even if it was a military or police air-craft, running surveillance along the border, it wouldn't be a problem, because the crew would be looking down, trying to identify anyone crossing into France by not using the roads. What he feared, though, was that news of their theft of the Piper Arrow had already been broad-cast, and that the Italian military was now involved.

'Give me that chart,' he demanded. Dekker handed it over.

Richter studied it for a few moments, then passed it back. 'We might be OK,' he said. 'The closest military base is near Caselle Torinese, just north of Turin. There's no way a gunship could have got from there to here by now, even if it had been crewed up and ready to launch the moment we stole this aircraft. And if the Italians were looking for us on the ground, a gunship wouldn't do them any good.'

'So you reckon that's maybe just a police chopper, something like that?'

'Most likely, yes, but just keep your eyes on it.'

Richter had now coaxed the Piper up to an indicated altitude of just over 5,000 metres, which felt pretty near its maximum ceiling because the rate of climb had fallen dramatically, despite the Lycoming engine still being at almost full throttle. The helicopter looked as if it was about 1,500 metres below them, and was heading south. It still appeared to be following the Franco-Italian border, which in that area ran more or less north-east to south-west. As the Piper was flying north, Richter reckoned they should get behind the helicopter within a couple of minutes.

Ahead of the aircraft, a group of four peaks loomed up, in an almost square formation. The westerly pair were the ones Richter had decided to fly between – Pointe de Charbonnel and L'Albaron – and as the helicopter passed down their port side, about four miles away, he started easing the Piper into a gentle left-hand turn onto a northwesterly heading. Looking down, he saw two small towns almost directly below them. From the chart, they looked like Margone and Usseglio, both on the banks of the Stura di Viù river, which told him exactly where they now were. His new course would take them across the French border as quickly as possible, and also allow him to keep an eye on the helicopter, just in case its crew spotted them.

'I think that peak is probably Croix-Rousse,' Dekker said, looking at the chart and mangling the pronunciation. 'And if it is, it's actually on the border itself. So, once we get beyond that, we should start smelling the garlic.'

Below and behind them, the helicopter continued on its southbound track, apparently oblivious to their presence overhead.

In fairness to Richter, he had his hands full. He was piloting an aircraft he'd never flown before, and was still getting used to its instruments and controls. He was flying over unfamiliar and potentially hostile territory, without any kind of flight plan or even a clear idea of where he was going. And a lot of his attention was focused on the helicopter below them.

Which was why he didn't see the *Aeronautica Militare* Aermacchi MB-339 until it roared past their right-hand wing tip.

Chapter Twenty-Three

Monday
Sluzhba Vneshney Razvyedki Rossi Headquarters, Yasenevo,
Tëplyystan, Moscow

'Even for an administrator, you've been very stupid,'
Zharkov snapped, sitting down opposite Abramov.
'What did you think you could achieve by approaching
the general directly?'

'I hoped he would make you do your job properly,'
Abramov replied, with spirit, hoping his action had
wrong-footed this man. 'I hoped he would order you to
carry out a proper investigation here at Yasenevo, and to
check what Raya Kosov claims to have discovered. And
have you found her?'

For the first time since he had met Zharkov, the colonel looked unsure of himself, and Abramov guessed that
he'd faced a fairly hostile reception from the general in
charge of SVR security. His manner also suggested his
men had failed to track down Raya Kosov, which the
colonel's next words confirmed.

'Not yet. But we know roughly where she is, and we
should have her by the end of the day.'

Abramov smiled inwardly at the man's response, recognizing that Zharkov probably still had almost no idea
where Raya had gone to ground, because if he had, she
would already be in custody.

'So where is she?' he asked.

'Northern Italy. We have all the borders covered, and our people there are working closely with the Italian police. Every means of transport she could possibly use is being monitored. She won't get out of the country, that I can assure you. Now, Abramov, since you suggested Kosov's ridiculous allegations are worth investigating, you can help us while we do so.'

'Does this mean you no longer believe I was involved in her defection – or whatever you're now calling it?'

Zharkov shook his head. 'The general seems convinced of your innocence, but I do not share his view. I will be watching you very carefully from now on. I have decided to let you assist in the investigation only because you are familiar with the security procedures and computer systems, but everything you do will be checked and double-checked.'

'Where do you want me to start? With the Top Secret files?'

'No, I've already assigned one of my men to check those. You can inspect this office Kosov claimed somebody was using illegally, and find out exactly where this Moscow telephone number is located.'

Checking the number didn't take long, and within a few minutes Abramov knew that the telephone which the unknown traitor – for, unlike Zharkov, he was prepared to accept that Raya had been telling the truth, until unambiguous evidence was provided to the contrary – had dialled, from Yasenevo, terminated in an office within the Lubyanka, in central Moscow.

'The number's in the Lubyanka?' Zharkov asked yet again.

'That's what the trace reports, yes,' Abramov replied.

'Right, contact the Lubyanka security staff and tell them to identify which office that telephone is located in, and to go there immediately. Anyone they find in the room is to be arrested. If it's empty, they're to seal it pending my arrival.' Zharkov stood up and walked to the door, then turned back to glare at Abramov. 'Get up,' he snapped. 'You can come along as well.'

London

Andrew Lomas had received three more 'wrong number' calls, each providing him, through the Russian website, with a continuing update of information on the hunt for Raya Kosov.

The last message had been the most encouraging. Moscow, through the Russian Embassy in Rome, had enlisted the help of the Italian police and security forces, and this had now paid dividends. A car had been spotted close to the French border and, when a police officer had tried to stop the vehicle, the driver had accelerated away. Then both of the pursuing vehicles had been immobilized by two extremely accurate rifle shots, which was almost a confirmation that Raya Kosov was the fugitive inside the car. Lomas already knew, from a brief telephone call to his other asset, both of them using public phones, that the defecting officer was now accompanied by an ex-military pilot called Paul Richter, and by a specialist sniper from the SAS.

The Italians hadn't caught Kosov yet, but the net was certainly tightening around her. The pursuers now knew, to within a mile or so, exactly where she was, and could concentrate all their resources in that area. The next message, Lomas was confident, would merely confirm that she had finally been captured. And then he, and more importantly, his senior asset in the SIS, a man code-named 'Nick', could relax. 'Nick' sounded suitably English, but was actually a contraction of *Vnutrennik*, a Russian word meaning 'insider', and was specifically used to mean a penetration agent. In this case, the use of this word was extraordinarily accurate.

Above Piemonte, Italy

The Piper rocked slightly sideways in the turbulence caused by the jet fighter powering past it, and Richter put both hands back on the control yoke.

'Shit!' Dekker said, and automatically reached for the case containing his sniper rifle.

Richter glanced sideways, saw what he was doing, and shook his head. 'Forget it. Now he's shown us that he's here, he'll stay behind us, where we're nicely within range of whatever weapons he's carrying. And any second now he'll call and tell us what he wants us to do.'

Dekker stared out of the side window. The Aermacchi was in a tight right-hand turn that would bring it up behind the Piper.

'How will he know what frequency we're on?'

'He'll call us on Guard, which is twelve-fifteen megahertz. All civil aircraft are supposed to monitor it.'

The radio speaker suddenly crackled, and a heavily accented voice filled the cabin. 'Unidentified aircraft, you are instructed to turn onto a heading of one one zero immediately, and commence descent.'

'What are we going to do?' Raya asked, her voice choking with fear.

'Well, not what he tells us, that's for sure,' Richter said. 'Not after all we've already been through.'

'But that's a jet fighter, for fuck's sake,' Dekker snapped. 'How the hell are you going to outrun it? He'll be all over us.'

'I can't outrun it,' Richter said simply, 'so I'm going to have to out-fly it. Make sure you're belted in, both of you, and get that rifle secured, Colin. I don't want that case flying around the cabin and braining someone. Your bag too, Raya. This is going to be bouncy.'

'Oh, God,' Dekker said, and jammed the rifle case under the seat.

Richter reached out and pulled the throttle back gently, reducing power and watching the airspeed dropping.

'You're slowing down,' Dekker said nervously.

'I know. Trust me, there's no point in trying to go quickly, because that jet's got a top speed about four times faster than we can manage. He can probably do about five hundred knots, and I already know this aircraft is flat out at around a hundred and twenty. But we do have one advantage: we can fly slower than him.'

'And that helps how, exactly?'

'His stall speed will be at least one hundred knots, almost as fast as we're going now, which means he has to keep travelling faster than that, or his aircraft will fall out of the sky. We can go as slowly as fifty knots and still keep flying.'

'But he can keep circling around us.'

'I know. But he can't stay behind us, and that's the point.'

As Richter spoke, the Aermacchi flew past them again, this time on the left side of the Piper, the pilot gesticulating for them to head back the way they'd come.

'He looks pissed off,' Dekker remarked.

'He's going to be a lot more pissed off in a minute. Now, let's see how good a pilot he is. Hold on.'

Richter pulled smoothly back on the control yoke, and simultaneously applied full right rudder. The Piper's nose rose high in the air, then the aircraft's right wing dropped with sickening suddenness. Instantly, the Piper started to fall, plummeting straight down towards the ground, the whole aircraft rotating clockwise, clearly completely out of control.

Above Rhône-Alps, France

'I hold visual contact with the target aircraft,' the U2 pilot reported. 'It's still in Italian airspace, but getting close to the border. Wait. There's also a military aircraft in the same area, behind the target. Waiting for identification now. Confirmed. The military bogie is an Italian Air Force Aermacchi MB-339.'

'What's your assessment?' Westwood asked. He was sitting in the luxurious cabin of the Lear 60 as the pilot taxied towards Fiumicino's active take-off runway, talking to the U2 jockey on a discrete Company UHF frequency. 'Is the Italian aircraft acting as an escort, or is it hostile?'

'Difficult to say. Standby . . . something's just

happened. It's definitely not an escort. The target aircraft has just started a spin, so it's possible the Aermacchi engaged it with a gun. Definitely not a missile, beause my systems would have detected missile launch.'

'Oh, shit,' Westwood muttered, a feeling of impotent disappointment flooding through him as he visualized the unarmed civilian aircraft crashing onto some unforgiving Alpine slope. 'Pinpoint the crash site,' he said. 'I'll get the emergency services moving.'

'Jesus fucking Christ,' Dekker muttered, 'you've bloody lost it.'

Richter calmly shook his head, keeping the controls in the same positions and alternating his attention between the instruments in front of him and the swirling landscape visible through the windscreen. 'We're in a spin. We're losing height very quickly.'

'I can fucking see that. More to the point, can you get us out of it?'

Richter nodded, looked again at the altimeter and then at the compass, its needle swinging wildly. He waited until the aircraft had almost completed another revolution, then removed his right foot from the rudder pedal. Almost immediately the Piper stopped spinning, but continued its uncontrolled plunge towards the floor of the valley.

'Where's that jet?' Richter asked.

'What?' Dekker couldn't tear his eyes away from the terrifying view through the windscreen.

'Where. Is. That. Jet?' Richter asked again, enunciating each word very clearly.

'It's a long way above us,' Raya said. 'It seems to be flying in a circle.'

'Good.'

As Dekker watched with horrified eyes, Richter pushed the control yoke fully forward.

'But that's the wrong way?' Dekker said. 'You need to pull back.'

'It's counter-intuitive, I know,' Richter said, his tone almost conversational. 'I'd stopped the spin, but the aircraft was still stalled, which means the wings weren't generating any lift. We were in free fall, if you like.'

'I kind of fucking guessed that.'

'So what you have to do is un-stall the wings, and you do that by pushing the control column forwards. Then,' Richter added, his words mirroring his actions, 'you increase power and ease back slowly, and that brings the aircraft back under control.'

Steadily, and without any drama, the nose of the Piper rose until the aircraft was flying level again, now only a couple of hundred feet above the high-altitude valley floor that stretched between the peaks of Pointe de Charbonnel and L'Albaron, and still heading west.

'Where's that Aermacchi? The jet? Where is it?'

'It looks as if it's still circling,' Raya said, 'but it's still quite a long way above us.'

'Good. We'll stay down here in the weeds. I tried to make it look as if the aircraft was completely out of control, so hopefully he's waiting to see the ball of fire that would mark our impact site.'

'He wasn't the only one expecting that to happen,' Dekker muttered.

Richter grinned at him. 'Have a little faith in me, Colin.'

'Now it looks as if it's descending,' Raya said sharply.

'Bound to happen.' Richter pushed the throttle as far forward as possible. 'Now let's try a bit of psychological warfare.'

He grabbed the aeronautical chart he'd been looking at previously, then selected the civilian Guard frequency, 121.5 megahertz, and pressed the transmit button. 'Mayday, Mayday, Mayday. This is French civilian aircraft Foxtrot Lima Yankee Charlie Papa. My position is near Bramans, about ten kilometres from the Italian border, and I'm under attack from an unidentified Italian Aermacchi fighter aircraft. Somebody, anybody, please help.'

Richter released the button and glanced at Dekker. 'That might give the Eyetie flying that Aermacchi pause for thought, simply because we *are* in France now. Shooting us down on the Italian side of the border is one thing. Following us into France and doing the same thing is a whole different ball game.'

'And that broadcast might be picked up by other aircraft or air-traffic control units near here as well?'

'Maybe, maybe not. We're surrounded by mountains here, so most probably not, in fact. Really, that was for the Aermacchi pilot's ears only. Where is he now, Raya?'

'He's climbing again, and he's started turning back the way we came, towards the east.'

'Forget the emergency services,' the U2 pilot corrected Westwood. 'I said it was in a spin, not crashing. The pilot's just recovered, and the target aircraft has now crossed the border. The Aermacchi's still in the area, but

I don't think there's anything he can do now that the civilian aircraft's in France. And . . . wait.'

There was silence on the frequency for a few seconds, then the U2 pilot transmitted again.

'OK, the guy flying the target is English, and he's cute. He just made a Mayday broadcast on twelve-fifteen – that's the civil emergency frequency – to say he's flying a French aircraft and he's being attacked by an Italian military jet.'

'We didn't hear anything,' Westwood remarked. The Lear had just lifted off the runway, and the pilot had been cleared by ATC for an unrestricted climb.

'You wouldn't. You're well out of range. In fact, I doubt if many people heard it, because of where he is, deep down in that valley. But it does prove he's listening to twelve-fifteen, if you want to talk to him. He's using the French call sign Foxtrot Lima Yankee Charlie Papa, which he's obviously just made up if the aircraft's on Italian registry.'

Then the radio speaker in the Piper crackled again, and the same harsh voice issued from it. 'Very clever, but it won't help you. We will be passing your details on to our French colleagues. They will undoubtedly take care of you.'

'Yeah, well, we'll see about that,' Richter said. He glanced again at the topographical chart. 'Change of plan. I was going to keep heading west, but that Italian comedian is right: the Eyeties *can* ask the Frogs to force us down somewhere, so that's starting to sound like a really bad idea. Especially as that fighter pilot will have noted our real registration number and description, and he'll also be able to give the French an accurate starting point for a search.'

'So?'

'So we'll head north-west, up into the Tarentaise area of France. It's home to some of the most expensive ski resorts on the planet – places like Val d'Isère and Les Arcs – and we'll try to find a flat bit of land where we can park this thing.'

Dekker studied the map for a few seconds. 'I won't be sorry to get my feet back on the ground, that's for sure. And if a simple soldier like me can make a suggestion, if you can land somewhere near either Séez or Aime, that would help us.'

This time it was Richter's turn to look puzzled. 'Why?' he asked.

'We could try to steal or even hire a car,' Dekker said, 'and that would inevitably leave a trail of some sort. But if you can get near either of those two places, we won't need to, because there's a railway line there. We can just buy our tickets for cash, and let the French railway system whisk us away. No paperwork, no paper trail.'

'As long as the trains are running, that sounds a very good idea. And railway tracks tend to run on level ground, so we might well find a convenient field to land in somewhere nearby.'

Still keeping the aircraft reasonably low, but mindful of the dangerous atmospheric effects, such as sudden updraughts and downdraughts, which could plague flying across mountains, Richter swung the Piper north-west, and increased their speed slightly.

*

'The target's changed course. He's now heading north-west, currently approaching the Pointe de la Grande Casse.'

'Copied that,' Westwood said, studying a map of the French border area. 'Thanks for your help. Stay in the area and monitor the situation, please. I'm going to call the aircraft now.'

'Roger.'

Westwood selected intercom on the control panel beside his seat. 'Give me twelve-fifteen megahertz,' he instructed, 'and a VHF chat frequency.'

'You've got the civil-emergency frequency on button two,' the pilot replied after a moment, 'and you can use seventeen-fifty-five on button three.'

'Thanks.' Westwood clicked button two, and then pressed the transmit key.

'Foxtrot Lima Yankee Charlie Papa, this is November Two Four. I gather you need some help.'

As they passed the peak of Pointe de la Grande Casse, and altered course to transit to the west of Mont Pourri, Richter gestured over to the right, where two lakes sparkled in the sunshine.

'Val d'Isère is somewhere over there,' he said, 'and Les Arcs is just ahead of us.'

'How far away now?'

'About twenty miles or so.'

From the twin peaks, the ground sloped away to the north dropping down towards the gentler slopes of the ski resorts, where the green and brown hillsides were cut through by the skeletal black lines of unused ski lifts.

Beyond them, at the foot of the valley, Richter could discern the town of Aime, with a road and the parallel glint of a railway line. More importantly, there were several areas of seemingly level ground, hopefully long enough to accommodate the fairly short landing run the Piper would need.

Then the radio speaker crackled again, but this time the voice was unmistakably American. 'Foxtrot Lima Yankee Charlie Papa, this is November Two Four. I gather you need some help.'

'What the hell?' Dekker muttered.

Richter picked up the microphone and depressed the transmit key.

'Thank you, November Two Four, but I think we're OK now.'

'Are you sure about that? The Italian fast jet has run for home, but how's your passenger? Is she OK?'

'What passenger?' Richter asked, looking genuinely confused.

'Sierra Lima minus one,' the American voice replied, then fell silent.

Richter looked at Dekker, then glanced back at Raya. 'What the hell's he talking about?' he asked, of nobody in particular.

'He means me,' Raya said. 'Sierra Lima minus one. Take one letter away from each and you've got Romeo Kilo – my initials. That's what he means.'

Suddenly Richter remembered what Simpson had said, and pressed the transmit key again. 'OK, let me use the same convention, Kilo Xray. Give me a frequency.'

'Neat,' the American replied. 'One seven five decimal five.'

'What the hell's going on?' Dekker demanded, as Richter changed frequency.

'If I'm right, the guy who's talking to us is a senior CIA officer named John Westwood, hence the "Kilo Xray" tag I gave him. "JW" equals "Juliet Whisky", and adding one letter in each case gives you "Kilo Xray". He's obviously worked out that Raya's travelling in this aircraft, and the fact that he's talking to us means he's also airborne somewhere nearby, flying in an American-registered aircraft, because of the "November" call sign.'

'So?'

'So let's hear what he has to say,' Richter replied, and pressed the transmit key. 'You there, Kilo Xray?'

'Do I know you?'

'Not yet, no. What can we do for you?'

'I think it's more what I can do for you. I'm in a Lear 60, way up above you, and I'm prepared to offer you and your passenger a lift, if she'd want one.'

Richter glanced at Raya before replying, and she shook her head firmly.

'The only problem with that, Kilo Xray, is that you'd probably have a destination in Virginia in mind. Somewhere near Langley, perhaps?'

'That's what I'd like to suggest, yes. But my first priority is your passenger's safety, because she's really important to us as well as to your own people. So if you accept my offer, I'm prepared to take you anywhere you want to go. Once you climb into this Lear, we can have you both in London in a couple of hours, no problem.'

'Give me a minute,' Richter said, and sat back in his seat.

'You're not going to agree to that, surely?' Dekker asked.

'I don't know. Raya, were there any leaks that you knew of in the CIA?'

'Not that I was aware of. If you hadn't turned up in Nervi, my next move would have been to approach the Americans.'

'OK,' Richter said. 'It might just be worth hitching a ride with the CIA, not least because the French are going to think twice about interfering with an American-registered and CIA-owned executive jet. And it might even give the Russians pause for thought. And we do have an ace in the hole.'

'What?' Dekker asked.

'You, Colin,' Richter replied. 'John Westwood thinks there are two people in this aircraft – just Raya and me. When, or if, we decide to meet him somewhere, you can stay out of sight and cover us with your rifle until we know for sure that we have the situation under control.'

'You really sure that's a good idea?'

'Listen, Colin, we've got a hell of a long way to go. The Italian authorities will know for sure that we've made it as far as France, and that means the Russians will know it as well. I really don't fancy trying to fight our way through teams of Moscow hit men all the way to Calais. If we can hitch a ride on that Lear, we can be in London *today*. In a couple of hours. We just have to make sure that's where we end up, and not in Virginia.'

'OK,' Dekker replied. 'So how do we do it?'

'That's the tricky bit. Let me have another look at that map.'

*

'I've now picked up two further contacts in the vicinity of the target aircraft, both heading north-east and in loose formation,' the U2 pilot reported to Westwood on the Company chat frequency. 'Slow-moving, so probably rotary wing. I'm waiting for the computer to confirm that.'

'Position?' Westwood asked.

'Just about to cross the E70 autoroute near St Michel de Maurienne. That puts them about twenty miles from where the target turned north-west, and twenty-five miles from its present position. Computer now confirms they're helicopters, most likely a pair of French Eurocopter Dauphin gunships. If they catch up with the target – and they will – they'll be able to blow him out of the sky.'

'Thanks.' Westwood switched frequencies. 'Foxtrot Lima, November Two Four, update. You have two probable helicopter gunships approaching you from the south-west. You can't outrun them, so I suggest you land as soon as possible, before they force you down, or worse.'

'That's it,' Richter said. 'Decision made.'

He called Westwood. 'OK, Kilo Xray, we'll grab a ride with you. If you can land the Lear at Chambéry, we'll put this thing down as soon as we can and meet you there. Agreed?'

'That's a deal. I'm up here with a friend, and we'll fly top cover for you until you're on the ground.'

'A friend?' Richter asked.

'One high letter and one low number.'

'Copied.'

'You're going to tell us what the hell he's talking about, I hope,' Dekker said.

'It's easy,' Richter replied. 'There's only one aircraft operated by the Americans that's designated by a letter that occurs late in the alphabet and also a low number. There's a U2 somewhere way up above us. That explains how Westwood found us, and how he's been getting information on other stuff flying around.'

'A U2? You're kidding.' Dekker glanced at Raya with new respect. 'You must be a hell of a lot more important than I thought,' he said. 'Makes me wonder why they sent a knackered old shag like Richter here to bring you in.'

Raya grinned at him. 'Because that's what I wanted,' she said. 'Somebody who wasn't a member of your SIS. And he's not that knackered, and I can prove it.'

Dekker glanced from Raya to Richter, and back again. 'Got it,' he said. 'Message received and understood.'

'OK,' Richter said, as the Piper covered the remaining distance, 'make sure your seat belts are tight, because the landing's going to be bumpy. I'll make a low pass over the field first, just to check for obstructions like cows or power lines, then I'll put it on the ground.'

Dekker was still looking at the topographical map. 'You're heading for Aime?' he asked.

'Yes, it's slightly closer, and the contour lines suggest there might be a bit more level ground there.'

A few minutes later, Richter throttled back, dropped the Piper down to about five hundred feet above ground level, and banked to the left as he studied the ground below them. A road and railway line were now clearly visible to the north, while below there was a largely open field, lying south of the railway line, which lay south of the N90 road. The field had clumps of trees growing at both ends, but there was an open area between which looked to Richter about five hundred yards long. It would be tight, but doable. And there was nothing else nearby that looked any better.

'I suppose it's a bit high here for growing most crops,' Dekker remarked, 'but I can see a few animals over to the north of the main road. Grazing the mountain pastures, I suppose.'

'Ski areas are a pretty depressing sight in summer,' Richter said, 'but they're also usually deserted, which suits us. That'll do fine,' he added, turning the aircraft left, to point back the way they'd come.

'There?' Dekker sounded horrified. 'It's like somebody's back garden. You'll never get it down into that space.'

'Thanks for the vote of confidence,' Richter said, 'but it's actually long enough, and quite wide. I just need to drop down as near to those trees at the north-east end as I can, and then get this thing stopped before we run into the trees at the other end.'

'Bloody hell,' Dekker muttered, and pulled his seat belt a little tighter.

'And, actually, there's nowhere else,' Richter added.

'The two helos have split, one left, one right,' the U2 pilot advised Westwood. 'It looks like they're starting a search for the target. The guy going north-east is going to spot the aircraft within a couple of minutes, if he stays on the same heading.'

'Roger,' Westwood said, and switched back to the frequency he was using to communicate with Richter. 'This is November Two Four. You need to get that thing on the ground right now. One of those gunships will be on you in about three minutes.'

'Copied. We're almost downwind, should be on the deck inside two minutes. And thanks.'

The field was covered with grass, but it was far from a bowling-green surface, looking rough and lumpy. But, on the good side, it was reasonably level, and just about long enough for the Piper to land in, with no obvious obstructions apart from the trees. Like all pilots, Richter had a well-deserved fear of power lines, telephone cables and the like, which could rip off a wing or propeller in an instant, and turn any landing into an uncontrollable and fatal crash.

He continued around in a tight turn – to start what would have been called the downwind leg if he'd been at an airfield circuit. That took him over what looked like a small, recently built housing estate. He eyed the trees carefully as he prepared to land, but their branches seemed almost stationary, so he knew there was no significant wind.

Richter reduced speed still further, selected full flap and then lowered the undercarriage, dividing his attention between the instruments in front of him and the open field to his left.

With the airspeed indicator showing just over seventy knots – on the plastic board, the stall speed of the aircraft was listed at fifty knots – he turned the Piper onto base leg and continued the turn until he was lined up with the field. Then he continued reducing speed slowly.

As always, the aircraft seemed to go faster the closer it got to the ground, an optical illusion Richter was very familiar with. The trees seemed to rush up towards them, the field in front now looking deceptively short, and the surface slightly worse than he'd expected. He held the speed at sixty knots, which would give him sufficient speed to go around again – to carry out a missed approach – if he wasn't happy with the look of the surface just before the Piper touched down.

Directly ahead was a short line of trees, at right angles to his line of approach, which marked the end of the clear area.

He watched the tops of the trees getting closer, and for an instant it seemed they were too close, that the undercarriage was going to clip them. Beside him, Dekker muttered something under his breath.

Chapter Twenty-Four

Monday
The Lubyanka, Moscow

Just under an hour later, Zharkov strode into a small office on one of the upper floors of the Lubyanka and looked around. Abramov and two of the building security guards followed him into the room. The security staff had found the door locked, with nobody inside, when they'd arrived to secure it. They'd also reported that it was normally only ever used as overflow accommodation for SVR officers temporarily appointed to the building.

And, indeed, the office's furnishings were extremely sparse. There were two desks, positioned back to back against the longer wall of the room, and a pair of swivel chairs. The desks were bare apart from a desktop computer sitting on one of them, two telephones, a few sheets of blank paper and a handful of pencils.

'So why would anyone phone here,' Zharkov mused, 'if there's nobody to answer?'

Abramov looked closely at the two telephones, then bent forward to peer, under the desks, at the wall sockets.

'They might not have been calling anyone actually in this office,' he said, reaching forward under one of them.

'What do you mean?'

'I mean this looks like a call diverter,' Abramov said, pulling a small oblong box out from the underside of one of the desks. One lead ran from the box to the line socket on the wall, and the other to one of the two telephones. A third, very thin lead ran to a power socket, but it was wired directly into the back of it, so that the main socket could still be used for a computer or any other piece of mains-powered equipment.

'Clever,' he said. 'This box is well hidden and, because the room's only used by temporary staff, probably none of them would ever wonder what it was, even if they'd noticed it.'

Abramov pressed the power button on the desktop computer.

'Can you find out what number the diverter's set to call?' Zharkov asked, seeming noticeably more subdued now that at least a part of Raya Kosov's story appeared to have substance.

'I already have done,' Abramov replied. 'As soon as this computer's working, I'll look it up in the directory.'

Zharkov nodded absently, and sat down in the other seat while they waited for the desktop's operating system and application software to load. After a couple of minutes, Abramov opened the directory program that would allow him to trace the number he'd copied down from the tiny digital display on the call diverter. He entered the digits in the correct field and then pressed the Enter key to obtain the details.

Then he sat back in the chair and looked across at Zharkov.

'Well?' the colonel demanded. 'Who is it?'

'It's you,' Abramov said, his voice hushed. 'According to this directory, the number the diverter calls is your Moscow apartment.'

Aime, Rhône-Alps, France

Then they were over the trees, the branches rushing beneath them so close that it looked to Dekker as if he could almost lean out of the window and touch them.

Richter eased the throttle back, dropping the speed still further, and lifted the nose slightly as the aircraft lost more height. By now they were committed to a landing. They dropped quickly towards the field, heading for touchdown.

The two main wheels of the tricycle undercarriage thumped on the ground. The Piper bounced once, then settled on the grass surface, as Richter closed the throttle completely. The nose-wheel dropped and the aircraft bounced and shuddered, seeming almost to lurch from wheel to wheel as its speed fell away.

He controlled the aircraft's direction with the rudder pedals, keeping it straight. There was another group of trees over to the left, which he needed to keep well clear of. As the aircraft slowed down, Richter opened the throttle again to keep it moving, aiming towards the far end of the field, which lay closer to the village of Aime, and which would mean they had a slightly shorter distance to walk once they stopped.

Beyond the far end of the field was another line of trees, about fifty yards clear of the main copse. Richter steered the aircraft over to the right-hand end of it, swung in behind it and braked to a halt. Then he switched off the engine and applied the parking brake. While the aircraft would still be easily visible from the air, stopping it in this spot meant that most people on the ground would only be able to see it if they looked from a certain point on the railway line running just to the north of the field, or actually entered the field itself. Of course, he'd landed so close to the housing estate that no doubt somebody from there would come wandering over fairly soon.

'Pretty bumpy landing,' Dekker observed, 'but on this surface it's not surprising. And you definitely know how to fly.'

'I've had the same number of landings as take-offs,' Richter declared, 'and in the Royal Navy that counts as exceptional flying ability.' He glanced behind him. 'Are you OK there, Raya?'

The Russian girl nodded shakily, unclipped her seat belt and grabbed her bag, ready to get out.

Dekker pulled his rifle case from under the seat, opened the door and climbed down. As soon as he was on the ground, he checked all around, looking for any sign of trouble. But, as far as he could tell, nobody had noticed them land – or at least there was nobody, in or near the field, watching them. Raya and Richter followed him out of the aircraft and stood beside him.

Then, with a roar that was deafening and a blast of air almost knocking them off their feet, a Eurocopter Panther gunship roared past above their heads, and then seemed almost to topple onto its side as the pilot pulled it around in a brutally hard turn, the sound of the rotors beating the air like distant thunder.

*

'One of the choppers is right over the target aircraft now, and turning hard.' The U2 pilot sounded calm and controlled.

'Thanks for the update,' Westwood replied, 'but there's nothing we can do to help them now.'

The Lubyanka, Moscow

'You're obviously mistaken, Abramov.' Zharkov's voice was low and menacing. 'You must have looked up the wrong number.'

Abramov glanced at him, then at the two Lubyanka security guards who'd accompanied them. He absolutely knew he'd got the correct telephone number from the call diverter and, unless somebody had tampered with the directory, that telephone line terminated in Colonel Zharkov's Moscow apartment. There were only two possible conclusions he could draw. Either there genuinely *was* a mistake in the directory, which seemed fairly unlikely, or Zharkov himself must have had something to do with the security breach that Raya Kosov claimed to have discovered.

Suddenly, the security colonel's obvious reluctance to initiate an investigation made perfect sense. And Abramov knew there was now only one thing he could do, despite the risks.

'I'm sorry, Colonel,' he said, 'but I have no option but to place you under close arrest until we can resolve this matter.'

'You what?' Zharkov couldn't believe his ears. The worm, classically, had turned – and it had turned on him. 'You will do no such thing. This is clearly a mistake. A stupid mistake made by somebody, and they will pay for it when I find out who they are.'

Abramov nodded. 'No doubt you're correct, Colonel, but I have no choice. Guards, you will place this officer under arrest, immediately.'

The two security guards had been following the conversation between them with bemused expressions, but a direct order was a direct order, even when delivered by the more junior of the two SVR officers involved.

One of them drew his weapon, covering Zharkov, while the other man stepped forward and removed the colonel's personal weapon from his belt holster.

Zharkov didn't react, but just stood perfectly still, which Abramov found more alarming than any blustering denial. 'You'll pay for this,' the colonel hissed. 'If it's the last thing I do, I'll make sure of that.'

'Take him away,' the major ordered.

Rhône-Alps, France

'Colin!' Richter shouted, grabbing Raya by the arm and turning to run towards the nearby trees. 'Try not to kill anyone!'

Dekker had already reacted and dived for cover. The gun case was now open beside him, and he was assembling the weapon with calm urgency.

The helicopter gunship swung around to face the Piper Arrow, then settled into a low hover over the open ground about a hundred yards away, as the pilot began lowering the retractable undercarriage ready for landing.

As he and Raya ducked into cover under the trees Richter could see, even through the glare of sunlight reflected off the twin windscreens, two figures in the cockpit, but he knew that the Eurocopter, in its AS 565 Panther configuration, could carry up to ten fully armed and equipped troops. If the French had found time to deploy that many personnel, he knew they were probably not going to get away this time.

'Stay down,' Richter instructed.

As he watched, the 20-millimetre Giat cannon swivelled towards the abandoned Piper Arrow. Then the muzzle shifted slightly to one side, and the gunner fired a short burst at the trees a couple of dozen yards away from where Richter and Raya had taken cover. The French airman was probably hoping such a demonstration of firepower would be enough to persuade the fugitives to give themselves up.

But that wasn't quite what happened.

Richter heard the flat crack of Dekker's sniper rifle, and suddenly smoke started pouring out of the Panther's starboard engine. Then there was a much louder bang, and the helicopter's engine seemed almost to explode, panels flying off it, and a sheet of flame erupted from the turbine inlet.

The helicopter lurched upwards, then swung sideways, the pilot fighting for control. Then the Panther crashed downwards to land so heavily that the right-hand main wheel collapsed under the impact. As the aircraft lurched violently sideways, the edge of the rotor disc clipped the ground, and that was enough to bring the aircraft's total destruction. In an instant, the four main rotor blades splintered and cracked, sending debris flying all around. The fuselage toppled further onto its side, the noise of the remaining engine rising to a scream, and then it finally crashed to the ground.

Dekker appeared suddenly beside Richter, as he stared across the field at the smoking wreckage. Two men wearing flying overalls and helmets were climbing shakily out of the ruined fuselage, but they now clearly posed no threat to anyone.

'That was either a pretty special bullet or a fucking good shot,' Richter remarked.

Dekker grinned at him. 'One round sent straight into the engine intake. No problem, at this range.'

'Right, so now you've pissed off the French as well as the Italians. It's time we got ourselves out of here. Let's go and find a car.'

Dekker kept the rifle slung over his shoulder, as the three of them ran towards the group of houses they'd spotted before they landed. There was no point in trying to be discreet, since the sound of the helicopter's Giat cannon would have alerted everybody in the neighbourhood. As soon as they reached the houses, Richter started looking out for a car. Preferably a fast one.

As they headed down the street, ignoring the curious glances of various residents who'd emerged from their houses to investigate the noise, a single man drove up in a newish four-door Renault saloon, which Richter thought might be a Laguna.

'That'll do,' he murmured, and strode across to the driver's door, just as it opened.

The driver looked at him enquiringly, then backed away quickly as Richter produced his Browning pistol.

'I'll drive, Colin,' he suggested, 'just in case we need your rifle again.'

Within seconds, all three of them were seated in the car, and Richter had swung it round to head back the same way the dispossessed driver had come.

'He'll tell the gendarmes, of course,' Dekker said.

'I know – which is why we need to get a move on. There aren't that many roads around here, so mounting roadblocks won't be difficult. I know we need to head south-west out of Aime, but where do we go after that? And how far is it to Chambéry?'

Dekker fished a map book of France out of the passenger door pocket, found the correct page and studied it for a few moments.

'Keep going as far as Moûtiers, then turn right up to Albertville. There's an autoroute there that we can follow all the way to Chambéry. It's not far away, in a straight line, but probably about ninety or a hundred clicks on the road because of all the valleys.'

'Bugger, that's further than I thought,' Richter said. 'And I think we'd better stay off the autoroutes, because they're the easiest to block.'

The road through Aime was good and wide and mostly straight, at least to begin with. When they reached the vicinity of Villette, it narrowed and became more twisty, but it was still good enough for Richter to keep their speed at well over one hundred kilometres an hour.

At Moûtiers, the N90 swung around to the south of the town and then headed north up the valley, but still they were able to travel quickly.

'Keep your eyes open for trouble,' Richter warned, as the Renault sped past La Bâthie. 'The guy we borrowed this car from will have certainly sounded the alarm by now, so we'll need to watch out for roadblocks.'

'Yeah,' Dekker agreed, still studying the map. 'In fact I'm wondering if we should try a small detour, just in case.'

'Where?'

'At Albertville, maybe. That's quite a big place, so there's bound to be a gendarmerie somewhere about, and blocking the main road would be obvious. I suggest once you get to the interchange in the middle of the town, you get off the N90, and instead take a left on a minor road which should be signposted to Grignon. After you cross the river, the road continues pretty straight all the way to a place called Le Mathiez, where you'll need to turn right.'

'Sounds like a plan, so let's do that.'

The interchange was easily spotted, because it was the only one on that stretch, so Richter swung the car down the slip road and headed south. After the relatively wide and open roads they'd been travelling on, the two-lane route to Grignon seemed instantly slower. But once they'd crossed the river, it at least became straight and almost empty of vehicles. And, just after they'd crossed the bridge, Dekker noticed how the traffic was backing up on the N90, which they could see over to their right, on the other side of the river. Though that might be due to an accident, he suspected a checkpoint on the road. Once they drove into the outskirts of Grignon, they lost sight of the alternative route.

'That's Le Mathiez over there,' Dekker said soon, pointing left, 'so watch out now for a junction to the right. It should be the D69, heading towards the autoroute, but you can go under it, carry on across the river again, and then pick up the D1090.'

As they approached the autoroute, they all glanced back, towards Albertville. The south-bound traffic was now very light, suggesting that there was still an obstruction of some kind.

'That was a good call, Colin. I wouldn't want to be stuck back there, whatever the reason. So we stay on this route, yes?'

It may have been just a minor road, but being a French minor road, it was straight and well surfaced and, twenty minutes later, Richter turned north-west at Montmélian. They were now approaching Chambéry.

'We have to go right through the town and out the other side,' Dekker advised him. 'There's a lake up to the north, with the town's airport situated just to the south of it.'

French gendarmes have a habit of lying in wait behind hedges and around blind corners, armed with radar guns to trap speeding motorists. Usually, by the time a driver has seen them, it's too late, and his speed and registration number would already have been recorded. A demand for money would pop into his letter box a few days later.

It was a little over an hour after they'd left Aime, and just south of a village named Challes-les-Eaux, south-east of Chambéry, when Richter powered the Renault down a straight stretch of the D1006, and headed straight past two gendarmes leaning across the bonnet of a dark blue car. One of them was holding a radar gun.

'Shit,' he muttered, watching in his rear-view mirror. He wasn't worried about a speeding fine, obviously, but he was certain the stolen car's registration number would be widely circulated by now. Even as he watched, he saw the two men gesticulating wildly, before they hurried around and climbed into their car. Only seconds later, it was turning onto the road behind them.

Sluzhba Vneshney Razvyedki Rossi Headquarters, Yasenevo, Tëplyystan, Moscow

'Are you absolutely certain of your facts?' General Morozov asked. He was the senior SVR security officer, and Zharkov's direct superior.

Yuri Abramov nodded. 'The number that the call diverter in the Lubyanka was set to contact is definitely the one listed in the directory for Colonel Zharkov's apartment in Moscow. Those are the facts, sir, and I submit that they're beyond dispute. Of course,' Abramov added, 'it's possible that the directory was wrong, and that—'

'No,' the general interrupted. 'I've already checked Zharkov's personnel file, and that directory listing is accurate. It's just that the colonel has always been considered one of my most trusted officers, and a man who I've always felt I could rely on absolutely. And now this.'

For a few seconds the general just sat in his chair, with arms resting on the wide desk in front of him, lost in thought and seeming almost to have forgotten that Abramov was still present.

Finally he roused himself. 'Right,' he said briskly, 'so

now we have to start investigating him, as well as repairing the damage caused by this disastrous defection of the Kosov woman.'

A thought suddenly occurred to Abramov. Knowing Raya's undoubted ability with computer systems, he wondered if perhaps she could have rigged the call diverter to falsely implicate Colonel Zharkov. But, for her to do that, there must have been some contact between the two of them in the past, something that caused such serious friction that she'd dare attempt something like that. But, as far as he knew, Raya had never even met Zharkov, because they worked in entirely separate sections of the SVR. But Abramov realized he was obliged to at least voice his suspicions.

'Sir, just a small point. Do you think there's any possibility of the two incidents being related? Considering that our suspicions over the colonel have been raised simply by what Kosov said in her email.'

The general looked interested now. 'You're suggesting Kosov might be trying to get revenge on Zharkov for some reason?'

Abramov nodded.

'I frankly doubt it,' Morozov said. 'I've already reviewed Zharkov's file, and there's no mention there of him even knowing she existed. But it might be worth checking her file as well, so I'll get one of my officers to do that.'

'And me, sir?'

'You can assist with the investigation into Colonel Zharkov's actions, since my team can probably make use of your specialist knowledge of the SVR computer systems.'

That sounded reasonable, but Abramov could read between the lines. Morozov had no intention of allowing him to check Raya Kosov's personnel file, in case he added or deleted something that might be germane to her defection. And having Abramov on the team investigating Zharkov was simply a way of ensuring that the general and his staff could keep an eye on him.

But at least he wasn't locked up in a room by himself any longer.

Chapter Twenty-Five

Monday
Near Chambéry, France

'How far now, Colin?' Richter asked urgently, getting as much speed as he could out of the Renault.

Dekker had been looking behind, but quickly glanced back at the map. 'About ten miles, that's all,' he replied.

'That car won't catch us,' Richter said, 'but by now he'll be radioing for back-up. Let's hope there aren't too many police cars between here and the airport.'

The road was virtually straight, but they were meeting more traffic now because of the built-up areas fast approaching, and Richter was forced to drop his speed.

'There's an airport,' Raya said urgently, pointing to the right as they drove out of Challes-les-Eaux.

'Yeah,' Dekker replied, 'but it's the wrong one.'

'That's just a little civilian field,' Richter added. 'It's probably used for gliders and light aircraft, that kind of thing. I doubt the runway's anything like long enough to handle a Lear.'

'Traffic lights ahead,' Dekker said, 'and go straight on.'

As they approached, Richter weaving past cars and vans whenever he could, the lights suddenly turned red. In his mirror, he could see the French police car maybe half a mile back, its headlamps on and roof lights flashing. Travelling quickly, it was now too close.

'Hang on,' he said, swerving around a slowing articulated lorry and pulling over into the right-hand lane. A horn sounded loudly behind him as the lorry driver expressed his displeasure.

Traffic was already driving in both directions across the junction, but Richter just powered ahead, past the red traffic lights. He hit the brakes hard as a white van passed a few feet in front of the Renault's nose, then picked a gap in the crossing traffic and accelerated hard. The driver of a small grey Peugeot did an emergency stop as Richter shot across in front of him, but the driver behind him didn't react as quickly. There was a rending crash as his vehicle smashed into the back of the Peugeot, but by then Richter was already well past.

'That might help,' he muttered, glancing back. 'Nothing like a traffic accident in the middle of a junction to slow everything down.'

The road swung around to the left and straightened up, then the traffic lanes got narrower as they approached a roundabout.

'Keep going straight,' Dekker instructed. 'There are three roundabouts, one after the other.'

As they drove around the third one, Richter spotted another police car, lights flashing, heading directly towards them, but it carried on straight along the road towards the junction where the crash had just occurred.

They were now close to the centre of Chambéry, where the traffic was getting much more congested. The bad news was that Richter had to slow right down, but on the other hand their car was now just one more anonymous Renault in a town filled with French-made vehicles, so spotting them was going to be much more difficult for the local gendarmes.

Dekker directed him onto the Avenue de la Boisse, a north-bound road that ran alongside a railway line and then past a station. 'Stay on this road,' he said, 'and maybe keep the speed down a bit. We're pretty close now, only about five miles away.'

They were still driving in a heavily built-up area, so Richter actually had little choice but to keep going with the flow of traffic. At the next intersection, following Dekker's instructions, he pulled onto the north-bound autoroute. It was a non-toll section, which meant there were no payment booths where they could be stopped.

Richter wound the speed up as soon as they cleared the junction. A couple of miles later, he hit the brakes and pulled off the urban autoroute, and back onto a normal road which ran to the west of a village named Voglans.

Dekker pointed ahead of them, towards another roundabout. 'Turn left there,' he said. 'We've arrived.'

As Richter swung round the roundabout, he saw another police car heading down the road straight towards them. There was nothing he could do about it, so he accelerated the Renault towards the airport, hoping that the gendarmes hadn't spotted them.

As the police vehicle carried straight on down the road towards Chambéry, Richter started to breathe more easily. He glanced to his left and saw what was probably a general aviation terminal, used by private pilots. Dwarfing the handful of light aircraft parked in front of the hangar was the unmistakable sleek black shape of a Lear 60.

'That looks like our ride,' he said, then glanced in his mirror again.

The French police car was performing a U-turn in the road, the lights on its roof bar now flashing.

'We've got more trouble,' he said.

'There's a surprise,' Dekker replied, turning round in his seat to look back.

'You'll have to stop him, or we'll never get on board that aircraft,' Richter said, swinging the car off the road and towards the terminal building. 'Then can you cover the pair of us as well?'

'No problem. Just drop me here,' Dekker instructed, seizing his rifle.

Richter slewed the car to a stop, waited until Dekker had climbed out, then surged forward, with tyres screeching, towards the Lear jet.

There was a pair of steel gates barring their way across to the hardstanding, but they looked more for show than security.

'Brace yourself,' he yelled to Raya, and powered the car straight towards the point where the gates met.

The Renault jolted under the impact, but the gates flew apart instantly. Richter pulled the car to a stop, about twenty yards from the Lear, and switched off the engine.

'Let's go,' he said, grabbing Dekker's rifle case.

'What about Colin?' Raya asked, picking up her bag.

'He'll be here any second.'

As if in response, they both heard the crack of a rifle somewhere behind them.

The passenger door of the Lear was open, and a dark-haired man wearing a grey suit was standing beside the aircraft, looking towards them. Above him, Richter could see two men sitting ready in the cockpit.

He hurried across the hardstanding, Raya beside him, and they stopped beside the aircraft.

'John Westwood?' he asked, and the man nodded. 'My name's Paul Richter, and this is Raya Kosov. If you can tell your guys to kick the tyres and light the fires, we'd appreciate getting this taxi into the air as soon as possible.'

Westwood nodded. 'You're very trusting,' he said with a slight smile. 'I could have a couple of guys inside the aircraft ready to shoot you down right now, and then take Raya straight back to the States with us.'

'You could certainly try,' Richter agreed, 'but you'd never get off the ground. There's a man behind me, watching you through the sights of a sniper rifle. If you try and pull a gun, you'll be dead, then he'll blow out the tyres on the landing gear, and we'd just take our chances at avoiding the French.'

Westwood glanced behind Richter, but apparently spotted nothing. His smile growing broader, he opened his jacket to show that he was unarmed. As he did so, a tiny red spot of light appeared in the exact centre of his chest.

'I told you.' Richter pointed.

'It was just a hypothetical scenario,' Westwood replied. 'I always keep my word.'

'Sure you do,' Richter didn't look entirely convinced, 'but I'm going to check anyway.' He pulled out his Browning, motioned to Raya to stay where she was, and climbed the steps up into the cabin, which was empty.

'Now I believe you,' he said, returning to the door of the aircraft. 'Right, let's go.'

As Raya climbed up the steps, Richter waved to where he thought Dekker might be hiding. Moments later, the SAS officer emerged from the bushes and ran across to the aircraft, the sniper rifle slung over his shoulder.

In seconds, all four of them were safely inside the Lear's luxurious cabin. Westwood closed the exterior door and stepped across to the cockpit entrance. 'We're all aboard, Frank. Get us out of here.'

'Yes, sir.'

A man emerged from the cockpit, glanced without apparent surprise at Richter and Dekker, who were both pointing pistols at him, and checked that the exterior door was properly secured. With a nod to Westwood, he then returned to the cockpit and closed the intervening door.

As the jet engines spooled up, Richter glanced at Dekker. 'OK?'

'No problem.' That expression seemed like a mantra for the SAS man. 'I just took out the front tyre on the plod-mobile, as it came around the corner.'

The speaker system switched on, and a Midwestern voice filled the cabin. 'Please make sure your seat belts are fastened. We've been instructed to hold here in dispersal, Mr Westwood, at the request of local law enforcement. But we guessed you probably wouldn't want to do that, so we're heading for the runway right now.'

The Lear swung around and started moving quickly, heading south down the taxiway leading towards the end of the runway.

Richter peered out of the window beside him. Chambéry had the usual range of crash and rescue service vehicles and, as he stared at one of the buildings, red-painted steel door shutters started to roll up, and the fronts of a couple of heavy fire engines emerged.

'They're going to try and block the runway,' he said urgently.

'Relax, Mr Richter,' Westwood said. 'The guys in the cockpit are ex-USAF fighter jockeys. They'll find a way past them.'

Richter doubted that any pilot, no matter how experienced or talented, could 'find a way past' a couple of ten-ton fire engines blocking the runway, but he lapsed into silence because there was nothing he could do about it. If he'd seen the fire engines, obviously the flight-deck crew would have seen them as well.

The Lear turned sharply to the north, and its engine noise rose to a crescendo as the aircraft began its take-off run.

Richter looked again through the window. The two engines were heading for the mid-point of the runway, the intentions of the crews obvious. It was all a matter of speed and acceleration and physics. The two vehicles were probably travelling at twenty miles an hour, and gaining speed slowly. He guessed that the Lear was already doing nearly a hundred knots, and getting near V1. And there was also the human factor. He doubted if the crash crews would actually want to drive directly in front of a jet aircraft travelling at well over one hundred miles an hour, because that way they would effectively be committing suicide.

And as he watched, the two fire engines slowed right down, and then came to a stop just off the edge of the runway. The aircraft roared past them, and Richter gave an ironic wave as they went by.

The Lear lifted smoothly off the runway and started to climb swiftly over the long, narrow lake lying immediately north of Chambéry airfield.

As they passed through about five thousand feet, Westwood picked up a phone.

'Frank,' he said, 'it's possible our guests here might have offended the French, so make a call to see if our friends can join us.'

'Friends?' Richter asked.

Westwood nodded. 'I've had a couple of F-16s from the 31st Fighter Wing at Aviano on standby, just in case we needed an escort out of here. They got airborne about twenty minutes ago. As far as the Italians are concerned, they're being sent over to Mildenhall on a liaison visit, so they're fitted with drop tanks to give them range. They're also carrying what I believe the pilots refer to as a "full rack".'

Dekker turned enquiringly to Richter.

'That means they're fully armed,' he said, 'just in case the Frogs decide their best interests might be served by having a couple of Mirages pop up beside us, to try to make us land at some French military airfield.' Richter glanced at Westwood. 'A U2, this Lear, and now a couple of F-16s? This has not been a cheap exercise for you. Why are you so interested in Raya here?'

Westwood shrugged. 'Mainly, I suppose, we got interested because the Russians were so keen to get you back, Ms Kosov. You simply had to be important because of the size of the operation they've mounted to find you. And I'm very glad they didn't succeed. The British, of course, denied all knowledge of your existence, and that was why I knew they were deeply involved.'

'So what's in it for you?' Richter asked.

'I work for the CIA, as I'm sure you know. Ideally, we'd like to debrief Raya ourselves, back at Langley, but now we know that's not going to happen. So our next best option seemed to be to help you get her out of the clutches of the thugs that Moscow sent after her, and then ask politely if we can share her material.'

Westwood turned to Raya. 'So who are you, exactly?' he asked. 'Our Moscow people first identified you a long time ago, but you haven't popped up on our radar for quite a few years. We guessed you'd been recruited by one of the organs, like the SVR, and that's why you seemed to vanish.'

'She's just a clerk,' Dekker said, holstering his pistol and peering out of the window at the fast-receding ground. The Lear was climbing rapidly. 'Goes up bloody fast, doesn't it?' he added.

'Like a fart in a bath,' Richter remarked. 'Like Colin said, Raya's a clerk.'

'No, she isn't,' Westwood said firmly. 'And Colin here is who, exactly?'

'Our guardian angel. He's the man with the long rifle to make sure the bad guys keep their distance.'

'Sounds reasonable,' Westwood said. 'And what about you? I presume you're the guy who was flying that little puddle-jumper you stole in Italy?'

Richter nodded and introduced himself. 'I'm ex-military,' he finished, 'and I kind of got suckered into this by taking a job that looked too good to be true. Which it was, of course.'

'So you're not SIS at all?'

'No, Mr Westwood,' Raya chipped in, 'because that

was one of the conditions I insisted on. There are at least two SIS officers on our Moscow payroll, and the one thing I wasn't prepared to risk was one of them being sent to meet me. That would be a sure and certain way of ending up back in Moscow. So I wanted London to send out somebody completely unconnected with SIS and I ended up with this character, who's so far proved quite good at keeping me alive.'

'OK.' Westwood nodded. 'Now we know who we all are, but no way is Ms Kosov just a clerk. Almost the entire Russian Embassy staff were out on the streets of Rome looking for her, plus a minimum of fifty experts flown in specially from Moscow to help. They wouldn't do all that for a defecting clerk, so just who the hell are you, lady?'

Raya glanced at Richter, then nodded. 'You may have just saved all our lives,' she said, 'so I think you at least deserve to know this. I was the Deputy Computer Network Manager at Yasenevo.'

'Holy shit,' Westwood muttered. 'Or maybe I should say the holy grail.' He glanced from Raya to Richter, and back again. 'Look,' he said, 'don't take this the wrong way, but I owe it to my bosses to at least make you an offer, just in case you might be interested. Whatever the British have agreed to pay you we'd double it at a minimum. You can have a new identity in the States, as part of the Witness Protection Program, and live wherever you want. This aircraft could take you to Virginia right now.'

Raya gazed at him for a long moment, then shook her head. 'There's more than one motive for betraying your country, Mr Westwood. Money doesn't interest me. I have a very different reason for being here.'

'And that is?' Richter asked.

Raya smiled at him. 'All in good time, Paul. Let's get somewhere safe – somewhere *really* safe, I mean – and then I'll answer all of your questions.'

'Our playmates have just arrived,' the captain announced over the cabin broadcast system.

As he made the announcement, there was a sudden roar audible even over the noise of the Lear's engines. Richter changed seats and peered through the window. One of the F-16s was just passing down the starboard side of the Lear, at the same level and maybe eighty metres away. Clearly visible on the rudder were the 'AV' letters that identified it as being based at Aviano.

'Now,' Richter said, leaning back in his seat, 'when I see a Fighting Falcon out there instead of an Aermacchi, I actually do feel safe. Just you make sure the jet jockeys driving this thing know we're heading for London, not Langley, Mr Westwood. Because, you're right, it *was* me flying that Piper Arrow over the Alps, and I'm perfectly capable of driving this executive knocking shop as well.'

Sluzhba Vneshney Razvyedki Rossi Headquarters, Yasenevo, Tëplyystan, Moscow

Yuri Abramov stood at the rear of Colonel Yevgeni Zharkov's spacious office and stared around.

Members of the search team the general had sent in were busily opening doors and drawers, looking for anything that might be construed as incriminating. As Abramov watched, one of the men pulled a drawer completely out of the desk, the more easily to inspect its contents. As he lifted it up, another investigator spotted a metallic glint from the drawer's underside, and muttered an instruction.

Working together, the two men swiftly removed the contents of the drawer and stacked them on the desk. Then they turned it over to inspect the base. Immediately, Abramov saw precisely what had attracted their attention. Secured to the underside of the drawer, with clear tape, were two flat keys. This find alone was enough to convince the searchers that they were onto something. If these keys were innocent – if they merely fitted a lock in the colonel's apartment or something in his office – then why were they hidden?

They studied the keys closely, then one of the men made a call. A few minutes later General Morozov himself appeared.

'Leave them where they are,' he instructed. 'I will invite Colonel Zharkov to explain what they are used for, and why he felt it necessary to conceal them.'

Then he turned to face Yuri Abramov. 'I hate to admit it,' the old man said, 'but it looks as if you were right and Zharkov is playing some kind of a dirty game.'

'Have you questioned him, sir?' Abramov asked.

Morozov nodded. 'Yes, but he merely claims somebody is trying to set him up. And there is one thing he's saying that makes sense. You found his apartment number on the call diverter recovered from that office in the Lubyanka. Zharkov's point is that the only reason for setting up such a diversion would be to link a computer terminal, here at Yasenevo, with another computer inside his apartment, so as to enable files and data to be sent out of this building. And because the call would apparently terminate in the Lubyanka itself, no suspicion would be aroused that anything was wrong.'

'That was exactly what I thought, sir,' Abramov agreed.

'But Zharkov doesn't own a personal computer, and claims he has never had such a machine in his apartment. Of course, it's possible that he may have secreted it somewhere else, if he became concerned that questions might be asked of him. What I would like you to do, Major, is examine that call diverter and see if there are any other numbers on it that you might be able to recover. Can you do that?'

'It depends on the way the diverter functions, but I will do my best.'

'And do it right now,' Morozov instructed, 'before I ask Zharkov to explain what we've just found here.'

One of the search team escorted Abramov back to his office, and stood watching while the major tried to analyse the diverter's history. It was quickly clear to Abramov that somebody had wiped any earlier numbers from the device, and apart from the telephone number that he now knew belonged to Colonel Zharkov's apartment, there was only one other recorded. He wrote it down on a piece of paper, then ran a check on the directory system. But that produced no information and, wherever that particular number terminated, it was not a location known to the SVR.

Back in the colonel's office, Abramov explained what he'd found.

'Leave it with me now,' Morozov instructed. 'I'll organize a back-trace of that number.'

London

The next message Andrew Lomas received from Moscow through the Australian website was completely unexpected, bearing in mind the earlier communications.

He had genuinely expected simply to receive confirmation that Raya Kosov had been captured somewhere in northern Italy, and then handed over to the Russian authorities. Instead, he was told that, against all odds, she had somehow managed to escape into France, and had then climbed into a North American registered executive jet, which had flown north. Moscow's assessment of the situation was that the aircraft was making for London, so it was now up to Lomas to ensure that Kosov was unable to pass on any classified information to the British. And, more importantly, he must make certain she wouldn't be able to betray the identity of the jewel in Moscow's crown – the high-level SIS officer who had been working for the Russians for over twenty years.

Lomas closed the Internet connection and sat back in his chair to consider his next move. The first thing to do was obvious: identify the destination of the aircraft in which Kosov was travelling. That was probably the easy bit because, if it was heading for London, it wouldn't land at any of the three major civilian airports, Heathrow, Gatwick or Stansted, for a variety of reasons. That left only one choice, RAF Northolt, a military airfield conveniently located just north of Heathrow, with easy access to London and also the benefit of being closed to the public. It seemed to him the only possible destination.

He knew he would never be able to gain access to

the airfield, but that didn't present an insurmountable problem. He didn't need to actually enter RAF Northolt, only find out where Raya Kosov was taken when she left the airfield. Once he knew that, he could decide exactly how to carry out the orders he'd received from Moscow Centre.

Lomas considered his next move carefully. It would mean breaking cover but, in the circumstances, he felt he had no option. There was no way that he could complete his assignment without help – and expert help at that.

Twenty minutes later he left his apartment and walked for about a quarter of a mile through the rain-soaked streets of West London. He picked a public phone box at random and made a call to a man he'd never met but whose name he knew very well. Although Lomas was using a public phone, he still had to be very careful in what he said and how he said it, because the man at the other end of the line was sitting in Harrington House at 13 Kensington Palace Gardens. It was home to the Russian Embassy in London, and all lines going into the building would almost certainly be monitored by British intelligence.

He used a series of code words couched in seemingly innocent and innocuous sentences to establish his bona fides, and finished by requesting a callback. He gave the Russian a telephone number which didn't exist, but which he knew was held in a highly classified file inside the embassy, together with the real number to which the callback should be directed. That was a pay-as-you-go mobile phone which Lomas used just often enough to keep it active, but which he never used for any kind of sensitive conversation.

Less than a quarter of an hour later, during which time the Russian SVR officer had to leave the embassy and find a phone box, Lomas's mobile rang. He answered it and then issued a series of urgent orders in Russian.

When he'd finished, Lomas used the public phone to make another very brief call. The man who answered sounded irritated, which was unsurprising. Most busy men would react that way if a car-insurance salesman called their personal mobile phone with details of some fatuous special offer during the working day. But, when Lomas ended the call, he felt certain that the other man had completely understood his message.

RAF Northolt, West London

The Lear 60 landed smoothly a little under ninety minutes later. The pilot had filed an in-flight flight plan while the aircraft was somewhere over central France. There had been no delays, caused by air traffic or otherwise, in their approach and final landing. Their escort duty over, the pair of F-16s had peeled off as the Lear crossed the coast of southern England, and then headed north for their own landing at RAF Mildenhall in Suffolk.

The executive jet followed the ground controller's instructions and taxied across to a hardstanding beside a small terminal building, well away from any other aircraft. As the twin jet engines spooled down, their roar dying away to a diminishing whine, the three of them unbuckled their seat belts and stood up. They followed John Westwood to the exterior door and waited while one of the flight crew emerged from the cockpit to unlatch it.

It had been hot and sunny in southern France and northern Italy, but Richter was unsurprised to discover that it was raining in London. The tarmac around the aircraft glistened in the early evening gloom, reflecting the sheen of lights that illuminated the hardstanding or shone from the windows of the terminal building.

'That's just bloody typical,' he muttered, as he splashed through a succession of shallow puddles between the Lear and the terminal itself. He had an umbrella in one hand with which he was trying to protect Raya's hair from the rain, while in the other he was carrying her bag.

'Yeah,' Dekker agreed. 'Say what you like about the bloody Frogs, but they do have better weather than us.'

John Westwood followed behind the small group, because there were things he needed to do inside the terminal, including paying landing fees for the Lear and arranging for a bowser to refuel it. The pilots were out of flying hours, so he wasn't going to make it back to the States until the following day. He needed to find accommodation, either somewhere on the base itself or in a local hotel, for himself and the two pilots.

Richter pushed open the door and walked inside the building. To his right was a waiting area sporting a few low tables and easy chairs, and on his left a reception desk behind which stood two uniformed senior RAF non-commissioned officers. He turned towards them and reached into his pocket for the diplomatic passport, which he hoped would be enough to avoid complications with the duty customs and immigration officers who might already be on their way over. He still didn't know exactly what they would make of Raya, or whether her Russian passport would even allow her out of the airport. And the Browning pistol in his shoulder holster was almost certainly going to raise eyebrows.

His plan, such as it was, was to try to talk his way through the ranks of officials he expected to meet and, if that didn't work, to call Simpson and let him sort it out. It was, after all, ultimately not Richter's problem.

But, before he reached the desk, he heard an unpleasantly familiar voice calling out to him from behind. 'And about bloody time, too.'

Richter turned immediately, and was rewarded by the unwelcome sight of Richard Simpson, as immaculately groomed as ever, rising from one of the easy chairs and walking over towards him. His complexion appeared slightly pinker than before, possibly an indication of the irritation he was doubtless feeling.

'Simpson,' Richter greeted him. 'And it's nice to see you, too.'

'You can cut the crap, Richter. Your bloody phone's been switched off ever since you last called me, when you told me a pack of lies about what you were doing and where you were going. As a result I'm seriously thinking about throwing you and Dekker straight back to the Italian authorities. And when they've finished with both of you, there are some highly placed officials in France who'd like a bit of a chat as well.'

There was a silence that seemed to last for minutes, while Richter tried to decide if it was worth shooting Simpson there and then, or if he should just settle for beating the crap out of him.

Then a cultured American voice broke in. 'Hi, I'm John Westwood. You must be Richard Simpson.' Westwood stepped forward, his hand extended.

Almost reluctantly, Simpson shook it. 'How did you recognize me?' he asked.

'Word gets around,' Westwood said somewhat enigmatically. Then he turned to face Richter. 'It doesn't look to me as if your talents are fully appreciated here, my friend. If ever you feel like a change of scene, you know where to find me. The Company can always use people like you.'

Richter nodded, then shifted his glance back to Simpson. 'Thanks,' he said, 'but for the moment I'll stick with the devil I know – and right now that isn't just a figure of speech. Let me ask you a question, Simpson. Have you any idea at all *why* my phone's been switched off while we tried to get out of Italy without having our heads blown off?'

Simpson shook his head. 'No, I just assumed you were disobeying every instruction I gave you, as usual.'

'My phone was switched off because somebody was using it to track us.'

'That's impossible.'

'Bollocks!'

Richter explained what had happened in Nervi, after following Raya's instructions about the rendezvous.

'This, by the way, is Raya Kosov,' he finished, 'who's probably just as sick of hearing your whinging as I am. The point is that she *wasn't* followed to Nervi.'

'When you called me, you told me she *had* been followed,' Simpson pointed out.

'I told you a porkie, just to see what happened. And, right then, I wasn't absolutely sure but now I'm quite certain that she wasn't being followed. Apart from anything else, if the bad guys had been behind her, why didn't they snatch her before she even got to the town? After all, *she* was the target, not me.'

Simpson didn't respond.

'The only other person who knew the location of the rendezvous,' Richter continued, 'was Colin Dekker, and we discussed that face to face, not over a telephone link. So the only way the bad guys could have known where we were was to track my phone.'

'They could have been tracking Kosov's mobile, or even Dekker's.'

'No, because Raya kept her unit switched off almost all the time, precisely so she couldn't be tracked. And the bad guys were already waiting in the square at Nervi, but Colin wasn't there. He was on a rooftop nearby, with his phone switched off and watching what was going on through the telescopic sight of his rifle. Just as well he was, otherwise I'd probably be lying on a slab in some Italian morgue, and I really don't like to even think about what might have happened to Raya.'

'That's not the point, Richter. You could still have used a public phone, just to let me know what was happening. I don't like being kept in the dark. And then there's the matter of the private jet I sent out to Innsbruck to pick you up. The one which is still waiting there for you, as a matter of fact. You'll be paying off the cost of that abortive mission for the rest of your life.'

'I don't think we'd have got anywhere near that airport,' Richter argued, 'because I think your organization leaks like a sieve.'

Simpson's eyes blazed. 'You'll retract that remark or bloody well justify it, Richter, and right now.'

'That's easy enough. When I called you, after we'd

got out of Nervi, I told you which town we were heading for, and even gave you the name of the hotel we were going to stay at. Exactly four people were privy to that information, Simpson – you, me, Raya and Colin.'

'So?'

'So we went somewhere else, but Colin found a perch where he could cover the hotel. Late that evening, a bunch of professional thugs arrived and checked everyone in the building. I hadn't told anyone else we'd be there, and nor did Raya or Colin. So that means you must have done or somebody you talked to did, because we were set up.'

Simpson went white. 'You're sure?' he asked. 'You're sure those people were looking for you?'

'As near certain as makes no difference,' Dekker intervened. 'They definitely weren't Italian security people, because they made sure they got the hell away from the hotel well before the *carabinieri* arrived. And they even beat up a couple of the residents who objected to being dragged out into the street.'

'Right,' Simpson said, 'that puts a different complexion on things. Assuming, of course, what you say is correct, Richter – and I will be running a check to make sure you're not just trying to cover your back. But you're still wrong about one thing. If there was a leak, it didn't come from my section, because I've not discussed this operation with anyone there. Somebody else is involved in this, and you can be certain I'm going to find out who.'

'Raya here might be able to help with that,' Richter suggested. 'She knows that the SVR had at least two SIS officers in its stable. Gerald Stanway was presumably one of them, but her information might help identify the other.'

Simpson shook his head. 'That probably won't be necessary. 'I know exactly who I told about your route through Italy. It must either be him, or somebody he discussed it with at SIS. You can leave that to me.'

Simpson turned to the other two. 'Welcome to Britain, Miss Kosov,' he said shortly. 'And thank you, Dekker, for your support in this operation.'

'How did you know we'd be on that aircraft?' Richter asked.

'I know almost everything, Richter, almost all of the time. In this case, it wasn't particularly difficult to deduce. First, you shot up a couple of Italian police cars then stole an aircraft from some poor sod of a farmer. Next you nearly crashed it in the middle of the Alps, by pulling off some hare-brained manoeuvre. To cap that, you sent a transmission on a distress frequency, in which you used a false call sign and accused an Italian air force pilot of attacking you. And all that, of course, was a mere bagatelle compared to what you achieved in France. Do you have any idea how much those helicopters cost?'

'Oddly enough, I do,' Richter said, 'because I used to fly the things. When you were busy talking to your chums on the east side of the Channel, did they mention that their helicopter crew opened fire on us with a heavy machine gun, before Dekker here gave them something else to think about?'

'According to my contacts,' Simpson said, 'they just fired some warning shots to attract your attention.'

'They certainly did that, but it all still comes down to the basic rule of engagement. If you fire at me, you shouldn't be too surprised if I decide to shoot back.'

'Yeah, well the French don't see it that way. They'd

like reparation for the loss of their very expensive helicopter, not to mention some clean trousers for the flight crew. Then there was the sudden appearance at a nearby French airfield of a North American-registered executive jet owned by a certain organization based at Langley in Virginia. The same jet then took off, in defiance of air traffic control instructions and the orders of the French police, and which was escorted all the way across France by two American fighters. Put all that stuff together and a conclusion wasn't particularly difficult to reach.'

'So what are you going to do about it?' Richter asked.

'Nothing at the moment. The Frogs and the Eyeties can simply wait until we're sure of exactly what happened, and what Miss Kosov here has brought with her out of Moscow. If your data is valuable enough, we'll tell them to sod off, and deny any suggestion that a British subject was involved. If we don't like your dowry, then we might just throw you back.'

For a few moments Raya just stared at him. 'I don't think I'm going to like you,' she said.

'I don't give a toss whether you like me or not. All I'm interested in is what you can give us, now you're finally here. In view of the pile of shot-up cars and wrecked aircraft Richter and Dekker managed to leave across Italy and France, I hope you haven't just brought us a few ordinary old files, from whatever section of Yasenevo you worked in.'

Raya smiled slightly. 'I've done a little better than that,' she said. 'I was employed as the Deputy Computer Network Manager for the SVR, and in my bag here I have a CD player that's been modified quite a lot. I took out most of the existing works and replaced them with a half-terabyte-sized hard disk. It's full of files that I copied from the Yasenevo database, and I think you'll find that what I can offer is essentially a snapshot of virtually all of the SVR's current operations. And if you're not interested, Mr Westwood here has already made me a counter-offer.'

'That,' Simpson muttered, unconsciously echoing Westwood's remark earlier, 'is the holy grail. You're most welcome, Miss Kosov.'

Raya favoured him with a sharp look. 'And just so you don't get any sneaky ideas – because you look like that kind of person – the hard drive is password protected, and the gateway program includes an auto-destruct routine that will wipe the entire drive if an incorrect password is entered more than three times.'

Simpson didn't look particularly impressed by this warning. 'We have computer experts who would be able to crack that.'

'I doubt it,' Richter interrupted. 'In case you hadn't realized it, Raya is an expert too. But aren't we all supposed to be on the same side here?'

Simpson rubbed his hands over his face. 'You're right,' he said. 'It's been a very long day. Right, let's get Ms Kosov settled in one of our safe houses, and we'll start analysing the data in the morning.' He turned to her with a slight smile. 'I'm sorry if we got off on the wrong foot, but I've spent most of today fielding angry calls from senior officials from both the French and Italian intelligence services. In fact, it hasn't been the best day of my life so far, not least because I was worried that Richter wouldn't get you out of Italy in one piece.'

'I'm sorry, Simpson,' Richter again intervened, 'but we've no intention of going to a safe house. Until we're certain that the leak's been plugged, we're doing our own thing. That means Raya and I will find a hotel somewhere and check in as Mr and Mrs Smith. I'll call you at Hammersmith in the morning.'

Simpson glanced from Richter to Raya, and then back again. 'Have you two become what the modern idiom refers to as an item?'

Richter shook his head. 'That's none of your fucking business.'

'It might be, if it clouds your judgement.'

'It won't,' Richter said sharply. 'You just tell me where and when, and I'll make sure we're there for the debriefing. And, just so you know, I'm hanging on to the Browning in case your little mole hunt takes you longer than you think. So I recommend you don't send any-body to follow us, because I'd hate to end up shooting one of your lot by mistake.'

West London

Evening traffic in West London is almost always heavy, and that night was no exception. Despite the rain, when their taxi emerged from the gates of RAF Northolt it joined a long stream of vehicles heading west. In those conditions it was almost impossible to tell whether any-thing might be following them. Richter did his best to check, turning to look behind at regular intervals, but all he could see was a forest of headlights following and of red tail lights preceding them.

He instructed the driver to just head west first, then told him to take the turning towards Uxbridge. As the taxi left the main road, Richter again checked behind, but failed to spot any sign of surveillance. With no specific destination in mind, he finally decided that one of the hotels near Heathrow would be suitably anonymous. Under half an hour after leaving Northolt, he and Raya found themselves standing in the lobby of a multi-storey airport hotel, as Richter booked them a double room.

Before taking a lift to the fifth floor, Richter peered out through the plate-glass windows lining one side of the lobby. Outside the massive building, cars, minibuses and motorcycles kept arriving and departing. In the end, he shook his head. Trying to look out for surveillance here was completely pointless.

'Are we safe now?' Raya asked, as he finally double-locked the hotel room door behind them.

'I bloody hope so,' he replied, walking across to a window that afforded him an excellent view of one section of the car park, and of Heathrow Airport itself. 'I don't fancy sitting in full view in some restaurant to-night,' he added, pulling the curtains across and turning away from the window, 'so would you be happy if we just ordered something from the room-service menu?'

'As long as I have something to eat, I don't care,' Raya replied.

Richter smiled at her, studied the menu, and then picked up the phone.

Five floors below, on the far side of the car park, two men sat in an anonymous dark-blue Ford saloon. One of them was watching the illuminated windows of oc-cupied rooms through a pair of powerful binoculars fitted with a digital camera able to record an image of whatever the user was focusing on. He had just been watching as the light in a fifth-floor room came on and a male figure had walked across to peer out of the window. In that brief period, he had taken half a dozen pictures.

'Is that them?' the other man asked, hearing the rapid clicks of digital images being recorded.

'I didn't see the girl,' replied the man with the binoculars, 'but I'm pretty certain that's the guy who was with her.'

'Sounds good enough. You stay here and I'll go and find a floor plan, so we know exactly which room they're in.'

He pulled up the collar of his coat as protection against the rain, took a compact umbrella from his pocket, opened the car door and walked swiftly towards the hotel entrance. Five minutes later he was back.

'You get it?'

'No problem. They're in number five one two, and I checked it twice. Getting inside the room isn't going to be easy, though. The room doors are thick and solid, and they're fitted with entry card readers that will be difficult to crack. And they'll have closed the deadlock on the inside, as well.'

'Not our problem. We picked them up, we followed them, and we know where they're staying for the night. Now we can hand over to somebody else.' He pulled a mobile phone out of his pocket and dialled a number. 'I'll call it in now.'

His companion nodded, pulling on his seat belt, started the engine and drove away from the hotel.

Chapter Twenty-Six

Tuesday
Hammersmith, West London

At Simpson's insistence, Raya Kosov's initial debriefing was held at the FOE building in the backstreets of Hammersmith. The reason, as he explained when Richter phoned in that morning, was because he wanted the location to be both totally secure and completely under his control. Although FOE had access to safe houses in several different parts of London, nowhere else would offer the same level of security and, until the second traitor working for the Russians within the SIS was identified, and apprehended, he was unwilling to place Raya at risk by meeting anywhere else.

Actually, that suited Richter just as well. Despite Simpson's abrasive manner, sarcasm and frequent rudeness, he still believed his short-term boss was straight – or at least as straight as anybody else in the murky business he had become involved with. Richter would rather Simpson controlled the situation from his Hammersmith offices than take the risk of involving officers or facilities from any other branch of the British intelligence machine.

They arrived just after nine-thirty by taxi, and were ushered through the main entrance by two bulky security guards. Richter's Browning semi-automatic created a Christmas tree of lights as he walked through the metal detector situated a short distance inside the building.

'I'll take that,' one of the guards announced, stepping forward.

'In your dreams,' Richter snapped. 'I'm hanging on to this pistol. If you don't like it, call Simpson and get his approval.'

While his companion watched the two new arrivals carefully, the guard picked up an internal phone and held a short conversation. Then he nodded and turned back to Richter.

'Right,' he snarled, clearly irritated. 'Follow me, both of you.'

He led the way to an inner hallway, and across to a pair of lifts with silver grey doors. The right-hand lift was already at their level, with the doors open, and the guard immediately stepped inside, Richter and Raya following close behind. He pressed the button for the third floor, and a few moments later they stepped out of the lift again and he escorted them down a narrow, cream-painted corridor towards a set of double doors at the far end.

He knocked twice and opened the door. Inside the room was a long table, around which were arranged about a dozen chairs. Two of them were occupied by men Richter had never seen before, both of whom stood up as he and Raya entered. On the table were sheets of writing paper and pencils, and a high-quality digital recorder to which were connected two microphones on table stands. There were also several cups and mugs, three insulated coffee pots, and a couple of plates displaying a somewhat limited selection of biscuits.

'You must be Raya Kosov, right?' one of the men said, extending his hand, and Raya nodded. 'My name's David Walters. We were really glad that you managed to get out of Italy.'

'I had some help,' Raya explained, glancing at Richter.

'And you're Richter, obviously,' the other man said. 'You're the guy who's been causing our boss such grief, not to mention leaving a trail of devastation halfway across Europe. I'm Masterson, by the way, Jeff Masterson. We're the debriefing officers, at least for the first phase of this operation, because both of us speak and read Russian.'

'I think "trail of devastation" is putting it a bit strongly,' Richter protested, shaking hands with both men. 'About all we did was blow a few tyres off a handful of police cars, though in fairness we did wreck an expensive chopper.'

'How did you do that?' Masterson asked.

'We had an SAS sniper with us, watching our backs, who popped a bullet down one of the engine intakes. That was all it took, so I think maybe the French need to take another look at the design of the Eurocopter, if they're ever expecting it to survive a real live firefight.'

'OK,' Walters said briefly, 'why don't you both grab a seat, pour yourselves a cup of coffee, and then we'll get started.'

A few minutes later, he started the recorder going, and made an opening statement.

'My name is David Walters and my colleague is Jeff Masterson. This is the debriefing of Raya Kosov, formerly in the employment of the Russian SVR, who has voluntarily sought asylum in the United Kingdom. Also present is Paul Richter, who is currently on attachment to this unit.'

He paused and glanced at his notes but, before he could say anything else, the door of the conference room swung open. Richard Simpson marched in, nodded to the four people already seated there, and took a seat at the far end of the table.

'Carry on, Walters,' he urged. 'I'm just here as an observer.'

Walters leaned towards to the microphone again, and added: 'Also now present is Richard Simpson, Director of Foreign Operations.'

He checked his notes once more, then gazed across at Raya. 'Let me just explain the way this is going to work,' he said. 'This is just an initial interview, the first of many, so today all we're going to do is cover the basics. There will be in-depth interviews later, to discuss specific aspects of whatever you tell us. Basically, we have to do three things.

'First, we need to establish that you are who you claim to be. To do that, we'll ask you a number of questions about the SVR and about Yasenevo in particular. We'll also discuss your career and your precise employment in Moscow.

'Second, we have to satisfy ourselves that you are a genuine defector. As I'm sure you're aware, in the past the GRU and the KGB, and latterly the SVR, have occasionally sent one of their employees to the West as a purveyor of disinformation. Obviously, we have to be sure that this is not the case here. Only when we have satisfied ourselves on these first two points can we then look confidently at the information you've brought out with you, and analyse its worth to us. Do you understand all that?'

Raya nodded.

'And, thirdly, would you be prepared to submit to a polygraph examination – a lie detector check?'

Raya nodded again. 'I have no problem with that.'

'Good. Now, are there any questions you'd like to ask me or my colleague before we begin?'

'No, I'm happy to start right away.'

For the next ninety minutes or so, Walters and Masterson alternated in firing questions at Raya, and took copious notes of her answers to supplement the recording. Two things quickly became obvious to Richter: the level of British knowledge of the internal workings of the SVR was quite extensive, but Raya Kosov very clearly knew an awful lot more than either of them.

'Now, Raya, obviously we'll need to run some further checks on your statements over the next couple of days, but personally I'm satisfied with your knowledge of Yasenevo,' Walters conceded. He looked towards the far end of the table, where Richard Simpson was still sitting in silence. 'Have you any questions, sir?' he asked.

'No,' Simpson shook his head. 'You two are the experts and if you're now convinced she's the real deal, then I'm happy with that assessment.'

'Fine,' Walters said. 'Let's take a short break and then start on phase two.'

He ordered fresh coffee and, as soon as it had arrived, the questioning started again.

'So far so good, Raya,' Masterson began. 'I think we're agreed so far that you were the Deputy Computer

Network Manager at Yasenevo. What we have to do now is find out why you're sitting here in West London instead of working at your desk on the outskirts of Moscow. This is a very simple question, but I suspect the answer might be quite complex. Why, exactly, did you defect?'

'Actually,' Raya replied, 'the answer is just as simple as the question. I did it for revenge.'

Walters looked up with interest. 'Revenge for what – and against what? Do you mean you were rebelling against the state itself, or just against the SVR?'

Raya shook her head. 'A bit of everything, really. I was trying to hit Mother Russia, I suppose, because of the totalitarian system there. To use the SVR as a tool seemed almost poetic, because that organization essentially applies the system. But, most of all, I was seeking revenge against one man – one who to me represented an instrument of that system.

'I wanted that man to suffer for what he once did to my family, and the weapon I decided to use against him was the SVR itself. Let me explain. In 1989 the KGB burst into our apartment to arrest my father. He wasn't a criminal, a terrorist or even an anti-Communist. All he had done was to voice mild criticism of a local Party official. Unfortunately, somebody overheard him, and registered an official complaint. They sent six men to make the arrest, in the middle of the night.

'They broke down the door, pulled my father from his bed, then beat him so severely that he died within hours – apparently even before he reached their headquarters. My mother and I were forced to watch, and I think both of us then realized it would be the last time we would ever see him alive. I was a mere child at the time, but in my memory I can still replay everything that happened that terrible night. My mother remembered the name of the officer in charge, who had directed the beating, and we vowed there and then that someday, somehow, we would make him pay for what he did that night.'

Raya paused and looked at the faces of the four men sitting around the conference table. They stared back at her, none of them making any comment.

'I deliberately chose to study languages and computer science, because I believed those skills would make me a more attractive prospect for recruitment into the SVR. By the time I'd finished my education, I had already been offered employment by the SVR. I've worked at the Lubyanka and Yasenevo ever since.'

'There are two obvious questions that need asking,' Masterson began. 'First, does this man who killed your father still work for the SVR? And, second, how come their entrance security checks didn't reveal the fact that your father had died as a suspected dissident? If that information had been available, I doubt if the SVR would have taken you on. Tainted blood and all that.'

Raya nodded. 'Yes, that vicious little Georgian bastard is now a colonel in the SVR. The second question is more complicated to answer. When my father died at the KGB headquarters or in the back of the car on his way there, the squad which had arrested him must have realized they were in trouble. They'd been sent out to bring in a middle-aged man for questioning about a minor offence, and they'd returned with a bloody corpse. I don't know exactly how that Georgian bastard, then a captain, managed it, but we were told a few days later that my father had died in a traffic accident, and the arrest record simply vanished. And in those days, nobody questioned anything that the KGB told them.'

'But this captain who's now a colonel,' Masterson persisted. 'Surely he might have recognized your name and checked into your background?'

Raya shook her head. 'No,' she said, 'because as I expect you know Russian names are complicated. Let me explain. The tradition is that a girl's first name is simply given to her. That's the easy bit. Her middle name is a feminized version of her father's first name, and her last name is a feminized version of her father's last name. My father's name was Pavel Ostapenko, so my full name as a child was Raya Pavlovna Ostapenka, and my mother's name was Marisa Hohlova Ostapenka.

'The year after my father was killed, my mother married a distant cousin. It was a marriage of convenience, purely to allow me to take a different name. The cousin's name was Alexander Kosov, so my mother became Marisa Hohlova Kosova, and I followed tradition and changed my name to Raya Alexandra, but I preferred "Kosov" as a last name, rather than "Kosova". Of course, any detailed search would have shown my previous name, but with the arrest warrant missing and my biological father tragically killed in a car crash, there would have been nothing to find. The only person who might have made the connection was the Georgian and, as far as I know, he never looked.'

'And does he have a name, this Georgian?' David Walters asked.

'Yes,' Raya replied shortly. 'His name is Yevgeni

Zharkov, and by now, with any luck at all, he'll be sitting in a cell at Yasenevo or the Lubyanka, staring at the wall and wondering just what the hell has happened to his life.'

Moscow

The SVR search team arrived in one car, and the armed troops in another. The searchers parked some distance down the street and waited for the building to be checked and the apartment secured. A few minutes later, two carloads of Moscow police appeared as well, to help control the scene.

Abramov peered through the car window at a small apartment building, which the Moscow police had identified earlier as the location of the other number he had managed to extract from the data contained on the call diverter. The building itself was undistinguished and anonymous: just another small block of flats in a street that contained little else.

The police officers set up a cordon, diverting all traffic away from the vicinity, then surrounded the building to ensure that nobody could leave it without having their identity confirmed. Then the armed SVR troops advanced towards the street door and took up positions on both sides of it. One officer stepped forward and inserted a key in the lock. Or rather he tried to, but the key wouldn't fit, so he slipped it back into his pocket and tried a second key. This one slid in smoothly, and moments later the door was open, whereupon the SVR team streamed inside the building and was lost to sight.

Abramov waited patiently in the car, expecting confirmation either that the apartment was empty or that any occupants had been arrested. After three or four minutes, a junior SVR officer emerged from the building, and walked across to the car.

'The apartment is empty, sir, and it doesn't look as if it's been occupied for months. There's only some very basic furniture inside, but there's a computer on a table in the main room, and it's switched on.'

Abramov immediately climbed out of the car. 'Order your men not to touch that machine,' he instructed. 'It might hold vital clues regarding this investigation.'

Moments later, the major was himself standing in the tiny living room of the first-floor apartment, and looking round. As the young officer had explained, on a plain wooden table, which was pushed up against one wall, sat a fairly basic desktop computer. The power light was glowing on the front of the system unit, though the screen itself was blank. Abramov deliberately touched nothing, but he checked the cables and connectors. As expected, the PC was attached to a modem plugged into a telephone point.

He took a handkerchief from his pocket, carefully covered the ends of his fingers to avoid leaving prints, and then powered up the screen. When he saw a standard screensaver running, he touched the space bar on the keyboard to clear it. He was surprised to note that the unit wasn't password-protected, which would certainly make the job of examining the contents of the hard disk a lot easier.

'Right, Captain,' he said, opening up his briefcase which he had placed on the table beside the PC. 'Witness this, please. I'm about to make a copy of the contents of this computer's hard disk, then we can shut the machine down and take it back to Yasenevo for full examination.'

Abramov connected a high-capacity external disk drive to one of the USB ports on the front of the system unit, then carefully – still using his handkerchief to prevent leaving prints on the keyboard or mouse – he initiated the copy routine. The dialogue box which now appeared suggested that it would take at least half an hour to completely copy the disk's contents.

'Why could you not do that at Yasenevo?' the captain asked.

'Because even though the screensaver wasn't password-protected, it's possible that the operating system itself might be. The last thing I want to do is shut the machine down and then find it takes us months to bypass the password in order to access the hard drive.'

The captain nodded. 'While we're waiting, I'll have my men collect everything here that might have retained fingerprints,' he said.

'Good idea,' Abramov replied. 'And you can start with these.' He pointed to a few pencils and a ballpoint pen which lay on the table beside half a dozen sheets of blank paper. 'Whoever was using this computer would almost certainly have left his thumb and forefinger prints on some of those.'

Hammersmith, West London

'As I said before, Raya,' David Walters reminded her, 'today is really more or less just an introduction. This discussion enables us to get to know you a little better, and hopefully will allow you to feel more comfortable talking to us.'

Raya nodded. 'I understand.'

'Right,' Walters went on, 'we'd now like to take an initial look at the material you brought out with you. I gather from Richard Simpson that you made copies of certain SVR files before you left Moscow, and that those files are held on some form of electronic data storage. Is that correct?'

'Exactly right. I couldn't risk leaving Russia carrying a laptop computer. Not even my SVR credentials would have enabled me to board an aircraft out of Russia carrying a laptop, so I brought out my personal CD player instead.'

Raya opened her handbag and pulled out an old and fairly battered battery-powered CD player, along with three or four CD discs.

Walters looked confused. 'You mean you copied the data on to those CDs?' he asked.

'No, the CDs are simply camouflage.' She opened one of the CD cases and slipped the disc into the drive slot on the player. A light illuminated on the front of the unit, but no sound emerged from the speaker. 'I removed almost all the internal workings of the unit to make enough space to install a hard disk,' she said. 'It's that hard disk which contains the data.'

'That's clever,' Masterson acknowledged. 'So how can we access it? And how big is this hard drive?'

'I just need a screwdriver, and a USB lead with a small terminator at one end, plus a computer to connect to the other end of the lead. The drive itself is half a terabyte, which was the biggest I could find that would fit into the available space inside that CD player.'

'That's really ingenious,' Walters acknowledged. 'I'll go and organize what you need.'

He stood up and left the conference room, returning a couple of minutes later with a laptop under one arm and a small toolkit in his other hand. He passed the toolkit to Raya, then plugged in the laptop and switched it on.

Raya opened the toolkit, selected a screwdriver, and removed a small plastic panel on the side of the CD player. Walters then passed her a USB lead. She inspected the terminator at one end, nodded on finding that it was the correct size, and plugged it into the female socket that was revealed after removal of the panel. Then she leant back in her seat and waited for the laptop to power up.

'If you pass me that lead,' Walters said, 'I'll just plug it in.'

But Raya shook her head. 'Not quite so fast, Mr Walters. These negotiations have been a little one-sided so far. You've asked me questions and I've done my best to answer them, but I'm about to provide you with access to half a terabyte of SVR files classified at top-secret level and above. What nobody has confirmed so far is whether or not I'm being granted asylum here. Before you even take a look at the directory listing contained on this hard disk, I want a positive assurance that I'll be able to stay in this country.'

Walters shook his head. 'The problem is, Raya, that until we see what you've brought us, we can't assess its value. And because of that—'

'Before you go any further down that route,' Raya interrupted, 'you should know that I've already had a firm offer of asylum from the CIA. So if you try and fuck me about, I'll be on the next flight out of Heathrow across the pond. And if that happens, my data goes with me.'

Masterson glanced from Raya to the modified CD player, and smiled. 'Managing that,' he said, 'might not be as easy as you think. Right now, we've got custody of both you and the hard drive.'

As a threat, it was somewhat less than subtle.

Richter looked at Raya, wondering if he should now intervene, but then he eased himself back in his chair and relaxed, because she seemed in complete command of the situation.

'Yes, you've got the disk, but you won't get the data,' she said simply, 'because the whole drive is protected, as is each individual file. Essentially, the data has been scrambled and, without the master password, that's the way it will stay. I wrote the program myself, and I've also incorporated an auto-destruct sequence which is triggered if an incorrect password is entered more than three times. So if you've got some idea about hooking my disk up to one of the Cray supercomputers in the basement of the Doughnut out at GCHQ, you're going to be disappointed when you try to crack it.'

Both Walters and Masterson stared at Raya with a mixture of irritation and respect, then Walters glanced down the table at Simpson, who gave him a nod.

'You've kind of painted us into a corner,' Simpson declared, 'but we've no wish for you to go and talk to the Americans. So let me suggest a compromise. Pick any file you like from the data you've accumulated, decrypt it – or whatever it is you have to do to make it readable – and let Walters and Masterson take a look at it. If they're satisfied that it's both genuine and valuable, then you'll get your offer of asylum. You have my personal guarantee on that.'

Raya looked at Simpson, then glanced behind her towards Richter. 'Is this man trustworthy, Paul?' she asked him.

'Buggered if I know,' Richter replied. 'Personally I don't trust him, but I do think he's straight. By which I mean that if he guarantees you asylum, he'll do everything in his power to make sure that happens. But ultimately, Raya, this is your life and your decision.'

'That was a somewhat backhanded compliment, Richter,' Simpson snapped irritably.

'It's all you're going to get.'

There was silence for a few seconds, then Raya nodded. 'OK,' she said, 'I'll let you see just one file.'

'Make it a good one,' Walters suggested, as he turned the laptop so that Raya could view the screen.

Raya plugged in the hard drive, opened up a program, checked to make sure nobody in the room could see exactly which keys she pressed, and swiftly entered a password. When the directory listing appeared, she worked her way down until she found the file she was looking for. She double-clicked on the icon to open it, decrypted it, and made a copy which she pasted onto the laptop's hard drive, before encrypting her own directory again. Before sliding the laptop back across the table to Walters, she disconnected the USB cable.

'That's one file that might be of interest,' she suggested.

Walters read the first few lines of the Cyrillic text,

then looked up at Simpson and nodded. 'This is classified *Sov Sekretno*, Top Secret,' he said. 'It's an analysis
of the state of battle-readiness of the Russian Northern
Fleet, so if this file is representative of the rest of the data
on that hard disk, it's dynamite. Grade-one intelligence,
straight from the horse's – or rather the Bear's – mouth.'

'Right, Miss Kosov,' Simpson announced, 'you've got
yourself a deal.'

Chapter Twenty-Seven

Colonel Yevgeni Zharkov was seated on an upright wooden chair. His hands rested on his lap, his wrists bound together with steel handcuffs, as he stared across the table at his accuser.

General Morozov stared back at him, his expression sombre and almost sad. 'Of all the officers in my department, you are the last I would ever have suspected of treacherous activities. I always believed that I could rely upon you absolutely and unreservedly, but I suppose that just proves that nobody can ever be considered beyond suspicion.'

Zharkov shook his head wearily. 'As I keep trying to explain to you, General, I have done nothing wrong. My loyalty to you and to the SVR has never wavered, and I'm wholly innocent of the ridiculous charge that I'm now facing.'

'Don't try and play the innocent with me, Zharkov!' Morozov roared, his voice filling the interrogation room. 'The evidence against you is overwhelming and unarguable. The two keys for the building and the apartment where you'd hidden that computer were found in your office, hidden in your own desk. Both keys had your fingerprints on them, and alongside the computer were found pens and pencils from which our technical staff have also recovered your fingerprints.'

'But I tell you I've never been inside that apartment, and I have never seen that computer before. Or those keys, or anything else. Somebody is clearly attempting to frame me.' Zharkov's voice remained strong, but was now tinged with desperation. 'Just look at that telephone number which Abramov found on a call diverter in the Lubyanka.'

'It was the number of your own apartment,' Morozov reminded him.

'I know, and that's the point. Why on earth would I reprogram a call diverter to dial my own number? It would be like waving a flag to admit my guilt straight away. But if somebody else wished to cast suspicion on me, it would be an obvious clue to plant. And why would I leave evidence as incriminating as those two keys in my own office, when I could just as easily hide them in my apartment or in my car – or anywhere else?'

Morozov glared at his subordinate. 'Very well,' he said, 'let us assume for the moment that you are an innocent victim of some complicated conspiracy. If that is the case, who is orchestrating it? And why? What could be their motive? And why have they picked on you?'

'I don't know,' Zharkov replied desperately. 'I have no idea who would want to do this to me. All I do know is that I'm innocent, entirely innocent, of these charges.'

General Morozov continued to stare at him, then dropped his eyes and shook his head. 'I'm sorry, Zharkov, but this matter is now out of my hands. I have received my orders, and you are to be taken for interrogation to the Lubyanka. You will know, as well as I do, exactly what that means. If there was anything I could do to prevent that I would, but my orders are unequivocal.'

On the other side of the table, Colonel Zharkov turned white and began quivering with fear. 'No, General. No, please . . . Please, anything but that.'

Morozov's eyes hardened as he studied the terrified man in front of him. 'Earlier today, Major Abramov said something interesting to me. He told me that when you began investigating the defection of Raya Kosov, you seemed very reluctant to even consider the allegations she had made about there being a traitor here at Yasenevo. He also claimed that you would only begin such an investigation if Kosov told the same story after you had her strapped to a table in the Lubyanka basement, with electrodes hitched to her genitals. It sounds to me as if you're happy enough to inflict pain on a helpless subject, but have no stomach for enduring the same yourself. That is not an attractive trait in any man.'

Morozov pushed back his chair to stand up, then he walked over to the door and opened it.

'He's all yours,' the general said to the two men waiting outside.

Hammersmith, West London

'Now, before you wet yourself with excitement, Walters,' Richard Simpson said, 'there's an urgent matter we need to discuss with Ms Kosov first.' He switched his gaze to the Russian girl. 'Richter has already told me that you knew of *two* people in the SIS who were regularly passing information to Moscow. We now know that Gerald Stanway was one of them, of course.'

'Yes,' Raya agreed. 'The most prolific source we had in your SIS was code-named *Gospodin*. I checked his file, and found that one of the earliest entries was the initial contact report, which mentioned the name "Stanway". He originally walked into our Paris embassy wearing a basic disguise, requested a meeting with one of the SVR officers there, then explained who he was and what he wanted. At first, they didn't take him too seriously, but Moscow Centre assigned a case officer – an illegal – to handle him in London, and then assessed the value of the material he supplied them. They probably expected it to be low-grade rubbish or even disinformation, but then discovered that it was actually the real thing.'

'When was that?' Masterson asked. 'When did Stanway make that approach?'

'I was appointed Deputy Computer Network Manager at Yasenevo eight years ago,' Raya replied, 'and one of my first jobs in that position was to handle the material that source *Gospodin* had just started sending us. I remember that he was very prolific.'

'Jesus wept,' Walters muttered. 'So that bastard has been working for the Russians for eight years. God knows how much information he's betrayed in all that time.'

Raya smiled at him. 'Luckily,' she said, 'I know exactly what he sent to Moscow.'

There was a short silence as the men sitting around the conference table absorbed this information. Then Simpson uttered a single word. 'How?'

'I was effectively running the Yasenevo network. I

was creating directories, deciding on the encryption routines and protocols, and implementing the access level to be applied to every file. And, as I said before, I already knew, long before I arrived at Yasenevo, that one day I would be defecting to the West. So right from the start I made sure that I assembled a dowry which would interest either the British or the Americans. I put a very simple routine in place.

'The files *Gospodin* supplied were in English, of course, and each was stored in encrypted form on our database, in the same language, together with a translation into Russian that we had prepared in-house, as well as a short summary of the file contents. Because they were your own files, I knew there would be no point in making a copy of any of those files to show you, so I simply recorded the name and reference number of every file that source *Gospodin* forwarded to Moscow. I have that list safely on my hard drive as well.'

Simpson shook his head. 'Stanway, it seems, was the most damaging penetration we've ever faced,' he said. 'But thanks to you, Raya, at least we'll soon know exactly what secrets he betrayed. And that's one of the most important things you have done for us.'

Raya nodded and smiled. 'It wasn't only files from your SIS,' she added. 'A short time ago, I was instructed to create a new directory to handle some additional material from source *Gospodin*. These new files needed a brand-new directory because they came from a different organization, and the name I was told to give to that directory was *Zakoulok*.' She paused and looked around expectantly.

Simpson looked blank. 'I don't speak the language,' he said.

'*Zakoulok* means "back alley" in Russian,' Richter informed him, 'but I don't know if that's significant, or even relevant.'

'Oh, it's relevant all right,' Masterson said. '*Zakoulok* is a slang term used by the Russians, in some of their signals and cryptograms, to refer to the Foreign Office in Whitehall. The name refers to that arched courtyard entrance leading to the FCO off Downing Street. It seems Stanway must have decided to start ransacking the FCO files as well.'

'That makes sense.' Simpson nodded. 'And you did the same with these new files, Raya, as you did before? So we will be able to identify exactly what information Stanway transmitted?'

Raya nodded again. 'Of course. If you'll allow me access to the laptop again, I'll give you all the directory listings right now.'

Walters spun the laptop round and slid it across the table. Raya again connected her concealed hard disk and a few minutes later pushed the computer back towards Walters.

He scanned the listing and shook his head. 'There are hundreds of file names here,' he said, 'so Vauxhall Cross is going to have to run a major damage-limitation exercise. I'm not familiar with most of these subjects, but it looks to me as if Stanway probably betrayed almost every ongoing SIS operation there is.'

'And that isn't your only problem,' Raya said. 'Source *Gospodin* sent us a lot of information, but essentially all he did was copy files. There was a second, much older, penetration at SIS. And that one was at a much higher level.'

She gestured for Walters to slide the computer back towards her. For a few seconds, Raya's fingers flew nimbly over the keyboard, then she passed the machine back to him again.

'That,' she said, 'is a recent copy of a file called "Appreciation", which is held in a top-secret directory at Yasenevo, named *Zagadka* or "enigma". I was puzzled by the directory, because no new material had been added to it for over five years. But, despite that, the "Appreciation" file was being accessed on a regular basis by SVR Directorate heads. When I studied the file myself, I realized why. There was a second source, here in London, who in the past had supplied Moscow with copies of classified files, much as *Gospodin* was doing. But for some time he's been doing something almost as damaging, and maybe even more damaging.

'This source – and I don't even have a code name for him, let alone his actual name, because his identity was kept that secret – has been providing the SVR with a regular summary of SIS policy and general strategy. And also, when he felt it necessary, with precise details of particular operations. My assessment is that he must be a very senior officer within the organization. I reckon Stanway was certainly damaging, but this other person is more dangerous by far.'

The Lubyanka, Moscow

Yevgeni Zharkov was powerfully built, and was now literally fighting for his life, so it took three burly SVR guards to manhandle him into the basement interrogation room at the Lubyanka, strip the clothes from him and get him strapped onto the table. Only then did the interrogators finally approach.

'You know why you're here,' one of them said, gazing down at the man who was still vainly struggling against the leather straps that held his naked body in position.

Zharkov shouted something unintelligible, and the interrogator stepped back and looked at his companion.

'I gather he's a senior officer in the SVR,' he said, glancing down at the information sheet he'd been given half an hour before.

'He's also a traitor,' the other man declared, 'and we need to get every scrap of information out of him before he dies.'

The first interrogator nodded, and inspected the foot of the information sheet, where the Cyrillic word полный was was ticked, accompanied by the signatures of two senior SVR officers. The Russian word translated as 'full' or 'complete', and meant that the interrogation was to be terminal. Their instructions were that the subject would die on the table.

The two interrogators stepped to one side of the room and donned waterproof aprons over their white coats. Then they sat down in a couple of chairs to await the arrival of one other man.

Five minutes later, the door opened and a doctor

stepped inside. He was carrying a small bag of special-ized drugs and other equipment, and glanced quickly at the table where Zharkov was still struggling against his bonds. He, too, then pulled on a waterproof apron, before he nodded to the two interrogators.

One switched on the overhead camera and micro-phones, announced his own name and rank, followed by that of his companion and the doctor, and finally the name of the man who lay on the interrogation table. The other attendant wheeled over a cart on which were laid out the tools. These included the generator and leads, and the pliers and knives and saws and steel bars and acid they would use to do the job.

And then it began.

Hammersmith, West London

Simpson left the debriefing session just after eleven that morning, leaving Walters and Masterson to continue their questioning of Raya. They stopped for lunch just after midday, then returned to the conference room.

Simpson reappeared just after the four of them had sat down again. 'Right,' he began. 'Walters, I want you and Masterson to go through that Appreciation docu-ment and see if there's anything in it that would help us to identify our man. I'm thinking about stuff like assessments, obviously. If there's some piece of informa-tion in the file that only Malcolm Holbeche or William Moore could possibly have known, for example, that would obviously tie one of them down. I don't think you'll find anything like that, because whoever it is that's been betraying us for twenty years is obviously no amateur. But maybe you'll turn up some dates: for instance a date when information was sent to the Russians at a time when one of the people at the top of the SIS either couldn't possibly have known the information, or couldn't have sent it because he was in hospital or something.'

'So who do you suspect, sir?' Walters asked.

'Right now, I don't know,' Simpson replied, 'I frankly can't believe it's Holbeche, because he's the man who's been coordinating and directing this entire operation. But what worries me is that he was the only person at SIS who knew exactly where Richter supposedly planned to stay overnight in Italy. Or, to be absolutely accurate, he was the only person at SIS to whom I mentioned Lodi. But, on balance, I suspect that he either briefed somebody else, or inadvertently let that information slip out. The problem is that if Holbeche is the traitor, I can't tackle him directly about it without revealing my suspicions. I'm still working on a way to either confirm that it is indeed him or else somehow prove that it isn't.'

'I don't think I can help you identify him,' Raya said, 'because he's not been sending actual files to us, only general information about SIS policy and direction. And I suppose almost any of the senior officers you have there would have sufficient access and clearance to do that.'

'Can you follow the money?' Richter asked. 'If this guy is being paid by Moscow, is there any way you can trace the funds?'

'He might not actually be on Moscow Centre's payroll,' Masterson said. 'If he's motivated primarily by ideology, there might be no money trail for us to follow. And even if he's a mercenary traitor, the funds will probably be paid into some offshore tax haven, or maybe a Swiss bank account.'

'Stanway was certainly in it for the money,' Simpson remarked. 'I had a call from one of his interrogators, and apparently he's singing like a caged canary. Mind you, they've been using a certain amount of chemical stimulus on him to loosen his tongue. We now even know the name of his handler, and we'll be paying him a visit any day now, once he's properly identified.

'Stanway knew only his handler's name, Andrew Lomas, and had no phone number or address for him. They communicated by chalk marks on walls and other old-school spy craft. Whenever they had to talk directly to each other, it was always from one public phone to another. But Lomas did have an unregistered and untraceable mobile phone for emergencies only, and we're checking that one now against the home and mobile numbers of all the senior SIS officers, just in case one of them ever called it. And we're waiting for the call records for Stanway's mobile as well.'

About an hour later, one of Simpson's men entered the conference room, carrying several sheets of paper. Walters broke off his study of the Appreciation file, and he and Masterson joined Simpson at the end of the table to study the data they had so far obtained. Richter peered over Walters's shoulder as the three men examined the phone records.

'That's the mobile that Stanway claims Lomas uses,' explained Simpson, pointing at one page.

'Is there any correlation?' Richter asked.

'Not that my people have been able to spot.'

Richter nodded, his eyes never leaving the pages spread out on the end of the table. The data had already been scanned, in an attempt to identify any of the senior SIS officers who might have been called by Lomas, but nothing had been found.

'One thing I notice from this,' Richter said, pointing at the same sheet, 'is that Lomas hardly ever made or received a call using this mobile, but he did so yesterday. Somebody called him during the afternoon. But what number is that?'

'Not one of our suspects,' Walters said. 'That letter "P" besides the entry means the calling number was a public phone, so it could have been absolutely anybody.'

'Can you get the records for that public phone as well?' Richter asked.

'Yes, of course.' Simpson nodded. 'If you can give me a good reason, that is.'

'Just a hunch right now,' Richter said. 'And can you also get the location of the mobile at the time when the call was received, the numbers and call records of any public landline phones near that location, and also the location of the public phone the call came from? And find me a decent-sized London A–Z, please.'

Ten minutes later, the same man reappeared with another half-dozen sheets and the map book.

Richter took them from him, and ran his eyes down the list of numbers. Then he compared the position of the public phone from which the call to Lomas's mobile had been made with one of the pages in the A–Z, and checked some of the other data on the lists. Then he sat back with a slight smile.

'What is it?' Simpson demanded.

'Three things,' Richter said. 'First, the public phone box is just around the corner from the Russian Embassy. Second, when Lomas received the call, he was standing here.' He pointed to a spot in the Shepherd's Bush area. 'He was then right beside a public phone box and, if you look at the records, about fifteen minutes before that, somebody had used that public phone to call the Russian Embassy. I've never been a big fan of coincidence, and I realize I'm quite new at this game, but I'll bet Lomas made that first call, and then whoever he spoke to at the embassy trotted outside the building to find a public phone, and called Lomas's mobile.'

'You're probably right,' Simpson said, 'but I'm not sure how that helps.'

'That's the third thing. It was raining yesterday afternoon, as I recall.'

'So?'

'When Moscow found that Raya had done a runner, I'm sure Lomas was given a whole list of instructions and orders to follow. He's too experienced a professional to use a phone that could be traced to him, which is why he used a public phone box to contact the Russian Embassy. I'm wondering if he could also have contacted his – what do you call it? – his agent-in-place from the same phone box, simply because it was raining and it would have saved him having to walk around looking for another one to use. I think it might be worth checking these phone records against the numbers you have for the SIS officers.'

Simpson rubbed his chin thoughtfully, then nodded. 'Do it,' he instructed Masterson.

Within a couple of minutes Masterson muttered an exclamation, and ran a green highlighter along a line on one of the mobile-phone records.

'Somebody called this mobile from that phone box just after Lomas finished his call. The call was probably innocuous in nature, just in case anybody was listening in, but my guess is it was Lomas, as the case officer, telling his asset to either lie low or maybe get the hell out of town.'

Simpson looked down at what his officer had found, and nodded. 'That was good work, Richter. I'll get the wheels in motion.'

'Who is it?' Richter asked.

'Holbeche,' Simpson replied shortly, and walked out of the room.

Heathrow Airport, West London

A grey-haired middle-aged man clutching a briefcase and a carry-on bag joined a short queue at the Business Class section of the Air France check-in desk. He was still waiting in line when two other men appeared beside him.

'Not flying the flag today, Malcolm?' Richard Simpson asked.

'Hello, Richard,' Holbeche replied. 'No, I couldn't get a seat on BA. The bloody flight's full, so I'm having to go with the French. I've a bit of business to take care of over in Paris. I didn't expect to see you here.'

'I'm sure you didn't.'

'Is there a problem?'

'Yes, there is,' Simpson replied. 'We know that Andrew Lomas called you yesterday afternoon, and I guess he told you to run.'

'Andrew Lomas?' Holbeche paled slightly. 'I don't think I know him.'

Simpson shook his head regretfully. 'Oh, I think you do, Malcolm. After all, he's been your case officer for probably twenty years. We know that now, because of the information Raya Kosov brought out of Moscow. And I also know that you're not really going to Paris. Or at least that's not your final destination. I guess there's an Aeroflot out of Charles de Gaulle later today, heading for Sheremetievo, and you're already booked onto it.'

Holbeche said nothing, and Simpson nodded.

'Now, we can do this the hard way or the easy way,' he said. 'The easy way is for you to simply turn around and walk out of the terminal with the two of us.'

Holbeche lowered his head, then reached inside his jacket and pulled out a 9-millimetre Glock 26 subcompact pistol. He aimed the weapon directly at Simpson's stomach and smiled bitterly.

'Did you really think you could get onto an aircraft carrying that?' Simpson asked, apparently unfazed by the threat.

'With my diplomatic passport and a carry permit issued by the Metropolitan Police, it wouldn't have been difficult,' Holbeche said. 'Now get the hell out of my way, Simpson.'

'I'm sorry, Holbeche, but you're going nowhere.'

Two other men appeared behind Simpson, each holding a semi-automatic pistol aimed at the Chief of the Secret Intelligence Service. A couple of passengers standing nearby suddenly noticed the drawn weapons, and a woman began screaming. Instantly, it seemed, chaos erupted in that particular section of the terminal. People were running and shouting, desperate to get away from these armed men standing near the Air France desk. But Holbeche, Simpson and the two other men remained stationary, seemingly oblivious to what was going on all around them.

Holbeche ignored the two armed men confronting him, and stared only at Simpson. 'I've had a good run, Richard,' he said. 'Twenty-odd years – nearly a quarter of a century – working my way up through the ranks in the service, and at the same time cementing my position as the most important single asset the SVR has ever had. Did you know that they've already made me an honorary general at Yasenevo?'

'But now it's all over,' Simpson snapped. 'You've nowhere to go.'

'I suppose you're planning a trial to be held, *in camera*, so that no one will ever know just how thoroughly compromised British intelligence has been. And I'd be pensioned off, stripped of my knighthood, questioned for months by one of those slimy reptiles that you employ. And then I'd end my days in contented obscurity somewhere. Not a bad deal really.'

Simpson shook his head. 'As I said to Richter only last week, the days when traitors to Britain could get just a slap on the wrist are over, at least as far as I'm concerned. After we've questioned you and we've milked you dry, I'll make sure that you die, and preferably painfully. You're a dead man walking, Holbeche. You just don't know how long you've got left.'

Holbeche shook his head. 'That's never going to happen, Simpson. You know it and I know it.'

Quite deliberately, he raised the Glock to point it at Simpson's head, and the beginnings of a smile appeared on his face.

The two men behind Simpson fired instantly, the two shots so close together that they sounded almost like a single report.

Holbeche was knocked backwards by the double impact of two 9-millimetre bullets smashing into his chest. He staggered backwards, the Glock tumbling from his hand.

Simpson stepped forward, picked up the weapon, and then knelt down beside the fallen man to feel for a pulse in his neck. Then he stood up and turned to face the men who'd just fired the fatal shots.

'Good shooting,' he said. 'I'm going back to the office now. I'll have a D Notice issued within the hour to cover this, so if the Met plods give you any trouble, refer them to me.'

Then Simpson turned on his heel and strode away.

Hammersmith, West London

The questioning continued through the afternoon, as Raya answered queries about various aspects of the SVR files she had copied from the Yasenevo database.

She was now sufficiently comfortable talking to Walters and Masterson that, when she left the conference room with Richter late that afternoon, she allowed the two men to retain her CD player and transfer all of her files onto the laptop for further analysis.

They met Simpson out in the corridor, heading back towards the conference room.

'Any news?' Richter asked.

Simpson nodded. 'Holbeche has resigned, permanently. We caught him trying to board a flight to Paris, and he admitted to me that he was a Russian mole.'

'And he resigned?' Richter asked.

'In a manner of speaking, yes. He pulled a gun on me and a couple of my men took him down. He was dead before he even hit the ground.'

'So that's it? We can all relax?'

'Yes, that's it. Holbeche is dead and Stanway's busy telling us everything he knows. We've now found and eliminated two very costly and dangerous penetration agents inside the SIS and, thanks to Raya here, we've obtained enough high-quality data about the SVR to keep our analysts busy for years to come. All in all, it's a good result.'

They all continued down the hallway towards the building's main doors, where they paused. Simpson shook hands with both of them.

'Don't worry about gaining asylum, Raya,' he said. 'As soon as we've finished this debriefing, I'll ensure that we find you a new identity and somewhere decent to live. In the meantime, are you still happy hanging around with Richter?'

Raya nodded. 'Perfectly, thank you. Tonight, we're going out for a traditional English meal.'

'Good. Just make sure he takes you to a reasonable restaurant, and doesn't try to make you pay half the bill.'

London

It was a reasonable restaurant. In fact, it was the oldest privately owned restaurant in London, Rules in Covent Garden. Richter had been lucky to find a table, because usually there was a waiting list. It served classic English food: no fancy bits, no nouvelle cuisine thankfully, just good solid food perfectly cooked. Raya opted for the fish and chips served, of course, in a copy of the *Financial Times*, while Richter chose one of his favourites, steak and kidney pudding – not pie.

Afterwards, they found a taxi in Bedford Street and, about half an hour after they'd left the restaurant, they walked into the lobby of their hotel near Heathrow and went straight up to their room.

They'd only been there about ten minutes when the phone rang, and Richter answered it.

'Mr Wilson?' Richter had chosen a fairly simple alias. 'This is the reception desk downstairs. I have a Mr Simpson here to see you. Can you come down?'

'What's it about?' Richter asked.

There was a pause and a muttered conversation in the background, then the female receptionist returned to the phone.

'He says something's come up about today's briefing, and he needs to see you. It will only take a few minutes.'

'OK, I'll come down.'

'How did he know we were staying here?' Raya asked.

Richter smiled at her. 'I haven't known Richard Simpson very long, but I do know that he's always very well informed. We could have been followed by one of his men that first night, when we drove here from Hammersmith. Anyway, I won't be long. Just keep the door locked until I get back.'

Richter checked the Browning was loaded, just in case, replaced it in his shoulder holster, then let himself out of the room.

As he emerged from the room and started walking down the corridor, a door further along opened and a man with black hair and almost black eyes stepped out. The door was marked 'Chambermaid – Staff Only' and in the small room behind it, a blonde-haired Polish girl lay helpless on the floor, her wrists and ankles secured with wrapping tape and a rough gag covering her mouth. She was still unconscious from the blow she'd received to the back of her head about five minutes earlier.

The man pulled the door closed, checked that it was locked, and then walked unhurriedly along the corridor to Richter's room. He paused at the door and glanced in both directions. A few seconds later, a second man, similar in appearance, strode briskly down the corridor towards him. The first man nodded, then used the master key card he'd taken off the chambermaid to open the door in front of him. They both stepped inside the room and closed the door behind them.

'Where's Mr Simpson?' demanded Richter, who had arrived at the reception desk to find no sign of the man he had come down to see.

The receptionist looked slightly flustered. 'I'm sorry,

Mr Wilson. He received a call immediately after I finished talking to you, and I think he stepped into the coffee shop to take it.' The receptionist pointed towards the open double doors to one side. 'He should still be in there, I think.'

Richter nodded his thanks, and walked through into the coffee shop. There were perhaps a dozen people in there, sitting at tables, but no sign of Richard Simpson.

He felt the first faint prickle of unease, and strode back out to the reception desk. The receptionist was talking to a middle-aged American couple. Richter simply and unceremoniously elbowed them aside.

'This man Simpson,' he demanded, 'was he about five-eight, slim build, pink complexion?'

'No, sir,' the girl replied. 'He was about six feet tall with dark hair and he—'

But Richter was already moving, running across the lobby to the bank of lifts. The doors of one were just closing, but Richter thrust his arm through the gap and forced them open again.

On the fifth floor he sprinted down the corridor, the Browning already in his hand, safety catch off and his finger on the trigger.

The room door was closed, he could see that as he approached. He pulled the key card out of his pocket with his left hand, thrust it into the slot, pushed open the door and stepped into the room, holding the pistol out in front of him.

But, before he could locate a target or pull the trigger, he felt a sudden stabbing pain in his right side as the twin darts from a Taser penetrated his skin. He shot a glance to his right, straight into a pair of dark, almost black, eyes set in a face that was memorable chiefly because of its ordinariness. He tried to swing the Browning around, but he was a lifetime too late.

Around 120,000 volts of electricity coursed through his body, and Richter tumbled backwards, rendered instantly unconscious.

The Lubyanka, Moscow

A little over four hours after they'd started work on Yevgeni Zharkov, the two interrogators stepped back from the table. The colonel had at last slipped into a comatose state where what little sanity remained within his conscious mind was finally and mercifully put beyond their reach.

'I'm not even certain he was guilty,' one of the interrogators observed. 'He never changed his story, not once.'

'Maybe he wasn't. But we'll never know now, that's for sure.'

They glanced back to watch as the doctor prepared a lethal injection. He found a vein on Zharkov's left arm, which the interrogators had broken in two places during questioning, and slid the needle into it. As he depressed the plunger, the colonel's body arched upwards and his face contorted in a sudden rictus of pure agony. Then Zharkov slumped back onto the table, finally feeling no more pain.

'One of these days,' the first interrogator remarked, hanging up his blood-splattered apron, 'I really must find out what he puts in that syringe.'

Chapter Twenty-Eight

Wednesday
London

When Richter came to, it was like surfacing after a long time under water. He became slowly aware of a light, a distant light, somewhere above him, and then of voices. The faint hum of conversation gradually began to impinge on his consciousness, the noise steadily becoming louder. He tried to move, to sit up, but his limbs seemed unwilling to obey. And he couldn't even separate his hands.

Then he began to understand what two of the voices close to him were saying.

'I think he's coming round.'

'Good. We need to talk to him, then get him to hospital for checks.'

Richter's eyes flickered open, and he stared up into the stern and unsmiling faces of two uniformed police officers.

'Right, Mr Wilson, now you're awake, we've got a few questions we'd like you to answer.'

Richter tried to ease himself up into a crouching position, and then slumped backwards, his handcuffed wrists making it impossible for him to stand without help. The two police officers grabbed him under the arms and helped him sit in a chair at one side of the room.

His eyes were only now starting to focus properly, but the room – and it was his hotel room, as far as he could tell – seemed to be full of people. But they weren't what immediately attracted his attention. What his eyes were drawn to first was the bed, and what lay on it.

Richter stood up and stepped forward, shaking off the restraining grasp of the sergeant. He walked across to the foot of the bed and looked down, utterly appalled at what he saw.

Raya's naked body lay still and silent in the middle of it, a huge pool of blood surrounding her like an obscene halo. Ropes had been attached to her wrists and ankles, and then tied around the feet of the divan so as to spreadeagle her across the sheets. It looked as if every square inch of flesh had been cut apart with a scalpel or knife. Her eyes were wide open and seemed to be staring directly at Richter, her mouth open in a silent scream.

Richter's eyes filled with tears as he looked down at the ravaged body. He stretched out his hands and stroked what was left of her cheek for the last time.

'Raya,' he muttered, 'I'm so sorry.'

Then he closed his eyes and dropped his head, unable to look at her any more. The sergeant had moved across to stand beside him, and was still talking to him, but Richter hadn't heard a single word.

'Why did you do it, Mr Wilson? Lovers' tiff was it?' the man repeated.

Richter turned his head round and stared at him as if he was mad. 'What the fuck are you talking about, you simple-minded idiot? This is nothing to do with me. Give me my phone. I need to make a call.'

'You can call your solicitor once we've got you down at the station,' the sergeant snapped.

Richter glanced back once more towards the bed, then stepped towards the officer. 'I'll give you one chance,' he said. 'If you still want to have a job tomorrow, get me my fucking phone, and get it now.'

For a long moment, the sergeant just stared at him, then he shrugged. He must have seen something in Richter's eyes that told him this man wasn't making an idle threat. 'Right,' he said. 'You can make one call, but I'm going to dial the number for you and listen to what you say.'

'Fine with me.'

The sergeant picked up the mobile, and Richter gave him the emergency number Simpson had provided him with, what seemed like weeks before, outside the casino in Ax-les-Thermes. Within seconds, he was connected.

'Yes, Richter. What is it?' Simpson sounded almost cheerful.

'The shit has really hit the fan. Raya's dead, and it looks like she was tortured to death. And I'm still in the hotel near Heathrow surrounded by woodentops who think that I did it. I need you and whatever people are needed to get here as soon as possible and get this situation under control.'

To give Simpson his due, he asked no questions, just one regarding the address of the hotel. He then promised he'd have a team there as quickly as he could, certainly within thirty minutes.

'Now let me talk to whichever plod there seems to be in charge,' Simpson ordered.

Richter moved the phone away from his ear and

looked at the sergeant. 'My boss,' he said, 'wants to talk to your boss.'

Three minutes later, the sergeant was removing Richter's handcuffs.

Simpson and half a dozen men arrived well within the promised half-hour. Simpson took one look at the butchered body lying on the bed, and pulled Richter out of earshot of everyone else.

'What happened here, Paul? Who did this?'

'I don't know,' Richter replied. He explained about the phone call from the reception desk, and then briefly seeing the man with the Taser.

'That knocked me cold, but I've got a puncture mark in my left arm, so I guess they pumped me full of something to keep me unconscious while they performed their butchery. But the phone call, Simpson? The man at the reception desk used your name. That's the only reason I bothered going down. You know what that means, don't you?'

'Yes, you don't need to spell it out. Holbeche knew I was running this operation, and he knew who you were as well, because I told him. I had to: I was reporting to him. He must have passed on everything he knew to Andrew Lomas. That's why whoever appeared downstairs – and there was obviously more than one of them – could use my name to put you off your guard.'

Richter glanced back towards the bed, where Raya's mutilated corpse was now mercifully covered with a sheet already stained crimson in several places.

'I still don't really know why they left me alive,' Richter said. 'Or why they had to do what they did to Raya.'

'I think I do,' Simpson replied. 'That was Moscow sending us a clear and unequivocal message. In the space of a week, we'd identified and eliminated their two most important penetration agents in Britain. That would be bad enough for the Russians, but instrumental in that operation was Raya Kosov, and the files she'd copied from the Yasenevo database. Killing her, and especially killing her the way they did, was Moscow – in the persona of Andrew Lomas – demonstrating that they possessed the reach and the resources to track her down and make her pay the ultimate price for daring to betray the SVR and Mother Russia. She was the target. You were incidental, just a bystander, a person of no consequence.'

'So you think Lomas did this?' Richter asked.

Simpson nodded. 'I'm certain he did. But, don't worry, we'll find him sooner or later.'

Richter shook his head. 'Is that job offer still open?' he asked, in an apparent non sequitur.

'Yes,' Simpson said. 'Why?'

'Because I'm going to take it, for one very simple reason. If I'm working inside British intelligence, some day I know I'll come across Andrew Lomas again. Because you're wrong about one thing, Simpson: you won't find him. That's because I'm going to beat you to it, if it's the last thing I ever do. I'm going to track down Lomas and finish him myself, and I can guarantee that it'll take him a long time to die.'

Simpson studied Richter for a long moment, then nodded. 'Welcome to FOE,' he said, extending his hand. 'I think you're getting the hang of things now.'